HIDE-OUT
I GET WHAT I WANT

LORENZ HELLER

INTRODUCTION BY GREGORY SHEPARD

Stark House Press • Eureka California

HIDE-OUT / I GET WHAT I WANT

Published by Stark House Press
1315 H Street
Eureka, CA 95501, USA
griffinskye3@sbcglobal.net
www.starkhousepress.com

ISBN: 978-1-951473-15-0

Book design by Mark Shepard, shepgraphics.com
Cover design by Jeff Vorzimmer, ¡caliente!design, Austin, Texas
Proofreading by Bill Kelly
Cover art from the Eton edition of *Hide-Out*

First Stark House Press Edition: November 2020

HIDE-OUT

Gangster Lew Markey knows when it's time to lay low, and with all the racketeering investigations going on, he figures he's a lot safer in Florida. He's got the perfect hide-out—no one gets in, or out. But Lew needs company, and he brings with him his watchdogs Vito and Yutsy, plus his lawyer, Harry Joyce, for intelligent conversation, and wise-cracking Goff to act as butler and maid. And there's his wife, Josie, of course, and her sister Nellie, who he plans to pair up with his brother Ozzie. But Harry and Nellie have other plans. Trouble is, they are locked behind Lew's iron gates, with no telephone, 20 miles from the nearest town. It's the perfect hide-out alright, and the perfect set-up for violence, hate— and death.

I GET WHAT I WANT

When Jeff Tucker first spots Letty on the dock, he knows he has to have her. It's love at first sight. But Letty is nothing but trouble, a fiery woman with a red-hot temper. And her uncle, a huge guy named Buster, is something else again. Jeff knows that Buster is trouble. First they hire Jeff to take them out in his boat. Then Buster suggests that maybe Jeff would like to get involved in some Cuban liquor smuggling. It's Letty that Jeff wants, but Buster is part of the package. So when the two of them leave town suddenly, and return a few days later with a man who has been shot in the shoulder—wanting to hold up in his cabin, no cops involved—Jeff knows he's going to have to go through Hell to get her.

7

Lorenz Heller
by Gregory Shepard

13

Hide-Out
by Lorenz Heller

137

I Get What I Want
by Lorenz Heller

161

Lorenz Heller Bibliography

LORENZ HELLER
BY GREGORY SHEPARD

"… the dialogue is crisp, the story edgy and populated by eccentric, volatile characters who just can't get a grip on life."
—Paul Burke, *CrimeTime*

Author Bill Crider called him "another one of those forgotten paperbackers who deserves to be remembered." Quite an epitaph. Lorenz Heller certainly does deserve to be remembered. He never quite achieved the heights of a John D. MacDonald, but as a fellow Florida crime writer, he kept close company. And he entirely supported himself with his writing, not something that a lot of 1950s authors could say.

Lorenz was born in West Hoboken, New Jersey, from fourth generation German-Americans, which might account for his first name. Lorenz is German for Lawrence. Everyone, of course, knew him as Larry. In fact, as Larry Heller, he wrote *I Get What I Want*, one of the two books in this volume. Lorenz wrote under many names, but he only wrote one other book as "Larry Heller"—*Body of the Crime*, published by Pyramid Books in 1962—plus one short story, publishing most of his novels under his "Frederick Lorenz" pseudonym.

As Frederick Lorenz he wrote six crime thrillers for Lion Books, beginning with *A Rage at Sea* in 1953 (a treacherous tale of revenge reprinted by Stark House Press, 2020), and quickly followed with *Night Never Ends* (a slice-of-life story involving an arrogant photographer and the couple he manipulates), *The Savage Chase* (a quirky kidnapping tale, reprinted by Stark House Press, 2019), *A Party Every Night* (about a bartender who is inadvertently framed for murder, also Stark House Press, 2020), *Ruby* (a man is unjustly accused of murdering the town tramp), and *Hot* (in which the brother of a bank robber must deal with his conniving wife); plus a juvenile delinquent novel for Chariot Books called *Dungaree Sin,* a seedy romp through the author's Jersey days. This final Frederick Lorenz book from 1960 reads like something pulled out of the bottom drawer, unfocused and poorly edited. But the rest of the Frederick Lorenz novels are tight, little gems.

And then there are all the books written as Laura Hale (crime fiction with strong female protagonists), not to mention the Larry Holden stories from the late 1940s and early 50s—over 100 of them—written for such magazines as *Detective Tales, Doc Savage, Dime Detective Magazine, Shadow Mystery* and *Thrilling Detective.* Seven of these pulp stories feature detective Dinny Keogh, who seems to solve most of his crimes through brute luck more than careful deduction. But when you're writing for *Mammoth Mystery,* you don't want a main character who is too cerebral. Fast action and heavy gunplay is the name of the game.

Heller wrote three novels as Larry Holden as well. The one in hand, *Hide-Out* (originally published in 1953 by Eton Books), plus *Dead Wrong* (reprinted recently as a Black Gat Book, 2020) and *Crime Cop* (a police procedural originally published by Pyramid Books in 1959).

But for all that—all the many pseudonyms, and all the various publishers he worked with, all the hardboiled titles—Heller was a character-writer more than an action writer. In a 1956 interview that appeared in the *Sarasota Herald-Tribune,* he confessed to being "interested in characters, not plots." This was his defining quality as a writer. In another interview, this one from the *St. Petersburg Times* later that same year, Heller said simply, "the plot is less important than putting characters in conflict." Characters, he said, "must be alive and have dimension. The reader should be able to see every character in the book." And because he placed more emphasis on characterization than plot, Heller was able to allow the action to take a lot of unpredictable turns.

Character is what makes *Hide-Out* such a tense and outstanding read. Heller takes a situation right of *Key Largo.* Nine people are holed up in an out-of-the-way mansion down in the Florida jungle, brought there and essentially imprisoned by a gangster who is trying to escape retribution from his fellow New Jersey hoodlums. Each one is either desperate to stay, or desperate to leave. Mob boss Lew Markey and his two henchmen control the situation. Markey's lawyer, Harry Joyce, and yes-man Goff, are brought along to provide Lew with conversation and lackeying. Lew's wife Josie and her sister Nellie are there to take care of the physical needs of Lew and his brother Ozzie. And then there's the poor sap who is thrown into a dark room under a trap door in the garage where he is beaten and starved, providing Lew with a convenient outlet for his impulsive fits of anger.

This isn't an action story, it's a taut drama about a group of trapped souls who are constantly cajoled and berated, and driven to the point of despair. Lew rules his little kingdom with a tight fist and an abusive tongue, but knows that he can't go too far. He's suspicious of Harry but needs him to provide a conversational sounding board. He knows that his brother Ozzie is weak, not too bright, and ruled by his libido. Ozzie keeps looking for ways to leave, but he is, after all, Lew's brother. His wife he constantly humiliates in small ways, making sure that everyone knows that she's his, but careful not to bruise his property.

However, as Lew's façade of strength is slowly chipped away, we see the scared little tyrant underneath emerge. Each character in turn reveals either hidden strengths or weaknesses as they are melted down in a crucible of fear. Locked behind Lew's iron gates, they have to overcome these fears just to survive. *Hide-Out* is a riveting story, right up to the explosive ending.

Heller always puts his characters through the wringer. He himself led quite an adventurous life. After running away to sea on a freighter at a young age, he then jumped ship with the entire crew and found work in Puyallup Valley, Washington, picking raspberries, baling hay and building barns. Heller then returned home and got serious about his life. He wrote his first book, *Murder in Make-Up*, in 1937 when he was 27, and got it published by Julian Messner, Inc, under his given name, Lorenz Heller. According to the St. Petersburg interview, it was his return home to West Hoboken that made him finally decide it was time to either get a job, or commit to his writing. Of course, like many young men, Heller took some time out of his life to serve in World War II, working at the Radio Aircraft Corp. war plant. But it wasn't too long after the war that his first stories began to appear. Then he moved to Florida.

Heller may have grown up in New Jersey, but he didn't grow old there. "I came down to Florida because I could not stand the snow," he said. First he moved to Nokomis, on the Gulf Coast, then built his own home in nearby Venice, sailing and fishing the Keys and islands when he wasn't working at his writing. The goal was to write 2,500 words a day, and sometimes Heller would be at it for 12 hours a day. But that's how you support yourself with your writing. And Heller was dedicated to it.

He wrote 18 novels in all, not counting the four Laura Hale books he adapted for Beacon Books from earlier works. Heller also wrote six TV scripts during the 1950s as Burt Sims. His last book appeared in 1962, the previously mentioned Larry Heller title called *Body of the Crime*, a cop drama reminiscent of the Ed McBain 87th Precinct mysteries. His only other Larry Heller novel, *I Get What I Want,* was published by Popular Library in 1956.

If *Hide-Out* is confined to its claustrophobic prison, *I Get What I Want* is about a prison of another sort—the bonds of emotional obsession. This one is set in what is presumably the Sanibel area on the Gulf of Mexico south of where Heller lived, renamed Sanibar here. The red tide—a "marine germ that kills the fish by the ton"—has come in and a local fisherman named Jeff Tucker, who refuses to leave, is temporarily out of work. Then a man and a woman come along wanting to hire his boat for a quick day trip. The man turns out to be a brash fellow named Buster. The woman is his niece, Letty, and as Jeff soon finds out, a total spitfire.

Jeff is soon pulled into their world, first by falling in love with Letty, then by letting Buster charm him into submission. Jeff himself is a stubborn, impulsive guy who, like many Heller heroes, is quite often his own worst enemy, always pushing at authority, sometimes more head-strong than head-smart. But it's his story, so we let him tell it in his own way.

In fact, *I Get What I Want* has more twists and turns than is usually found in a novel of this length. We start off thinking we're reading one of those stories about a guy who gets manipulated into committing a crime by a scheming woman. Not so. Jeff falls for Letty, but she and Buster immediately leave town, and Jeff goes on a drinking binge. At this point Heller introduces a subplot involving a redneck goon and his cousin, a local police detective who's got his eye on Jeff. Then Buster and Letty return, and the plot takes another turn as they bring a friend with them who has just been shot while trying to rob a bar.

The reader really has no way of knowing what to expect next. The characters of Buster and Letty keep things on edge with their contradictory ways—Buster being an amiable schemer filled with bravura cunning; Letty having grown up in the school of hard knocks, always coming out swinging—and keep us involved in the story. As Jeff says at one point, "They were the kind of people you couldn't scrub off with sulfuric acid once they got on you." Buster and Letty hold a fatal attraction for our narrator. They fascinate us as well.

As Alan Cranis wrote about Heller on *Bookgasm.com*, "Lorenz's characters are what keep the pages turning, as we wonder what new complications the players will encounter." Neither *Hide-Out* nor *I Get What I Want* disappoints in this regard. Heller gives us two great stories, filled with interesting characters, and doesn't waste a word doing it.

—June 2020
Eureka, CA

Sources:

Rita Billingham's "Profiles from Venice" from the *Sarasota Herald-Tribune*, Sunday, October 14, 1956

Woody Thayer, *St. Petersburg Times Suncoast Skyway* Edition, July 22, 1956

HIDE-OUT

LORENZ HELLER

writing as Larry Holden

CHAPTER ONE

The three cars fled southward on the Tamiami Trail through the soft darkness of the Florida night, the motors thrumming with the senseless urgency of sheer speed. In the rear seat of the Cadillac two women lay sleeping. One was blonde and beautiful; the other was brunette and, though not beautiful, lovely in a special way that came from inside her, even in sleep.

The blonde girl was dreaming, and once in awhile her arms or legs twitched, her fingers made vague clawing motions, and her wide sensual mouth drew back from her teeth in a grimace that was pain, shame and protest. She whimpered and her hands clenched tightly to her breast. It was a recurrent dream.

She was walking naked through a kind of zoo. There were cages all around, and the paths between the cages were so narrow that she had to walk in the exact center so that the animals could not reach her through the bars. The paths didn't go anywhere but led into other paths, like a maze.

And it was a special kind of nakedness. She had never felt as naked as this, except in this dream. It was the kind of nakedness she wanted desperately to cover up but couldn't. Her full breasts thrust themselves, against her frantic will, into the pitiless public gaze, and though she tried to keep her long-thighed legs primly together as she walked, she could not. She knew that she looked wanton and lascivious, and she wanted to cry out that she really wasn't. There was actually no one to see her nakedness but the animals, but the horrible thing was that all the animals were watching her avidly. Then suddenly they began coming out of their cages. They made a ring around her and she crouched, trying to hide her breasts behind her inadequate hands. Then a huge kind of thing, that she knew was a man but not really, came and began to feel her all over as if she were some kind of animal, and he kept whispering and leering, "Sweetheart...."

She awakened with a moan, but slowly succumbed to sleep again.

It was almost dawn when the three cars rolled through the gateway of the twelve-foot wall. The Cadillac and Lincoln rolled up the driveway and into the six-car garage, but the Ford stopped inside the wide gateway. A squat, bowlegged man slid out, stretched, then closed and barred the heavy high gates. He drove into the garage and parked at the opposite end from the other two cars. He switched off his lights and motor, then twisted around and reached back over his seat to prod experimentally at the unconscious man lying bound on the floor.

That was all the squat man wanted to know. He had no personal interest in the unconscious one. He knew what Lew wanted done, but he had to wait until everyone left the garage. He sat stolidly in the car and watched them plod toward the big house with shambling, fatigue-drugged steps—the two women, three men, and finally Lew himself. Lew turned in the doorway and made a slight movement with his hand.

"I told Yutzy to help you, Vito," he called. "You know what to do now." He obviously did not expect an answer, for he turned and followed the others.

Yutzy, a huge man with a stupid, placid face, had been unloading the baggage from the trunks of the Cadillac and Lincoln. He went over to the Ford when Lew walked away. He opened the rear door and poked at the bound man with his foot. The man moaned faintly.

"Still alive," Yutzy shook his head. "Dumb bastard." That was all he had to say. Yutzy never had much to say. He stood waiting for Vito to show him what to do.

Vito was already busy. He had opened a trap in the floor of the garage and turned on the basement light, revealing a set of concrete steps. He was light and quick on his stubby legs. He had thick curly blue-black hair and a shallow inch of forehead. His face was heavy and immobile with something of the quality of meteoric rock. His features were not clearly defined, as if his Maker had never quite decided whether to make him human or animal, and as a result he looked neither human nor animal but something between the two.

He motioned Yutzy to help him carry the bound man into the basement of the garage. It was a light burden and they were both tremendously strong. The basement, lighted by only the twenty-five-watt bulb, was imbedded in shadow, but Vito had obviously been down here before. He walked into the darkness for about fifteen paces and backed into a small room. They threw the bound man on the floor and went out without untying him. Vito closed the heavy door and snapped the lock.

"Don't you want to stick a towel in his mouth or something?" Yutzy asked. "Suppose he yells?"

Vito gave him a brief expressionless glance and tugged at the lock to make sure it had snapped. Yutzy looked away uneasily. He could not figure out this Vito at all. He wasn't like anybody else. For instance, he never said anything to anybody except Lew, and then it wasn't in any kind of language. It was just grunts. Yutzy had a funny feeling about Vito. Not that he was afraid of him physically. He wasn't. He wasn't afraid of anything or anybody physically. But there was something dark about Vito. Like that basement under the garage. It was dark and something else, too. Yutzy did not like it down there. He struggled with his inarticulateness to let Vito know how he felt.

"Damp," he said finally.

Vito paid no attention to him. He turned his back and walked up the stairs with the seeming singlemindedness of a dog going home. Yutzy followed, wishing that Vito would say something once in awhile instead of just giving you those looks.

They took the baggage into the house and stacked it in the gloomy hall, a cavern ill-lit by bracketed amber lights. The house was the Spanish-Mediterranean type popular during the boom of the Twenties with ornate plaster ceilings and tiled floors, furnished with dismal taste. The drapes were blood-red velvet suspended on rods that resembled spears. The furniture was massive, dark and uncomfortable. It reminded Yutzy of a movie house, and he rather liked it. He grinned at Vito, waved his hand to indicate their surroundings.

"Lana Turner," he said. "Coming attractions." That was as close as he could get to explaining in as few words as possible that this reminded him of a movie house and that he liked it.

Vito gave him a blank stare, and Yutzy mumbled, "Aaah, go to hell." He sniffed the air. "Coffee?"

He could use a cup of coffee. He could use a bed, too. They had driven straight down to Florida thirty-six hours from Newark without a break. His whole body felt as if it were humming from the vibration of the car. In less than an hour, up in Newark, Lew had loaded the whole lot of them in the three cars and set out, but that was the way Lew was. Lew never had to sit around making up his mind. Lew was smart. Yutzy had never met anybody as smart as Lew. And when Lew told you to do something, you did it. There was no fooling around with Lew. You did it or you got what Grizzard was going to get, Grizzard tied up in the basement of the garage. Dumb bastard.

Yutzy looked at Vito. "Coffee?" he repeated loudly as if Vito were either deaf or a foreigner.

Vito grunted and padded down the hall on his light cat-feet. Yutzy followed him grumbling because he could never get an answer out of

Vito, and Vito would lead him to Lew. He couldn't go to bed till Lew said so.

Lew was in the kitchen with that lawyer of his—Harry Joyce. Yutzy and Vito walked in.

"Okay?" Lew said casually to Vito, and Yutzy knew he meant about Grizzard being put down in the basement of the garage.

Vito grunted, and Lew said, "Hang around. The coffee'll be ready in a minute."

Lew didn't drink liquor but he was crazy about coffee. Yutzy never saw anybody so crazy about coffee, strong and black like tar, no milk or sugar. Ten, twelve pots a day. All the time coffee.

Vito squatted down on his heels, crossed his forearms on his knees and stared impassively straight ahead. Yutzy leaned against the wall and looked around, marveling at the size of the kitchen. He had never seen a kitchen this big outside a restaurant, but it was cleaner than any restaurant where he had washed dishes, and Yutzy had washed dishes in restaurants in every state and almost every major city in the country. Just bumming around until he tied up with Lew steady. Everything in the kitchen was stainless steel and gleamed like a mirror—counters, tables, sinks, stoves. There were three electric stoves and a big walk-in refrigerator.

"Some place, eh?" Lew was saying to Harry Joyce. "Twenty-five rooms. Wait'll you see the rest of it in the day. Patio, swimming pool, bowling alleys, squash court, poolroom, moom pitcher room, television room, all kinds of rooms. Even a pianna as big as a goddam freight car, the fancy kind they use in opera. Biggest goddam pianna in the world."

"And a twelve-foot wall," said Harry Joyce, "to keep out the Indians."

Yutzy looked at him. There it was again, this kind of stuff he could never figure out about Harry Joyce. Indians. What kind of a crack was that? You only got Indians out West, not Florida. Yutzy looked at Lew to set Harry straight, but Lew just laughed.

"Naaah," he winked, "to keep the Indians *in*."

Harry started, "How long ..."

"In the morning," said Lew. "There's lots of things we got to talk about in the morning, Wiggins."

Yutzy knew what Wiggins meant. Wiggins meant that he and Vito were listening in, and Lew had things to say to Harry that he didn't want him and Vito to hear. That was all right with Yutzy. He did not want to have to think about things anyway. He was more than happy to let the thinking part of it up to Lew.

Then Harry Joyce said, "I can't figure out what happened to Grizzard."

Lew gave Vito and Yutzy a quick warning glance. "Aaaah," he said, "he's probably still squattin' in some gas-station john up in Virginia, that dope."

"Vito just drove off and left him?" Harry said.

"You know what I told everybody on them stops. Stay with it or get left. Grizzard got left."

Vito grunted something and Lew added, "He says it was the Sunoco station inside Richmond where we had them samwidges."

Harry Joyce murmured, "I can't figure out how Grizzard got himself left. He was smarter than that."

Yutzy felt himself go tense when Lew said, "It makes a difference?" as though he was wondering if maybe Harry Joyce was tied up with Grizzard some way. Christ, that would be a thing—Lew's own lawyer tied up with Grizzard!

Then Harry Joyce made one of the dumbest cracks Yutzy had ever heard from anybody. Harry lifted one shoulder and said, "I don't think Grizzard ever made any difference to anybody in all his life." Yutzy looked at him with wonderment. How could a guy as smart as that, a lawyer, be so dumb sometimes? Yutzy knew what had happened to Grizzard. He knew what, why, and when. It had happened on that road in North Carolina when Vito signaled with his horn that he was in trouble with the car and everybody stopped while Lew went back to see. The Ford had been back behind the curve. Lew had been there fifteen minutes, then came back saying indifferently:

"Dirt in the carburetor."

Yutzy had immediately known better. If it had been dirt in the carburetor you would of heard Lew from here to Hoboken, goddam carburetor, goddam this, goddam that, goddam the other thing. Lew raved even when his cigar-lighter wouldn't light. Goddam cigar-lighter.

But Lew had only said, "Dirt in the carburetor."

He couldn't fool Yutzy. Yutzy looked back at the first town they came to and saw Vito still driving the Ford, but he couldn't see Grizzard sitting beside him. That was when he knew. He knew Grizzard. Grizzard was dumb, always griping when he thought Lew couldn't hear. Well, this time he had griped to the wrong guy, namely, Vito. You couldn't gripe to Vito against Lew. Not ever. That was why Vito had signaled Lew with the horn. Grizzard had said the wrong thing. So Lew went back, and between him and Vito they had taken care of

Grizzard. At first Yutzy thought they had cooled him and dumped him in the piney woods, but when he thought about it more, he didn't think so. Yutzy knew that this unexpected trip to Florida was no pleasure trip, even if Lew did this kind of thing all the time. There was something in the air. Lew had been too edgy in the beginning, relaxing the farther they got away from Newark, but still driving too hard. There was something in the air. And that was why Grizzard had to be taken care of, and that was why they hadn't just dumped him in the bushes. Everybody knew that Grizzard was one of Lew's boys, and if Grizzard turned up in the North Carolina bushes, it would point out that Lew had gone that way. So Grizzard was in Vito's car, but taken care of.

And that was why Yutzy had been surprised to find him still alive in the back of the Ford out there in the garage. And that was one of the reasons he'd had that funny feeling down there in the basement. He knew that Lew wasn't going to kill Grizzard the easy way. When Vito locked that heavy door, Yutzy knew what they were going to do, or had a good idea. They were going to starve Grizzard to death and beat him up while they were doing it.

Yutzy suddenly lost a lot of respect for Harry Joyce. Harry Joyce wasn't smart. He was dumb. He couldn't even figure out a thing as plain as this with Grizzard. That was dumb. It was something anybody could see.

Lew snapped, "What the hell's eating you, Yutzy?"

Yutzy jerked upright and flushed. He couldn't tell Lew what he had been thinking because Harry was Lew's lawyer and he couldn't tell Lew things like that about people he liked. Yutzy struggled with his inarticulateness.

"Rain," he said finally. "Feels like rain."

Lew said, "Oh, hell," and glowered, but before he could say anything else, the door opened and Josie walked in.

Josie was Lew's wife, a flaxen blonde, and when she came in, the very air seemed to change. That happened every time Josie walked into a room. No matter what you were doing, you had to turn and look. This time she was wearing a nylon nightgown and negligee that didn't actually show anything but gave the appearance of being about to reveal something wonderful, which it could have if she took it off.

She murmured, "Somebody said coffee." Her low, husky voice made if sound very intimate.

Yutzy's eyes roved from the curved press of her thighs against the negligee to the high lift of her breasts. He did not look at her face. Lew patted her fanny and drew her over to the table.

He said, "Hi, sweetheart," and nuzzled a kiss into the curve of her neck. He put his hands on her thighs and began to knead them gently. Yutzy licked his lips and looked quickly at Harry Joyce and Vito. Vito's shoe-button eyes were wide and shiny. Harry Joyce was looking down at the cigarette in his hand. Yutzy tried to look away from what Lew was doing, but his eyes kept coming back. This was the way Lew got sometimes, and he never paid any attention to anybody when he got this way, even if he was in a nightclub. Yutzy had seen him time and time again. First he'd play around with the dame and finally take her outside in the car and give it to her. It didn't make any difference to Lew if there were a million people around. Like now.

He was kissing Josie and doing that stuff with his hands and running them under the negligee even after she tried to push him away.

She said sharply, "Cut it out, Lew. I'm tired. All I want is coffee."

Lew looked at Yutzy, Vito and Harry. He flapped his hand at them.

"Beat it," he said heavily. "Beat it. I'll see you in the morning."

As they walked down the hall away from the kitchen, they heard Josie cry out in anger and pain.

Yutzy struggled to say something and finally managed, "Lew ... his own wife ... he hadn't ought do that ... in front of guys...."

He was sweating. And for once Vito did not seem to notice that Lew had been criticized.

CHAPTER TWO

It was afternoon when Harry Joyce awakened. He blinked into the bright sunlight that shafted through the window, rolled over on his side and pulled the cover over his head. That was a thing that had been growing on him lately, this reluctance to awaken, this desire to slip back into sleep or to crawl back into the womb or the semblance of it. But this time he realized he was doing it. He lay for a moment with his eyes squeezed shut, and then angrily threw off the covers and sat up. He reached for the package of cigarettes on the night-table beside the bed.

There was a sodden weight at the back of his neck and he raised a lean brown hand to massage the muscles, though obscurely he knew that massage would not knead it away. Lately he had been awakening every morning with that same sodden burden back there. It pulled down his head and slumped his shoulders. It made thinking difficult and somehow meaningless. Nothing was worth the effort while he was carrying that extra burden, whatever it was, wherever it came from. He had experimented with hard pillows, softer pillows, with no pillow at all, but every morning it was there as inexorable as dawn. A physical check-up at the doctor's had not shown a thing. His health was monotonously good. His long fingers manipulated the muscles. He rolled his head, listening to the grinding at the base of his skull. It wouldn't do any good, he knew. It would go away as the day wore on, or perhaps it just seemed to go away because he became accustomed to it. It didn't matter much. He wasn't going any place, and he wasn't going to do anything. He drew disinterestedly at his cigarette.

After awhile Joyce swung out of bed and plodded into the bathroom. He stood dully under the cold shower as the spray needled his wide shoulders and lean flanks. He was lean but not thin and had the look of a fast light heavy weight after a particularly grueling match. His thoughts wandered meaninglessly, more tactile than intellectual, and he seemed almost to have forgotten the rushing hiss of water that splashed him. Then he turned and let it play over his face and chest. He turned it off, stepped out of the shower and toweled himself slowly.

Joyce looked into the mirror and fingered his chin. It took him some minutes to decide to shave. Afterward he brushed his teeth and rubbed his face with a stinging lotion. His skin tingled and he had the momentary illusion of well-being. It faded quickly. He plodded back into the bedroom. He pawed over his clothes without interest, finally putting on a pair of old tennis shoes, shapeless white ducks and a T-shirt. He dressed slowly as if reluctant to go downstairs and join the others. What was there to join, anyway? Lew, Vito, Yutzy, Josie? Then there was Ozzie, Lew's kid brother. Ozzie got out of bed in the morning with the sole purpose of getting back there again as soon as possible with the first willing female he could find. He had no other discernible object in life and wanted none other. When he wasn't getting it, he was talking about it, and when he wasn't talking about it he was either thinking about it or looking at pictures of it. Ozzie was a real bundle of joy, all right.

Another bundle of joy was Goff, the misanthrope. After talking two minutes with Goff you couldn't help wondering why he hadn't gone off some place and shot himself years ago.

And then there was Nellie, Josie's sister. Harry Joyce had purposely avoided thinking of Nellie. Nellie disturbed his growing vegetable lethargy. It was because of Nellie that Harry was reluctant to leave his room. He wanted, in effect, to hide from her.

He wandered to the window and looked out. There was a lot of ground, but it was difficult to see what lay beyond. The foliage was thick and the palm trees were towering, clustered islands of verdure. All kinds of palms—royal, cocoanut, date, plumosa, traveler, pandanus. That was the top layer. Below them were the flowering trees, gold, orange, red, white, none of which Harry could identify. There were vines with trunks as thick as hawsers, and hibiscus bushes with blooms the size of dinner plates, colors from pure snowy white to flaming crimson. There were gardenias and camellias. There was cactus. It was a hodgepodge, a jungle.

Below the window were the fat balusters of the patio, and beyond, the circular aqua-tiled swimming pool. Lew was splashing and snorting in the crème-de-menthe water, clowning to conceal the fact that he could not swim. A pair of very shapely ivory-tinted legs protruded from under the canopy of a canvas deck chair. That would be Josie. Josie hated the sun, for it did ugly things to her delicate complexion.

Somebody was playing tennis, for Lew could hear the distinctive ponk-ponk of the hit ball, but the trees hid the court from his sight. It couldn't be anyone but Nellie and Ozzie, and Harry felt his stomach coil at the thought of Nellie and Ozzie doing anything together, anything at all. Suddenly he wanted to get out of his room and go downstairs.

He took a package of cigarettes from the carton in his bag and went through the long, wide tunnel of the corridor and down the dark stairway. The house had many windows but none of them seemed to admit any light. Probably because of the crowded trees outside.

Goff was sitting on the patio leafing through an old copy of *Life*. He was a slender little man with straw-colored hair and eyebrows, and a narrow bony asymmetrical face, a face of gnawing melancholy. He gave Harry a slanting upward glance.

"What, no tennis racket?" There was always a thin edge of derision in his voice. "No swimming trunks? No football uniform? Better watch your step, buster, or they'll throw you out of the athletes' union. We're all athletes around here. Even me. I'm Lew's towel boy. I carried his towel down to the pool for him. A towel and a piece of soap. Somebody ought to tell him that's a swimming pool, not a bathtub."

"You tell him."

"I did. I said, 'Lew, you're a filthy swine.' And do you know what he said? With the tears streaming down his face, he said, 'Please don't be mean to me, Mr. Goff. I'll reform.' Those were his exact words."

"I'll bet."

"What's the matter, Mr. Joyce? You sound like *Massa's in de Cold, Cold Ground.* Something you swallowed, like your conscience, for instance?"

"Go to hell."

"Why bother? We're here, or didn't you know?" Goff waved his bony hand. "Welcome to Alcatraz. Take a look at that wall around the place. Two feet thick and broken glass on top. What are we in for, life?"

"Ask Lew. He's the boss."

"The warden, buster, the warden. Have you heard the latest communiqué? We're all on K.P."

"On what?"

"Yutzy's the cook, Vito sweeps and cleans around, and I wait on tables and make beds. I don't know what your girl friend does."

Harry compressed his lips. "My who?"

"Do you mean to tell me that Nellie isn't your tootsie-wootsie?"

He laughed when Harry flushed.

"See?" he said. "Don't ever try to kid me, buster."

Harry controlled himself. "Do I have a job too?" he asked.

"You'll have to get that from the horse's mouth. Or is it a mouth? It looks more like something else."

"*Your* mouth'll get you in trouble one of these days."

Goff's eyes darkened with a kind of yearning sadness and for a moment he seemed on the verge of making a bid for friendship, but he had either lost the knack or didn't know how for his mouth twisted bitterly and he looked away.

Lew called from the pool. "Hey, Harry, come on down, want to talk to you."

Goff made a mocking gesture with his skinny hand. "Your turn, stooge."

Harry gave him a hard glance and stepped over the balustrade. As he passed Josie, she looked up from her manicure.

She said, "Hi, Harry," and gave him the kind of caressing glance she gave all men except Lew.

He said, "Hi. Have a good sleep?"

"Some sleep!" she darted a smoldering glance at Lew in the pool. "Harry ...?"

"Yes?"

"What ... what did those men say after, well, after, you know, last night after they went out the kitchen?" She blushed.

Harry said quickly, "They said good-night, that's all."

"I can't stand it when Lew mushes around like that in front of people!"

"Don't worry about it, Josie. Everybody was too tired to notice."

"How'd you like it if he always ran his hand up your leg in public? How'd you like it? And sliding his clammy fingers down the front of your dress and playing with you where everybody can see. How'd you like it?"

"Take it easy, Josie...."

"I've taken it easy and I've taken it hard and I'm sick of it!"

"We all get sick of something once in a while, I guess."

She gave him a quick warning glance and picked up her bottle of nail lacquer. Lew was climbing heavily out of the pool. He dabbled his feet in the water. His chest was plump and hairless.

"Siddown, kid," he said to Harry. He blew his nose in his hand and splashed his hand in the pool.

Harry pulled over a folding stool and sat beside him. Lew pursed his lips and gave Harry a shrewd, heavy-lidded glance.

"I suppose you're wondering what this is all about," he said.

"Well—it was pretty sudden."

"Not so sudden. I had this in the back of my head for a year. This place," he laughed when Harry looked surprised. "Yeah, for over a year. In some ways I'm dumb, Harry, and some ways I'm smart. This is one of the ways I'm smart. Would you call me a big shot, kid? Be frank."

"Big enough."

"Yeah, big enough. You goddam lawyers," Lew mocked him good-naturedly. "Maybe a big shot to a guy like Yutzy, but you and me, we know better. I'm a medium-sized shot, or maybe just a shade under. What I'm getting at is something I seen coming for a long time now, all over the country. Senate investigating committees, state committees, city committees, committees to investigate committees, a big clean-up. I blame it on this Russian stuff. Beginning to get the picture?"

"It's a big picture," said Harry warily.

"Big," Lew agreed. "Now there are two kinds of guys that ain't going to be touched by these committees—the big ones and the little ones. The big ones are too big, and the little ones ain't worth going after."

"But the ones in the middle ..."

"Get it in the neck." Lew paused, glanced back at Josie and lowered his voice. "A guy took a shot at me about a week ago. I didn't tell Josie, so don't mention it because I don't want her to worry. Now, hell, I been shot at before, but this time I got a feeling. And I been hearing things. A guy knocked off in Philly, a few more in Chi, a couple in Cincy, St. Louis, Detroit. Guys like me, guys in the middle. I ain't been up in front of no committee but suppose I am, what happens? I tell what I know or I get sent up for perjury or contempt. If I start telling what I know, the big shots—the real big shots—they won't like it, and when they don't like something they get rid of it. I don't want to be got rid of. On the other hand, if I don't talk I get sent up. I don't want to get knocked off, Harry, but on the other hand I don't want to do time either. So I'm on the short end, no matter how you look at it. Oh, I seen it coming, Harry, but like everybody else I didn't think it meant me—until that guy took a shot at me last week. And I think this is just the beginning. The real shake-up is still to come."

Harry felt a twinge of unaccustomed excitement, a touch of dread, a presentiment. "So now what?" he asked slowly.

"Who knows? I got out while the getting was good, but what good is getting out? You still know what you know, don't you? And if some big shot decides you're better off with a hole in you, you get a hole in you, like they tried to do with me last week. It's no good getting out unless you *hide* out too. And that's just what I'm doing, hiding out."

"For how long?"

"That's the sixty-four-dollar question, kid. Till I can go out again. I got enough dough to last me the rest of my life, as far as that goes, and this is a nice place. Everything here you could want—swimming, bowling, pool, television. Right now Ozzie and Nellie are playing tennis. We got that, too. Anything else you can think of, I'll put it in. So what difference does it make how long we stay?"

Harry felt something knot inside. "But what about all these people you brought with you?" he asked levelly.

"What do you mean what about all these people? Vito and Yutzy never had it so good."

"What about Goff?"

"Goff does what he's damn well told!"

"All right. Take Ozzie then."

"Ozzie?" Lew looked surprised. "He's my kid brother. I got to look out for him. But I know what you're thinking. Ozzie likes to play around. But don't worry about that," Lew winked. "I got an idea that Nellie'll take care of that end of it. It's about time Ozzie was thinking of getting married and having kids, and how much better can he do than my own wife's sister? She's a smart kid, she's stacked, and I if I know my stuff she'll make a good lay, so what more could Ozzie ask?"

"Yeah," said Harry harshly, "what more?" If Ozzie as much as laid a finger on Nellie, he'd beat his face in. But it wouldn't come to that. Nellie couldn't stand Ozzie.

"I suppose," said Lew, "that you're coming around to yourself next."

"I wasn't thinking of that." It was the truth. He hadn't given himself a thought. It was Nellie. He'd stay as long as Nellie stayed, and Nellie wouldn't go as long as Josie remained. Nellie always looked after Josie.

"I'm glad you didn't have yourself in mind," said Lew calmly, "because I need you around in case anything turns up. You're the only lawyer I'd trust, and that's a compliment, kid. Anyway, you along makes it an even number when we choose up sides for bowling." He grinned.

But God, Harry thought with dismay, *he's out of his mind; he can't play with people's lives like this!*

"I'm a lousy bowler," said Harry mechanically. So Goff was right. Alcatraz.

"You'll learn. You got all the time in the world." Lew glanced at Josie, who had one leg raised and was lacquering her toenails. His glance intensified and he chuckled. He slapped Harry on the leg with the back of his hand and clambered awkwardly to his feet. "Here I go again, kid," he said out of the side of his mouth, "All I got to do is look at that Josie and I can't control myself. But that's what you get married for, ain't it?" He dropped his hand on Harry's shoulder and tightened his fingers. "But in the meantime, in case anybody asks, nobody leaves here without my say-so. I don't want to get tough about it, but you can see how it is."

Lew walked away. As he passed Josie, he rumpled her hair. "Come on, baby," he said, "a little service." He kept walking, sure that she would come. Josie flushed and followed with reluctant feet. Harry saw Goff look her up and down as she passed him on the patio.

Nobody leaves.

Harry hunched forward, his hands clenched. Christ, Lew doesn't know what he's doing. You couldn't just lock up a bunch of people like this. Something would have to give sooner or later. This was actually the payoff; this showed them where they stood. They were all inextricably bound up with Lew Markey. On the outside there had been an illusion of freedom, an illusion of free choice, but right here was where the illusion burst. Perhaps there had been a choice in the beginning....

In the beginning, Harry had a dusty office on Market Street and just about enough practice to pay the rent with something left over to buy needle and thread to darn his socks. Then the offer had come from Lew. Lew had a suite of offices in the McCarter Building on Broad Street. It was called Investments, Incorporated. Lew had sent for him, and he had gone. Lew's layout was dazzling—mahogany desks, clerks, stenographers, a receptionist, and a business-like air of subdued activity.

He had known who Lew Markey was, of course. Everybody in Newark did. In a general way. A kind of racketeer. Harry had expected a left-hand offer which he was prepared to turn down flat. In fact, he had gone to Lew's office more out of curiosity than anything else, and he wanted no part of any crooked deals.

But Lew had been like silk. After telling Harry that he had looked up his record, that he was a bright boy, and congratulated him on the top marks he had gotten in school and all that, he got down to business.

"To hear a lot of people talk, Harry," he said, "I'm nothing but a crook. Just because I made some mistakes when I was young and ran around with a tough crowd. That was years ago, but they still hold it against me. See this layout? Strictly on the level, strictly legitimate...."

And it was, too. Lew had his fingers in many legitimate businesses—a chain of laundries, a part interest in a brewery, a wholesale liquor distributing company, a big printing business, and many others.

"That'll be your job, Harry," he said. "I need a lawyer I can trust to keep his eye on things. They call me a crook, but some of these so-called honest businessmen around can take me to the cleaners and don't think they can't. They've done it. That's why I need a bright guy like you...."

And that was it. Strictly legitimate. Harry couldn't find a hole in the proposition, so he took it, and before long he found out that he was nothing more than Lew Markey's legal errand boy. This side of Lew was, as he had said, strictly on the level, but there were other sides, and the take from the other sides was what fed the money into the legitimate side.

Harry himself was strictly honest, but how long can you compromise with your self-respect without losing it? Lew never asked Harry to do a dishonest thing, and in fact respected his stubborn honesty. But Lew himself was crooked, and that was the heart of the matter.

Up there in Newark, it had seemed to be a matter of choice. He could work for Lew Markey, or he could quit. It was choice. And compromise.

But now he remembered how Lew had always warned him to keep this under his hat or that under his hat.

"It's all on the level as you can see, Harry, but I want my name kept out of it...."

Like the brewery. Lew owned stock in that through a dummy. He controlled the wholesale liquor distributing company through a dummy.

"Keep it under your hat, Harry...."

He had kept it under his hat, but he had been kidding himself all along that he'd had any choice about quitting. Lew would never have let him quit.

What Harry had felt before was self-disgust—and now he began to hate Lew Markey.

CHAPTER THREE

Harry turned his head and looked steadily at that sprawling caricature of a house with its silly wrought-iron balconies and narrow Gothic windows. But behind the facade, the house itself was not silly. It was grotesque, but not silly. It was dark and very solidly built and there were wrought-iron bars on the windows, bars meant for decoration but bars none the less and of hard metal. Only when you likened the house to Lew did it become sinister. It was Lew's house, and the house was Lew, and each was symbolic of the other. It was an easy house to hate, now that it had become a prison and Lew the warden.

Harry heard Nellie's voice coming toward him through the trees from the tennis court, and he jumped up from his stool with an eagerness that would have surprised him an hour earlier when he had wanted to avoid Nellie without knowing why. Now he knew, and within the last few minutes he had cleansed himself of Lew Markey, though he was not rid of Lew yet. It was as if he stood in the middle of a jungle and had just discovered the way out. There was an exhilaration in that—but the distance had still to be covered and it was a dangerous path.

He walked around the pool as Nellie and Ozzie appeared in the path that wound through the columnar palms, carrying tennis rackets. Ozzie's face was flushed and sullen. Nellie saw Harry and waved her racket, smiling.

"You two look as if you could use a swim," he said, deliberately noncommittal. Now that Lew had earmarked Nellie for Ozzie, he had made up his mind to pay her no unusual attention in public.

Ozzie threw his tennis racket on the grass and said angrily, "The goddam thing's all warped. The hell with a swim. I'm going for a drive."

He was tall and well aware of his handsomeness, but here was a Levantine softness about him. In Lew that softness was an envelope concealing the inner hardness. Ozzie was soft all the way through, and always Ozzie was conscious of himself as if he knew there was someone around the next tree with a waiting camera. He had a full petulant mouth.

He scowled at Harry and walked around the pool toward the garage at the end of the long house.

"What's the matter with him?" Harry asked. "I suppose you beat the pants off him."

Nellie laughed. "I beat him 6-1 and he hated it. He hates me too at the moment, thank God."

Harry grinned at her, telling her with his eyes that he loved her. She was as unlike Josie as a sister could be. She was small and slender with hazel eyes and a wide, thought full mouth. She took his arm.

"Let's walk through the tree-garden," she said. "It's fabulous. There are acres of it. It was planted in the Twenties by a Colonel MacDonald. There are trees and things from all over the world. Lew was telling us about it, and he made it sound as if the colonel had grabbed everything at gunpoint."

They walked slowly under the sculptured spread of a flowering royal Poinciana tree.

"That's the way Lew would have gotten all these things," said Harry. "In the beginning, that is. At the moment he's giving one of his imitations of respectability. He probably bought this place in the usual way, congratulating himself for weeks on his sterling honesty."

"Harry!"

"What?"

"What's gotten into you? I've never heard you talk like that before about Lew. And when we came up to the pool you looked furious."

He looked back over his shoulder. They were screened from the house by the fan of a towering traveler palm. He bent and kissed her quickly.

"I'll tell you in a moment," he whispered.

"Tell me now." She smiled up into his eyes, raised herself to tiptoe and kissed him lightly on the lips.

There was the gritty sound of someone coming rapidly down the path and they broke away from each other. It was Ozzie. He was purple like a baby about to burst into a tantrum.

"Something wrong, Ozzie?" asked Harry just a shade too casually.

"You're goddam right there's something wrong!" Ozzie's voice rose shrilly. "I try to go for a goddam drive and the goddam gate's locked. Where's Lew?"

"In the house."

Ozzie strode toward the house without even a muttered thanks.

"Number one," said Harry drily.

Nellie gave him a quick questioning glance. "Number one what? You're being awfully mysterious today, darling."

This time he cupped her elbow in his hand and led her deeper into the tree-garden and away from the house. Then slowly he told her everything that Lew had told him. He had expected her to be alarmed or concerned, but she was only bewildered.

"I don't see anything to get upset about," she said. "After all, it's Lew's problem, not yours."

"Honey, listen carefully to me. It *is* our problem. It is more our problem than Lew's. He intends to keep us here indefinitely."

"I still don't see why you're getting so excited."

"What do you think 'indefinitely' means?"

"Well ..." she hesitated, "... a month or two."

"Make it a year or two and you'll be getting warmer. These investigations aren't a flash in the pan this time, honey. There are going to be more and more of them. This is no longer a peaceful, sleepy country. Lew was shrewd about one thing. He blamed the investigation on the Russians. In a way, he's right. The country is becoming anxious not only about the menace outside the borders, but about the termites inside, too. Lew intends to stay here as long as he has to. He has enough money to last all of us the rest of his life. I know. For the past six months, I've been liquidating some of his biggest holdings in Jersey. He'll stay here for ten years if he has to."

"But ... why did he bring *us* with him?"

"He brought Vito and Yutzy as guards. They were his goon squad up north. He brought me because I'm his lawyer and he needs a lawyer. He brought Josie for the obvious reason, and you go with Josie. Ozzie's his kid brother and he has the idea he has to take care of Ozzie, and how right he is. Goff... Goff's a question mark. Goff hates his guts. Goff hates everybody's guts, but Lew's in particular. I have an idea Lew brought him along as a butt, a whipping-boy. Lew can't do without a whipping-boy."

"But why does Goff stand for it?"

"Why do any of us stand for it?" asked Harry wearily. "He's got us all tied up, one way or another. He tied me up with a juicy fee. Oh, it sounded legitimate enough in the beginning, and he never tried to mix me up in his rackets. Even when I found out he was a crook I didn't leave him. I was making more money than I had ever seen before in my life...."

Nellie laid her hand against his mouth. "Don't, darling," she said gently, "don't. You've never done anything dishonest. You're just punishing yourself now. Anyway, do you actually know that Lew is a crook?"

"You mean, do I have any legal evidence? No."

"There you are. It's only what people say. Just the same old gossip about him." There was an uneasiness in her was voice and, avoiding his eyes, she said quickly, "You said he had us all tied up, one way or another. That's not true. He doesn't have me tied up."

"He's got you tied through Josie. You wouldn't be here if it weren't for Josie."

"But, Harry, I've always looked after Josie. Ever since we were children."

"Why? Is she a Mongolian idiot or something?"

"Harry, please, let's not quarrel. We've gone over this time and time again, and you know as well as I do that if I weren't around, she'd always be in trouble."

"Why can't Lew look after her?"

"That's the trouble she'd be in," said Nellie flatly.

Harry said, "Well, now...." and let it dangle. He knew what she meant. Josie had given him those come-on looks, too, and he had seen her give them to others.

They had taken a side path that turned back on itself and now through the trees they saw the garage and Vito backing the Cadillac into it. He came out a few moments later, putting something into his pocket. He gave them a lowering glance and walked around the end of the garage.

"He gives me the shivers," muttered Nellie. Her fingers tightened on Harry's arm.

"Five'll get you ten he took the keys out of the cars," said Harry.

"Let's look."

They went into the garage and peered into all three cars. Last night the keys had been dangling from the ignition locks; now they were gone.

"And that," said Harry, "is why Lew brought Vito. Object lesson number one."

He heard Nellie suck in her breath, and he turned. Vito was standing in the mouth of the garage watching them suspiciously. He motioned them out.

"We want to sit in the back seat and neck," said Harry.

Vito shook his head and waved his hand peremptorily. They walked down the driveway toward the gate, knowing he was still watching.

"Well," whispered Harry, "I found out one thing, he understands English. I'll have to remember that."

"He's an awful man. I'm afraid of him sometimes." She was actually shivering. Harry covered her hand with his.

"That proves you've got good sense."

They came to the gate and stared at the obviously new hasp and padlock that had been put on that morning.

"Goff called this place Alcatraz," said Harry. "I thought he was just being Goff. He also told me that the walls were twelve feet high and had broken glass set into the top of them. I made a joke about the wall last night. I asked if it was to keep out the Indians, and he said it was to keep the Indians *in*. I thought it was funny at the time. I don't think I like your brother-in-law anymore, honey."

She covered his mouth with her hand. "Don't say that," she said in a panicky voice. "Don't even think it!"

"He's a mind reader?"

"Sometimes I think he is."

A feeling of discouragement swept over Harry. It was as if in her fear Nellie had allied herself with Lew, and her growing nervousness was evidence of it.

She turned him from the gate, saying hurriedly, "We'd better get back to the house. I ... I promised Josie I'd do her hair this afternoon."

As they walked back in the deep shade of the high trees, Harry said quietly, "Well, what are we going to do—just sit, or try to figure a way out? The longer we sit, the worse it's going to get, and I know what I'm talking about. Lew has to have lots of people around him telling him what a wonderful guy he is, and I'm afraid the present company is a little too small and a little too reluctant to feed his damned ego twenty-four hours a day."

Nellie gave a cry of delight and, darting to the side of the path, plucked a white blossom. He gently took the flower from her and threw it into the dense underbrush of the tree-garden. He tilted her face with light fingers under her chin. His arm went around her.

"This is serious, honey. I like to smell flowers, but this isn't the time for it. We're going to have to make up our minds if we're going to be subjects of King Lew the First, or if we're going to try to find a way out of this."

She pulled her chin from his fingers, straining away from him. "Stop it, Harry," she said sharply. "You're hurting me."

"I'm not hurting you, honey. Listen to me. Believe me we're in a bad spot here...."

"I *don't* believe you."

"Please just listen...."

"I won't listen. I think you're dramatizing yourself. This is the first time I've known you to do this. Now stop it. I know what's the matter with you. You're all mixed up because you've suddenly decided to leave Lew. That's all right, Harry. Leave him if that's what you want to do, but please don't make a production out of it." She was still pushing against his chest with her hands, turning her face away from him.

"I'm not just thinking of myself, honey," he pleaded. "Nor just of you, either. When we find a way out of here, we can take Josie with us. I never meant to leave her."

"I never heard anything so silly in all my life." She had succeeded in thrusting herself away from him and she gesticulated with her hands. "Why should she go? She has no reason to go. She has everything she wants, and in his way Lew is very good to her."

"If he's so good to her, then we can leave her."

She looked away from him and went on talking in that hurried scolding voice, "You shouldn't talk so silly, Harry. What would she do without me? She can't even put up her own hair."

"She could get a maid," said Harry savagely. "Other people get maids, why can't she?"

She answered earnestly as if she had given the matter a good deal of thought and had come to the conclusion that among all others this was the only right one. "No. No she couldn't, Harry. Other people can get maids, but not Josie. She can't handle maids. She spoils them. She had a maid in New York and all they did all day was play gin rummy and drink Benedictine. That's her favorite drink. Benedictine in a tall glass with vanilla ice cream." Her voice disintegrated into a giggle, then steadied. "No, you're wrong, Harry. Lew would get her a maid in a minute. Actually, Josie couldn't have a better husband. He gives her everything she wants. He's very good to her. She has no reason to dislike him, and she shouldn't make eyes at other men...."

"No reason to dislike him ... except that every time he lays her the whole neighborhood knows it and has seen all the fingering and slobbering that went on before. Dislike him! By Christ, if she hit him with a meat-ax, I'd hold him while she did it a second time."

"That's all very true, Harry. I realize that Lew is the amorous type, but he'll calm down. I've told Josie that she simply has to learn to handle him. Josie isn't as stupid as you think."

Deliberately brutal, Harry said, "You may have the opportunity of learning to handle one of the Markey men yourself, darling. Lew is about to play Cupid. He has just made up his mind that you'd make a good wife for Ozzie."

It was more effective than a direct slap. Her prattling stopped with her mouth open and she stared at him with drained eyes.

"Oh no ..." she said, "... oh *no!*" She turned and fled down the path ahead of him.

When he reached the patio, Goff was still there, lying back in the chaise with the magazine over his face. He was not sleeping, for when Harry stepped over the low balustrade, he raised the magazine and peered from under it with one eye. Harry dropped into the chair beside him.

"As one good little stooge to another good little stooge," Harry said, "how's about a drink?"

Goff let the magazine drop back over his face, but his shoulders hiccupped with silent laughter.

"Who woke you up, sleeping beauty?" his voice came thinly. He took the magazine from his face and looked at Harry. For a moment it seemed that he was about to say something else, something friendly, but he did not know how, or did not want to take the chance.

"Yeah, two good little stooges," he said.

CHAPTER FOUR

Lew was in rare high humor at dinner. Harry knew that mood and was wary of it. Lew's level of humor was to jerk a chair out from under you; or give you a hot foot. However, at the moment he was too hungry to do anything but eat, which he did sloppily and voraciously.

Only the family and Harry ate in the gloomy high-vaulted dining-room. It would have taken six men to lift the massive banquet table that seated twenty-four. Harry would much rather have eaten in the kitchen with Vito, Yutzy and Goff, but again he had no choice. And, then, too, there was Nellie.

Harry had been in love with Nellie for over a year. Up in Newark, emotions had run thin, and of course he had seen her only at night, about three times a week. Now the very thought of her made his heart beat more richly.

Lew sat at the head of the table with Josie to his right and Nellie to his left. Ozzie sat beside Josie—he had not forgiven Nellie for beating him at tennis—and Harry sat beside Nellie. Nellie sat in white-faced silence, eating quickly and neatly, not looking up from her plate, answering Harry only in monosyllables. Finally he gave up and watched Ozzie across the table. Ozzie had maneuvered his chair closer and closer to Josie, watching Lew with veiled hating eyes.

My God, thought Harry, *did Lew bring anyone with him who didn't hate him?*

He watched Ozzie with contemptuous detachment knowing what Ozzie was up to, wondering what Josie's reaction would be. He did not have a high opinion of Josie. Ozzie plied his fork with his right hand, but his left crept stealthily under the table. Josie started and angrily pushed his hand away, saying nothing. Ozzie grinned and blandly reached for the pepper, with which he sprinkled his food until it was black. His hand began to slide under the table again. He must have made a bolder move, for Josie's face became fiery. She half rose from her chair and swung her right hand in a full-armed slap. Ozzie's hair bounced from the force of it.

"You do that again," she shrilled, "and I'll stick you with a fork!"

Lew's head jerked around. "What's going on?" he demanded. He looked from Josie to Ozzie. "What's the idea?

Josie said furiously, "Your lousy brother was feeling me under the table, that's what."

Goff stopped in the doorway with a tray of food and watched Lew intently, a sharp little grin lifting one corner of his mouth. Lew's eyes narrowed and he placed both hands flat on the table. His mouth hung open and he began to breathe in short audible breaths. This was his usual prelude to a burst of rage. Ozzie licked his lips and said hurriedly:

"I was just tickling her and she makes a production."

Lew hung over the table edge and then threw back his head and gave a bray of forced laughter.

"Aaah, don't pay any attention to him, sweetheart," he said to Josie. "He's just a growing boy. Ain't you, kid?"

Josie said grimly, "The next time I'll scratch his eyes out," and looked at both of them with open hatred.

Lew laughed again as if determined that nothing disturb his good humor. He was the life of the party and he it was going to go on being the life of the party. He looked around for a victim and found Goff.

"Hey there, Jeeves," he snapped his fingers, "get me a toothpick toot sweet."

He grinned broadly. He liked that. That was real wit. Jeeves. That was the kind of stuff he got a kick out of.

"Hey, Jeeves, there's a crumb on the floor. Pick it up."

"Hey, Jeeves, this toothpick is blunt. Get me a sharp one."

"Hey, everybody. I just got an idea. I think we ought to get Jeeves here a butler's suit like that guy in the movies. Arthur Treacher. What do you think?"

He kept Goff running on trivial errands until Goff's face shone with perspiration. It was hot.

"Hey, Jeeves, wipe off my chin. There's something wrong with this succotash. It leaks."

Ozzie tittered and took the opportunity to lay his arm across the back of Josie's chair and play with her back hair with his forefinger as if deliberately goading her. She paid no attention. Harry looked at Nellie, who pressed her lips together and stared fixedly at her plate. This was bad, and Harry knew it. Lew had given Ozzie a kind of carte blanche to go after Josie, though what Lew would do if Ozzie did go after her Harry did not want to think. Lew could turn very nasty in the middle of a joke.

At the end of dinner, Lew said to Goff, "Listen, Jeeves, you can't serve dinner looking like a slob no more. Hereafter wear your tux. The one thing we need around here is class. And from now on when I talk to you, come to attention and salute."

Harry took one look at Goff's tight face and said to Lew, "You don't want a butler then, Lew, you want an orderly. Orderlies salute. Butlers just butle."

"An orderly? Like in a hospital?"

"No. Like in the army. If you want him to be an orderly, you'd have to get him an orderly's uniform."

Lew thought Harry was going along with the gag and he nodded eagerly, "Yeah, yeah, that's right. We'll get him an orderly's suit. What's it look like?"

"Well, like a Boy Scout's, but longer. Why not just let him be a butler and come out to the patio and say, 'Dinner is served.'"

"And salute."

"If he's a butler, he can't salute. It's against the rules. The orderlies union would get after us, and orderlies being in the army, that means Uncle Sam, and the last thing we want is Uncle Sam after us. Right?"

Harry knew what he was doing. It was still part of the gag, but he knew Lew wouldn't like any reference to Uncle Sam being after him. That wasn't funny. It was the end of the joke, in fact.

Lew stood up and said abruptly, "Who's for bowling?"

It wasn't a request; it was an order, and he led everybody down into the basement to the bowling alley. He divided them into two teams, his own team being Vito, Yutzy and Josie, all good bowlers. Josie was surprisingly good, rolling a consistent one-eighty. Ozzie and Goff threw their balls as if they did not care if they reached the other end of the alley or not. Harry had bowled less than a dozen times in his life, and Nellie had never bowled. But it was the kind of contest Lew loved, and he crowed and whooped and jeered as if his team were winning a tremendous victory.

Goff, of course, was pin-boy.

Lew had a wonderful time.

Harry did not get to talk to Nellie all evening.

After everyone else had been sent to bed—it was an order—Lew and Vito went out to the garage. Vito carried a Coleman lantern. They went down into the basement of the garage to the room into which Grizzard had been thrown. The man had managed to prop himself up against the concrete wall and he was sitting there, his eyes slightly crazy, when Lew and Vito walked in. The left side of his face was swollen and discolored. A trickle of dried blood from the corner of his mouth had rusted on his chin. There was motor grease in his almost white blond hair, and his forehead was smeared with it. He was a gaunt man, a rack of bones. He blinked painfully into the brilliant light and his mouth twitched and trembled as he tried to grin ingratiatingly at Lew. He was so weak he was barely able to sit upright even though propped against the wall. The hard white light of the Coleman lantern threw fantastic shadows of Lew and Vito against the wall.

Lew looked down at Grizzard and rolled his cigar from one corner of his mouth to the other.

"What was that crack you made to Vito?" he demanded suddenly.

Grizzard looked terrified and moved his jaws, but seemed unable to utter anything but a croaking sound.

Vito grunted something and Lew said impatiently, "Okay, okay, get him some then."

Vito went out and returned in a few minutes with a milk bottle of tepid water. He knelt beside Grizzard and let the man drink, a sip at a time. The man was frantic for water. He clutched at the bottle and sucked desperately at the few drops Vito was allowing him. Vito watched impassively. He looked up at Lew and made a thick-fingered gesture, signifying that it would be a little while before Grizzard would be able to talk.

Lew said, "Call me," and went out of the room. The lantern partially lit the basement and Lew looked up at the heavily timbered ceiling. Thick. He glanced around the basement. It was littered with empty oil cans and drums, waste, rusting car parts, molded cartons, and scattered unidentifiable debris. It was about a hundred feet long, thirty wide, and nine feet high. Lew nodded thoughtfully. With a little soundproofing on the ceiling, it would make a good shooting gallery. Lew loved shooting galleries. Shooting galleries, Coney Island, hot dogs, rides on the roller-coaster, the crowds. For a moment he felt inexpressibly lonely. To be at Coney Island right now! The people around you, the women.... For a moment he had a wild idea to build his own roller-coaster right here on the ground, a roller-coaster and a merry-go-round, a hot-dog stand. He gave his head a hard shake. It was crazy. Forget it. This is your hole, boy; don't horse around.

But he could have a shooting gallery. Vito could pick up a half dozen .22 rifles in town, and they could rig up some moving targets. Lew loved to shoot. He grinned a little, thinking of Josie with a gun. You'd sure have to duck fast when she started pulling that trigger.

That was it, a shooting gallery with clay birds and ships and a pendulum and all the other things that moved, like at Coney Island. He'd get Vito and Yutzy to work on it tomorrow. It wouldn't take more than a few days. With Goff's help.

And kites. They could fly kites from the roof of the house. He'd have Vito pick up a dozen kites in town. Jesus, all the fun you had when you were a kid. Kites, shinny, one-o'-cat, run-sheep-run, and smacking each other with stockings filled with flour on Hallowe'en, and the way some of the gang used to put stones in their stockings, and stones in the snowballs, too. Kids were the ones that had the fun, all right.

He was on his second cigar and wrapped dreamily in plans of organizing some of those good old kids' games when Vito appeared in the doorway and motioned. Grizzard began to babble the minute he walked into the little room.

Lew said, "Shut up."

Grizzard stopped short and looked up at him with pleading eyes. Lew said nothing, unnerving Grizzard still further with a long, stony stare.

"Now what was that crack you made to Vito?" he said abruptly.

"Nothing, Lew, nothing. Honest to God...."

"You said, 'Too bad the wop didn't get Lew that night.' Remember?"

"Sure, Lew, sure, but honest to God I didn't mean nothing. It was just one of them things like drop dead. It didn't mean a thing. Honest to God, Lew...."

"Shut up. I don't give a damn about that. All I want is, how'd you know it was the wop took a shot at me that night?"

"I ... I guess I heard you and Vito talking or something."

"The hell you did. If you heard us talking, it wouldn't be about that."

He grunted something to Vito, who was squatting in the corner, watching with flat black eyes. Vito shook his head. Lew looked back at Grizzard.

"You're a lying son-of-a-bitch," he said in a conversational tone. "Me and Vito never talked about nothing."

"Lew, for crissake, I never had nothing to do with it. Listen, Lew, listen to me. Jesus, Lew, honest to God...."

"Shut up. I'm thinking."

Lew was as outwardly calm as when he had told Harry Joyce his reasons for the flight to Florida. It had been easy to be calm with Harry. He was secure behind his twelve-foot wall—but this with Grizzard was something else again. He was sure Grizzard had nothing to do with the wop. In the first place, Grizzard was too dumb, and in the second place, he didn't have the guts, and in the third place, he didn't have the dough. A guy like the wop didn't go around shooting guys as a favor. You had to lay it on the line. Well, the wop wasn't going to point a gun at nobody no more, for love or money. Vito had taken care of that.

But there was little pleasure in the thought for Lew—now. At the time it had been a pleasure. A real pleasure. Vito could take a guy apart when he was told. But now was something else.

Grizzard had certainly overheard *somebody* talking about the wop. Was it Goff? Christ knows Goff hated his guts. Or Yutzy. Yutzy wasn't as dumb as everybody thought, and you never knew what was going on in Yutzy's head. And Harry Joyce. Or even Vito. No, no, no, not Vito. Never Vito.

Grizzard could not have heard it on the outside. Lew knew damn well he couldn't have heard it on the outside. Nobody would tell Grizzard a thing like that. Everybody knew Grizzard worked for Lew. Anyway, Grizzard never went outside. He was Lew's driver, and he ate, slept and screwed in the room over the garage, and he never saw anybody but Yutzy, Goff, Vito, or Harry Joyce, the cadre of Lew's organization. Sure there was a whore two or three times a month, but a guy had to have his tail, and they didn't count, anyway.

Jesus—Lew felt a prickle as the sweat burst from his forehead—*had he brought along with him down here to Florida in this very house the very guy that wanted to rub him out?*

His hand trembled slightly as he took the cigar from his mouth and hunkered down on his heels in front of Grizzard.

"You wouldn't hold out on me, would you, Grizz?" his voice was almost wheedling. "We slapped you around a little, but you had it coming, a crack like that. But I always treated you right, didn't I?"

A flicker of hope showed in Grizzard's eyes, and he said eagerly, "Sure, Lew, sure."

"Okay then. Who'd you hear talking about the wop taking a shot at me?"

Grizzard whimpered, "Honest to God, Lew, I thought it was you and Vito."

Lew brought his hand across in a stinging slap. Grizzard's head bounced back against the wall. Lew slapped him twice again, back and forth across the cheeks.

"I don't want any more crap now! Who'd you hear talking?"

Grizzard cried out and tried to hide his face in the hunch of his shoulder, babbling, "Honest to God, Lew...."

"Who, who, *who?*" Lew struck him with his fist, shouting, "Come on now, who, who, who?" Each time he yelled 'who,' he struck again. "Who? Goddam you, who?"

He lost all restraint and battered the face with his knuckles until Vito reached out and tapped his knee, indicating that Grizzard was unconscious. Vito had no tenderness for Grizzard. He was thinking only of Lew. In this mood, Lew would kill Grizzard. Vito knew that Lew did not want to kill Grizzard. All he wanted was for Grizzard to answer the questions. Therefore, Grizzard had to be kept alive. For a while.

Panting, Lew pushed himself to his feet and slapped the dust from the knees of his slacks with the back of his hand. There was madness in his eyes, but it was fading.

"The dumb son-of-a-bitch," he said heavily, "trying to put something like that over."

It never crossed his mind that Grizzard might actually be telling the truth, that Grizzard had actually overheard him talking to Vito about the wop. You didn't talk to Vito. Vito wasn't any guy to talk to.

He took a fresh cigar from his pocket and lit it shakily. "Let him lay there and think it over," he said to Vito. "Let him lay there and think over all the things he ever heard in his life. He'll remember, all right. You hear that, you dumb bastard?" He leaned over Grizzard and angrily twisted an ear. "Lay there till you remember who you heard, and every once in awhile we'll come in and help you with a smack in the snoot. We'll talk to him again tomorrow, Vit'. He'll remember."

He turned and walked out. Christ, he shouldn't get himself worked up like this. There was that ringing in his ears again. No, just one ear. The right ear. Every time he got himself worked up, there was that ringing in his ears. He felt a little dizzy as if his eyes were out of focus, like that.

As he approached the house, he saw the red glow of a cigarette on the patio and his heart gave a lurch. Then he saw that it was only Goff.

"What the hell are you doing up?" he demanded angrily. "I told you to go to bed."

Goff's hand tightened around the neck of the bottle on the floor beside his chair, and then pulled away as he heard Vito's footsteps on the shell path. No such luck as catching Lew alone in the dark. There was always Vito.

"Just smoking a cigarette," he said. "It was hot upstairs. I came down to get cool. Is there a law?"

The back of Lew's hand smashed across his face, sending the cigarette flying in a spray of sparks, and Lew snarled:

"I'm getting tired of your cracks all the time. I'm warning you, cut it out."

Goff said tightly, "You're the boss."

"Keep it in mind."

"Always, Lew, always."

"Is that another crack?"

"I was just telling you that I was keeping it in mind. Is that a crack?"

"Beat it. Go to bed. You bother me."

"Can I have a fan in my room?" Goff asked with exaggerated politeness. "It's hot."

"Go to bed, goddam it. Roast for all I care! Get the hell out of here or I'll beat your brains out."

Goff warily picked up the bottle and lunged toward the door. It was on the tip of his tongue to say, "Sweet dreams, Mr. Markey," but he bit it off. Vito had come out of the shadows of the trees and was approaching the patio. He did not want to be worked on by Vito.

He went into the house without a word. He knew that if he opened his mouth, the loathing would stab through his voice like barbs on a wire.

Lew glowered after him, his hands clenching and unclenching, and when Vito came up he said heavily, "Think it could of been Goff, Vit'?"

Vito shrugged his simian shoulders and rubbed his thumb across the tips of his fingers. Lew understood. It took money to hire a guy like the wop and Goff didn't have that kind of money.

Lew muttered to himself, "I wish to hell I'd left him up in Newark."

He wished he had left them all up in Newark—all except Josie, Ozzie and Vito.

CHAPTER FIVE

With cynical amusement, Goff watched Lew turn into a moody Caligula, one day laying down the law with threatening scowls and dark hints of reprisals, the next day clowning raucously to persuade everybody that he was really a good-natured fellow at heart and everybody's friend. It was Goff, more than anybody, who saw how sharply Lew watched them all. Goff was delighted. Lew was cancerous with the fear he had brought with him from Jersey. It was a malignant growth eating at his brain, sapping his sanity. One of these days Lew would go crazy entirely and do something so bestial that they would have to kill him, he would do in the open what he was doing to Grizzard in secret.

Goff knew about Grizzard. He knew that every day Lew went down into the basement of the garage with Vito, and he knew what went on down there, for he had followed them into the garage one day and saw the open trapdoor in the floor. He had listened until his ear brought the mumble of voices into focus.

"Well, how's the kid today?" Lew said, strangely jovial. "The memory getting any better? No? Tell you what we'll do, Grizz old kid, we'll help it along a little."

Goff flinched at the cry of pain that followed. He wanted to go away but a horrible fascination kept him frozen at the mouth of the trap. He heard Lew ask the same question over and over:

"Who'd you hear talking, Grizz? Who was it? You're not doing yourself any favors clamming up, kid...."

At times Lew's voice was oily and friendly, at other times wheedling, but finally it gibbered with insane fury pierced by the feeble cries of pain.

An hour later, when Lew came up from the basement, Goff saw him turn in the doorway and throw something back into the garage. Goff waited until Lew and Vito went into the house, and then he went into the garage and found what Lew had tossed on the floor. It was a kind of knout, made of five strands of twisted copper wire fastened to a short wooden handle. The ends of the wire were knotted and stained with blood. Goff threw it over the wall.

It took him several days to muster courage to go down into the basement. He selected the inevitable hour in the afternoon when Lew took Josie up to their room for "a little service here, sweetheart." He found the room down there, but there was a padlock on the door. Vito and Yutzy had started building the rifle range and there was a false wall between the door of the room and the range.

Goff put his mouth close to the door and said as loudly as he dared, "Grizzard? Can you hear me?"

He was answered by a moan.

"This is Goff, Grizzard. Can you hear me?"

Grizzard croaked, "Drinkofwaterdrinkofwaterdrinkofwater...."

"Sure thing, Grizzy, soon as I can figure a way around this goddam lock they got on here. Are they giving you anything to eat?"

"Drinkofwaterdrinkof water...."

"Sure, sure, sure."

Goff felt an unaccustomed wrench at his heart. He had never been friendly with Grizzard. He had never even liked him. But this was something else. From the ever-germinating soup of his mind rose a childhood memory of a silly dog he had named Sir Lancelot, probably the least Lancelot-ish of all canines, a foolish animal that had managed, in a gruesome fashion, to throw himself into the lawn mower. The bewildered whimpering of Grizzard behind that door reminded him of the pathetic Sir Lancelot. Goff could weep over animals, though he was cynical of humans.

He tugged futilely at the padlock, swearing under his breath. For a reckless moment, he considered taking a hammer and knocking it from the door, but he had enough sense to realize that this would help neither Grizzard nor himself.

He whispered at the door, "Be back in a minute, Grizzard," and went outside to the partially constructed rifle range. He knew that every minute he spent down here sharpened the risk he was running, and his eyes darted, seeking an inspiration. He did not know what he was looking for, but he had an opportunist's mind and when his glance fell on a brace and a case of bits, he knew that was it. Upstairs in the garage he had seen a coil of garden hose hanging on the wall. He ran up the stairs and hurriedly cut a two-foot length. He drilled a hole as low on the door as he could, down in the shadows, picking up every scrap of angered wood and putting them into his pocket. He thrust the hose through.

"Come on over to the door, Grizzard," he said urgently; his ear was tense for the sound of a footfall descending the steps to the basement. "You'll find a piece of hose. Suck on it. Make it snappy before somebody comes."

The other end of the hose lay in a pan of water which he refilled as fast as Grizzard could suck it up. He cut Grizzard's babbling gratitude short.

"Shut up!" he snarled. "I'd do the same for a dog. Now listen. I'll try to get some soup down to you. When you hear this shave-and-a-haircut knock, come right over to the door because I don't want to get caught feeding the animals."

"Thanks, Goff, thanks, Jesus, thanks, fella, I always said you were a right guy, I always said ..."

"Shut the goddam hell up goddam it! I'm not doing this for you so get that idea out of your head. I'm just practicing to be a major in the Salvation Army. I don't want your lousy thanks. Be back later, and don't forget that shave-and-a-haircut knock."

There was a dryness in his throat when he crept up the stairs and looked stealthily around before emerging into the garage.

Until recently, Goff had been certain that Harry Joyce was just another Lew Markey lapdog, growing fat and sleek on the Markey bounty. But lately Harry Joyce had begun to get that lean and hungry look. There had been a sharpening of Harry's features, a hardening of the eyes. Very little escaped Goff. He had a shrewd, hard mind. He could evaluate what he saw. He had made tentative overtures to Harry Joyce, subtly, and Harry had rebuffed him every time.

Harry Joyce was only another question mark in Goff's book. He knew that Harry was having trouble with Nellie, and that alone made Harry untrustworthy in his eyes. Nellie was too close to Josie, and Josie was Lew's. Goff knew by this time that Lew had plans for Ozzie and Nellie. Lew could be very sentimental, Goff knew. Lew was the kind of guy who could wear a carnation on Mother's Day, even though the old lady had died cursing him. Up in Jersey, Lew had been a real cemetery fiend, haunting the graves of his family, piling them high with flowers, erecting marble in various conventional forms to perpetuate their memory and his ego. Yes, Lew could be as sentimental as an old whore, and when Lew conceived a sentimental notion, such as brothers marrying sisters, he would never let go. Lew would marry

Nellie off to Ozzie whether they liked it or not, and Harry Joyce, with other plans for Nellie, would be six feet under when the nuptials were consummated. Harry, in Goff's estimation, was a bad risk.

It was at the end of the week that Lew, casting about for humiliating tasks, had sent Goff out into the tree-garden to pick a bouquet for Josie.

"What's them flowers there, Harry?"

"Periwinkles."

"Yeah, periwinkles. But they're all pink. Josie likes the white ones. Goff, c'mere. Listen. I want you to pick a bouquet for Josie. White periwinkles. A big bouquet, enough to choke a horse. But only white ones, understand? Stick one pink one in and I'll make you eat it with mustard. Now get off that dime...."

Humming to himself, Goff wandered idly around the tree-garden picking a white periwinkle here and there, taking his time. On the way back to the house, he saw Lew and Vito walk into the garage, and he knew from former experience that they would be down in the basement for at least an hour.

Josie was sitting alone on the patio when Goff walked up with the flowers. She was wearing a halter and skirt and her feet were propped up on the foot-rest of her deck chair, generously displaying her perfect legs. Her legs were always generously displayed. Goff's eyes went automatically to the shapely curve of thigh. Of all the men in the house, only Harry Joyce did not seem interested in the inventory of Josie's charms, but then Harry's emotions were otherwise committed.

Goff had never, physically, been this close to Josie before. Up in Newark, Lew had practically kept her isolated, and down here in Florida Goff had simply not bothered. He had dismissed her as a beautiful moron and let it go at that. He was surprised. He had never really looked at her before. Her beauty was overwhelming, but in her face there was a hurt, bewildered wistfulness.

"For me?" she cried when Goff handed her the bouquet. She gave him one of those languishing glances. "How'd you know I like these kind of flowers?" She held them to her face though they had no odor.

"All beautiful women like flowers," he said, sitting on the balustrade.

Her eyes melted on him. "They're beautiful," she said. "You know something? Nobody ever picked flowers with his own hands for me before. Isn't that funny?"

Those glances she kept throwing to him from under her lashes sent his pulses racing. "Where's everybody?" he asked.

She pouted. "Gone."

"Where?"

"I don't know. Ozzie's out there looking for Lew, and Harry and Nellie're playing tennis, and Yutzy's fixing stuff for dinner in the kitchen."

Goff's hands were moist. This was dangerous, but it appealed to him. It would be getting back at Lew, for one thing. He leaned forward.

"I'm supposed to make your bed in the morning," he said. "But you weren't up today."

"I like to lay in bed," she said archly.

"Yes, but what I want to know is, is there any special way you want me to make your bed. I don't want to make it just any old way. Know what I mean? I want to fix it nice," he winked, "for you."

She giggled. "It's funny, a man making my bed."

"Show me how you'd like to have it made," he said softly.

"Well ..." she glanced quickly around, "... sure."

He followed her up the stairs. His heart was beating quickly. He could see from the way the fabric of her skirt clung to her haunches that she was wearing nothing under it. Josie never wore any more than she had to. He went into the bedroom after her and locked the door quietly. He went over to the bed where she was standing uncertainly.

"I'm not so hot at making beds," he said. "How do you go about it?"

"Well ... you kind of straighten the bottom sheet first."

As she bent over to show him, he touched her lightly. She jumped and looked wildly at the door.

"Don't do that! Suppose he walked in on us?"

"He won't. He'll be gone for an hour."

"But suppose ..."

He took her in his arms and, before she could recover from the surprise, kissed her hungrily. She pushed against his chest with her hands, turning her face away from his probing lips. He held her with one arm and turned her face back with his other hand. He was much stronger than she had thought.

She wailed, "No, no, he'll kill us...." She had not thought this far ahead when she had given him those languishing glances, nor had she even considered that this would actually happen. No one, after her marriage to Lew, had ever taken her up like this. They were all too afraid of Lew. And Vito.

Goff whispered, "He won't kill anybody. He's scared to death himself. That's why he's hiding out here. He's scared to death."

He kissed her again more fiercely, pressing her back toward the bed. She fought him, and then suddenly let go and began wildly returning his kisses, digging into his hard shoulders with her fingernails, clinging to him.

Goff's bitter little world inexplicably exploded. She had a depth of emotion that had never been tapped, that had been surging close to the surface waiting for someone to set it flowing.

Lew never considered her for a minute. He had married her, so what more could she expect? He took her when he wanted her, when the hunger was on him, never bothering to arouse her first, never really stirring her. He simply threw her on the bed and, in his own words, "let her have it." She had never been able to respond. There was never any tenderness, never any prelude.

Goff's hands fled over her with all the little tendernesses. His kisses, growing more urgent, led her rather than drove her toward the vortex of the shared emotion.

Out of his hatred for Lew and the chaos of savage desire came this new thing. His mounting need of her cut like jagged lightning, but the aliveness of her against him, her soft clinging cries and her yielding response all tempered the violence in him. A different thing than he had ever experienced came over him and he slowed his tempo so that he was not running ahead of her, so that he was no longer alone, but the two of them together, merging and blending.

He unbuttoned her skirt and slid it down over her hips. He ran his hands over her thighs while she stood there with her eyes closed, trembling slightly. Then he swung her up in his wiry arms and lowered her to the bed. Hesitating, he hovered over her, ashamed suddenly that this had started out of his hatred for Lew. Her eyes opened.

"Please, please," she said tremulously, *"please!"*

He pushed up the scanty halter and cupped her breasts in gentle hands. He cried, "Oh Jesus!" and flung himself down beside her, pulling her to him.

After a while they were lying there, looking at each other with dazed wonder as if this had been something neither of them had ever thought or dreamed of. Something had been shorn from Goff—the thin bitterness, the protective cynicism. He was the kind of man to whom a thing like this came but once, if at all. He was fiercely monogamous. Among all the twisted, tangled threads of his life, that one thread ran straight and true.

And Josie knew that this was the first man who had not taken more from her than he had given. He had given her a completeness. As she looked down into his lean, crooked face, she wanted to mother him, yet also to be mistress to him, lover and loved.

He kissed her lightly and in a curiously tender and protective gesture pulled over the sheet to cover her nakedness.

"I'd better get out of here, honey," he whispered. "I don't want to get you in trouble."

And he meant exactly that. It was she of whom he was thinking.

She held him to another lifting kiss, and then he twisted out of bed and walked shakily from the room.

CHAPTER SIX

Harry Joyce was alone in the billiard-room, just off the bowling alley, glumly practicing massé shots. It had been somebody's whim to make the billiard-room "Olde English" with beamed ceiling and hunt prints and mullioned windows. The walls were oak paneled. For some reason, the felt on the billiard table was brown instead of the conventional green. It was not a cheerful room and, in fact, it could have been used to illustrate some of the gloomier passages of Oliver Twist.

But actually Harry preferred this room to any other in the house for the simple reason that Lew never went there. Lew had neither the patience nor finesse for billiards. Lew's game was bowling. He liked the heavy smashing ball and the thunder of tumbling pins. As no one else played billiards, Harry had come to think of this room as his sanctuary.

He heard the door open and vaguely saw that it was Goff. He did not bother to greet him. Then he heard the key grate in the lock and he looked up sharply.

"What's that for?" he demanded.

"Can I talk to you for a minute, Harry?"

The wiry little man's face was pale and there were pebbles of perspiration across his upper lip. He avoided Harry's glance.

Harry said curtly, "Beat it. I don't feel like talking." He turned to the table and leveled his cue for another shot.

Goff mumbled, "I did you a bad turn today, Harry."

The masseter muscles bunched at the ends of Harry's jaws, but he did not answer. The cue made a dull *tuk* as it struck the ball. He remained bent over the table watching the cue-ball carom sharply from the cushion and miss the white ball by inches. A bad shot. He straightened up and reached mechanically for the chalk.

"I want to tell you something, Harry," Goff's voice sounded strained. "I sicked Ozzie on Nellie today."

Harry laid his cue across the table and turned. "You did what?" he asked carefully.

Goff took an involuntary backward step. Harry's eyes had dilated until they were a blaze of white in his lean dark face.

Goff took a breath and said, "I told Ozzie Nellie was crazy about him."

Harry said, "Oh, hell," and the violence drained from his face. "She can't stand him. What was the idea?"

"To make trouble."

"You know, I don't know what's keeping me from smacking you straight on the jaw."

"I expected you would."

Harry gave him a long, hard stare. "You're up to something," he decided finally. "Let's have it. What's on your mind?"

"You're not worried about Ozzie?"

"Hell no."

"Well you ought to be! Listen to me for a minute. I know a million guys like Ozzie. He thinks he can do anything because his brother is Lew Markey, and in this house maybe he can. Keep that in mind. He's a potential rapist and you can take my word for it. The next time you see a picture in the paper, take a look at the kind of young loobies that are up for rape. All cocky young rats like Ozzie. I wanted to warn you."

Harry said harshly, "You must have told him quite a story to get him that steamed up."

"You don't have to steam up a bird-brain like Ozzie. That's the way he's built."

"So you've warned me. So what?"

"For God's sake, man, don't act like that. Warn Nellie. Tell her to watch her step. Tell her not to go any place alone with him, don't let herself get caught in a box with nobody around. He won't try anything if there's anybody around. That's all there's to it."

Harry turned his back. "Beat it," he said. "You make me sick to my stomach."

"There's more," said Goff, pleading; he had come to make a bid for Harry's help and he felt it slipping away. "You're on Lew's shit-list. I don't know why, but you are."

"Peddle it some place else, will you? I'm not in the market."

"He's been giving you looks all week. I know him better than you do. I've seen him give that kind of look before. I've been with him three years, and when he gives you that kind of look, watch your step. He's thinking something over. Something you've done, maybe. Or something he thinks you've done. He's weighing you. He's trying to make up his mind."

"Balls."

"Just listen to me, Harry, please. I see a lot more that goes on here than you think. This place is getting unhealthier every minute and I've got an idea that you and I, we'll need each other before this is over. You asked me before what was my idea in telling you all this. Okay. That's it."

"Count me out," said Harry flatly.

"You don't trust me?"

"Trust you!" Harry turned and looked derisively at him. "I wouldn't even take your word for which way is up. You're too glib and you're too damn clever for anybody's good except your own. You like to make trouble and then sit back and laugh when it starts. Well, sonny-boy, I'm not going to give you the chance to laugh at me, so trot along and make trouble some place else."

Goff had expected this. He had never given anybody any reason to trust him, and now he desperately needed somebody *he* could trust. He knew he could trust Harry Joyce. Harry was not like the others. Harry was not a crook. He was Lew's lawyer, but Goff's bright, shrewd eyes had noted many things about Harry, and he knew that Harry had finally turned against Lew.

There was only one thing left. If he wanted Harry to trust him, he'd have to take the chance and trust Harry. Implicitly. It would have to come to that in the end, anyway.

"All right, I'll tell you something," he blurted. "I'm in love with Josie and I want to get her out of here."

Harry said incredulously, "You're what!"

"I'm in love with Josie. I want to get her out of this time bomb we're living in."

"She wouldn't move a step with you."

"She'll come ... I mean ... a girl like that ... a girl like that, she wouldn't ... I mean, unless she were in love too ... she wouldn't ... not that way...."

Harry pursed his lips and whistled softly. He looked at Goff with sudden and profound pity. He felt no shock that Josie had gone to bed with Goff. It was one of those things he had expected to happen sooner or later. Not with Goff, particularly—anybody. Josie couldn't go on indefinitely throwing come-on glances around without somebody cashing in. There was no doubt that Goff was telling the truth now.

Something had happened to Goff, something had shaken him deeply. A roll in the hay with Josie must have been quite an experience.

Through these wry speculations, a kind of hope was struggling in Harry's breast. Suppose, by some wild chance, Josie actually was in love with Goff. Nothing could be wilder, but just suppose. You had to suppose something sometime, and this could be a ray of light in this murky madhouse. If Josie were in love with Goff, it was just possible that she might be willing to run off with him. And if Josie left, Nellie would go, too. It was crazy, but the whole thing was crazy. Despite himself, Harry felt a stir of growing excitement.

"If you don't mind my asking," masking his excitement behind sarcasm, "had you thought that getting out might not be quite as simple as leaving a telephone booth, my friend?"

"I've been thinking about it," Goff glanced over his shoulder at the locked door and dropped his voice. "It won't be easy. Yutzy and Vito take turns watching the gates all night, and it would be suicide during the day."

"Do you think we could get to Yutzy?"

"There's an outside chance."

Neither of them even remotely considered the possibility of getting to Vito. Vito was Lew's watchdog. Vito was not human. Vito was deadly. It would be worse than stupid to fool with Vito.

"I don't know about Yutzy either," worried Harry. "He does everything Lew tells him. Maybe we'd better leave him alone."

"We'd never get through that gate without help, Harry—day *or* night. And if we did get through, where would we be? Outside, and that's all. The nearest town is twenty miles south. I know, because I've checked the speedometer on the Ford every time Vito's gone to town. It registers forty miles on the nose. We'd have to walk twenty miles and that would take at least five hours with the girls along. We couldn't use any of the cars because Vito's taken out the distributor heads. Hell, I don't even know where we are! We're in Florida, but where? Do you know?"

Harry shook his head. "I just followed Lew's tail lights that night we rolled in here. I vaguely remember passing Tampa, but that's all."

"So we're on the west coast. You know what they call the west coast? The mangrove coast. If we set out for town on foot, we'd have to stick to the road or get lost in a mangrove swamp and that's sure death. Mosquitos and snakes. We'd never make it on foot. We'll have to have a car. There are other things to think about, too. We'll need money, for instance. Lew's taken every cent we had. We'll have to think this over damn seriously before we move a finger. I don't have to tell you what'll happen if we go off half cocked."

Harry nodded somberly.

Goff looked down at the palms of his hands, spreading the fingers. They were shaking. "I ... I suppose," he stammered, "you're going to check up on ... well, what I told you about Josie?"

"Wouldn't you, in my place?"

"I guess so ... but for God's sake, be careful with her. If you scare her, it'll be all over between her and me. She'd deny everything. Go at it easy. If you spoil it for me," Goff's voice edged, "you'll wish you hadn't, that's all."

"I won't spoil it for you. I'll get Nellie to handle that end of it."

"Yes, that would be the best way. And tell Nellie to watch her step with Ozzie, and in the meantime I'll see if I can cook up something to fix the little bastard's wagon."

"I'll tell her. Now let's get out of here. If Lew finds us in here with a locked door, there'll be hell to pay. He's jittery these days."

"He's scared to death."

"So am I," said Harry shortly.

Down in the small room in the basement of the garage, Vito threw a bucket of water over the unconscious Grizzard. Lew had spent an hour and a half down there today. He was developing a technique. He was beginning to learn just how far he could go before Grizzard passed out, and each day he was able to extend that period just a little longer.

Grizzard's face was hardly recognizable as a face. The skin was puffed and purple and cut, the eyes swollen, the lips like sausages. Vito looked down at him with stolid curiosity. A man like that was beyond his comprehension. If Grizzard did not know the answer to Lew's question—and Vito was disinterestedly certain that he did not—why didn't he make up an answer, just give any name? Harry Joyce, for instance. That was the name Lew wanted to hear. Lew had given Grizzard enough clues on that. If Grizzard had any brains he'd have said Harry Joyce before this. That was what Vito would have done. Getting beaten up like this all the time was crazy.

CHAPTER SEVEN

The *New York Times*, as usual four days late, was tossed over the wall by the newsboy from town, and in it was the story that Lew had predicted. It was a very short story, buried near the financial news, but it was there in black and white. Lew, and several other Jersey men, were being sought for questioning by the Essex County crime investigating committee. Lew was not the only one who had disappeared in the nick of time. Former members of Lew's Newark organization had already given testimony against him. The ship, thought Harry, was deserting the sinking rat.

Lew laughed about it, loudly and too much, burlesquing the search for himself, looking around trees, in the swimming-pool, up the flat sides of the twelve-foot wall.

"That Lew Markey," he kept saying, shaking his head. "He's a slippery one. You can't trust him for a minute. You turn your back, and he's gone. Where *can* he be? Dear, oh, dear, where can he be? My, my, my, my, slap my wrist. Where is that naughty man? Aha, I know! Here he is!"

He lifted Josie's skirt and leered under it. She flushed and jerked it out of his hand.

"That ain't funny, Lew!" she said sharply. Her eyes fled to Goff.

Harry could hardly have missed that, it was so obvious. Goff's face was so tight that his nostrils looked pinched. Harry looked quickly around to see if anyone else had noticed, but Ozzie as usual was gaping at the long flash of Josie's legs, and Nellie was staring down into her lap, ashamed that her sister could be so lewdly treated without protest.

Lew yelled at Josie, "What the hell's the matter with you all of a sudden? I'll look up it all I damn well want!"

He threw up her skirt. She was not wearing any panties. For a moment, even Lew looked nonplussed at what he had done. Her palm came down across his cheek with a ringing slap and before he could recover, she turned and ran from the patio. Harry grasped Goff's quivering arm and held him tightly.

Lew looked around and tried to clown his way out of it. This was one time he was wrong and knew it. "That Lew Markey," he said noisily, "you never know where he'll turn up. She might have had him hidden up there all the time."

Yutzy was the only one who laughed, but then Yutzy always laughed when Lew indicated something as being funny.

Goff was muttering, "I'll kill the son-of-a-bitch, I'll kill the son-of-a-bitch...."

Lew caught the mutter, but that was all. "What was that, Jeeves?" he demanded nastily.

Harry tightened his fingers on Goff's arm. If Goff answered cockily now, it would be the end of Goff. Lew's mood had soured.

But Goff's answer was unexpectedly disarming. "All I said, Lew, was that there's one place where you forgot to look for this guy Lew Markey."

"Where's that jerk?"

"Right there," Goff pointed to the flagstone on which Lew was standing.

Lew's face was blank for a moment, then he burst into a roar of laughter. "Yeah, yeah, and it's the one place they'll never look. That Lew Markey, they'll never catch up with him. He's always where they ain't." He brayed again.

But he could not laugh that uneasy look out of his eyes. He stopped clowning abruptly.

"Okay, okay," he growled. "Break it up. The show's over. Beat it, I want to read the paper in peace."

Yutzy gave him an odd glance and walked into the house to start dinner. He looked back once over his shoulder with painfully puzzled eyebrows and gave his head a short shake. Vito left the patio to check the padlocks on the gates. On Lew's orders, he checked them several times a day now. At no time, actually were the gates without surveillance. Goff looked at Harry, compressed his lips, and then went upstairs to change into the tuxedo that Lew now made him wear every night while serving dinner.

Lew gave Harry one of those surly, measuring glances—he seldom talked to Harry these days—and plodded down the walk to the swimming pool where Vito had placed a lounge chair from the living-room under the shady spread of the banyan tree. He lowered himself into the chair with a grunt and opened the paper in front of his face, a deliberate gesture to show Harry Joyce that he was a pariah and Lew wanted nothing to do with him.

Harry lifted his eyebrows and shrugged. He had noticed Lew's growing coldness, of course, but he had not taken it personally. Now there it was. Goff had warned him.

Nellie rose from her chair and started toward the doorway, but

Harry took a step and wound his fingers around her upper arm.

"I've *got* to talk to you," he whispered.

She resisted, keeping her face turned from him. "I have to go up and see Josie," she said woodenly.

"Later. I have to talk to you first."

Nellie glanced swiftly at Ozzie who was sitting on the balustrade, watching them with a smoldering expression on his soft, handsome face.

"Let her alone," he ordered Harry in a petulant parody of Lew's peremptory manner. "Want to go for a little walk, Nell?"

Harry tightened his hand on Nellie's arm and said sweetly, "Oh, I'm so sorry, Ozz, but Nellie has promised *me* this waltz." He warned her again with the pressure of his fingers.

"Later, Ozzie," she said. Then unwillingly to Harry, "I'd love to see the pandanus, but I have to be right back. I promised to do Josie's hair."

With astonishment, Harry saw that she was terrified. He gave her arm a reassuring squeeze and pretended to point out the more exotic trees as they strolled into the tree-garden.

She paid no attention to him and the moment they were out of earshot, she said distractedly, "Don't ever do that again, Harry. Please don't ever do that again. Lew'll be furious."

"Just because we take a little stroll together?"

"You don't understand."

"What's there to understand?"

"Please, Harry, just take my word ..."

"Sure. But for what?"

"Lew'll be furious. Don't make Lew mad at you, Harry. Please don't. I don't want anything to happen to you!"

She clung to his arm and looked appealingly up into his face—but not, however, without first throwing a frightened glance back through the trees toward the house. Harry patted her hand. He wanted desperately to kiss her and take her in his arms, but he knew that if he did, her panic would burst into flame.

"What is it, honey?" he asked gently.

She shook her head. "Please don't ask me."

"Is it this business of Lew making a match between you and Ozzie?"

She gasped. "How did you know?"

"It's hardly a secret. Who told you? Lew?"

"Josie. She told me that Lew thinks you're trying to ... well, beat Ozzie's time, and he's furious with you. He asked Josie to keep an eye on you and tell him everything you do. She told him she would, but she won't."

Harry nodded thoughtfully. "How do you feel about it?" he asked.

"Ozzie doesn't want to marry anybody," she said scornfully. "All he wants ..." she flushed. "Well, you know all he wants."

"That's what I wanted to talk to you about."

"Ozzie?"

"Let's keep moving. I'll tell you while we walk."

They walked in silence. It was as if the same sense of unreality had crept over both of them at the same time. These grotesque trees, the brooding shadows, that immense house back there with its dark corridors and corners that swallowed even the echoes.

And Lew.

In Newark, Lew had been remote—but here they felt his full weight smothering them. Everything they ate, drank or did was censored by his likes or dislikes. There was nothing unreal about that. It was there twenty-four hours a day. They could see it, taste it, hear it, feel it; it enveloped all their senses. The unreality was what it was making of them.

They had to keep their eyes open as they walked. If Lew had told Josie to spy on Harry, it was a foregone conclusion that Vito and Yutzy had the same orders. Probably Ozzie, too.

Nellie said tensely, "If it's something about Lew, I don't want to hear it. I don't even want you to say it."

"It's about Ozzie. He had a talk with Goff, and Goff led him to believe that you're really in love with him, but you're playing hard to get."

"That's silly!"

"Wait. I thought so, too, but Goff brought up another point that isn't silly. He's afraid that one of these days Ozzie will, well, attack you. He says that's the way Ozzie's built. So don't go anywhere with him alone. Always be sure that either Goff or I is around. Or anybody, as far as that goes. Excepting Lew or Vito. I think they might get a kick out of seeing Ozzie ... well, you know what I mean. Be careful."

"Oh, no, Harry. You're only fooling."

"Not about this, not ever where you're concerned honey, so promise me you won't take any chances."

She pulled her arm from his hand and faced him angrily on the path. "Now, Harry," she said, "this has gone far enough. You're letting your antagonism toward Lew affect everything you do or think. I'm not afraid of Ozzie. He's nothing but a ... a spoiled brat, and don't try to make him out worse than he is. The last person on earth that I'll ever worry about is Ozzie."

"All right. Don't worry about him. Just watch yourself."

"If you only knew how ridiculous you sound!"

"I'm willing to sound ridiculous," he said stubbornly. "I ..."

"Oh, stop it, stop it, *stop it*...."

She covered her ears with her hands. He could see that she was close to hysteria. It was not just this thing with Ozzie. She had the strength to take that. The strain had been building up all week.

Harry said quietly, not touching her, for he knew that she would go to pieces at his touch, "I've been talking to Goff. I think he can be trusted."

Snap her out of it, he was thinking, *make her realize what kind of mess this is, don't let her run away from it this time.*

"Yes," he said deliberately, "I'll trust Goff. He's in love with Josie." He watched her eyes widen.

"He's what?" she said incredulously.

"He's in love with Josie. And from what he told me, she's in love with him."

"That's not true, Harry. I refuse to believe that. It's not so. He's lying."

"She went to bed with him. He wasn't lying about that. I could tell. And these days and in this house, it's not the kind of thing to lie about, not even in a joke. Now here's what I want you to do. I believe Goff, but I want you to check up. I want you to see if you can get Josie's side of it."

"Lew'll kill them. He'll kill both of them."

"He's not going to get the chance."

"He'll find out. He'll kill them. In Newark he almost killed a drunk who tried to get Josie to dance with him in a nightclub. They had to take the man to the hospital. Oh, God, Harry, he'll kill Josie. He'll kill her!"

Harry seized her shoulders and shook her. "Stop it, Nellie! He's not going to kill anybody. We're going to get out of here before he gets the chance."

She twisted frantically in his grasp, thrusting at his chest with both hands. "I've got to talk to Josie. I've got to talk to her right away. Oh, God."

"You're not going to talk to Josie, the state you're in." He slapped her sharply across the cheek, slapped her again when she continued to struggle insanely. She stiffened and looked at him with huge eyes. She touched her cheek.

"You ... you hit me," she said in a small, wondering voice.

Then her tears came in a relieving flood. Harry held her tightly. She pressed herself to him. The warmth of her body flowed into him. He kissed her hair and murmured soothingly. The sobbing stopped as abruptly as it began, it spilled out and that was the end of it.

She pushed herself away from Harry. He let her go.

"I'm all right now," she said calmly. "I'll talk to Josie. I'll find out if Goff is telling the truth."

"Don't scare her, honey."

"I won't. I can handle Josie." She was in full possession of herself and spoke calmly.

Harry said, "You realize how much depends on the way you handle Josie, don't you?"

"Yes."

"We're going to get out of this madhouse, honey, and we're going to take Josie with us."

She started stiffly, "I hope ..." and then the stiffness evaporated and she cried, "Oh, Harry!" She flung herself into his arms and kissed him passionately. Never before, even in Newark had she kissed him like this, so recklessly and with such complete surrender of her lips. His pulses hammered and they swayed as if they were on the brink of consummation. He was sharply aware of every point of contact—the swell of her breasts against him, the long thrusting line of hip and flank, of her lips burning on his. In that kiss was the essence of the act of love itself. It was Harry who broke the kiss.

"This is crazy," he said thickly.

They looked at each other with smoky, frustrated eyes. They had been within a breath of the affirmation of their love—and had to pull back. This, more than anything else, brought home to them the iron-fisted completeness of Lew's tyranny.

Without a word they turned and walked hand in hand, but when the white walls of the house showed through the tangle of trees, they dropped hands and walked sedately side by side, not touching. Harry felt swollen from the rage that churned within him.

CHAPTER EIGHT

Lew had seen them walk down the path and into the tree-garden, but he ignored them. He scowled behind his paper, and he let them go. The hell with them. All the same, that Nellie was a nice little piece with those high pointy breasts and that cute little behind that seesawed just enough when she walked to make you want to put both open hands on it and pull her hard against you while she hung on your mouth in one of those warm, wet kisses.

Lew felt himself begin to simmer at the thought of it. Josie had been getting worse and worse. You might just as well go to bed with a rubber doll. She couldn't give you enough of a toss to make it worth the effort. And that business today when he was just horsing around. Slapping him even! Was it his fault that she didn't wear something under her skirt? He felt a little defensive about that. But what the hell did she think marriage was—a box of candy and a kiss on the cheek?

He glanced covertly at the path again; Harry and Nellie had disappeared behind the row of six limequat trees. That little Nellie was stacked, all right. What a dope he'd been not to have noticed it before. Well, one of these days he'd make up for lost time.

He heard someone coming down the shell path toward him, and he kept the newspaper up in front of his face to show that he didn't want to be bothered. It was Ozzie.

"Did you see that?" Ozzie demanded petulantly.

Lew pretended to read. "See what?"

"That lousy Harry Joyce made Nellie take a walk with him."

"What'd he do, point a gun at her?"

"He took her by the arm and wouldn't let her go. She didn't want to go."

"Why didn't you stop him then?" Lew wasn't interested in Ozzie's woes at the moment. Furthermore, he wanted to take a shot at Nellie himself. Better if she didn't get interested in Ozzie right away. You couldn't go around laying your kid brother's girl friend. It was a point of etiquette.

"How could I stop him?" asked Ozzie peevishly.

"Give him a poke in the snoot."

"He's bigger than me."

Lew lowered his paper and looked disgustedly at Ozzie. "Afraid of getting your hair mussed," he jeered.

Ozzie flushed and Lew laughed shortly.

"If you want a dame, kid," he advised, "you got to go after it, not let some guy waltz her out from under your nose."

"Maybe I'll take a shot at Josie instead."

It was Lew's turn to flush. "Talk sense," he growled.

"Talk sense? What do you mean talk sense? The way you showed off her snatch today in front of everybody, I got the idea you were inviting us to give her a jolt. In case you're thinking of standing at the door and collecting from us as we go in, and I wouldn't put it past you, keep it in mind that you took all our money. Of course, if you're giving it away for free...."

Lew struck up at him with a sweeping backhand blow, catching Ozzie across the mouth with the knuckles of his right hand. Ozzie staggered and fell with a bleating cry. Lew's jaw dropped at the enormity of what he had done. Never, never before had he as much as laid a finger on Ozzie, and he hadn't meant to this time. It was that business of showing off Josie's snatch. He hadn't meant to do that either, and Ozzie shouldn't have thrown it in his face.

Lew half rose from his chair, stammering, "I ... I'm sorry, kid. I didn't mean that."

Ozzie snarled at him like a spitting cat and scrambled to his feet. A trickle of blood wavered from the corner of his mouth and sluggishly crept across his chin. Ozzie touched it and goggled incredulously at the incarnadine stain on his fingers tips. His eyes dilated and he looked up at Lew.

"I'll fix you!" he screeched. "I'll fix you for that!"

He spun around and ran for the house, holding a handkerchief to his mouth.

Lew ran a few steps after him, calling to him. Ozzie did not even look back. Lew stopped and clenched his hands.

"The hell with you," he yelled.

He returned to his chair, shook out his paper angrily, and slumped down behind it.

What was the matter with everybody, anyway? They never had it so good. Were they going crazy or something? One after another—Josie, Ozzie, Harry Joyce.

By this time Lew had convinced himself that Harry Joyce was acting peculiarly. He had not made up his mind yet that Harry was mixed up with Grizzard or the wop who had taken a shot at him that night. But Harry was acting funny, all the same.

Was there something between Harry and Josie?

This was a new thought and it brought furious blood pounding into his face. Harry and Josie. His hands tightened into hard knuckly balls. He'd kill them. He'd string Harry up by the thumbs and let Vito go to work on him.

But he wouldn't kill Josie. He'd figure out something special for her, maybe strip her bare ass naked and let Vito and Yutzy have her, or turn her over to that guy in Tampa that traded in women, or maybe ... His mind fingered grim obscenities with which to scourge her.

He'd catch them together, that's what he'd do. He'd keep his eye on Harry Joyce. He'd have Yutzy and Vito keep their eyes on him, too.

He turned his head and saw Harry and Nellie coming toward him through the tree-garden, hand in hand. The evil dream exploded. What a jerk he was! Harry had never even looked at Josie. It was Nellie he was after. What was the matter with him, thinking things like that about Harry? He missed Harry. Harry was the only one in the whole damn place he could talk to. You couldn't talk to Vito or Yutzy, Ozzie was just a kid, Goff was only a stooge, and Josie didn't have a brain in her head. But what fun he and Harry had when they first came down here. When you talked to Harry you had to keep on your toes. Harry was smart. He was a smart kid, and a laugh every minute when he got going, like in those games of gin rummy. Harry would never two-time him.

Hell, he'd practically taken Harry out of the gutter back there in Newark. A guy doesn't forget a thing like that overnight. And had Harry ever two-timed him? Never, and he'd had plenty of chances up there in Newark. Christ, when you came right down to it, Harry was the best friend he had; honest, a guy you could trust.

When Harry and Nellie came out sedately from the cool shadows, Lew threw his paper aside and called, "Come here a minute, Harry. Come here a minute, kid, I want to talk to you."

Nellie sucked in her breath, but Harry gave her a reassuring smile. There was nothing menacing in Lew's tone. Lew watched him approach with that light, springy step of his, head high, mouth slightly smiling.

Lew said affectionately, "Sit down, kid," hooked his foot in an aluminum lawn chair and swung it around for Harry.

Harry sat down, still smiling lightly. Lew leaned forward and laid his hand on Harry's knee.

"What's the matter between us, kid?" he asked.

Harry quickly noted that moist, sentimental glisten in Lew's eyes. It didn't surprise him, but he wondered what had brought it on.

"Why, Lew," he said easily, "I didn't know anything was the matter between us."

"Don't kid me, kid. You think I'm a jerk, don't you?"

"I never thought you a jerk, Lew."

"Well, then you think I'm a bastard."

"Why should I think you a bastard?"

"You think I'm a bastard because I stuck my nose in you and Nellie. Well, let me tell you something, kid," he patted Harry's knee earnestly,

"I'm sorry. I apologize. I'm a jerk. Don't deny it. I know I'm a jerk. The best friend I have and I try to futz him up. That's the jerk in me."

Harry smiled without answering. You never knew in what direction Lew would take off during one of these self-pitying sprees.

"I apologize, Harry. I can't do more than that, can I? I apologize."

"There's nothing to apologize for, Lew."

Jesus, he was thinking, *don't let him get too deep into this; don't let him wallow; he'll remember it tomorrow and hate your guts.*

"Forget it, Lew," he said firmly. "There was no harm done."

"Well ... there could of been, kid. Why didn't you tell me you were nuts about Nellie? It wasn't nothing to be ashamed of. Why didn't you tell me when I was flapping my blap about Nellie and Ozzie? I didn't mean nothing by it, kid. I wouldn't of given it a thought if I knew how it was between you and Nellie. You should of told me, Harry," he said with humid reproach.

Harry still smiled. He wanted to laugh. He had not believed that this was what had been on Lew's mind all the time, even when Nellie had told him. This was the kind of thing Lew used as camouflage—and it still nagged in his mind that there was, or had been, something else.

"Well," he said, "we were sort of keeping it a secret. Knowing how you feel about Ozzie."

"That clown!" Lew made a contemptuous chopping gesture with the edge of his hand.

"Wait a minute, Lew," it was time to step in and stop it again; for the time being he was in Lew's good graces, and he wanted to keep it that way; he did not want to give Lew anything to brood over later; not for a while, anyway. "There's nothing actually wrong with Ozzie...."

"You mean nothing that a swift kick in the ass won't cure, don't you?"

It would take more than one, and with a bigger foot than either you or I have, Harry thought.

But he said, "He's young, Lew. Make allowances. He's full of energy." (*God forgive me, but I did have my fingers crossed, didn't I?*) He smiled sweetly, "Maybe he needs something to do, Lew, as an outlet for his high spirits. Give him something to do. Let him help Vito and Yutzy with the shooting gallery."

He almost laughed aloud on that. If Lew put him to work, Ozzie'd be so mad he'd bite clean through his teething ring. Give him one of those home-permanent sets, he thought, and let him wave his hair all day.

"You're right, Harry," Lew nodded solemnly. "He's had it too good."

"Wait a minute, Lew. If you're going to put Ozzie to work, don't do it as a punishment. Do it as a favor."

"Come again?"

"Don't punish him. Do it for his own good."

"You got a point there, kid. But Jesus, Harry, I'm glad you're not sore at me. We always had a lot of laughs together, didn't we? How about a little game of gin rummy after dinner tonight like we did when we first came down?"

"Let's play 'Accident.' You'd like that, and everybody could join in."

"Sure. How's it go?"

"Well, you get everybody in a small room, say about ten feet square. One of us is blindfolded and is given a baseball bat. At the word 'go,' he is allowed to take three healthy swings. If he hits anybody, it's called an 'Accident,' and he scores one point and takes three more swings. But if he doesn't get anybody, the next man around takes the bat. The last man on his feet wins. If we don't have a baseball bat, we could use a gun."

Lew listened, nodding delightedly. When Harry finished, he cried, "Yeah, yeah, yeah, let's play that. But we'll blindfold everybody and give them all baseball bats. But you and me, we'll duck out and watch the fun," he whooped and pounded Harry's knee, doubling over with mirth. He wiped his eyes with the back of his hand. "Know any other games like that, kid? We'll play them all."

"Sure. We could play Mexican roulette, too."

"How's that one go, Harry, how's that one go?"

"Well, you get everybody in this room again, and then you take a loaded gun and cock it...."

"Yeah, yeah?"

"Then you throw it up and hit the ceiling with it."

"*Bam!*" whooped Lew. "*Bam!* Right?"

Oh, God, thought Harry, *why did I ever start this? The next time he turns sour, he'll make us play it!*

"It's not a very good game," he said. "The ceiling gets all chipped from the gun bouncing against it. The game I like is gin rummy."

"The hell with gin rummy, kid. You can't play it with baseball bats. Name me another game with baseball bats."

Lew could never really go along with a gag; he always grabbed it by the neck and dragged it to death.

"What's another game with baseball bats, kid," he urged, an anticipatory grin tugging at the ends of his mouth.

"Baseball," said Harry. "And I know one with billiard cues. Billiards."

Lew was convulsed. That Harry Joyce! A real comedian. Better than Jerry Lewis. A laugh a minute. Good old Harry. How could you be sore at a guy like that?

"I love you, kid," he gasped. "Honest to God, I love you. Together again, eh, kid. Together again." He reached out and squeezed Harry's knee fondly. Then, fumbling for Harry's sympathy and understanding, "What'd you think of that Josie today, popping her wig like that? I didn't mean nothing by it. Know what I think, kid? I think she's trying to get herself elected Miss Jerk of 1953."

"Just a moment, Lew."

"Listen to me first, kid. Listen to my side of it. You'll see I'm right. I'm not a bad guy. I level with everybody. That's a fact, ain't it, Harry? I always leveled with you, didn't I? I always give Josie everything she wanted. She wants a Caddy. Okay, I buy her a Caddy. She wants a fur coat. What do I do? I buy her a fur coat. Everything she wants, I give her. No questions asked." Lew's voice rose indignantly. "And what do I get in return? A slap in the puss. I been too good to her. That's the whole thing. She's spoiled. She needs to be slapped around a little, that's her trouble. I'm going to give you a piece of advice, kid. Don't ever treat them too good; they turn on you. Right? Okay. Now I got my rights too, ain't I, Harry? I'm married to the dame. She's married to me. She had no call slapping me like that. So what I say, if it's six of one, it's a half dozen of another. If she can slap me in the snoot, I can slap her around, as of now. Right, kid? Right?"

Harry said gently, "No, Lew."

"No? What do you mean, no?"

"I've got news for you."

"News? What kind of news?"

Harry stalled, desperately trying to think of something to say. If Lew hit Josie, Goff would go at Lew and Vito would go at Goff, and it would be a mess.

"You mean you've got no idea?" he asked.

"Idea of what?"

"You've no inkling?"

"If you got something to say, kid, say it," Lew was getting peevish. "Come on, come on."

"Josie hasn't told you?"

"She told me all right. She told me with a slap in the snoot. Tell me what?"

"She's pregnant, Lew."

Lew's face went stupid with surprise. He clutched the arms of his chair. "She's ... what?"

"She's going to have a baby, Lew. She didn't tell you? She didn't say a word?"

"You're nuts!"

"No I'm not, Lew," he said. "I've got eyes in my head. I know the signs. She likes to lie in bed these mornings, doesn't she?"

Lew made a meaningless gesture with his hand. "She always did. So what?"

"There's a difference, Lew. She used to be full of pep, but now she gets up from bed and lies in the deck chair all day. Her ankles looked a little swollen to me today. That's a sure sign. This morning I heard her being sick in the bathroom. That's another sure sign. And there are other things, too. She's touchy, she flies off the handle at the least thing, she can't bear to have you near her. This is just a stage, Lew, that all pregnant women go through."

"What the hell do you know about it?"

Harry ignored Lew's glare. Lew hated being surprised. In another moment he'd begin to yell.

"Hell, Lew," Harry smiled, "my old man was an obstetrician."

"What's that make me?"

"He was a baby doctor, Lew," Harry lied. "So for God's sake, I should know a pregnant woman when I see one, shouldn't I?"

Lew gripped the arms of his chair. "Christ, Harry," he said, "do you know how long I been trying to have a kid? Since I was married. Every time I give it to Josie, I say, 'Come on, kid, let's make one this time.' No dice. I think something's wrong with her. Of all the dames I can pick, I pick her. A half dozen times I was going to kick her out on her ass. Jesus," he began to grin, "so finally she's knocked up. I'll be a son-of-a-bitch!" he jumped up, grabbed Harry's hand and pumped it excitedly. "What the hell do you know about that, knocked up! I'm goin' right up, kid. I'm goin' right up," he looked back over his shoulder at the house, "I'm going right up and tell her when the time comes she's going to the best fuggin' hospital in the country and she's going to have the best fuggin' care any broad ever had...."

"No, Lew," Harry interrupted quickly. "This is the wrong time. She's upset. Let her calm down."

"Let *her* calm down! What about me?"

"Use your head, Lew" (Harry cursed inwardly, cursing the wayward thought that had brought this on). "This is a critical time in her life...."

"It's a critical time in my life, too. Who's been trying to make this fuggin' baby, me or her?"

"Do you want a baby, Lew?" asked Harry sharply. "All right, let her alone, then, or she'll have a miscarriage. You've kicked her around enough for one day. You've got to treat her with kid gloves."

Lew yelled, "I'll treat her with ..." he stopped. He rubbed his hands up and down his thighs, breathing heavily. "Get your ass out of here," he snarled. "I got to think this over."

Harry walked swiftly into the house. He bounded up the stairs to the second floor, taking them three at a time. He knocked softly but urgently on Nellie's bedroom door. There was no answer. He had a moment of unreasoning panic, thinking that she might have gotten caught by Ozzie, and then he remembered that she was going to go to Josie. He rapped at the next door, Josie's. He heard someone cross the room inside.

"Go away!" it was Nellie's voice, sharply.

"It's me, honey," he whispered, his lips close to the panel. "I have to talk to you. It's important."

The door opened and she slipped out into the hall. She kissed him quickly and put her fingers to her lips.

"She's hysterical," she said in a low voice. "She'll be all right. It's that awful thing Lew did to her down on the patio."

"I've got it fixed so that he won't do that again. Listen. I told him she's pregnant."

"Oh, no!"

"It was the only thing I could think of offhand. He was brooding about that slap she gave him and he had just about made up his mind to give it back to her with both hands. And you know what Goff ... did she say anything about Goff?"

"She loves him, all right. I can't understand it. What can she possibly see in that ..."

"Please, honey, listen to me. He might take it into his head to come up here at any minute. Josie has to act pregnant, but tell her to do it as if she didn't know she was pregnant. There's something the matter with her, but she doesn't know what it is. Get the idea? If she starts babbling about babies, she'll ham it up. She doesn't know what's the matter with her. Tell her she has to pretend to be sick every morning even if she has to lock herself in the bathroom and stick her finger down her throat. Tell her to complain about her ankles. Tell her to be cranky and whiny and not want anybody to touch her, especially Lew. And food. She has to get a sudden craze for something. Mangoes. And ... well, you probably know better than I do the way a pregnant woman would act. You tell her."

"I've never been pregnant, darling. But after we get married we'll change all that, won't we?"

"Nut," he kissed her. "I don't think you'll have to worry about Ozzie any more. Lew has given us an official blessing, you and me. For some reason or other, he loves me again. We're going to play gin rummy tonight, and just now he laughed at all my jokes. Some day I'm going to try to figure out what lives in that swamp he calls a mind. But keep Josie coached, will you? We're walking a narrow line."

"All right, darling. I'd rather get back to her now. Watch your step with Lew. I don't trust him even when he's being nice."

"I trust him least when he's nice," said Harry emphatically.

They heard someone coming up the stairs, and Nellie ducked back into the bedroom. It was only Ozzie. Harry walked toward his own room. Something crawled on his face and he brushed at it. It crawled again. It was cold perspiration.

CHAPTER NINE

Goff knew that something had happened. He had not been able to talk with either Josie or Harry before, during or after dinner, but he saw the change in Lew. All through dinner he was exceptionally solicitous toward Josie, and Harry Joyce was the white-haired boy again. Goff folded his lips tightly but kept his eyes and ears open. He watched Harry with smoldering suspicion. And in the midst of everything, Josie suddenly emptied her plate of steak and French fried potatoes on the floor and said calmly that she wanted a mango.

Goff sucked in his breath, expecting Lew to explode, but instead Lew turned on him and barked, "You heard her. Get it!"

Goff said, "Yes, sir," and ducked out into the pantry.

"And you, for crisake," Lew leaned over the edge of the table, glaring at Josie. "Coming down here emptying your plate on the goddam floor and all that stuff. Stay up in your fuggin' room, hear me? That's my kid you're carrying around in your belly, and you're not taking any chances with it."

He looked ready to erupt. Harry started, "Lew ..." when Nellie interrupted.

"Is this your idea of treating your wife with kid gloves?" she asked coldly.

Lew was taken by surprise. "Well, Jesus Christ," he began to purple, "I'm trying to take care of her, ain't I?"

"Then don't shout," Nellie was icy. "What do you want to do, give her a nervous breakdown?"

Lew looked around the table, swelling with impotent fury. He clenched his hands, but under Nellie's steady, accusing eyes, he did not shout again.

He said heavily, "She should be in bed. She should take care of herself. We been trying ever since I got married to make this fuggin' kid, and she shouldn't take chances...."

"I want," interrupted Josie calmly, "a dill pickle."

Harry jumped up before Lew could interpose. "One dill pickle for the lady with the baby," he said brightly, and walked quickly out of the dining-room toward the kitchen.

Harry met Goff in the butler's pantry between the dining-room and the kitchen.

He whispered hurriedly, "Come up to Nellie's room tonight after everybody goes to bed."

"What's going on here?" Goff demanded suspiciously.

"I'll tell you later. Now let's get back to the kitchen with that mango. Josie wants a dill pickle. Don't look like that. Everything's under control."

Goff said shortly, "I hope so."

He stood in the doorway of the dining-room when Harry gave Josie the pickle. She wrapped it carefully in her napkin and pushed back her chair.

"I'm going to eat it in my room," she announced. "I want Nellie to come up with me. I don't want anybody else." She looked straight at Lew. "I don't want anybody but Nellie near me tonight."

To Goff's astonishment, Lew said, "That's okay, sweetheart. I'll sleep in one of the other rooms. Go upstairs with her, Nellie. Stay with her. If she wants anything, anything at all, you get it for her, understand?"

Goff could not understand this suddenly solicitous Lew at all, but he had an idea that Harry Joyce had gotten the needle into Lew some way. And it didn't take any clairvoyance to see that for the moment Harry was in and Ozzie was out. There had been some kind of hassle between Lew and Ozzie. Ozzie's mouth was pinched and furious. Lew ignored him coldly.

Goff had to clear the table when Lew finished eating. This was a rule. Lew had decided that soiled dishes were offensive to his finer sensibilities. He liked to sit at the table and smoke a cigar after dinner and give everybody the word on a few general subjects, but it upset him to have to sit there in the middle of all that garbage, as he called it. Goff stacked the dishes on a tea cart. For this task he had to wear a frilly organdy apron that Lew had found in one of the closets.

"This is a high-class place," he said, "and all high-class places have maid service."

Such indignities merely amused Goff. It was not he who was being degraded by these petty cruelties; it was Lew, who had invented them.

But tonight Goff was jittery, not knowing what Harry Joyce had up his sleeve. This sudden friendliness of Lew was unnatural, and it was a thing that could explode in their faces. Lew had to be handled like nitroglycerin. No one alive could handle Lew one hundred per cent of the time, and alive was what you wouldn't be if you handled him wrong. Goff could see the tension in Harry's face. Harry was really working at it. Goff's hands shook a little as he removed the soiled dishes, and they were going to shake, he knew, until after that conference in Nellie's room. It wasn't a matter of trusting Harry Joyce—he had to trust him—but it was a matter of knowing what was going on. And something was going on because Harry was drawn as tight as a wire.

"Now take women, kid," said Lew. "Have you ever really stopped to think about women. I don't mean quiff; I mean *think* about them."

"Give us the word, Lew," smiled Harry lazily.

"Okay. You take us guys. We futz around, have ourselves a time, and the next day it's somebody else. Right? Okay. But you take a woman. Every woman, kid, is a mother in her heart, and when you stop to think about it, what right have we got to fool around with something like that? What right have we got to say that this dame is just a piece of tail, or that dame is a tramp. For all we know, it's the mother instinct," he shook his head. "All my life I've been a jerk. I admit it."

Ozzie cackled and rolled his eyes at the ceiling. Lew looked at him.

"Go upstairs!"

Ozzie snarled, "Go to hell!"

Lew rose slowly from his chair and walked toward him. Ozzie bleated and crossed his arms protectively in front of his face. Lew twisted his fingers in Ozzie's collar, jerked him from the chair and shoved him toward the door.

"Go upstairs," he said heavily, "and lock yourself in. And don't come down till I tell you to."

Ozzie fled. Lew went back to his chair at the head of the table.

"I don't want to be too hard on him," he said. "I was the same kind of jerk when I was his age. You know what a woman is to him, kid? Just a lay on legs. But he'll get over it. One of these days he'll realize."

Goff reached under Lew's gesturing hand and whisked out the coffee cup. Unfortunately, Lew as usual had spilled coffee in the saucer and, in taking it from the table, Goff spilled a few drops on Lew's slacks. He saw it happen and instinctively ducked, but he was not fast enough. Lew's furious backhand swing caught him across the face. It was a heavy blow and he staggered, back-heeled, caught in the rug and sprawled on the floor. Lew leaped from his chair and straddled him, slapping him back and forth across the face. Goff cried out and struggled. Lew swore and shoved the heel of his hand into his face. Harry Joyce jumped at Lew and grabbed him in a hammerlock. Lew was strong, but Harry had him short. Two chairs went down as Lew lunged furiously. A look of fear clenched Lew's face and he screamed:

"Vito! Vito!"

Goff saw Vito hurtle from the doorway and clutched frantically at his knees. He was flung back as if he had tackled a plunging tank with his bare hands. He crashed against the wall and when he scrambled to his hands and knees, Vito had Harry Joyce in a bear hug and Harry's face was slowly purpling as Vito's arms tightened around his chest. Lew leaped to his feet and slapped at Harry's face, screaming obscenities. He drove his knee at Harry's crotch, but Harry turned it with his thigh. Despite the punishment he was taking and that terrible pressure around his chest, Harry was still managing to smile.

"Don't excite yourself ... Lew," he gasped. "That's ... bad. You're about ... to become a ... father."

Lew's slapping hand jerked midair. "Huh?" his face was stupid with rage.

"Damn ... fool," Harry struggled to squeeze the words out. "I only ... stopped you because ... the racket ... would upset ... Josie. Damn fool!"

Lew's mouth went slack with dismay. He whirled and looked at the door. "Oh Christ!" he said. "Jesus, kid, I never gave it a thought. Let him go, Vito. Let him go, godammit!"

Vito unlocked his arms and stepped back warily. His hand slid under the white jacket Lew made him wear and closed around the gun butt under his arm. Harry stood, gulping deep breaths of air. His eyes were glittering pinpoints, but he held that manufactured smile on his mouth.

"Lew," he said, "as much as I like you, there's only one thing we can do with you for the next seven or eight months—tie you up and throw you in a soundproof room. God, Lew, you scared the pants off me when you started that rumpus. Do you want your baby to be born with two heads or something? Use your brains, man! This is a crucial time in Josie's life," Harry was talking fast now. "Upset her just that much, Lew, just *that* much, and it has an effect on the baby. Prenatal influence. Why, I've heard of pregnant women, frightened by, say, an airedale, and the baby is born with a dog's snout. You've heard of that, haven't you? Where do you think Ringling got his Dog-faced Boy? From just that kind of thing. You've got to mend your ways, Lew, you've got to mend your ways!"

Goff edged toward the buffet on which stood a massive wrought iron candelabra, but to his amazement, Lew burst into tears. Harry motioned to Goff to beat it. Goff walked out quickly and quietly. He went into the kitchen where Yutzy was washing the pots and pans.

"Picture this, Yutz," he said. "Lew's back there in the dining-room crying his eyes out."

Yutzy grinned uncertainly. He never knew how to take Goff. You had to be on your toes or the next thing you knew you were getting the horse laugh.

"You don't believe me?" asked Goff. "Take a look for yourself. It's running down his face as if his roof leaks."

Yutzy said, "Aaaah," and glanced toward the door to the butler's pantry.

"Take a look," Goff urged slyly. "You'll never see anything like it in your life again. Crying as if his pointed little heart would break."

Yutzy hesitated, and then walked toward the door, shaking the soapy water from his huge hands. Goff laughed softly. This was going to set Yutzy back on his heels; this was catching Lew with his pants down. In Yutzy's lexicon, men didn't cry. Yutzy returned a few minutes later wearing a puzzled frown. He made some vague motions with his hands and asked:

"What's he crying about?"

"Somebody broke his yo-yo."

"His yo-yo?"

"His yo-yo. Somebody broke the string."

"You're kidding?"

"Ask him yourself."

"But ... why's he in there asking Harry Joyce to smack him on the jaw?"

"Is that what he's doing?"

"Yeah. 'Smack me, Harry,' he's saying. 'Smack me, I'm a jerk.' I don't get it."

Goff dropped his voice, "Say, Yutz ..."

"What?"

"Do you think Lew's quite right in the head? I mean, why should he bust into tears and ask Harry Joyce to poke him in the snoot? That sounds crazy to me."

Yutzy went back to the gleaming stainless-steel sink and scrubbed uneasily at the frying pan with a piece of steel wool. Goff was undermining his faith in Lew and he didn't like it. He scowled. He glowered over his shoulder at the little man.

"Lew never had a yo-yo," he said heavily. "You're just trying to get the laugh on me again. Lew never had a yo-yo."

Goff swore under his breath. He had failed just because he hadn't been able to stifle that stupid impulse to put something over on Yutzy. He had always considered Yutzy fair game for a joke, and now the chickens had come home to roost. The horse was on himself this time.

"No, Yutzy," he said, trying to regain the lost ground, "Lew doesn't have a yo-yo, and I don't know why he's crying. Maybe he doesn't even know himself. When you start fluffing your duff, you cry and laugh for no reason at all, and you ask people to smack you on the jaw for no reason at all. Just between you and me, Yutzy, what's going to happen to us if Lew blows his stack? Are we going to have to stay locked up in here with a crazy man? I'll tell you frankly, Yutz, the mere idea scares the pants off me. All the time I keep thinking, what's going to happen next, what's going to happen next? With a crazy man, you never know. I read in the paper about a feller went crazy out in Kansas City and chopped up his whole family with an ax, wife and four kids. When Lew starts swinging an ax, I want to be far away from here."

Yutzy turned, grabbed him by the shirtfront and shoved him angrily against the wall. "What're you trying to do?" he demanded. "What're you trying to do, huh? What're you trying to do?"

"Nothing, Yutzy," said Goff in a defeated voice. "Not a thing."

"Then shut up. I don't want to hear no more. You open your trap again and I'll tell Lew. You're the one that's talking crazy, so shut up."

"Okay, Yutz. Anything you say."

Goff lowered his eyes. He was exulting. It wasn't entirely a fizzle. Yutzy was disturbed. That clumsy mind had finally been needled into motion, and that was good enough for a start. There'd be a next time and a time after that.

Yutzy released him and went back to the sink. He was struggling to articulate a tangle of thoughts. "A feller that believes anything you say," he gestured bitterly, "he's crazy. I don't want to hear nothing you say no more. Leave me alone."

Goff knew when to let well enough alone, and this was the time. Let Yutzy brood over this, and hit him again another day. He walked over to the table. A plate of steak, french fries and string beans had been set out for him, but tonight he had no appetite.

"I think I'll eat this outside," he said. "It's cooler."

Yutzy pointedly ignored him. Goff went through the kitchen door carrying the plate. He darted to the dining-room window and, standing on tiptoe, looked inside. Lew and Harry were back at the table, smoking cigars, and Vito stood watchfully in a corner of the room. Goff trotted toward the garage. He went down into the basement and rapped on the door of the room in which Grizzard lay prisoner. He heard a heavy, sluggish stirring inside and a mumble as if Grizzard were trying to talk.

"It's me, Grizzard," Goff called in a low voice. "I've got some chow for you. Make it snappy."

He winced as he heard Grizzard drag himself slowly across the floor to the door. He cut the steak in thin strips and fed it through the one-inch hole he had bored at the bottom of the panel. It took Grizzard a full fifteen minutes to eat everything, but at the end he seemed a little stronger.

"Thanks, pal," he said thickly. "Sorry ... to take so long but I ... only got a couple teeth left."

"That's okay, Grizz. I'll see if I can sneak you some soup in the morning."

"That's ... better. Don't have to ... chew it."

Goff slipped away. He felt sick. He had barely come from behind the partition when the trapdoor lifted and Vito's bowed legs came into view on the steps. Goff darted into the shooting gallery, and he was standing there when Vito caught him by the arm and swung him around.

"Hey," he said, "what's the idea?" He tried to pull his arm away but Vito's fingers dug into his muscle until he could have cried out from the pain.

"What's the matter with you?" he said. "I was just looking at the shooting gallery. It's almost done, isn't it?"

If Vito would only say something! If only there were some expression in that impassive slab of a face!

"It's looking pretty nice," Goff said desperately. "I always liked shooting galleries. When's Lew thinking of opening it to the public?"

Vito seized him by the hair and thrust back his head at an agonizing angle. He stared into Goff's face with black, impenetrable eyes, and then with a grunt he gave Goff a heave that sent him staggering toward the cement steps. He motioned curtly for Goff to get out and stay out.

Goff did not have to be told twice. He turned and scrambled up the stairs as fast as he could go. His heart was a fluttering nausea in his breast. He lurched into the bushes beside the garage and bent over, retching.

CHAPTER TEN

The slow hours had piled up like drifting snow. It was three-thirty. There was no moon and the only light in the room came from the ember of Nellie's cigarette which brightened and faded as she drew nervously at it. Josie lay curled and sleeping on the bed. Goff was a hard upright silhouette at the window.

"See them yet?" asked Nellie.

How many times had she asked that question framed in exactly those words! But she had to say something. The silence was a living thing that bit and worried the fringes of her mind.

Goff said, "No."

"They've been gone almost eight hours. Where could they be?"

"Your guess is as good as mine."

"Don't be like that! Harry had no choice. He had to go with Lew."

"Did I say anything?"

"You don't have to *say* anything! It's your tone, it's the way you stand there. You know as well as I do that Harry had no choice. Lew was drunk, and he made Harry go with him. You don't think Harry went because he wanted to, do you?"

"Listen, chum," said Goff wearily, "if you'd seen as much two-timing in your young life as I have, you wouldn't trust Jesus Christ."

"Don't judge everybody by yourself!"

"You're in love with the guy. I'm not."

"Go to hell."

"Where do you think I've been for the last eight hours? You think what you want to think, and I'll think what I want to think. Don't try to fight with me. I'm not interested. Wait a minute...." He pulled back the drape from the window. "Something's coming."

Nellie sprang up from her chair and stood trembling at his side, peering southward through the window. Through the treetops they could see the white stab of a pair of headlights rushing toward them.

Goff said, "Finally."

Ten minutes later the horn blared at the gate, and they saw Vito come down the driveway. The Cadillac rolled slowly up the drive and disappeared into the garage. A few minutes passed and Vito came from the garage carrying Lew in his arms. Harry Joyce trudged tiredly behind them. He glanced up once at their window before he followed Vito into the house. It was a quarter of an hour before they heard his light rap on the door. Nellie sprang to open it for him, and she was in his arms the moment he stepped into the room, kissing him fiercely.

"We were so worried, darling!" she whispered. "We were so worried."

He held her tightly. Her kiss warmed him and made him feel less tired.

"Lew wanted to celebrate," he said. "He bought Josie a sterling silver punch bowl, the biggest thing in the shop. He bought you a wrist-watch, and he gave me a dozen boxes of cigars. He got a hundred-dollar rod and reel for Ozzie, but don't ask me why. Then we hit every bar in town. There are only three, but he kept buying drinks for the house and nobody wanted him to leave. He finally passed out. It wasn't too good an evening. I imagine yours wasn't much better. Did you think I ran out on you?"

"Something like that," said Goff.

Nellie said vehemently, "*I* didn't!"

Harry looked from her to Goff. "I don't blame anybody for getting worried tonight," he said. "It was a bad night."

Goff mumbled, "I'm sorry, Harry, but ..."

"Let's forget it. Do you think you can make anything of these?"

Goff peered at Harry's outstretched hand. On the palm lay two blank keys and a whitish blob of something else.

"What is it?" asked Goff.

"When Lew was buying that rod and reel for Ozzie, I had a brainstorm and picked up one of those fat plumber's candles. I had an idea that if I could get enough liquor into Lew, he'd pass out. He did, but I can tell you this much," he laughed wanly, "the scotch distillers won't go broke this year. Anyway, after he passed out, I softened the candle by the heat of the motor and took an impression of the key to the padlock on the big front gate, and an impression of the key to the side gate. He has a set and Vito has a set and Yutzy has a set. I didn't want to take the keys because if he missed them in the morning, he'd just change the locks. I had a wild idea of slugging Vito when we rolled into the garage, but there was Yutzy with a shotgun, and I never argue with a shotgun. Anyway, Vito stood six feet back from the car when I got out. Sometimes I think he can read minds. Where was I ...?"

"The keys."

"Oh, yes," Harry blinked wearily. "Do you think you can make a pair of keys with these blanks? I picked them up the same time as I picked up the candle."

"If I can get a file," said Goff. "You didn't happen to pick up a file too, did you?"

"A file? Of course you'd need a file, but I never gave it a thought...."

"Don't worry about the file." Goff gloated over the two blanks and the wax impressions, handling them very gently. "There are files in the garage. I'll sneak one."

Josie sat up suddenly in bed. "Oh God," she said, staring at Harry, "look what the cat dragged in. I thought you went back to Newark."

"Lew took Harry to town," Nellie told her gravely, "and bought you a sterling silver punch bowl."

"A punch bowl? What do I want with a punch bowl?"

"You can wash your feet in it," said Harry. "It's big enough. But look. Before we get all tangled up in a bunch of wisecracks, let's sit down and see if we can talk things over. Otherwise, we're never going to get out of this place. I found out one thing tonight—Vito has taken the distributor heads out of all three cars. But I think you told me that before, didn't you?"

Goff nodded. "I've been trying to find out where he hides them."

"Yes, you told me. I remember your telling me," Harry's voice mumbled off into nothingness. He gave his head a foggy shake and rubbed his eyes with his fingertips.

Nellie looked at Goff and said, "Why don't we postpone this till tomorrow night? He's worn out."

"I'll be all right," said Harry. "Is there a drink in the house? Believe it or not, I haven't had a drink all night. I kept feeding mine to Lew."

Nellie objected again, but he smiled at her and plodded across the room to the bathroom. A moment later they heard him splashing his face with water. Nellie pushed Goff toward the door.

"Don't just stand there. Get him something to drink. There's a decanter of brandy on the buffet in the dining-room."

She opened the door and looked warily into the corridor, then stepped aside for Goff, who looked at her reproachfully and said:

"I'm still on your side, Nellie. If we're going to start grudges, we're never going to get anywhere."

"All right. No grudges."

"I'm sorry for doubting Harry tonight, but you know how it is."

"That's all right. Just get the brandy for him."

Harry was sitting on the edge of the bed when Goff returned with the decanter. Josie had drawn up her legs and sat clasping her knees. She blew a kiss to Goff when he came in. Harry looked much fresher. He drank two glasses of brandy, one right after the other. Nellie sat beside him, fondling his hand and looking earnestly up into his face.

Goff gestured toward the door and whispered, "Ozzie's downstairs in the living-room. Stewed to the gills and talking to himself. He's saying, 'I'll fix his lousy son-of-a-bitchin' wagon, I'll fix him.' Looks like we've got reinforcements, hey Harry?"

"Do you want him? I don't. Anyway," Harry frowned, "sooner or later Lew's going to make up with him. He always does, and it'll be at somebody's expense. I wish they were friends so we'd know where we stood."

"Oh God, I never thought of that!"

"But I have an idea we won't have to worry about that. Listen...."

He motioned Goff closer. Josie leaned forward, resting her chin on her knees, her eyes wide.

"Lew told me tonight," Harry whispered, "that Vito and Yutzy will have the shooting gallery finished sometime tomorrow afternoon, and tomorrow night after dinner we're all going down for a shooting match. He bought a bagful of prizes in the drugstore tonight. Vito was able to get only two .22 rifles. From here on it's up to us, Goff. In some way we'll have to manage it so that we two will be shooting at one time tomorrow night. Are you any good with a rifle?"

"I used to be."

"All right. You cover Lew and Yutzy and I'll take Vito. If Vito goes for his gun," Harry took a breath, "I'll let him have it right between the eyes. You, Josie, and you, Nellie, stay up here in your room. Don't leave the room no matter what happens. Goff and I will come and get you if ... we'll come and get you."

There was a catch in Nellie's voice as she said tremulously, "Does it have to come to shooting, Harry?"

Harry and Goff exchanged a flickering glance. As long as Vito was around, they knew it would have to come to shooting. He would never put his hands up. Yutzy would and Lew would, but Vito would keep coming at them until he was dead. That first bullet would have to be the one.

Harry was thinking, *I've never shot a man, but you can't point a gun and not pull the trigger when the moment comes at you like an express train and there's no sidestepping it, you have to pull the trigger, oh God,*

I hope I'll be able to pull that trigger!

Aloud he said, "There won't be any shooting. We'll have the rifles and they won't."

"But there's another way, isn't there, Harry? Let Goff make the keys. We can slip out that way at night. There are four of them and only two of you, and don't tell me Ozzie doesn't count. He can always grab you or something. Harry, please!" She shook his arm and her face strained toward his.

Goff watched Harry narrowly. If there were any weaknesses in Harry Joyce, now's when they'd show. It was all right for Harry to butter it up with Lew. That was only common sense, but if he let himself be led around by Nellie, that was something else again.

Harry kissed Nellie and said, "There are worse things than shooting, honey, and I don't intend to hang around here and let Lew show me what they are."

Goff said deliberately, "You were wondering what happened to Grizzard. I'll tell you what happened to him. He's locked up in a dark little room in the basement of the garage. Lew goes down there every day for a workout," he hesitated over the detail of the copper-wire knout and decided against telling it. "Lew is trying to starve him to death, but I've been sneaking him a little chow every day. That's what Harry means when he says there are worse things than shooting."

Harry said harshly, "Why didn't you tell me that before! We've got to get him out of there."

"And what happens when Lew goes down there tomorrow afternoon? Do you think he'll just stand around and say, 'Well, well, he vanished, think of that.' Don't try to kid yourself. Or me. You can't do a damn thing for Grizzard, except feed him, until we're ready to crash out of here."

Harry nodded somberly. He looked at Nellie. Her face was strained with the horror that pulled her lips back from her teeth.

"Forget what I said about shooting," she said. "Forget it! I take it back."

Harry said quickly, "I think it's about time we break this up. If you come across anything tomorrow, Goff, tell it to Nellie and she'll relay it to me. We'll need some sleep, anyway. We have a big day ahead of us."

Josie came off the bed and stretched. She took Goff's arm.

"See me to my door, sweetie," she smiled.

There was a connecting door between her bedroom and Nellie's. They stopped at the door. Josie waited a moment and said, "Don't I even get a good-night kiss?"

Goff was suddenly shy in the presence of Nellie and Harry. He kissed Josie's lips quickly and drew back. She laughed warmly, put her arms around his neck and kissed him back, pushing herself hard against him, showing plainly how she hungered for his hard, wiry body. Goff responded fiercely, spreading his hands across her shoulders to hold her tighter. Then he pushed her away and walked out of the room very quickly, his head down.

Josie stood looking after him, her mouth an O of bafflement, and slowly she smiled, a smile of complete tenderness.

"I shouldn't have done that to him," she murmured. "He's bashful. Good-night you two...."

She went to her bedroom and closed the door.

"She's wonderful," said Nellie to Harry. "She acted so pregnant, I was scared for a minute. And let me tell you something, Mr. Know-It-All, she didn't need any coaching from me. Don't ever tell me again that's she's dumb."

"You're right," said Harry solemnly. "She's wonderful. She should have been on the stage. She was, wasn't she?"

"Now don't be mean."

"I wasn't being mean. I thought she was wonderful. When she played the Rivoli in Newark, I went every night to see her."

"You *are* being mean. Just because she was in burlesque...."

"Don't say a word against burlesque. I love burlesque. Good burlesque, and Josie was the heart and soul of burlesque when she was up there behind the footlights. I never told you this before, but when Josie stood up there and started taking it off, she made you feel that she was doing it just for you, and you alone, that she wouldn't do this for anybody else, and she was only doing it because she loved you."

"Oh, stop grinning like that! Josie was never a stripper and you know it. All she did was stand on a little pedestal behind the dancing line, wearing more clothes than ... oh, I don't know why I ever take you seriously!"

Harry laughed and pulled her toward him. They were both laughing when they kissed. Nellie pretended to struggle and turn her face from his lips. They were sitting side by side on the bed and during the mock struggle they fell back and it was no longer a game. The fear that had smoldered in Nellie ever since Harry had spoken of guns now flamed fiercely and in her arms was a frantic strength as she strained him to her. When he drew back, whispering incoherently something about this not being the time, she followed his lips with hers, half rising, dipping her head over his, pressing down, holding his shoulders with constricting fingers. She wanted to cry out that this was the time, that this time might never come again, that this was the time, *this was the time, now, now, now!* She sprang from the bed and in a single lithe movement swung off her dress, bending as she pulled it over her head. She stepped out of her panties and threw them across the room. The satin straps of her brassiere burst when her hasty fingers could not find the tiny hooks and she ripped it from her. There was no coquetry, no conscious posturing, nor was it like the way she had imagined it would be, for her imaginings about it had always been a little misty and not quite real, for she had never been naked with a man before, nor had she ever felt this soaring urgency as she lay on the bed, tightening her arms around him, parting her lips as his face came down, *oh that lovely face but so tired! now, darling, now, there, there, right there, now, now!*

There was a brief, a very brief moment of confusion, of temporary chaos when her body seemed to be reaching and reaching for his, arching, not merely to establish contact but to draw him, to make him part of the pulse, of the beat that rhythmically surged through her, then suddenly there it was and she felt snatched up from the bed and whirled away.

It was a long while afterward before she became conscious of his gentle arms and the tendernesses he was whispering, lightly brushing her ear and hair with his lips, yet strangely she knew he had been whispering for a long time and she could remember everything he had said, all the little caressing words that, themselves, were like fleeting kisses, warming, yet cool and soothing, so necessary, so dearly loved after the roaring blast that had swept them upward like burning leaves. She turned and lightly moved her lips across his. She put both hands to his cheeks, touching his eyes, the flanges of his straight-bladed nose, the flat planes, the hard, lean thrust of his jawbones, his lips firm as they kissed her fingertips. She touched him as if she wanted to remember him through her hands. He cradled her breasts in his palms and she lifted herself so that he might remember her, too, this way, just like this, for always.

It was necessary that they remember, but her mind closed before the why of it could dangle the bony specter of her fears for him. She sought his lips again and smoothed them slowly from side to side with hers, smiling tenderly behind the velvet of the kiss.

They stiffened at the sound of the first crash on the stairs outside in the corridor. The crash was followed by another, and someone snarled thickly. A bottle broke in thin angry splinters on the terrazzo steps. The voice cursed it, not so much in words as in the frustration of tone.

Harry said, "Ozzie!" and Nellie felt his arm harden around her.

They heard him lurch against the wall and swear again. Then he shouted thickly:

"Nellie! Where th'ell are y', f'crisake. Nellie. C'mon, c'mon…."

He stumbled against the wall again, closer down the corridor this time. Harry reached out and killed the bedside lamp with a savage jerk on the dangling cord. He started to rise, but Nellie held him down, whispering:

"No, Harry, no! Let him go. He's not hurting anybody. You'll just get yourself in trouble."

Harry grated, "I'll break his God-damned neck!"

Nellie knew why Harry felt this way and she held him closer, whispering into his ear, kissing him, holding his face to hers. This drunken, shouting lout was a desecration, a spoiler, an obscene interruption, a crawling thing that had to be stepped on and ground into the earth. She held him desperately, for she knew that Harry would kill Ozzie if he went out there into the corridor. He was as rigid as steel in her arms, and she knew that she could not hold him for long. Ozzie was beating on the walls, apparently with his fists, as he lurched down the hall, calling:

"Nellie! C'mon, you bitch, where are you? Nellie, Nellie, godammit!"

The door opened from Josie's room, and Josie swept in. "Stay where you are, kids," she said. "I'll get rid of him."

She was barely in time. Ozzie had reached Nellie's door and thundered on it with his fist. He rattled the knob and slammed the door back against the wall. He stared stupidly at Josie, who confronted him, clad only in the negligee she had hurriedly thrown around her.

"Where's Nellie?" he demanded truculently. "Where is she, godammit? I wan' Nellie."

"Go to bed. You're soused."

"So'm soused. So what? Get outta m'way. I wan' Nellie."

"Get out of here. She don't want you."

"How d'y'know she don't? Wha' d'you know about it, anyway? I wanna get laid, see? I wanna get laid. I don't need you 'r anybody else t' tell me. When I wanna get laid, I wanna get laid, so get outta m' way or I'll smack y'inna puss. I'm not kiddin' aroun', unnerstand?"

Nellie held Harry desperately. The bed was out of the path of light thrown through the open doorway from the corridor, and Ozzie could not see them there, screened as they were by Josie.

Harry hissed, "If he raises his hand, I swear to God I'll beat his brains out!"

Josie snapped, "Go to bed. Nellie's sleeping."

Ozzie swayed, staring blearily at her. He reached out and steadied himself on the doorframe.

"She is? Well maybe I don't need Nellie at all. Y'know what? You're kind of a nice piece y'self. Let's you an' me go down my room. C'mon, let's go down my room, c'mon...."

He pawed at her. Josie's hand darted. There was the cold wink of steel. Ozzie cried out and staggered back, holding his hand. He stared incredulously at the creep of blood from his fingers. Josie held the long nail file ready and said:

"Go to bed or you'll get worse than that!"

Harry slipped out of bed. This time Nellie did not attempt to hold him back. He crossed the room in two silent bounds on bare feet and stood in the shadow behind Josie.

Ozzie backed away, hugging his torn hand to his belly, whimpering.

"I'll fix you, you bitch," he wept. "Just wait and see. I'll fix you." He looked from side to side and, out of sheer impotence, spat at her.

He turned and staggered down the corridor, bent over his slashed hand. Josie closed the door. She looked at Harry and attempted to grin but her lips were like rubber. She looked down at the long, ivory-handled nail file in her hand.

"I should of shoved it down his throat!" she said.

She shuddered, walked to the window and flung the nail file out into the darkness. She walked to her door, turned and tried to say something, but her feeling was too deep and her vocabulary too inadequate.

CHAPTER ELEVEN

Harry did not awaken until two the following afternoon. When he saw the time, he was out of bed with a bound. He dressed quickly and ran down the corridor and knocked at Nellie's door. He had told her to keep Josie in her room all that day, if possible. It was going to be a rough day. Lew was going to wake up with a terrific hangover, and there would be hell to pay.

Nellie answered the knock and spoke to him through the panel without either unlocking or opening the door.

Harry whispered, "I overslept. Everything all right?"

"It's all right now. Lew came up this morning and insisted on giving Josie the silver punch bowl. We were petrified. He had a hangover, and his eyes looked like something you'd expect to find under a butcher's block."

"Did he make any trouble? Don't open the door!"

"I love you, darling!"

"I love you, too, but don't open the door. Yes, open it for just a moment, quick!"

She opened the door and they surged into each other, holding tightly, kissing as if they had been parted for months. She stood on tiptoe and rubbed her cheek against his, whispering into his ear:

"Why did we wait so long? I didn't know it could be so wonderful. I love you so much, I'm exploding all over. Come in for just a moment, darling."

He held her away and groaned, "Don't think I don't want to, but we can't now. It wouldn't be for just a moment. I love you, darling. Listen. Let's be sensible. This is important. We have to be sensible. I have to find out about Lew. What kind of mood was he in?"

"Lew came in with that awful punch bowl and he fawned all over Josie. He kissed her feet. She was lying on the bed, and he kissed her feet. It scared me, darling. If he ever finds out she's not pregnant ..."

"He won't have time to find out. We're making the break tonight. Then he was in a good mood?"

"You never saw anything like it, the way he slobbered over Josie's feet, kissing her toes. Yet I couldn't help feeling sorry for him too...."

"Don't ever feel sorry for Lew!"

"I know, I know. It was only momentary. But it's going to be a terrible shock to him if he ever finds out he's not really a father. We're going to be out of here before then, aren't we, Harry? He'll be a maniac...."

"We'll be out tonight." He dipped, kissed her and pushed her gently back into the room. "Now stay there with Josie. Don't come out. I'll sneak up later."

"Later," she smiled mistily, yearning after him as she watched his back and the wide spread of his shoulders as he walked quickly and lithely toward the head of the stairs.

He met Goff at the foot of the stairway in the lower hall. During the day, Goff had to wear a white houseman's jacket. He had a broom and was sweeping the ubiquitous Florida sand toward the wide front door.

"'Old Blood and Tears' is waiting for you out by the swimming-pool," he said from the side of his mouth as he swept industriously at the tiles at the base of the steps. "The shooting gallery was finished this morning. I heard them popping away down there with the .22s. Watch yourself. He's restless. He went up to see Josie, and she kicked him out. He took it, but he's randy."

Harry said, "I'll watch it," and walked by as if they had not exchanged a word.

Yutzy was standing down the hall at the kitchen door, drying his hands on the apron he wore while cooking. He did not give them a glance. His shoulders were slumped and he looked unhappy.

Harry walked outside, blinking in the bright sunlight that washed the patio. Lew was sitting in the lounge chair by the swimming-pool and, ten feet behind him, Vito was squatting on his heels, laboriously making marks in the sand with his stubby forefinger. He looked up from beneath suspicious eyebrows as Harry approached. Lew stirred heavily and discontentedly in his chair.

"Hiya, kid," he said. "How's the head?"

Harry said, "Terrible," and pretended distress. "I'm never going out barreling with you again. What were you trying to do, drink the country dry?"

Lew gave a short barking laugh. There was no mirth in it, but it pleased him to feel superior.

"I didn't feel a thing this morning," he boasted. "Sit down, kid. Take a load off your brains."

Harry stretched out on the cushiony St. Augustine grass beside Lew's chair. "How did Josie like her punch bowl?" he asked.

"Fine, fine. She was crazy about it. Uh, say, tell me something, kid. How long's she going to be like this? I mean, I hate to see the poor kid feeling so lousy. Know what I mean?"

Harry knew what he meant, all right. Lew was already becoming bored with this particular phase of paternity.

"Oh, for awhile," he said. "It's called morning sickness. Nothing to worry about. They all get it."

"When she going to have this kid, Harry?"

"Be patient, Lew, be patient. This isn't something you can rush. You can't point a gun at Josie and make her have it this afternoon, you know."

"Harry, I'm telling you, I wish I could. I'm going to be a nervous wreck." Lew sucked at his teeth and let his glance rove glumly over the proud tossing plumes of the royal palms that flanked the far side of the swimming-pool. He pointed at the palms. "Them trees. You know

I first thought they was made of cement. I had to feel them to find out. The hell with them. I'm sick of trees. Say, how's about going down and shooting off a couple loads? We finished up the gallery this morning."

There was a hot surge of excitement in Harry, but he said casually, "You did? How's it look?"

"Beautiful. Just like Coney Island. Let's go down."

"Sure. I was never much good with a gun, but why not?"

Lew pushed himself up from the chair, waggled his finger at Vito, and started toward the garage, leaving Harry to follow him. He never waited for anybody. He cheered up as they descended the stairs to the basement and turned on the lights.

"Pretty nice, eh?" he said to Harry. "Just like Coney Island. We got all the stuff from a place in Tampa."

It was, Harry had to admit, just like Coney Island. There was a wooden counter and on it lay chained four .22 rifles. The range was no more than seventy-five feet, the target end illuminated by concealed lights. Lew pushed a button. There was a faint hum and the targets began to move. At the lower edge there was the usual row, however, of stationary ducks, and above them a line of battleships moved sedately from right to left. The pendulum target swung to and fro. At either side was a little house with a window and at intervals a soldier's head appeared in the window. It must have been surplus stock from the World War II period, for the soldiers were exaggeratedly Japanese. Above the moving battleships was a row of stationary white pipes, and over these a column of tiny tanks marched from left to right. Suspended from the ceiling was a small plane that made swooping figure 8s.

Lew watched with beaming delight. "I guess I'm just a great big kid," he said. "I get a bang out of this stuff."

He picked up one of the rifles and fired six fast shots at the swinging pendulum. Each time he hit it, a bell clanged. He grinned at Harry.

"Your turn, kid."

Harry took the end gun. He turned from the counter to make sure that the chain was long enough and that he could command that whole end of the basement with the rifle. He felt an icy tightening as the muzzle swept across Lew's stomach, but Vito was standing back in the shadows with his arms folded over his chest, his hand probably on the gun under his left armpit.

"Now how does this thing work, Lew?" Harry asked. "You pull this thing and shove it forward?"

"That's right. It's a pump gun. You pump it. You mean you never handled one of these things in your life?"

"I had a B-B gun when I was a kid."

"Then you're all set. The slug comes out the same end. Better duck when he starts shooting, Vit'. He'll probably spray the joint like a hose." Lew threw back his head and laughed noisily.

Harry turned back to the counter. He laid down the gun and wiped his hands on the sides of his thighs. They were sweating.

"Go ahead and shoot," prodded Lew, grinning. "Go ahead, it won't hurt."

Harry raised the rifle to his shoulder hesitatingly. He had a choice. The swooping little plane was the hardest target, and he knew he could nick it ten out of ten. That would give them some respect for his marksmanship and Vito would not be so likely to go for his gun when the time came. It was a temptation.

"Go on," said Lew, impatient for the laugh. "What're you waiting for, the Fourth of July?"

Harry deliberately fired six clumsy shots, one of which actually slapped through the plywood panel far below the targets. Lew whooped.

"Hey, look at that, Vit', he actually got all six down the right end of the gallery. You're doing swell, kid, but I can see right now what your trouble is. You should be closer, seventy feet closer!" He guffawed again and raised his own rifle and winked. "I'll show you how it's done."

He pumped six shots again into the pendulum target. It was actually the easiest target in the gallery, but a bell clanged each time a bullet slapped into the big black bull, and Lew liked that.

They shot off a few more loads, but Lew was getting bored with it now. He had shown off, and he was not interested in anything else. Harry was glad enough to stop. There was no fun shooting with Lew, and he had found out all he wanted to know. The chains were long enough to swing the rifles in any direction, and if they needed ammo, there was a case of cartridges behind the counter.

Lew took a cigar from his pocket, bit off the tip and spat it out. His face had fallen back into sagging lines of discontent. He eyed Harry for a moment and said:

"Say, didn't you used to do some boxing down the YM?"

"A little," said Harry warily.

"Don't give me that 'little' stuff. You were light-heavy champ for the county that year."

Harry shrugged, "Amateurs."

Lew's eyes thinned speculatively. "Think you could take Vito?"

Harry said emphatically, "No."

"Why not? He ain't never done no boxing. Come on, let's go up on the grass and you and Vito mix it up a little. Just friendly, know what I mean?"

"Count me out, Lew. You haven't any gloves, and there's nothing friendly about bare knuckles. Furthermore, what's the point if Vito doesn't know how to box? If he doesn't box, he's a slugger, and how friendly would that be?"

"Yella?"

"Nope, but I'm not going to mill with Vito unless I have to. All you want, Lew, is blood, and I don't donate blood to anybody except the Blood Bank."

Harry was angry. Lew saw it and mumbled, "Aw, what're you getting sore about? It was just an idea. Forget it. I thought we could have a little fun. Let's get out of here." He switched off the lights.

Vito walked up the stairs silently after them. Harry was becoming conscious that whenever he was with Lew, Vito was always somewhere behind, *always behind*, padding softly like an animal, watchful and suspicious.

Lew stopped in the mouth of the garage and stared down the driveway at Yutzy, who was checking the padlock on the high front gate. Yutzy was on guard duty. Lew plucked the cigar from between his fleshy lips.

"Hey, Yutz'," he called. "C'mere."

Yutzy came ambling up, wearing his usual empty good-natured grin. He grinned at Lew. He looked at Harry and grinned at him. He did not appear to see Vito, or perhaps it was that his grin became dimmer when it passed over Vito. Lew stood smiling.

"You used to be in the ring, didn't you, Yutz'?" he asked.

Harry said, "Oh God!"

Lew gave him a scowl. Yutzy's fingers touched one gnarled ear and slid to his flattened nose.

"Yeah," he said. "The ring."

"And you were pretty good, eh?"

"Yeah, pretty good," Yutzy grinned happily. He was being noticed by the boss. "Had fifty, sixty fights."

Lew looked sidelong at Harry and the tip of his tongue darted across his running smile. Harry's expression was carefully noncommittal.

"Where's everybody, Yutz'?" Lew asked.

"Everybody?"

"Yeah, everybody, you dumb lug. Don't you know what everybody means?"

"Sure, sure. In the house."

Lew put his cigar back into his mouth and rolled it from side to side, looking beyond Yutzy at the St. Augustine lawn that flanked the driveway.

"Let's go over there," he said, pointing toward a cleared space in front of the citrus grove. "Come on, Harry."

He kept Harry beside him as they walked across the driveway.

"This ought to be pretty good," he whispered. "Wait'll you see it. Yutzy's in for the surprise of his life."

"What's Vito going to use, a knife?"

"Vito don't need nothing. Just wait."

Lew settled himself comfortably in the shade of one of the trees. There was an aluminum tag on the tree that said Tangelo, Mineola. He squatted on the ground and leaned against the trunk, looking up at Yutzy and Vito.

"Just take a look at them," he said to Harry. "What a pair of gorillas. Yutz' is the missing link, and Vito's an ape. Ain't they a pair of beauties now? Jesus. Sometimes I think the human race is going backward instead of forward. Okay, you two mutts," he flapped his hand imperiously, "take off your shirts." He winked up at Harry. "This'll be a treat."

Harry shrugged. "They're your bodyguards."

"Watchdogs, Harry, watchdogs. The accent is on the dog."

Yutzy hesitantly took off his shirt and stood holding it in his hand. Under his shirt he was wearing a shoulder holster from which protruded the heavy butt of a .45. His chest was smooth except for a few graying hairs down his breastbone, but Vito was a mass of hard, shiny, black curling hair from his throat to his waist. It matted his shoulders and joined the shaggy growth down the nape of his neck. He, too, was wearing an underarm holster, but in addition to this was a sheath and knife at his left hip with the handle of the knife protruding forward so that it could be grasped quickly with a right-hand flip. Yutzy looked puzzled, but Vito was stolid, a full head shorter.

Yutzy was running to fat. It bulged over his belt in a soft roll, and his belly was a veal-white vulnerable mound. Beside him, Vito was a rock, wide-necked, solid, long-armed.

Harry suddenly understood. Vito was a wrestler.

Lew chuckled softly, "Place your bet, Harry. Look 'em over. Yutzy or

Vit'. Go ahead. You take one and I'll take the other."

Harry said, "I'll take Yutzy," because he knew that that was what Lew was expecting him to say, but he added wickedly, "and I'll be Yutzy's second."

"Nix, pal, nix. Next you'll be wanting a referee and the ticket concession. I know you shysters. But I'll tell you what. I'll let you have the hat-check concession for fifty grand."

"It's a deal. You hold my hat."

Harry's quick eyes spied Goff on the patio, leaning over his broom, and Ozzie on the second floor of the wrought-iron balcony outside his bedroom window. He looked for Nellie and Josie, but the window of Nellie's room was a dark empty mouth.

"Can I kibitz?" he asked Lew.

"Kibitz? Sure. What the hell. Anybody can kibitz. But let's go—or do you want to announce the next bout? Okay, you two, get rid of your heaters. We're in Madison Square now, and no plugging each other in the clinches."

Vito placed his harness and gun carefully on the grass beside his shirt, but Yutzy, unbuckling his holster, still looked puzzled.

Harry said, "Tell Vito to get rid of that shiv. He might not use it, but it's a mental hazard."

Harry's words were hardly out of his mouth when the knife was lying beside Vito's gun. He had scarcely seen Vito move. Lew winked.

"Just watch," he said, "just watch. That Vito, he's something." He waved his arm. "Okay, square off, you guys. Put 'em up. We want action. There ain't going to be no rounds and no referees. Anything goes. If you can put Vit' down for the count, Yutz', you get the genuine barbed-wire bathtub, and if you put Yutz' down for the count, Vit', you get the genuine, absolutely guaranteed ball-bearing medal of honor. Now go to it and let's see a little action!"

He leaned back against the tree, grinning slyly, rubbing his forefinger up and down the side of his nose. Nothing happened. Yutzy looked uncertainly at Vito, and Vito looked blankly at Yutzy.

Lew's eyes narrowed and he said sharply, "Smack him, Yutzy, go ahead, smack him! Give him the old one-two. Come on, you were in the ring, wasn't you? Give'm the old one-two. Wake him up. He's asleep. He don't know what's going on. Let'm have it down in the bread-basket. Them dumb wops can't take it down there. They're like niggers. Give it to him in the bread-basket! Come on, a little action!"

Yutzy lifted his hands uncertainly, but he made no move to smack Vito in the bread-basket or anywhere else, and Vito stood there just glowering at nothing in particular, his arms dangling at his sides, his curled hands just slightly below his knees. He had tremendously long arms, but Harry could see, from the tense hardness of his muscles, that he was resentful of this shaming display.

Lew's face clotted and he shoved himself angrily to his feet, shouting, "Come on, come on, doggammit, start swinging, smack it in there, what the hell's the matter with you...." He ran heavily across the grass and shoved Yutzy at Vito, cursing him.

Yutzy collided with Vito from the force of Lew's shove, and he immediately grasped Vito by the upper arms, steadying him in case the collision had been upsetting. But Vito had been braced, had not moved an inch. In fact, it was Yutzy who had been bounced back.

Harry, disgusted, cried out, "Oh let them alone, Lew. They don't want to fight. Let them alone!"

Lew swore and shoved the two together again. Yutzy reached out with an unenthusiastic jab and Vito circled away from him. Lew marched back under the tangelo tree. He held up his wrist-watch.

"I'm giving you two minutes," he said, "before I come out and beat up the pair of you myself."

It was not an idle threat. He would do exactly what he said, Harry knew, and neither Yutzy nor Vito would dare strike him in return. Lew stood breathing heavily, his shirt pulled open, showing that he, too, wore a gun in a shoulder holster.

Yutzy pawed reluctantly at Vito with that jab again, but this time Vito seized his wrist, turned and threw him over his shoulder. Yutzy struck the ground heavily. He rolled to his hands and knees, shaking his head.

Lew yelled, "Finish him off, Vit', finish him off!" but Vito seemed as unwilling for this encounter as Yutzy. He stood back and let Yutzy climb slowly to his feet. Lew snatched a fruit from the tree and hurled it furiously at him. It struck Vito on the side of the head. It must have hurt, for the ripe tangelos were heavy with juice. Vito scowled and shuffled toward Yutzy, who backed away unhappily pawing out with that long left. He tried to snatch it back when Vito leaped at him but Vito was much faster and he got Yutzy this time in a wrist-lock. Yutzy cried out from the unexpected pain and slugged Vito on the side of the neck. Vito grunted and dropped to his knees.

Lew was screaming hoarsely, his eyes shining, hooking the air with both fists. Harry, standing about ten feet to his right, saw the black gleam of the gun again under Lew's left armpit, and as he stared, the butt of the gun appeared to get larger and larger and thrust itself toward him. With the gun in his hand and Yutzy and Vito fighting on the lawn, in thirty seconds he would be in command instead of Lew and it would be all over. He began moving slowly and tensely toward Lew.

Vito was on his feet again, facing Yutzy. By this time, Yutzy knew better than to lead with that long left again. He kept his hands in close. His face was pale and worried. He knew that Vito would hurt him if he fastened another of those punishing holds on him, and he knew nothing of wrestling and he did not know what to do to break such a hold except to slug with both fists. Vito was on him, shedding his light ineffectual chops, and he groaned as Vito shoved his arm up behind him in a hammerlock.

Harry was within two paces of the screeching Lew, moving stealthily. He gathered himself for the leap. Two short paces, no more than four feet, but the distance between was the chasm between freedom and this peculiar form of slavery in which they were existing.

He did not have the opportunity to make the leap. Vito cried out a guttural warning, thrust Yutzy from him and dived for his gun on the grass beside his shirt. Lew whirled, snatching out his own gun, but by that time Harry was placidly reaching up into the tree to pluck a ripe tangelo. He looked at Lew and Vito and their guns with well-simulated surprise.

"Well!" he said. "What now? Are we going to play William Tell or something?" He placed the tangelo on his head. "Go ahead. I know I'm just a sucker, but never let it be said that Harry Joyce couldn't go along with a gag. Don't mind if I close my eyes. I never did like people pointing guns at me."

Lew gaped stupidly at him. His face darkened and he swung around and strode across the grass at Vito, slapping at him with the flat of his gun.

"You didn't want to fight, did you! I'll give you fight. I'll give you all the fight you'll ever want. I'll learn you to break it up when I tell you to do something!"

Vito dodged the gun, but he kept his hot, black eyes on Harry. He knew that Harry had clowned his way out of a tight corner.

Harry drawled, "Oh let him alone, Lew. I don't blame him a bit. It's too hot for exercise. Forget it."

Lew stopped, panting. He, too, was drenched with sweat from his brief exertion. Vito and Yutzy were dripping. Ozzie's voice drifted down thinly from his balcony:

"Smack him, Lew. He's chicken."

It was all that was needed to tip the scale. Ozzie, for the moment, was out of favor. Lew gave Vito a shove.

"Beat it," he growled. "Go on, get out of here before I let you have it."

Vito moved off a few yards and stopped obstinately while he put on his harnesses and shirt. He felt no ill-will toward Lew. Lew had the right to do anything he wanted. He was Lew Markey. Lew had cuffed him around before, and it was all right. But that Harry Joyce, he was up to something, the way he was trying to make at Lew just then. They were all up to something—Ozzie, Yutzy, Goff, Harry Joyce. None of them loved Lew the way he did. Some day Lew would know this.

A throb of yearning for that day passed over Vito, and he felt very warm and loved Lew more than ever. He would protect Lew. That was what he was there for. He would protect Lew against anybody.

He moved off into the tree-garden and lay down on the grass behind a clump of prickly pear. Between the cactus pads he could see everybody without being seen.

Yutzy shambled toward the garage, rubbing the arm that Vito had wrenched up behind his back. Harry Joyce watched him thoughtfully. Yutzy had been used very badly and he would be less than human if he felt no resentment.

Harry was peeling the tangelo when Lew thrust the gun back into its holster and turned. Harry offered him a piece of the fruit.

"Try it, Lew. It's better than an orange."

"Don't bother me."

Lew clumped over to the lounge chair beside the swimming-pool, picked up his newspaper and hunched down behind it. Harry strolled away, eating his tangelo and bending slightly to keep the juice from dripping on his shirt. He approached the house circuitously, and when he reached the patio Goff was inside, sweeping the hall. Goff's face was pale and his hands shook.

"God, Harry," he whispered, "my heart was in my throat when I saw you begin to creep up on Lew out there."

"Was it as obvious as all that?" asked Harry ruefully.

"Only at the end when you kind of crouched. I knew you were going to jump him."

"Another split second and I would have."

"And you'd have been dead right now, too. Jesus, doesn't that Vito ever miss anything?"

"Not where Lew's concerned, I guess. What lousy luck! In another minute I would have had Lew's gun and it would have been all over. We'd have been on our way by this time. Well, we'll have another chance tonight down in the shooting gallery."

"Harry …" Goff licked his lips, "… let's call that part of it off."

"What!"

"Wait a minute. Just think it over. Vito'll be there. Honest to God, Harry, just knowing he's standing behind me, I'll be paralyzed, I won't be able to move. This is one time I'm admitting I'm scared."

"Let *me* worry about Vito."

"That's just it. I don't know what kind of fast talking you did out there, but I do know you didn't fool Vito for a second. Even from here I could see that. From now on, Harry, he'll have his eye on you. If you try anything tonight, he'll put a slug in you so fast you'll never know what happened. We'll figure out another way.…"

"You can back out if you want to," said Harry coldly, "but I'm going through with it if I have to do it myself."

Goff moved his hands helplessly, hopelessly. "Okay, we'll go through with it. But do me a favor and think it over. Just think of the fix we'll be leaving Josie and Nellie in if we miss."

"We won't miss … and that brings up something else. We may have a third gun down there tonight. I think Yutzy might be in a mood to be talked to, if we hit him now while he's hot. Vito gave him a pretty rough going over. I'm going to brace him when he comes in to start dinner."

Goff closed his eyes like a man at whom the hazards have been coming too fast and too often. He could talk about these things, and he could plan, but there was a cringing of the flesh when it came to direct physical action. For too long had he been jeering from the sidelines, holding aloof from anything that implicated him personally.

But because of Josie he was committed to action, and he could not remain in hiding behind his closed eyelids forever. He opened his eyes.

"It would be better if I talk to Yutzy," he said. "You're too close to Lew. He'll be suspicious of you. I've talked to Yutzy before, and I know how far I can go with him. I'll sound him out when he comes in."

He was grateful when Harry just nodded shortly and said, "I think you're right."

CHAPTER TWELVE

There were only three of them at the dinner table that evening. Ozzie was permitted to leave his room for meals, but Lew ignored him, and he sat hunched over his plate, his face looking clotted and poisoned. He radiated hate, and in Ozzie hate was such a mean and petty thing that it was scarcely more than petulance, a peevish, spiteful emotion, so shallow that the gift of a toy would have appeased it. Lew was in one of his rare periods of seeing Ozzie for what he was, and when he looked at that handsome, pouting face, it was only with distaste.

Goff served the soup. His underlip looked swollen, as if he had been struck in the face, and when he caught Harry's eye, he gave his head an almost imperceptible shake. Yutzy had not listened, would not listen, and had slapped out with the back of his hand.

I told you to shut up about Lew. I don't want to hear nothing so shut up or the next time I'll bust you wide open!

If the dining-room had not been so distant from the kitchen, separated by the butler's pantry, Lew would have heard the unexpectedly shrill pitch of Yutzy's voice. It was as if Yutzy's grip on reality depended wholly on Lew's infallibility. He did not have Vito's blind devotion. His loyalty could be shaken, but not yet and not in this fashion. The only hopeful sign was that Yutzy had not told Lew the things Goff had said, if that could be called hopeful. Further needling, Goff realized, would be worse than dangerous. It would be foolhardy. Yutzy *wanted* to believe in Lew.

Goff lingered a moment in the dining-room. Vito had driven off toward town a few minutes ago in the Ford, leaving his uneaten dinner to grow cold on his plate in the kitchen. There had been a sudden order from Lew, and Vito had marched swiftly from the kitchen. There had been an air of urgency about the whole thing, and Goff wanted to hear if Lew would say anything about it.

But Lew was not very talkative. He snapped once at Goff to ask if Josie had been served her dinner, and Goff, coached by Nellie, had answered that Josie had wanted nothing but cold asparagus. (That afternoon she had ravenously eaten two cold roast beef sandwiches and a bag of potato chips.)

Goff wheeled the empty soup plates to the kitchen on his cart and returned with the broiled red-snapper steaks, french fries and string beans that Lew had ordered. In the few minutes he was gone, Lew's mood had changed and he was rallying Ozzie.

"Come on, kid, cheer up," he said. "Take the crepe off your snoot. What's the matter? What's on your mind? Let's get it off your chest."

Ozzie said, "Go to hell."

Lew laughed tolerantly. "That's the way it goes," he said to Harry. "When I was a kid, I didn't have nothing. When I wanted something, I had to go out and get it for myself," he held up both fists. "There wasn't nobody around to hand me a C-note or two if I wanted to take a babe out for the night. I don't know, maybe kids are different these days. When I was his age, if I had a place like this to live in, I'd think I was in heaven. That's the honest-to-God truth. Heaven. I don't know, Harry, I just plain don't know."

"What about the shooting match after dinner?" asked Harry. "You got all the prizes last night, didn't you? I hope you got a booby prize, because that's the one I'm going to win."

"Prizes, I got a boxful of them!" Lew winked delightedly. "Wait'll you see them. You know what's one of the prizes? A box of Trojans. And you know what's another? But this is just for the women. A douche bag, and it's got a million attachments. I can't wait to see Nellie's face when she opens it. It'll be a riot. And you know what I got for Josie?"

"Don't tell me. Let it be a surprise," said Harry woodenly.

Lew waved the objection aside with a flap of his hand. He was leaning over the edge of the table, grinning.

"It's one of them doctor's thermometers, the kind you stick up your ass. There's a drawing comes with it, showing you just how to do it. Harry, I'm telling you, you never seen anything like it in all your life. There's a picture of the ass and the hand shoving it up and everything. Honest to God, she'll pass out when she opens it in front of everybody!" Lew guffawed, leaning back in his chair and slapping his thigh. "What do you think of that, kid? What do you think of that now? And you should see some of the others. I got a prize for everybody. Everybody wins, nobody loses. Everybody gets a prize."

"Let's start the shooting match as soon as we finish dinner," said Harry quickly. "It sounds better than Coney Island."

"Hell yes! You never got prizes like this down at Coney."

Ozzie raised his head and sneered at Lew. "Why don't you grow up?" he said loudly and defiantly.

Lew's head jerked around in surprise, and then winked at Harry. "Another district heard from. Don't worry, Oz old kid, we got a prize for you, too."

"Sure. The Trojans, and what do you expect me to do with them, blow them up like balloons and carry them around on a stick? Why don't you drop dead?"

Lew stared down at the plate that Goff had set before him. Finally he said quietly to Ozzie, "If you want to get laid, kid, why didn't you just say so instead of horsing around like you did for the last few days?"

Ozzie glowered at Harry and snarled at Lew, "Will you for crisake drop dead!"

"Okay, kid, okay," Lew waved a placating hand. "I know just how you feel. It's nothing to be ashamed of. There's times a guy's just got to be laid. You don't have to tell me. I know all about it. You got to be laid and that's all there's to it. Right, Harry? Okay. Tell you what I'll do, Oz. I know a guy in Tampa. He's got a stable of dames. I'll have Harry give him a ring. For six hundred bucks he'll send down six dames. I've seen them before, and they're okay. First they put on a little show, and afterwards you have a little party. Christ, I wish I'd thought of this before. We could all use a party, and there'll be a babe for everybody, and with these babes anything goes, I mean it. I've seen them in action. How's that sound, Oz? Okay? Okay, kid?"

Ozzie said sullenly, "You're kidding."

"The hell I am. I'll have those babes down here Saturday night. How's that?"

"You mean it?"

"Sure I mean it. And any kind of babe you want, kid, you name it. Blonde, redhead, brunette, all you got to do is name it and it's yours."

Ozzie asked avidly, "What kind of show they put on, Lew? Tell me about the show? Like in those smokers?"

"Better than that."

"Will they ...?" Ozzie started obscenely.

Harry interrupted, "Where's the phone, Lew? I'll call that fellow right away."

Goff knew what Harry was after. There was a telephone wire to the house from the pole outside the wall, but they had been searching in vain for the phone itself inside the house. A telephone would be an instrument of liberation, once they found it!

Goff felt the hope go out of him when Lew answered, "I had it taken out. You'll have to call from town in the morning. But don't mention any names over the phone, kid. All you'll have to do is tell the guy that six hundred cash will be waiting in advance. He'll deliver the babes in the evening and pick them up in the morning."

Goff stolidly set out the dessert beside each plate—baked apple with wine sauce—and wheeled his cart back into the kitchen. He now had at least forty minutes to himself. There was an electric percolator on the table, and Lew would not miss him until the time came to clear away the soiled dishes.

The moment he was in the kitchen, Goff said to Yutzy, who was frying himself a steak at the electric range, "Guess what, Yutz'. Lew's bringing in six babes from Tampa Saturday night for a party. I just heard him tell Ozzie. I thought we were supposed to be hiding out down here. Now all of a sudden we're getting six witnesses to tell the world where Lew Markey's holed out."

Yutzy pretended not to hear, and Goff did not stop to develop the theme. That could come later, but right now he had only forty minutes. He hastily heaped a plate with food and ducked out the side door of the kitchen. He trotted out to the garage and down into the basement. This time he had a flashlight and did not have to turn on the overheads. He had been caught down there once by Vito; if he were caught a second time, he'd wake up with a chestful of broken ribs and Lew's foot in his face. Like Grizzard.

He crouched at the door of Grizzard's prison and gave his identifying rap. He put his ear to the door to hear if Grizzard were stirring. Lew had not been down there that afternoon, and Grizzard ought to be in better shape—but what he heard tightened the thin flesh of his scalp. Grizzard was howling softly like a dog in the cold madness of the moon, an empty sound punctuated by a chatter of gibberish and the hee-hee-hee-hee of meaningless giggles.

Goff shivered. He knocked again and called soothingly, "It's Goff, Grizzard. Come and get your chow."

He was answered by a snarl, and a moment later the door shook under the impact of Grizzard's lunge. Goff flinched and in the silence that followed, he thought that Grizzard had knocked himself out in his assault on the door. He listened hard at the panel, wondering if to call to Grizzard again but hesitant because it might provoke another outburst.

Then Grizzard's voice came craftily, "That you, Lew? Been expecting you. You didn't come. I'll bet you're mad at me!" He broke into a high cackle of laughter.

Goff's horror was smothered in a wash of pity for Grizzard, and for Lew a profound loathing. All day Grizzard had been expecting Lew to come and beat him up again, steeling himself desperately, dreading the moment. Solitary confinement in that dark hole was bad enough, but the anticipation of further torment was worse and Grizzard's mind, feeble at best, had snapped like a rusting guitar string.

Goff put his mouth close to the panel of the door and said cajolingly, "Come and eat your dinner, Grizzard. This is Goff, not Lew."

"Come on in, Lew. Come on. We'll have a real party. Come in all by yourself, Lew...." Grizzard's voice grated and he broke into a snarl again.

"It's Goff, Grizzard, Goff, Goff, your friend Goff."

"Goff?"

"That's right—Goff. I've got some chow for you. Remember that little hole I bored at the bottom of the door? I'm going to push some food through to you. The little hole at the bottom of the door...."

"Hole," said Grizzard dully. Goff heard his hands aimlessly scrabble on the door. "Hole?"

"Yes, right here, Grizzy. Look, I'll shine my flashlight on it. Now do you see it?"

Grizzard giggled. "I know you, Lew. You're a rat and you're coming in through the hole. Come in, Lew, come in. I'll catch you when you come through. I'll wrap my hands all around you and I'll squeeze and squeeze and you'll drip through my fingers. *Come on in, what are you waiting for?*"

Goff hesitated and then pushed a piece of fish through the hole. He heard Grizzard snatch it up and devour it noisily.

Grizzard's voice came pleadingly, "More? More?"

In this fashion, like an animal, Grizzard ate the food that Goff had brought. There were still some French fries left on the plate when Goff heard the Ford roll into the garage overhead. He shut off his flashlight and crouched, scarcely breathing, wondering frantically if he had remembered to close down the trapdoor when he descended the steps to the basement. He felt his way along the damp wall until he came to the steps. He did not have to look up. The darkness was complete; the door was shut. He breathed again.

Up in the garage, a deep, unfamiliar voice was saying, "I'll be darned, I didn't know anybody was living in this old place, though I should have expected somebody to snatch it up. The tree-garden was famous in its day. Still is, as a matter of fact. The most complete collection of exotic trees in this section of Florida. I'll have to ask Mr. Smith if he'll permit a group of school children to come through one of these days. But first we'd better take a look at our patient, eh?"

Look at a patient? This was a doctor? O, my God. Lew's gone and sent for a doctor to examine Josie! We should have known this might happen. Christ, I'll have to get out of here and warn Harry. In just about a half hour there's going to be all hell to pay. Oh, Jesus, what a thing to happen now! This is the time bomb we've been sitting on, and here she goes up in our faces. Josie, Josie!

Goff heard Vito and the doctor walk out of the garage, the doctor's hard leather heels thumping hollowly on the floor overhead, but he dared not raise the trapdoor and slip out, not until he had given them plenty of time. This was not the moment to get caught half out of the trapdoor. Goff hunched on the steps with his ear to the trapdoor, but the hell of it was that Vito moved so softly, like a cat, that you could never be sure when he was there or when he was not there. He was all around, always, all the time, and you never could tell. Goff beat his fist impotently against his knee. His mind writhed in its peculiar form of agony again. Here was reality pushing and crowding him again, forcing him to perform an act of positive action, and again the flesh was cringing from it, conjuring up an impossible super-Vito, Argus-eyed and omnipresent.

Grizzard's muted howl came desolately from its black hole, and in a flash of clarity, Goff identified himself with that broken insanity, realizing that this omnipresent Vito existed only in his mind, and he surged up through the trapdoor more recklessly than he would have had he not tormented himself with those chimerical terrors.

The garage was empty, except for the three silent cars. Goff ran to the Ford and lifted the hood. His heart leaped when he saw that the distributor cap was still in place. Vito had forgotten to remove it. And the keys still dangled from the ignition lock.

For a fantastic moment, Goff held freedom in his hand. That morning he had filed a key to the padlock on the big front gate. It had fit perfectly into the wax impression Harry Joyce had made of Lew's master key. All he had to do was leap in the Ford and within a few minutes he could shed the anxieties and the responsibilities. He could disappear into the anonymous world outside and find a niche where he could spin himself into another cocoon and never again be forced to emerge. That was the freedom he held in his hand and he could almost feel the feeble flutter of it before it died.

He had to warn Harry. That was the first thing he had to do. He had to warn Harry that Lew had brought in a doctor. He left the garage and trotted down the side path toward the house. A figure loomed out of the darkness. He sprang to one side, clubbing his flashlight, but it was only Ozzie leaning against a cocoanut palm, moodily sucking at a cigarette. Ozzie glowered at him and said peevishly:

"What's the matter with you?"

"I was just eating out here. I like the peace and quiet. Now I have to get back to work."

"Wait a minute," Ozzie planted himself in the path and said truculently, "I thought you were going to find me a way out of this place. That's what you said."

"And I said something else, too. For a couple C-notes I said I *might* be able to find you a way out. I don't see any C-notes, and right now I've got to get back in the house...."

Ozzie shoved him back. "Come on," he said. "I'm getting tired of this run-around, understand? I can take just so much horsing around, and then it's too bad." He pulled in his chin and hunched his shoulders in his feeble imitation of Lew.

Goff's hand clenched around the flashlight but relaxed as a sly grin was born on his lips.

"Okay," he said, dropping his voice and moving closer. "I can get you out, but you've got to promise to pay up when you get your hands on some dough. It's a promise?"

He almost laughed aloud when the promises boiled eagerly out of Ozzie. Ozzie's promises were worth their weight in stardust and just as collectible, but this was something here and now that only Ozzie could deliver. Goff took him by the arm and pulled him still closer. This was the kind of conspiring shenanigan that would appeal to a goon like Ozzie.

"Listen now," he hissed, "you've got to keep my name out of this no matter what happens. I'm the only one who can get you out of here without Lew knowing, understand? If you turn me in, you're stuck until Lew unsticks you. I'm only doing this because it's a shame to see a young fellow like you not able to come and go when he wants to. Hell, there are girls in this little town down that road that'd fall all over themselves if a handsome young fellow like you as much as looked at them. So if you keep me out of it, you'll be able to have a little fun whenever you feel like it."

Ozzie was so eager to promise anything, anything at all, that he fairly stammered.

Goff said impatiently, "All right, all right, don't spit all over me. Now listen. You can use the Ford in the garage. It's all set to go. Give me ..." he figured rapidly, ".... fifteen minutes. I'll have to pick that lock with a piece of wire. It's going to take time, so don't crowd me. You know what'll happen if you come charging down to the gate in the Ford and I don't have the lock open. Better make it twenty minutes just to be sure. Twenty minutes and not a minute before."

Ozzie began to babble his thanks but Goff cut him short. Time also was growing short.

"Now look, Oz," he said impressively, "if you do happen to get caught, blame it on Vito. Tell Lew that Vito left the gate open. Get me? The whole thing is Vito's fault. Know what I mean?"

Ozzie snickered. "He'll kick the shit out of Vito. It'd almost be worth getting caught to see that. Vito's the son-of-a-bitch that's keeping us in here. He's the bastard that turned me back the first time, and I owe him something for that."

Goff exulted but kept his face straight. Keeping his hold on Ozzie's arm, he urged him toward the garage.

"Now go and sit in the Ford, and in exactly twenty minutes, Vito," he winked, "is going to have that front gate open for you. Good old Vito, eh?"

"Good old Vito," gloated Ozzie.

Goff sprinted down the diverging path to the front gate. It took him a second to open the padlock with his newly made key and hang it on the staple, thrusting the hasp back against the gate. He felt naked in the spotlight that hung from the royal palm at the side of the driveway. His frantic shadow jeered him, hard and black before his eyes. He darted obliquely into the fringe of the tree-garden and ran for the house. From the Ford at the end of the garage, Ozzie could not see the gate. The gate was visible only from the center of the garage between the avenue of royal palms. Anyway, Ozzie would be sitting there, his eyes glued hungrily on the dial of his wrist-watch, waiting to jump the gun thirty seconds before the twenty minutes were up.

Goff panted into the kitchen. Yutzy was sitting at the stainless steel table, forking huge gobbets of beefsteak into his mouth, but though his eyes slid sidelong, he did not look up at Goff. His mind had set like cement. From here on in, he was ignoring Goff.

Goff hurriedly swung into the white jacket and white apron that Lew had decided he should wear while clearing off the dishes. That was the conventional busboy's uniform, and Goff had to wear it. He hurriedly wheeled his cart into the dining-room.

Harry was sitting alone at the table, worriedly turning his cigar in his mouth, his hard, lean face harsh in the overhead lights. He gave Goff a flickering glance but otherwise disregarded him. Goff pushed his cart against the table and began loading soiled dishes on it.

"Vito just brought in a doctor," he whispered liplessly, "to examine Josie. For the love of God, have a story ready!"

Harry reached out to tip his cigar into the ashtray on the table, and as he did he managed to point it significantly at the open doorway to the hall outside. Goff understood. Vito was lurking out there. Harry nodded. Just once. He lifted his eyes toward the ceiling and clenched one hand prayerfully. Goff understood that, too. From here on in, it was up to the ingenuity of Josie and Nellie. It was a matter of symptoms, of swollen ankles and sudden desires for odd tidbits, and how well they could mislead the doctor. A positive diagnosis of pregnancy depended on laboratory tests. Goff remembered that from some dim corner of his mind. Laboratory tests. That would be a brief respite, but transient at best. Josie would not long be able to conceal from Lew that she was not really pregnant. Oh, Jesus.

Harry sat hard and stony while Goff cleared the table as quickly as he could. Goff wheeled his cart out into the kitchen. Yutzy had gone. Goff scrabbled at the knife drawer, selected a long, horn-handled carving knife, which he thrust into his belt, and a short, sharp paring knife, which he held up his sleeve with his curled hand. He ran his cart back into the dining-room.

Harry was sitting upright. His hands were fists and the knuckles were white and pointed. He was staring toward the door. Goff heard the mumble of voices as Lew and the doctor descended the stairs from the second floor.

Goff could see them through the arched doorway. The doctor was marching solemnly, carrying his black satchel in his right hand, and Lew plodded beside him, hunch-shouldered, looking from right to left, his lips pulled back from his teeth in the kind of grin he put on when he was furious.

The doctor was saying patronizingly, in that too-tolerant tone doctors use when describing a perfectly obvious medical fact to a layman, to whom no medical facts are perfectly obvious:

"I've seen it time and time again, Mr. Smith. It's really nothing to get upset about. It's false pregnancy. She's not going to have a baby. I can see by your face that you're going to blame it on your wife, but stop to think that it can equally be your fault. Have you had a complete physical examination recently? Why don't you drop down to my office say around ten tomorrow morning and let me give you a good going over? The radio tells you to see your dentist at least twice a year," he laughed with professional heartiness, "well, the same goes for your family doctor, Mr. Smith. A great many things can happen to the human body in six months."

"Sure, Doc, sure," interrupted Lew in a heavy tone that said plainly don't bother me with this crap. "But what about all this other stuff, her puking in the morning, all the time she wants pickles, and her ankles are all swelled up. What about all that?"

"We-ll, her ankles aren't really swollen, you know. Perhaps a little from the heat, but not really swollen. Nothing to speak of."

"But why does she puke in the morning? That's supposed to be a sure sign, ain't it?"

"A sure sign of what, Mr. Smith? That her stomach's upset, perhaps? Not a sure sign of pregnancy."

They had descended the stairs and were standing at the pointed Gothic front door with its three-foot black wrought-iron strap hinges and ostentatious screwheads as big as marbles. The doctor wanted to leave and was becoming irritable, but Lew clung to his sleeve.

"Wait a minute, Doc, I want to get this straight. How can you be sure she's not going to have a kid? She's showing all the signs, ain't she? How can you be sure by just poking your mitt in her gut? How can you be sure? What about she wants pickles and ... stuff all the time? That's another sure sign, ain't it? Why don't you take an X-ray or something? I can pay for it. I'll lay the cash right on the line. I want my wife *examined*, get me? I'll pay for it. What the hell good is it poking her in the belly with your thumb? *Examine* her! Take X-rays, take pictures, show me! Why should I take your word for it anyway? You're nothing but a jerkwater sawbones that wouldn't even know whooping cough if it hooped in your face. She's pregnant. I know goddam well she's pregnant, so what do you mean telling me she ain't going to have a kid? She's going to have a kid and it's mine? You understand it? It's *my* kid she's going to have. My kid, mine!"

Lew had the doctor by the lapels against the door. His face was purple and he was shouting. It wasn't the ordinary kind of shouting that he did all the time. There was a different note in it. There was fury, of course, but there was also frustration, as if he was realizing that nothing he could do or say would make the doctor change his mind or his diagnosis, and even if he were able to force his will on the doctor, it still would not change the fact that Josie was not pregnant. He wanted kids. He had always wanted kids. Now they were trying to stop him from having them.

"There's no sense acting like this, Mr. Smith," said the doctor with some asperity. "Bring your wife to my office tomorrow, if you wish, and we'll give her the usual tests. We'll give her a thorough examination."

"The hell with you! I'm getting another doctor."

"You may do exactly as you wish, Mr. Smith, but I'll stake my reputation that your wife is no more pregnant than I am."

Harry jumped up from the table, muttering, "Why can't he keep quiet!" and walked hurriedly toward the hall door. The doctor was saying stiffly, "Now kindly take your hands off me. In my opinion, it's you who needs treatment, Mr. Smith. You've worked yourself into a tantrum. You're not normal. I don't blame your wife …"

Harry jumped forward and grasped Lew's arm. In another moment the doctor would have received one of those famous backhand slaps across the face.

Vito was standing not ten feet away but he did not interfere when Harry pulled Lew away from the doctor. Lew lunged furiously to tear himself from Harry's arm-locking grip. The doctor was pale, but he had not moved.

"I wish you had let him strike me," he said primly to Harry. "It would have given me great pleasure to have had him arrested for assault and battery. There's only one place for his kind, and that's jail."

"For God's sake," Harry cried to Vito, "get him out of here. Take him back to town. I can't hold Lew all night!" Lew stopped struggling and grated over his shoulder, "Get away from me, Harry, I'm warning you, get away from me!"

"As soon as the doctor goes. Get him out of here, will you, Vito!"

The doctor stood there bleating, "This man is mentally sick. He needs a psychiatrist. This man is mentally sick.…"

But no one was paying any attention to him now. Goff had come to the door of the dining-room and was watching narrowly, his right hand still curled stiffly from the wrist to keep the knife ready up his sleeve. Vito walked over to Lew. He made no attempt to help him break from Harry, but instead whispered urgently in his ear, gesturing at the doctor. He shook his head warningly and repeated several times:

"*Sbirro, sbirro!*"

"That's right," said the doctor with satisfaction, "we've got police down here and they're very efficient when it comes to handling situations like this."

Vito pushed at Harry's shoulder. Harry hesitated. Lew was rigid, but he was not struggling anymore. Harry released him and stepped back warily. He had made up his mind that if Lew turned on him now, he'd let him have it and take his chances with Vito, but Lew did not turn.

He looked at the doctor and said in a stifled voice, "Sorry I blew up, doc."

The doctor nodded once, severely. "You should be, and for your own good I'd suggest that you see a psychiatrist at your earliest opportunity. Good-night to you."

He opened the door and walked out. Vito went after him with a last warning glance at Lew. Lew waited until the door closed, and then whirled and ran up the stairs to the second floor. Harry started after him, and Lew turned on the top step and pointed his gun at him.

"I warned you!" he yelled. "I warned you!"

Harry stopped. Lew glowered at him over the gun. He turned and ran along the upper hall without firing. A moment later Harry heard him hammering on Josie's door with the butt of the gun. Goff darted to the foot of the stairs and tossed Harry the horn-handled carving knife. Harry sprang up the stairs. Lew was beating on the door with his fists.

Harry stopped in the shadow of the upper hall and flattened against the wall. All the doors in the house were of heavy oak and nothing short of a fireman's ax was going to break them down. Goff ran up the stairs but stopped before his head showed above the landing when Harry waved him back. Lew rattled the doorknob, gutturally telling Josie exactly what he was going to do to her when he finally broke in the door. Neither Josie nor Nellie answered him. He kicked at the door. He looked around, rolling his eyes savagely, and spied one of the high-backed Spanish-type chairs that stood against the wall in the hall. He ran to it, dragged it back to the door, but it was too heavy and cumbersome to swing. He threw it on its side and swore at it. He kicked it. The red-hot rage that had sent him sprinting up the stairs was beginning to cool. There were glitters of it left in his eyes, and the wildness and the senselessness had drained out of him. He looked at the door and laughed harshly.

"Okay," he said. "You got yourself locked in, so now you can stay locked in. When you get hungry enough, you'll come out. Or maybe I won't let you come. Maybe I'll have Vito nail the door. You got something coming to you, sweetheart, and you're going to get it one way or the other...." He laughed again.

Goff whispered, "Let's jump him when he comes. We can't wait till he figures a way to break in that door."

Harry nodded and motioned Goff down the stairs. The first floor would be better. They were too exposed on the stairs and Lew had a gun.

They ran lightly down the stairs and Harry pointed to the dining-room.

Harry whispered, "Start clearing the table. Rattle the dishes. I'll get him when he comes in the door."

He stood against the wall beside the door. Goff went to the table and noisily started loading the soiled dishes on his cart. From where he stood, he could see the stairway. He threw up his hand, warning Harry that Lew was coming. Harry tensed and clubbed his right hand, but before Lew reached the bottom of the stairs, the front door burst open and Vito ran in, gobbling excitedly. Lew sprinted down the remainder of the stairs, and he and Vito ran out of the house.

Goff clapped his hand down on the table and exclaimed, "That's Ozzie, I'll bet!" He darted to the window.

Harry crossed quickly and stood beside him, trying to peer through the tangle of bougainvillea vine that grew up the side of that part of the house. "What about Ozzie?" Goff told him rapidly how he had opened the front gate for Ozzie and that Vito had left the distributor head in the Ford that had been used to bring the doctor from town. "And I've got the lunkhead primed," Goff gloated. "When they bring him back, he's going to blame it on Vito, and you know what'll happen to Vito. Leaving that front gate open is the one kind of mistake Lew won't forgive. Goodbye, Vito!" He laughed exultingly.

Lew's voice called sharply from outside, "Get away from that window, you two, and stay in the house!"

Harry and Goff stepped back from the window, and Lew went down the front of the house bellowing for Yutzy. Harry and Goff ran up to the second floor. There was a balcony at the end of the hall and by crouching below the iron grille, they could see the garage, the driveway and a part of the gate. The Ford was standing in the driveway in front of the gate.

"I thought you said he took the Ford," Harry whispered.

"I told him to take it. It was all set to go, ignition keys and everything. Maybe Vito caught him before he could get out the gate. Damn it to hell, can't we ever have any luck!"

"I don't think they caught him. He must have gone without the car."

Lew and Vito were standing on the driveway. Yutzy came lumbering from the tree-garden, carrying a long chrome-plated flashlight. Lew strode to meet him. He pointed angrily at the gate and slapped Yutzy back and forth across the face.

Goff chattered, "Here we go again. Christ Harry, I'm telling you, I can't look at Lew's hand anymore without wanting to nail it to the floor with a railroad spike!"

Harry gripped his shoulder. "I know just how you feel, fellow," he murmured. "There goes the posse. I guess Ozzie got out all right."

Yutzy ran into the garage and Lew and Vito ran toward the Ford. Lew held the gate open. The Ford sped through and turned toward town. Yutzy came out of the garage in the Cadillac. He went through the gateway and turned north.

Goff said shakily, "I hope you're thinking what I'm thinking."

Harry nodded and said grimly, "Let's go."

They lingered a moment to watch Lew close the big gate and stand there examining the padlock. The floodlight was on him and they could see him turn the lock in his hands, looking for scratches that would show if it had been forced.

Harry wanted to stop and reassure Nellie and Josie, but time was so precious now that he could not spend it, even for that. He sped down the stairs behind Goff. They ran down the hall to the kitchen and out into the side garden through the kitchen door. Goff stooped and picked up a coquina rock the size of a baseball from the border of the path. They stopped halfway to the garage and tried to listen, but there was a strong breeze from the west and the palm leaves rattled drily overhead, covering any other sound they might have heard. But it did not matter. Lew would walk up the driveway and take the main path to the front of the house. They would get him where the two paths curved to within three feet of each other at the clump of date palms. They were running hard to reach that spot before Lew did when suddenly there was Lew standing spread-legged in the path not twenty feet dead ahead. He lifted his hand and Harry saw the glint of moonlight on the barrel of the gun in his hand. He gripped Goff's hand and called out:

"What's going on, Lew? We saw..."

"None of your goddam business. Get back in the house!"

Harry tightened his fingers around Goff's arm until Goff softly dropped the coquina rock into the grass beside the path.

"Something happen, Lew?" asked Harry. "We just heard two cars...."

"I said get back in the house goddammit! I'm not kidding around. Get back in the house!" The gun came up in a short, hard arc.

Harry said, "Sure, Lew, sure," and backed toward the house, pulling Goff with him.

Lew followed, pacing them heavily, until they went into the kitchen.

"Now go up to your bedroom and stay there," he yelled after them. He went back toward the garage. Goff beat his fists together, saying hysterically, "Oh, Jesus, can't we have any luck? Can't we ever have any luck? Is everything going to blow up in our face all the time?" His face kept twitching and his knuckles showed bloody where they had scraped across each other.

"We're lucky to be alive," said Harry. "That's luck enough for one night. Tomorrow's another day."

"Who're you trying to kid, me or yourself?"

"Both of us, I guess, for the time being. This can't last forever. We'll keep our eyes open and take the first break that comes along. In the meantime, we'll try to figure another way out of this place."

Goff went up the stairs ahead of Harry. He looked back over his shoulder and said bitterly, "Lew tells us to go to bed, and like two good little stooges we go to bed. How do you like it, counselor?"

"There are worse places than bed tonight, Goff."

Want me to tell you the trouble with you, counselor?"

"Go ahead."

"Nellie."

"That's right."

"She's taken the guts out of you. You went to bed with her once and you've been gutless ever since. I'm serious. I mean this. You're afraid to take chances anymore. You're always looking over your shoulder. You get a chance at Lew, like tonight, but you pull back. You keep saying to yourself, 'I can't let anything happen to me. If anything happens to me, Nellie'll be in a worse fix than she is now.' See what I mean? She's taken the guts out of you."

Harry did not interrupt. Goff was just talking. It didn't mean anything. He was just talking out his own momentary impotence. Goff had changed. He had come a long way from the cynical little man who used to sit on the sidelines and make remarks just to start trouble. Tonight Goff had actually been the aggressor. He'd had to hold Goff back out there. Goff would have hurled that coquina rock at Lew, and that kind of recklessness was no good.

It had been fine in the old poems to charge into the cannon's mouth, because in the old poems death was always glorious with a hint, by way of encouragement, that you would be an inspiration for posterity. It would be no inspiration for anybody to be lying dead out there with your face grinding into the shell path and two of Lew's bullets through your chest.

My God, thought Harry, *maybe he's right! Maybe I have become too cautious. Maybe I do keep looking over my shoulder. But there has to be something in your favor when you take a chance. I've been taking chances. We took a chance tonight. If we'd gone six more steps down the path, Lew would have hammered the full load into us. We couldn't have charged him....*

Goff stopped waving his arms and stood shamefaced. "What are we fighting about?" he mumbled. "And what right do I have to talk? Only this afternoon I was practically on my knees begging you not to go through with that shooting gallery idea. Are we going to be stuck here for the rest our lives, Harry? I don't give a damn about myself. It's Josie...."

He looked ready to burst into tears, but he didn't. There was no self-pity in him.

Harry said mildly, "I think it's about time we let the girls know we're still alive."

They went down the hall together. Harry knocked on the door, and Nellie answered eagerly, recognizing his knock. Through her voice came Josie's voice, asking anxiously, "Is Goffy there too? Is he there, Nell? Ask if he's there."

"Yes, he's here, we're both all right," said Harry swiftly. "Don't open the door."

"Not even for a minute, Harry?"

"Not even for a second."

"What ... what's Lew going to do?"

"I don't know. For the moment I think he'll just try to starve Josie out. Has this door got bolts on it as well as a lock?"

"Yes. There's one right up here and one down at the bottom that fits into the floor."

"Good. Keep them both bolted. And here's another idea. Take Josie into your room. Lew has either forgotten or doesn't know about the connecting door. If he knocks on Josie's door, open the connecting door and have her answer him, but if he starts to break in, close your door and lock it. And if he *does* break in, take Josie down to my room and lock and bolt yourself in. I don't think any of this is going to happen, but if it does, be ready for it. And don't get panicky. Goff and I will be doing all we can."

"We won't get panicky, darling. Can't I open the door for just a moment?"

"No!"

"I love you, darling."

Goff offered, "I'll watch by the stairs if you want, Harry."

"Both stairs?" asked Harry, looking significantly toward the rear of the hall where another stairway led down to the kitchen. He turned back to the door. "I love you too, honey. Don't make it tough for me."

"I won't, darling, I won't. I'm sorry."

Josie's voice broke in again, "I want to talk to Goffy. Can't I have a chance too?"

Harry whispered, "I'll see you later, honey," and stepped away from the door.

Goff stood close to it, talking eagerly. His right hand softly caressed the door as if he were actually touching Josie through the wood. Harry walked down the hall and stood where he could see into the main stairwell. Goff joined him in a few minutes, and they went to the little balcony at the front of the house, crouching so that they would be hidden by the wrought-iron grillwork. They were both quiet and subdued.

The white path of the shell driveway was empty under the floodlights. Lew was not in sight. They scanned the paths, the patio, the yawning black mouth of the garage, each hoping that Lew had taken a definite post. If they had spied him standing in any one place for a length of time, they would have taken a chance on a second sally from the house, but to go out blind was folly. The grounds were too extensive, the tree-garden too thick. Even in daylight it would have been impossible to find anyone in that jungle if he really wanted to conceal himself.

Finally Goff asked, "What do you think Lew will do to Vito, Harry?"

"Nothing."

"You're crazy! As far as he knows, Vito's the one who left the gate open for Ozzie to get out. The least he'll do is lock Vito up down there with Grizzard."

"The most he'll do is beat him up and maybe give him some nasty job to do, or something humiliating like doing the laundry. But people like Lew are too smart to cut off their right arm, and Vito's more than a right arm. He is also Lew's eyes and ears. No, he'll slap Vito around a little, and Vito will expect it, and that'll be the end of it."

"You're talking through your hat," said Goff heatedly. "This is the end of Vito, one way or another. Lew never gives anybody two chances. I'll lay money on it. Five'll get you ten. Here, I'll tell you what ..." He retreated into moody silence and refused to answer Harry except in monosyllables.

It was a long wait, squatting there behind the grille of the balcony, staring down into the jungly tree-garden, watching the roads for the sign of a returning car. It was Vito who returned first from the south in the Ford. He blared his horn at the gate and Lew appeared from the shadows of the citrus grove. He opened the gate. The Ford rolled in fifteen feet and stopped. Lew ran over to it while Vito climbed out and closed the gate. Ozzie slid out and faced Lew defiantly.

Goff unconsciously gripped Harry's leg with both hands and whispered, "Here it comes!"

Harry shook his head but did not take his eyes from the foreshortened group down on the driveway. Lew was yelling. They could hear his voice. They saw him step up to Ozzie with his clenched fist raised. Goff's heart lurched. If Ozzie told Lew who had really opened the padlock, the time to start running was now. But Ozzie did not utter a word. He turned on his heel and walked sullenly toward the house. Lew ran after him. He trotted at Ozzie's side, talking, pleading, looking up into Ozzie's face, touching Ozzie's arm. Ozzie shoved him away and walked faster. Lew ran and caught up with him. It looked exactly as if Lew were begging for a handout. Harry turned away, disgusted.

"Here we go again," he said. "Lew's going to blubber all over him and promise him the moon and when it's all over, Ozzie'll be in the catbird seat again. Here's a practical object lesson in dictators, Goff. Hitler was the same way. Let me know when Yutzy comes back."

He walked to the main stairwell and hung over the rail listening as Ozzie and Lew came in the front door. Ozzie went straight into the dining-room, with Lew trotting anxiously behind him.

Ozzie snarled over his shoulder, "For crisake let me alone!" and disappeared through the dining-room door.

"Listen to me, kid, just listen for a minute, won't you?" Lew implored. "I want to do everything I can for you. Just tell me what you want, that's all. Just tell me what you want."

The door slammed and the voices were cut off. Goff whistled and, when Harry turned, signaled that Yutzy had just driven in with the Cadillac. Harry ran back to the balcony. Yutzy and Vito were walking toward the house. Yutzy was talking to Vito and shaking his head, but Vito just walked stolidly, not answering. Harry and Goff had seen Yutzy and Vito walking together dozens of times, and it was always the same—Yutzy doing all the talking, shaking his head in that same bewildered manner, and Vito answering only in grunts or not at all. And that was the way the night was ending.

But instead of going to bed, Harry and Goff lingered tensely in the upper hall, leaning over the rail trying to hear what was going on in the dining-room, wondering if all this was a prelude to an assault on Josie's door by Vito and Yutzy. Lew might just take it into his head to get even with Josie there and then.

Suddenly there was a thunderous crash from the dining-room, as if someone had upset the huge banquet table, followed by the unmistakable crash of breaking glass.

Harry ran back to the balcony with Goff at his heels. As they peered through the wrought-iron grille, they saw Yutzy running heavily down the path toward the garage. Lew burst from the shrubbery, pursued him for a few yards, swearing, and then stopped, leveled his gun and fired two shots. Yutzy ran on for three paces, stumbled and fell. He pushed himself to his hands and knees and lunged forward, disappearing into the shadows at the turn where the cluster of date palms grew so lushly.

Lew took two following steps and stopped. He turned as Vito came from the house, staggering a little. He was bleeding from a cut that ran diagonally from his forehead to his cheekbone. Lew pointed down the path. Vito seemed to gather himself together, shake off the numbing effects of the blow, and ran down the path just taken by Yutzy. He blended with the shadows of the date palm cluster. A shot rang out. After an interminable stretch of time, Vito appeared in the patch of moonlight this side of the date palm cluster. He raised his hand in a triumphant gesture and vanished into the shadows again.

CHAPTER THIRTEEN

Harry lay tossing on his bed, neither quite asleep nor quite awake, reliving the day in troubled half-dreams. The reality had been nightmare enough; the dreams could hardly contort it further, but the dreams did one thing that added horror—they took the events and shredded them slowly, sifting them, examining the minutiae with ghastly fascination, deliberately lingering over the shards that brought him the most pain, and on him rode the horror of guilt, gibbering at his inner ear. Here is your blame, here and here and here....

The shooting gallery. When you swung the rifle around and the muzzle bore directly on Lew for that moment, why did you not pull the trigger? After pulling it once, you could have swung it still farther? Vito could not have drawn his gun and shot before you pulled the trigger a second time. What held you back?

But you couldn't shoot down two men in cold blood, no matter in what loathing you held them. You couldn't do that, you couldn't, you couldn't!

Very well then, but what of your opportunity when Lew had set Yutzy and Vito fighting? Why did you move so slowly? Why did you not cross that distance in a rush? Lew was unsuspecting. He was not watching you. You could have been upon him before he turned, and even if he had turned, you could have hit him, knocked him down and taken his gun before either Vito or Yutzy could snatch up their guns? What made you hesitate? Why did you move so slowly?

I had to move slowly. I had to! I was too far away. I had to move slowly at first so that when I did rush I could be reasonably sure. I was too far away.

Well, perhaps Lew would have detected such a sudden movement, and I grant that you did have to get him with the first blow, but what stopped you when you were wrestling with Lew in the hall after you had pulled him away from the doctor? There was a fraction of a second there when you might have snatched his gun and swung him around as a shield between you and Vito. Aha! the thought of that did not strike you until just now, did it? Goff was right, wasn't he? That thought of Nellie always in the back of your mind has made you gutless, gutless, gutless!

But I couldn't have snatched his gun. I needed both hands to hold him. There was nothing I could do!

You're making excuses, Harry Joyce. Do you realize that if you had seized any one of those three opportunities, Yutzy might still be alive? Poor Yutzy. You can't class Yutzy with Lew and Vito. He wasn't bad. He was just a stupid, lumbering sheepdog. Everybody liked Yutzy. He was misled by Lew, but in your heart you know that he was nothing but a big good-natured simpleton whose life you might have saved.

Yutzy, Yutzy....

And Goff had gone nearly crazy when they killed Yutzy. In his odd way, Goff had obviously liked Yutzy. He was contemptuous of him, yet he had been quite fond of him. Perhaps as you might be fond of a dog or a horse. And, too, Goff blamed himself for Yutzy's death. He was the one who had opened the gate for Ozzie. It had been no good to point out that though Lew must have believed that Vito had left the gate open, the blame had been put on Yutzy. The reason was clear. Yutzy was on guard. He was supposed to check the padlock. But Yutzy had not been killed for that. If that had been the reason, he would have been shot down in the dining-room. Lew had undoubtedly started to slap him around and suddenly Yutzy had gotten a bellyful. His dim slow mind had suddenly rebelled. God only knew what the thunderous crash down in the dining-room had been, but certainly Yutzy had slugged Vito before leaping through the dining-room window. Goff was no more to blame than Harry. Or Josie or Nellie, for that matter. It was a thing that had been brewing.

But Goff had been in an agony of self-condemnation, and hysterically had run to the stairway with only that pitiful little paring knife in his hand to attack Lew, to wipe it out in more blood.

The memory of that dreadful struggle at the head of the stairs in desperate silence, their breath hissing between their teeth! A short, hard right to the jaw had finally settled it, and now Goff was locked in his room until sanity returned. Lew in a killing mood was no man to attack with a paring knife.

The aftermath had been the clowning ghoulishness. With Yutzy lying dead somewhere out in the tree-garden, Ozzie and Lew had become quite drunk in a kiss-and-make-up orgy that meandered from the dining-room to the patio to the swimming-pool to the living-room where now they both lay snoring and stinking. They had sung. They actually had sung with their arms around each other's shoulders. They had stood down by the swimming-pool, singing *Come Back to Sorrento*, laughing and crying in each other's arms. Staggering back to the house for another bottle. And then the final besotted silence.

Harry had gone crazy, too. Not crazy like Goff, not hysterically. He had crept down the back stairway. He had his knife, the long horn-handled carving knife that Goff had tossed to him. The mind can take just so much, and he had crept down the back stairway, no longer squeamish about killing in cold blood. But the blood wasn't cold.

But there was the frustration and the impotence again. The door to the kitchen at the foot of the stairway was locked at the other side. In his bare feet, he ran to the main stairway. He was half way down when Vito appeared in the doorway of the living-room and pointed a gun at him, motioning him back.

"I want a drink!" Harry snarled, taking three more slow steps downward, measuring the exact step from which he would spring at Vito, unmindful of the gun—until Vito had crouched and sighted along the barrel. Harry had looked straight down into the muzzle, twenty feet below him, a round, black hole. The insanity beckoned and tugged, urging him to leap into that hole. Death lived in that round black hole. It lived there like a spider. It had leaped and caught Yutzy, and now it was ready to leap and catch Harry. Vito was nothing. Vito did not exist, but the death that lived in that round black hole did exist. Even in madness, Harry could see it in there, could see its bright and shattering smile, could feel the challenge. He could take four quick steps down and spring. *Which of us will be the faster?* There was a spark of reason left, a spark of reason that told him that there was not just one death living in that round, black muzzle, but several. Vito had fired only one shot at Yutzy. Had expended only one of the deaths. *Come, come, let us see which of us is the faster?* It was a deliberate snare. There was more than one death in that hungry muzzle. One could miss, and another could miss, but there would be a third and a fourth and a fifth.

And even an idiot could not miss at that distance.

The victory was Harry's. Despite the madness, he was not drawn into that cunning trap, into that glittering joust. The insanity evaporated.

"Throw me a bottle so I can celebrate with the rest of the boys," he said. "I haven't had a drink all day."

Vito shook his head and pointed up the stairs.

But in the half-dream, Harry said, "Poor Vito. Yutzy was one of Lew's eyes too, and Lew plucked it out because it offended him. Lew is mad, and he will pluck out his other eye if it offends him. I am not the one to watch, Vito. Lew is the one to watch." And still in the half-dream, Vito had wept, and inexorably had pointed up the stairs.

The dream was not the nightmare. Reality was the nightmare.

The bedroom door opened. For an instant, a towering muffled figure was outlined against the dreary amber light of the hall outside. Still enmeshed in the half-dream, Harry dropped silently over the side of the bed and crept along the wall. The figure appeared again, this time silhouetted against the stony moonlit window. He sprang at it. It was like smoke in his arms, unresisting, and a cry:

"Harry!"

Had she not cried out, he would have strangled her, for his forearm was already a constricting bar across her throat, his right hand pulling the wrist, his knee in the small of her back, breaking her across his thigh.

"Oh God, Nellie! Did I hurt you, honey, did I hurt you?"

He held her against him. He heard her gasp. He released her, lifted her in his arms. He carried her to the bed and laid her gently down. He knelt beside the bed, anxiously clasping her hand.

"I should have knocked," she said. "But all I could think of was to get out of the hall as quickly as I could."

"You shouldn't have come, honey. You shouldn't have taken the chance."

"We were frightened, darling. We heard the shots. We didn't know what to think. What happened?"

"Nothing, nothing. Lew and Ozzie got drunk. They broke a window."

"But the shots?"

"Don't worry about it."

"Is Goff all right? Josie is almost out of her mind."

"He's fine. He's in bed, sleeping."

"I have to tell Josie. I'll be right back."

"No, no. Stay in your room."

She kissed him lightly, slipped from his arms, and ran from the room. He pressed his face against the mattress, praying to her to lock herself in her room, praying for her to return. He jumped up and ran to the door. She was standing at Josie's door, whispering against the panel. He watched the stairway. When she came back, he opened the door wider, pulled her quickly inside, and closed it again.

He kissed her fiercely. She clung to him, and he could feel the long tremors run down her body. Her lips were hard against his, not returning his kiss but taking warmth from him, just as her clinging arms were more frightened than caressing. When he lifted his lips, she immediately burrowed her face into the side of his neck as if to get even closer to him. Her fingers dug convulsively into the muscles of his shoulders.

"What *were* those shots, Harry?" she whispered.

"Nothing, honey. Lew saw one of those white herons over by the swimming-pool, and he was using it for target practice."

"He ... he didn't hit it, did he?"

"No, thank God. He was so drunk he couldn't have hit Broadway from the Times Building."

"I'm glad. I couldn't have stood it if he shot it."

He knew she was identifying herself and him and Josie and Goff with the fictitious heron. He held her tightly, cursing Lew behind his clenched teeth. Through the thin nylon of her robe, he could feel how rigid she was. He kissed her hair, murmured to her and after awhile when she began to soften, the relaxing of her body was like a sigh.

"Darling," she breathed.

She lifted her face, stood on tiptoe and kissed him on the lips. Very softly. The lightest brush of a kiss. "I love you, darling," she whispered.

A pulse hammered in his throat, but he returned her kiss just as lightly as she had given it. The restraint was a terrible constriction around his chest, but this was not the time for anything else. She had come to him because she had been afraid. She wanted gentleness. She wanted ...

Her arm went around his neck and held him when he started to withdraw his lips. She kissed him as if she were pouring herself into him through her open mouth. Her tongue, thrusting, demanded. The restraint he had put upon himself a few moments before made him incapable of instantaneous response. She tightened her arms around his neck and moved her lips to and fro across his.

"Harry, Harry! Put your hands under my robe."

Her robe was open and he felt the long coolness of her, thigh to thigh, her hands urgent now in the small of his back. She moved against him.

"Harry!"

Still he held back. He wanted to thrust her away and cry out to her all the things that had tormented him in his half-dreams.

"Harry," he could feel her breath through her kisses, "when you love someone, you want love from him, and right now this is what counts."

She threw back her arms and he heard the whisper of nylon as her robe dropped from her.

No, Nellie, no, wait till I tell you….

He wanted to take her when he was clean of torment, not just bury that torment in her. He did not want to use her. Her kiss came again, passionately alive, breaking through his dammed-up bitterness and frustration. He met her reaching mouth with violence. He swung her up in his arms and bore her to the bed. He took her with a panting desperation as if he had just run a long way at top speed to meet her there.

Afterward, trembling slightly, she lay beside him, one arm across his chest, one hand cool against his cheek. She whispered, "Harry…"

"Honey…."

"That was the best. Each one is going to be the best. I know it."

"Each one will always be the best," Harry said.

The room was faintly and coldly glowing as if illuminated by light reflected from a white stone wall, giving everything the subtle illusion of a photograph in black and white, robbed of color. It also gave a subtle magic to the sweet lines of her body, slim rounded thighs, breasts lifted. Her cheek rested in the hollow of his shoulder, and she looked up into his face through her lashes, smiling. She stroked his cheek.

"Darling," she said.

"Yes, honey?"

"I love you so much, darling."

He shifted, cupped her chin in his hand and kissed her. Her lips spread softly. Her hand pressed against the back of his head and pulled him deeper into the kiss. His fingers fled lightly down the curve of her breast, touched the swell of ribs, the rise of hip, and lingered on the outside curve of her thigh before turning inward at the knee, returning, feathering the caress to the smoothest and most satin at the inside of the thigh. Her body rose to his touch, and he took her again, not in fury and not in haste, but on the lift of their blended emotion.

After awhile, as they lay side by side, he said slowly, "I've been thinking, honey."

"And Josie and I have been thinking. Is there any chance of the police getting Lew?"

"Not exactly. He's wanted by the Essex County Crime Investigating Committee. As far as I know, there are no criminal charges against him. Anyway, it's not the committee he's worried about. He's afraid that some of his gangster buddies will knock him off to keep him from testifying."

"But wouldn't there be a warrant or something out for him?"

"There could be. Whether it's worth anything is something else again. It's a purely local investigation, not like that nation-wide Kefauver business. I doubt that Lew could be extradited even if the warrant could be served. I happen to know that Lew does have some political connections in Dade County down here in Florida. I don't know exactly where we are in Florida right this minute, but it's dimes to dollars that we're safely inside Dade County somewhere. So I don't think Lew would have any trouble with extradition. Why? Did you have some idea of letting the police know where Lew is?"

Nellie said, "Yes," in a discouraged voice. "It wasn't a very good idea, was it? Josie and I talked it over, and we decided that all four of us trying to get out at one time is too much. One would have a much better chance than four, and we thought you would be the best one. Please, Harry, before you say anything...."

Harry squeezed her hand. "Right," he said, "and I've got an idea I think will work. I can get out of here. Goff has a key to the gate. I won't be followed. I'll rip the ignition wires out of all three cars. That part is set, and that's where I always bogged down. I didn't want to go and leave you, Josie and Goff. Now I've got that figured. I'll leave a note that Goff will give Lew about six hours after I go. It will take me just about six hours to reach town on foot. In the note I'll tell Lew to turn you three loose or I'll send telegrams to every newspaper between

Miami and New York, *telling them where Lew Markey is hiding out.* He'll know what that would mean. Within fifteen minutes after the papers hit the streets, his gunmen pals will be converging on this place from the entire eastern seaboard. But just to protect you while I'm gone, you and I will stage a little scene before I go. You'll slap me, scream that I've broken your heart and ruined Josie's happy home when I told her she was pregnant. All my fault, see? I think Lew will buy it if you really lay that slap on. I'll have a cab waiting at the gate to get you away from here. How does it sound?"

"Yes, Harry, yes!"

He lifted himself to one elbow and looked tenderly down into her face. "You didn't think I'd leave here without first being absolutely sure that nothing would happen to you," he whispered. "It was the only way I could think of to work it."

She raised her arms and clasped him around the neck, pulling him down to her reaching lips. Her body arched to his, breasts thrusting. Something leaped within him again and as he buried his lips in hers, he reached for her....

Whether it was minutes or hours, he never knew, nor ever would know, but suddenly he saw that the stony moonlight had gone and the light through the window was soft with the coming dawn.

He said, "Christ!" and jumped from the bed. He turned his hand to look at his wrist-watch, but he had taken it off before going to bed. He darted to the night-table. It was six o'clock! He shook off a grasp of panic. Nellie was sleeping, her head turned into the pillow that she hugged to her, her lips slightly parted. He bent over her, lightly kissed her breast, and then shook her gently.

As she opened her eyes, he said, "Up, honey. It's six o'clock."

She smiled, lifted her arms to him, and then with a gasp saw that dawn was rising. She sprang from the bed. "Harry! We fell asleep!"

She snatched up the nylon robe she had dropped from her in the earlier darkness and hurriedly swung into it. She went to him for a last kiss and ran to the door. He had pulled on his shorts.

"Let me go first," he whispered.

He opened the door and ran lightly down the hall. He went to the stairway. Below, hunkered on his heels, squatted Vito, who lifted his shiny shoe-button eyes the moment Harry appeared at the head of the stairs.

Harry waved cheerfully to him and, to cover Nellie's return to her room, said, "You shouldn't miss your sleep like this, Vito. You're a growing boy. You need all the sleep you can get." He started down the stairs.

Vito pushed himself up from his squat and showed the gun in his hand. His face was sodden with fatigue, but his vigilance had not relaxed. He stolidly motioned with the gun for Harry to go back up the stairs. Harry shrugged peaceably and turned back.

The hall was empty. Nellie had gotten back to her room. He darted into his own room for the key to Goff's door, but before unlocking it, he went back to the stairway to make sure that Vito had not decided to come up. Vito was still there. Harry ran back to Goff's room. He quickly opened the door—and froze, feeling as if every drop of blood in his body had been driven into his bursting face.

Goff and Josie, side by side, were sitting up in bed, staring at him with terror-stricken faces.

He quickly closed the door, locked it, and strode toward them, saying harshly, "Are you two crazy? Jesus Christ, of all the dumb stunts you could have pulled, this is absolutely the bottom."

Josie shakily pulled up the blanket to cover her bare breasts. The terror drained from her face. "We wasn't taking much of a chance," she said defensively. "I went downstairs about a half hour ago and there was Lew and Oz plotzed on the floor in the parlor, dead to the world, so what chance did we take?"

"The chance that he'd come up and start nosing around your bedroom, that's the chance you took."

"Aaah, you don't know'm when he gets plotzed. I seen him so many times, I wouldn't count if I could. He's good till two-three o'clock this afternoon. So what chance?"

"*You* should have known better," Harry snapped at Goff. "My God, at a time like this!"

Josie sprang out of bed and blazed at him, "Don't you go blaming Goffy. I did it all by myself, me! He tried to brush me off, but I wouldn't brush," she was stark and magnificently naked and unaware of it as she stalked toward Harry, defending Goff. "Anyways, who was that in your room all night, Minnie Mouse?"

Goff threw the blanket at her and muttered, "Cover yourself up for godsake, sweetheart."

She slapped the blanket down. She was furious. "Who's he think he is, a cop or something? I got feelings, too!" And then she burst into sudden tears and fumbled blindly on the floor for the blanket. "I'm just as crazy about Goffy as you are about Nellie, and you ain't got no call coming in here saying we're crazy." She stood, now covered from neck to ankle by the blanket. The tears gleamed on her cheeks, and there was a lifting dignity in her when she faced Harry. "I love him," she said, "and last night I loved him so much, I couldn't stay away from him this morning, and I don't care what you say."

Harry, shamed, said quietly, "I apologize, Josie, I apologize to both of you. I had something on my mind. I talked out of turn. I'm sorry. But I think you ought to go back to your room now, Josie."

"Well, if you had something on your mind, that's different. I know how it is, but," she tightened the blanket defiantly around her, "I want to hear what you got on your mind. It's about us?"

Harry could see that he would only make matters worse by attempting to chase her back to her room, so rapidly in a low voice he told them the plan he had just given Nellie. Goff nodded, his hostility evaporating.

"Sounds good," he said tersely.

Harry held out his hand. "You've still got the key to the front gate?"

Goff got it from the pocket of his trousers that hung over the back of the chair beside the bed. He opened his mouth. He wanted to say something cheerful, something encouraging.

"Aaah, why kid ourselves?" he said finally. "It's going to be close, but it's got to be our turn for a little luck, doesn't it? Lew can't have it all the time."

CHAPTER FOURTEEN

It took longer to compose the note to Lew than Harry had dreamed. It had to be just right, and everything had to be in it. He rewrote it four times before he got a draft that finally satisfied him. He folded it, wrote "Lew Markey, Personal" across the back and propped it against the mirror on his chest of drawers. That was where Goff was supposed to find it after Harry had gone.

He shaved and dressed very carefully. He had no money. Lew had taken the money from everybody on the first day. He would have to talk the local bank into cashing a check for him. It wouldn't be easy, but it could be done—if he looked prosperous. He was barely finished when he heard a pounding in the hall. He had an idea what it was, and when he looked out, there was Vito nailing Josie's door shut. Vito did not give him a glance. When he finished, after driving in six heavy spikes, he picked up the remainder of the nails from the floor, put the hammer in his back pocket and walked down the hall toward the stairway.

Harry was relieved. For the time being, at least, Lew did not intend to break Josie's door in, but it pointed up more than ever the necessity for getting out of here as quickly as possible. Lew was not long going to be satisfied merely with starving Josie. That was too subtle and too prolonged a procedure. When Lew was thwarted, sooner or later he had to wash it out with violence.

Harry walked down the stairs. Lew was in the lower hall and he turned when he heard Harry's descending steps. He hadn't shaved and his eyes were bloodshot. His head hung between rounded shoulders as if it were too heavy for him.

He waved his hand and said hoarsely, "Hey, come here a minute, kid. I want to talk to you."

To Harry's surprise, he seemed friendly despite his obvious hangover. He was even smiling a little as he rubbed the stubble of his blue-black jaw with his thumb.

Harry was saying, "Well, welcome to the land of the living," when Lew caught him across the face with a smashing backhand slap.

It was a heavy blow and unexpected. Harry staggered and threw out one hand to the wall to keep from falling. Lew's thick fingers had slapped across the bridge of the nose. He braced against the wall and shook his head.

Ozzie was standing behind Lew, lounging in the doorway to the dining-room, grinning slyly around the cigarette that dangled from his lips. He was turning a gun in his hands, and he looked eager to use it.

"That was for sticking your nose where it wasn't wanted," Lew's voice was still mock-friendly. "You're just lucky I didn't get to you last night. I'd have kicked your teeth in. You're a jerk, and I don't like jerks, but today I got a hangover, and I don't feel like taking the trouble. Maybe later on I'll perk up a little and work you over. I don't know. I haven't made up my mind. In the meantime, you're the new cook. I didn't like our last cook so I canned him. Vito tells me you think you're pretty good, so put on your apron. You're elected. Me, I want tomato juice with Worcestershire and Tabasco and an egg beaten up in it, a couple slices of toast, medium brown, and a cup of coffee. What's your order, Oz?"

"He can scramble me a couple eggs, a half-dozen slices of bacon crisp, orange juice, hot rolls, and a whisky sour. And if the scrambled eggs are mushy," he scratched his ear with the muzzle of the gun, "I'll wash your face in them. Right, Lew?"

"Right. Okay, on your way, chef. And when you get finished making breakfast, I got some shoes for you to shine."

Harry knew that Lew was watching him narrowly, watching for a glimmer of resentment, so he merely shrugged and said, "You're the boss, Lew." He touched his nose. It was bleeding slightly. He walked toward the kitchen.

"Hey, Lew," Ozzie said loudly, "you forgot Vito. Vito eats, too."

"The hell with Vito. Open him a can of dog food, chef. Keep an eye on him, Oz. I'm taking a shower."

Ozzie followed Harry into the kitchen. He found Goff's frilly apron hanging on the door of the broom closet and threw it at Harry.

"You need an apron, chef, and here's a pretty one."

Harry laughed and tied the apron around his middle. The best thing he could do, he knew, was to treat this as a joke. Ozzie was aching to use his gun.

"It's about time somebody appreciated my talents," he said.

"You look like a fairy in that apron. Are you a fairy, Harry? I'll bet you're a fairy. I'll call Vito in to give you a nice big kiss, how's that?"

"Please! I'd rather kiss a band-saw. How's about a little green pepper and onion in your scrambled eggs? Sure cure for the morning after."

Ozzie was baffled. He had expected Harry to resent this new indignity, and now that Harry didn't, he was at a loss. He made another attempt to anger Harry so that he would have an excuse to use his gun.

"How long have you been a fairy, Harry? I always knew you were a fairy. I could tell the minute I saw you, the way you wag your ass when you walk. Tell me something about fairies, Harry, I've always wondered...."

He became increasingly obscene and detailed. Harry just laughed at him. Ozzie's purpose was so obvious.

Goff came into the kitchen about ten minutes later. He gave Harry a sharp glance, but he was shrewd enough to see what had happened. He went over to Ozzie.

"What gave last night?" he whispered. "The Ford was all set up for you. You could have been in Miami by this time."

Ozzie looked uneasily at Harry and called, "Make a little noise over there, Harriet. Did you know Harriet's a fairy, Goff? Just look at him in that apron. Ain't he sweet? When Vito comes back, he's going to give Harriet a great big kiss, and Harriet's going to love it. Harriet's just crazy about Vito."

"He looks real sweet," said Goff gravely. "But are you sure you're not trying to make Harriet yourself, Ozzie?"

Ozzie flushed but said noisily, "Naaah, he ain't my type."

Harry knew that Goff wanted to talk to Ozzie, so he rattled his fork in the frying pan.

Goff asked in a low voice, "What happened last night, kid?"

Ozzie muttered, "That lousy Vito had the Ford disconnected. I stepped on the starter and nothing happened. Can you still get me out of this crumb bin?"

"Sure. But I thought you and Lew had kissed and made up."

Ozzie said savagely, "... Lew!"

Goff whistled, noting that Harry had gradually decreased the noise he was making at the cooking range. He raised his voice slightly so that Harry could hear.

"How far you get down the road before Vito caught you last night, Oz?"

"A couple miles. I want to get out of here, Goff. He wants to keep me here. He's bringing in a load of whores Saturday night, but who wants whores? I want out."

"Okay, kid, okay," Goff looked over his shoulder at Harry and inched closer to Ozzie, still keeping his voice high enough to be heard across the room. "I'll get you out, and this time you won't get caught. Is that worth something to you?"

"I ain't got nothing! You know damn well...."

"Hold it, boy, hold it. I changed my mind about that wrist-watch. How much you say Lew paid for it?"

"Five hundred," said Ozzie eagerly. "He showed me the bill from the jewelers."

"Okay. Slip me the watch and I'll give you the out."

Ozzie unbuckled the watch and slipped it furtively into Goff's waiting hand. Goff dropped it into his pocket.

"Here's the deal, Oz," he said. "But you'll have to cooperate a little this time. Okay?"

"Don't talk like a jerk! Sure!"

"Now listen. This is your part. While Vito's eating his breakfast, you slip out to the garage, reach up under the dashboards of all three cars and pull off all the wires you can grab. Get it? If they don't have a car, they can't pick you up once you're out. Rip out all those wires, kid, and it'll take an expert mechanic a month to put them back, and you can be in Miami Beach by that time, and all the girls you want and the hell with Lew's whores. But you got to do something for me, too, kid."

"What's that?"

"The gun, kid, the gun. I'm going to be left here with Lew, and if he decides that I opened the gate for you, you know where I'll be. I want the rod, just in case...."

He held out his hand.

Ozzie almost gave it to him. His hand moved—but he pulled it back.

"I'll leave it in the bushes at the side of the gate," he said.

Goff shrugged. He had not really expected to get the gun that easily. But it had been close.

"Okay," he said. "I guess I'll have to trust you, but don't cross me. In the meantime, you watch your chance and rip out all those ignition wires. Make a mess of them. I'll get you out, but don't get caught fooling with those cars. Where's Vito now?"

Ozzie wanted to rush right out, but Goff restrained him.

"Look, kid," he said. "I want to help you, but we don't want to get our ass in a sling, do we? Okay. So take it easy. Just kind of wander around outside, spot Vito. Don't go looking for him. Spot him and watch him, and report back to me. I'll give you the word when to rip out the cars. I let you out last night, didn't I? You can trust me, can't you? So do me a favor and do it the way I say, will you? You gave me your watch, and I want to earn the money. I don't want any slip-ups this time. Now, just go out and keep your eye on Vito."

Ozzie protested feebly, "But Lew told me to keep my eye on Harry."

"I'll keep an eye on Harry. I'll guarantee he won't disappear. Okay?"

Ozzie gave Harry a petulant glance and left the kitchen through the side door. Goff leaned against the wall and frankly wiped the sweat from his face.

"For a minute, Harry," he said, "I actually thought the little squirt was going to hand me his gun. I thought of taking it away from him, but he might have squawked, and that would have been a mess."

Harry looked toward the door through which Ozzie had just slipped.

"I don't know how smart that was," he said.

"Why not? Let him do the dirty work for us."

"It sounds fine, Goff, but I wouldn't trust him to open a window without breaking the glass. He'll fumble it, or get himself caught, or something. I would rather have taken the chance of doing it myself."

"So he gets caught, Harry. So what? He won't let on to Lew that I ..."

"That's not the point. Suppose he gets caught before he finishes the job? Suppose he leaves them a car that operates? If I'm going to get to town, they can't have a car."

"I'm sorry, Harry. I never thought of that. I'll call him off. I'll tell him I'll take care of the cars myself. You heard what I told him, didn't you? I told him not to do anything till I gave him the word. I'll call him off. Harry, I can't tell you how sorry I am. I thought I was helping...."

"Cut it out," Harry growled, turning back to the bacon sizzling in the frying pan. "It probably is a good idea. I'm all on edge, that's all. I feel as if somebody tightened every nut and bolt in me with a Stillson wrench. I'd feel a lot happier if we didn't have to use a lightweight like Ozzie. It's not just me I'm thinking of—it's the girls and you, too. I don't want anything to go wrong anywhere along the line."

"Sure, Harry," said Goff meekly. Now he could see how tightly drawn Harry was. There was no trembling of the hands, or anything like that.

There was a tenseness in the hard line around his mouth, in the thinning of his eyes.

"See if you can get him back in here," Harry motioned sharply at the door. "I don't want Vito to catch him dodging around out there. Vito's no fool. All he has to do is find Ozzie peeping at him from behind trees and he'll damn well know something's in the air."

Goff said, "Sure, Harry," and went swiftly to the door.

Harry was making coffee when Goff returned ten minutes later with Ozzie. Ozzie was flushed and in a high state of elation. Harry had only to look at him to see that he had already been at the cars. Harry said nothing and slowly stirred the creamy scrambled eggs in the frying pan.

Goff had slunk in after Ozzie and was leaning against the wall, looking miserable. Harry gave him a quick grin and a wink, signaling him not to worry about it. Goff looked grateful.

The door opened from the butler's pantry and Lew looked into the kitchen. He saw the frilly apron on Harry and he raised his eyebrows.

Ozzie giggled. "That's Harriet. Ain't she sweet?"

Lew was in no mood for jokes. "Cut out the horseplay," he growled. "Where's breakfast? I'm hungry."

"Any time you're ready, Lew," said Harry cheerfully.

Lew ignored him. Without looking at Harry, he said, "There's another order for orange juice, toast and coffee, and make it snappy. Bring him in when he's ready, Oz."

He gave Goff the kind of incurious glance you'd give a fly and closed the door after him.

Orange juice, toast and coffee. That would be Nellie. She's come down for breakfast. Harry's heart both lifted and tightened. Nellie was in there in the dining-room, waiting for him to appear so she could go through her part of the business. His hands were not quite steady when he dropped two pieces of bread into the toaster. It was getting closer.

Goff wheeled over his cart, getting ready to serve the breakfast. Ozzie waved him back.

"You've been promoted," he said. "Harriet's the new waitress. From now on, you're Harriet's boss in the kitchen, when nobody else is around. Serve breakfast, Harriet."

Harry almost laughed aloud. Here he'd been trying to figure a way to get into the dining-room without it looking as if he'd walked in for the specific purpose of being slapped in the face by Nellie, and now

Ozzie handed it to him on a platter.

Goff protested, "But Lew told me...."

"I'll take care of Lew," said Ozzie grandly. "Serve the breakfast, Harriet."

Harry loaded the breakfast things on the cart, trying to look as if Ozzie were taking all the joy out of life, and he managed to slide Goff a glance to tell him everything was under control. So far. He wheeled the cart into the dining-room, followed by the swaggering Ozzie.

Lew was seated at the head of the table, lumpishly gnawing at an unlit cigar. Nellie was standing at the window. She was pale and nervous, but to Harry she had never looked lovelier. He had to keep his eyes from her for he knew that Lew was watching him. He began laying the plates on the table. He heard the swish of nylon skirt as Nellie crossed the room. She was coming. He turned as if he were going to the cart to make it easier for her. She came around the back of Lew's chair saying sharply:

"I've been wanting to talk to you!"

Harry saw her hand coming in a full-arm swing. It cracked across his cheekbone, striking sparks. He did not have to pretend. She had put muscle and velocity into that swing. Harry put his hand to his cheek as if dazed. Lew looked up at them with dulled surprise.

Nellie put on a good show. Her voice was shrill and only half coherent. She stood in front of Harry, twisting her hands at her breasts as the choking, bitter words tumbled out of her, and there actually were tears in her eyes.

"Why couldn't you leave us alone?" she cried brokenly. "Oh why couldn't you leave us alone!"

She covered her face with her hands and ran out of the room. Lew looked heavily at Harry. Ozzie tittered and glanced at the doorway. Lew scowled.

"Serve it up," he said. "Come on, serve it up. I want to eat, dammit. Sit down, Oz. I'm driving in to town right after breakfast. Anything you want me to get you?"

Harry started and knocked over the salt on the cart, and Ozzie looked as if he were choking. Lew, unnoticing, started pushing toast into his mouth, making a noise like someone walking on crushed glass.

Ozzie, stammered, "Could ... couldn't you wait till this afternoon?"

"Why?"

"I ... I want to make up a list of things you should get me."

"Make it up now."

"I can't make it up now. I got to go through my stuff upstairs. I need shirts and socks and stuff like that. And I want some magazines. Anyway, why can't I go with you this afternoon?"

"Are we going to have another scrap, kid?" asked Lew wearily. "We agreed last night..."

"Okay, okay, okay," said Ozzie. He looked down into his plate, veiling his eyes. "Wait till this afternoon so I can give you a list."

Lew shrugged and grumbled, "You're worse than a woman...."

Harry wheeled the cart from the room, feeling as if he were walking on inflated inner tubes. That had been close, too damn close. Goff was waiting anxiously in the butler's pantry. He had been listening.

Harry followed him into the kitchen, pulling off his apron. He balled it up and threw it on a chair. Beads of perspiration pebbled his upper lip.

"What did you have to tell Ozzie?" he demanded.

"I told him I couldn't get to the padlock before noon. I told him Lew keeps me busy all morning, and I wouldn't have a chance to get out of the house before then. I told him that to give you plenty of time, Harry."

"Well, time's running out, and it's running out fast. I've got to get out of here before Lew decides to go to town after all. I left that note where I told you, propped against the mirror on the chest of drawers. Here's the key to my room...."

Goff pocketed it quickly as Vito walked in through the side door from the garden. His eyes flickered suspiciously over them, and then he sat himself down at the table with a grunt. Goff placed a bowl before him, set a box of corn flakes and a quart of milk at his elbow.

Harry put the milk and sugar and three coffee cups on his cart and wheeled it out of the kitchen. Vito did not even look up as he went. He left the cart and walked quickly down the hall. The dining-room door was partially open and he could hear Lew's voice rumbling to Ozzie about the party projected for Saturday night. Lew seemed to be in good humor. Harry took a breath and walked past the open doorway. No one called out to him or stopped him. He opened the front door and stepped out of the house.

He had, he knew, exactly ten minutes before Vito would finish his bowl of corn flakes and walk out onto the grounds to make his rounds again. Ten minutes. Goff had told him that. Vito spent ten minutes eating as fast and as much as he could cram into himself, and then he was off. Ten minutes was the margin.

Harry ran lightly across the grass, keeping off the path, for the crunching shells would betray him. There was an open space beyond the patio and he had a bad moment forcing himself to stroll to the trees beyond. If he were seen or stopped, he did not want to be running. But once in the dense tree-garden he sprinted for the front gate. The low fan-branches of the areca palm whipped his face, and he held up his arm to ward them off and sped on.

He was panting heavily when he reached the gate and he leaned against it for a moment to steady himself. He had a panicky moment when he dug into his pocket for the key and could not find it, but then he remembered that he had put it into his watch pocket. He wiped his hands down the sides of his thighs, looked briefly back over his shoulder and thrust the key into the padlock. It stuck. He swore, pulled it out, turned it upside down. It stuck again. He thrust harder, but it would not enter the lock at all—and then he saw that the padlock had been changed. The key had the Yale imprint, and the new padlock was a Kwikset, larger and stronger than the previous lock. A redness seemed to roll across Harry's vision like fog rolling in from the Gulf and he attacked the lock with his bare hands, jerking futilely at it, swearing hoarsely. The redness cleared away and he stared dully at the new mockingly shiny lock. Take your time, boy, take your time. You'll never do it with your hands without a key. A file. Goff had a file to make the key. He'd have to get the file. Take your time, boy, *take your time!* Get back to the house. Get the file from Goff. This is only a temporary setback. With a little luck, Lew won't look at the cars for hours. You've got three hours before lunch. Get back to the house and get the file from Goff.

He faded back into the shrubbery beside the driveway and trotted back toward the house. He slipped in through the front door. Lew and Ozzie were still talking in the dining-room and they were laughing about something. The cart still stood in the hall where he had left it, and he wheeled it back into the kitchen.

Goff's jaw dropped when he walked in. Vito was gone, and Goff was clearing the table. The bowl slipped from his hands and crashed on the floor.

"They changed the lock," Harry said tersely. "Where's the file you used to make the key?"

Goff's face squeezed together and he began softly to beat his fist against the side of his leg. Harry gripped his arm.

"Cut it out," he ordered. "Pull yourself together. It's not a tragedy. Get me the file. Or a pinch-bar. I can break the hasp quicker with a pinch-bar."

"They... locked all the tools away," Goff whispered. "But I still have the file, but it's awfully fine for that kind of work, Harry. It'll take you forever. That hasp is steel."

"Let me worry about that. Get me the file. You still have it?"

"Up in my room."

"Get it for me."

"Okay, Harry."

Harry leaned both hands on the edge of the sink and bowed his head over them. Don't start wailing about luck, boy. This is one time you're going to have to make your own luck, so forget the luck end of it or you'll start corning apart at the seams like poor little Goff. He opened his eyes. He looked down at his hands and clenched them. He poured himself a cup of coffee and sat down at the table to drink it.

Nothing had been lost. This was only a temporary setback, just a temporary setback. Maybe they would have to set fire to the house after all, to get Vito away from the gate while he was filing through. That had just been a sort of joke when he told it to Nellie, but now it didn't look like so much of a joke. He could not think of anything else that would keep Vito occupied for any length of time. But it was risky, risky. This was an old house, and it could flare up like tinder. Josie would have to be gotten out of her room first....

The coffee was good. It was hot, black and strong. Harry went over to the range and was pouring himself another cup when the scream exploded the silence. He stood frozen. Nellie's scream came again and he sprinted out into the hall. The scream came the third time from outside the house. He dashed down the hall. Lew appeared in the dining-room doorway. He waved his gun.

"Get back in your hole, pal," he said. "This ain't none of your ..."

Harry flung the coffee pot at him. Lew cried out as the hot liquid splashed over him. Harry dashed by and darted through the front door. Nellie was screaming from the tennis court. Harry leaped down to the path. He heard Lew's gun boom, but it seemed as remote and impersonal as someone blasting a tree stump in another county. He came upon Nellie and Ozzie at the turn of the path, on the fringe of clipped grass that surrounded the tennis court. Nellie was struggling in Ozzie's arms. Her dress was torn, but she seemed to be holding her own with teeth and fingernails. Ozzie was grinning. He was letting her struggle a little before he really went to work on her.

He lifted his hand to cuff her when he saw Harry. Fear flamed in his eyes. He shoved Nellie from him and clawed at the gun in his waistband. It stuck and he bleated in terror as Harry's fist caught him on the side of the head. He staggered and ripped the gun free. Harry hit him four times in the face and the gun went flying across the grass. Harry saw him only through a furious mist and kept pumping his fists into that shrieking face until the face became a formless redness. He heard Nellie scream again, and something exploded against the back of his neck. The darkness was sudden and complete.

CHAPTER FIFTEEN

Harry lay unconscious on the grass, face down. Lew was kicking at him, and Vito stood by impassively, his gun held down at his side. Lew kicked only three times and in such blind fury that his foot struck Harry only glancing blows on the hip. Ozzie was crawling sightlessly on all fours across the hard-packed clay of the tennis court, moaning. Blood ran from his face. Lew stopped kicking and ran to Ozzie. He dropped to his knees and put his arms around him.

"Did he hurt you, kid?" he blubbered. "What did the bastard do to you? Are you okay, kid? Here, here...."

He ran back, seized Harry by the arm and dragged him across the grass. He flung him in front of Ozzie.

"Smack him, kid," he pleaded. "Go ahead, smack him. Do anything to him...."

Goff limped warily to Nellie's side. He had been flung from the path into a coquina-stone rock garden by Vito, who had been the first to reach Harry. Nellie stood swaying, her face waxy.

Goff hissed, "Get out of here, Nell. Get back to the house. Get out of here or you'll be next...."

He lurched toward Lew, crying, "Leave the kid alone, Lew. Get him into a bed, get a doctor. Just look at his face, Lew!"

Ozzie had crawled another few feet and fell over on his side. It was not a face. It was just a raw and bleeding thing. The nose was smashed, teeth broken, lips cut, eyes swollen, and the right cheek was split from the side of the nose to the hinge of the jaw, and the jaw itself hung askew, either broken or dislocated. Lew's face purpled and seemed to swell. He ran at Vito and clawed the gun out of his hand, gibbering. Goff grabbed his arm. Lew hit him with his clubbed fist. Goff staggered back flailing but managed to keep his feet.

"Ozzie might want to do that himself, Lew!" he cried. "Ozzie won't thank you if you knock the bastard off. When he snaps out of this, he's going to have ideas of his own. Let him take care of Harry himself!"

Vito grunted in agreement. Lew stopped. His eyes were maniacal, but he nodded, showing his teeth.

"Yeah, yeah, that's right. We'll let Oz take care of him.... Oh Christ, Vit', look at the kid. Look at his face!"

He ran back to Ozzie and began dabbing at the blood with his handkerchief, the tears streaming down his own face. Ozzie screamed, a horrible, bubbling scream, and clawed Lew's hand away. Lew gently, very gently, picked him up in his arms.

"Throw that bastard down in the cellar," he said thickly to Vito, "then go get a doctor."

Nellie was still rooted where she had stood before. She was frozen in horror.

As Lew passed her, he said, "I'll take care of you later, sister. I'll take care of you myself."

Vito thrust the gun back into the holster under his arm and motioned for Goff to give him a hand with Harry. They carried him down the path toward the garage. Nellie ran after them and tried to touch Harry with fluttering hands. Goff shouldered her roughly away.

"Get away from him," he snarled. "You started all this. You'll get yours from Lew. Get in the house before somebody gives you a swift smack in the jaw!"

Nellie stared at him with disbelief. She turned and ran into the house, choking. Vito grunted impatiently and motioned Goff on down the path.

At the concrete stairs to the garage basement, Vito took Harry by the collar and dragged him down, his feet bouncing limply from step to step. Goff ran down after them. Harry was alive, he knew, for he had seen the rise and fall of his chest, but that was all he knew. Vito had hit him savagely enough to break his neck. Goff went down on one knee beside Harry when Vito turned to unlock the door. Harry stirred and moved his head, mumbling. A dizzying flood of relief washed over Goff. At least the neck wasn't broken. Nor the arms, for Harry lifted them slowly and painfully to touch his head. Goff looked up to find Vito eying him suspiciously. Goff grinned.

"I was afraid for a minute you'd broken his neck, Vit'," he said. "Lew wouldn't like that."

Vito grunted and opened the door. As he stood to throw Harry into the room, Grizzard scuttled out on hands and knees like an animal. He darted up the narrow passage and turned, facing them with a snarl. His eyes darted from side to side.

"Where's Lew?" he said. "Where's Lew?"

Vito pounced and seized him by the shoulder. He shoved and kicked him back into the room, flinging Harry in after him. He shut the door quickly and snapped the padlock. He licked his lips uneasily and rubbed his hands on his shirt. Then he looked at Goff and twiddled his fingers questioningly at his temple.

"That's right," said Goff. "He blew his stack. He's nuts. Did he bite you, Vit'? If he did, wash it out right away. That's the worst thing you can get, a bite from a crazy man."

Vito looked at his hands and shook his head, but his eyes squinted anxiously. He was superstitious about crazy men. He wiped his hands again on his shirt. Goff backed toward the stairway.

"I ... I better get back to the house and see if I can help Lew with Ozzie," he said. "You better wash your hands off with gasoline, Vit'. Don't take any chances. I wouldn't touch a looney for a million bucks...."

Time, time! He wanted time to think, just think.... He had to get back to the house. He knew he had to get back to the house. He had to get back to the house before Vito found out that Ozzie had ripped the ignition wires out of all three cars.

As always, when faced with the need for direct and physical action, Goff was in a panic. He had done all right saving Harry from Lew out there on the tennis court. But there was too much now, too much to have to think about, too much to do, and no time in which to do it. His mind whirled as helplessly as a motor with a broken driving shaft. *No time, no time, no time!*

He burst into the kitchen and looked wildly around him. He pulled open the broom closet—mops, brooms, dusting cloths, Brillo, Bon-Ami, soap powder, Shinola, Fab, Flit. The cabinets—pots, pans, water kettle, a case of Coca-Cola, vinegar, pepper, chili powder, turkey seasoning. He ripped open the drawers—and when he saw it, he knew that that was what he had been looking for, though not specifically, with design or forethought, but looking for something just like this.

The meat cleaver, thick, heavy, sharp, gleaming steel with a sturdy maple handle, copper riveted. He picked it up and it was a new muscle, a new strength. He scuttled to the kitchen door and peeped out, breathing heavily. There was a flash of white shirt among the trees and it was Vito running toward the house. Goff slipped out and slunk among the bushes until Vito passed on the path to the front door, and then he pelted toward the garage, running as hard as he could. There was no conscious thought in any of this. The trapdoor to the basement was still folded back to the floor and he dived down the steps, flipping on the lights with a slash of his hand as he sped by the switch. He had the cleaver in both hands and was swinging it as he leaped for the door of Grizzard's prison. He brought it down smashing across the lock and hasp. It took several blows before he could rip the padlock from the splintered wood.

He cried, "Harry!"

Harry was standing shakily with one hand against the wall. Grizzard crouched back in the farthest corner of the evil-smelling little room, baring his teeth.

Goff flung his hand toward the cement steps and babbled, "He'll be back, he'll be back! He just went to tell Lew about the cars!"

"Just give me a minute," said Harry unsteadily. He shuffled toward the open door, still holding to the wall. "I just came out of it," he felt the back of his neck and rolled his head painfully. "That would have been Vito." He was gaining strength.

Grizzard made a desperate scramble past them and skittered out into the passageway. He ran up and down, calling shrilly for Lew, exploding into cackles of laughter.

Harry took the cleaver from Goff's now nerveless fingers.

"Let's go," he said.

He staggered on his first few steps, steadied himself against the wall, walked on more strongly. He turned into the shooting gallery. The light .22 rifles still lay chained to the counter, which Harry attacked with slashing blows of the cleaver. The soft pine, though thick, cracked and splintered. Harry seized one of the chains, pulled it from the shattered wood. He tossed the gun to Goff.

"There's a case of cartridges under the counter," he panted. "Grab a handful."

He grasped the edge of the broken plank, braced his foot against the front of the counter and ripped it free, tearing the counter down the middle and loosening all the guns. Grizzard, who had been chattering insanely from the foot of the steps, made a dash at him and tried to wrest the gun from his hands. He bent and bit frantically at Harry's fingers.

Harry said, "Take it, you poor bastard," and snatched up another, cramming his pockets with the cartridges that Goff had piled on the ruined counter.

Grizzard hunched at the foot of the stairs, looking fearfully up at the oblong of light from the trapdoor. He hesitated as Harry and Goff ran up the stairs, and then scrambled up after them.

As they burst from the mouth of the garage, Vito came loping down the path from the house. He snatched for the gun under his arm, and they dived back. Grizzard battered them out of his path and leaped out into the driveway. They saw him stagger under the impact of Vito's first shot, and he threw his gun up to his shoulder and began walking toward Vito, shouting and screaming, firing as fast as he could pump the gun. He was struck twice and sprawled flat on the hard shell, and he squirmed up on him, and screeching, fired again and again.

Harry flattened on the floor and squirmed to the doorway. He poked the rifle out ahead of him. His finger relaxed on the trigger. Vito was still standing in the middle of the path, but his gun had wilted in his right hand, and his left arm was clasped across his belly. His knees sagged and he bent very slowly over his pressing arm, as if making a reverent bow. His gun dropped, his knees melted. He raised his head. His mouth opened and he croaked at the glaring blue of the empty sky. He fell forward.

Harry leaped up and ran toward the house. A shot cracked from the second-floor window, and he dodged into the path to the kitchen. Within a few paces, the angle of the building covered him and he sprinted for the door. He ran through the kitchen, kicked open the farther door and sprang into the hall just as Lew was dashing down the stairs. Lew turned at the newel post and fired twice at him before he could bring up his rifle. Harry dropped to the floor and managed to get in one shot before Lew jerked open the front door and darted outside.

Lew had disappeared into the tree-garden before Harry could reach the front door and run out to the patio. He vaulted the balustrade and sprinted down the path. At the bend by the date palm cluster he came upon Goff trying weakly to rise to his feet. There was a deep gash across his forehead. Goff waved him on.

"Nothing, nothing," he mumbled. "Just smacked me...."

Harry ran on. Just ahead, the path opened to the driveway, and he saw Lew leap over Vito. But Vito had turned and he grasped at Lew, crying out in a begging voice. He managed to hook his fingers in the cuff of Lew's slacks and Lew fell heavily. Vito cried out again in that feebly pleading voice. Lew kicked savagely at him, jerking himself from those clutching fingers, scrambled up and ran for the front gate.

Something must have snapped in Vito's rudimentary mind at that moment. Perhaps he suddenly realized that Lew would never put his arms around his shoulder and call him his friend, his only and truest friend; or perhaps he realized there had never been any possibility of that; that he had always been to Lew exactly what he was now— something to kick out of the way when nothing else would do. But whatever it was, it caused Vito to raise himself in an agony of effort and call out hoarsely:

"Lew! Lew!"

And when Lew did not even look back, the gun exploded in Vito's hand.

Lew spun into one of the royal palms that lined the driveway, rebounded and sprawled on the grass. He pushed himself to his feet, ran a few steps and fell again. He was crawling toward the gate on his hands and knees, the blood streaming down the side of his face, when Harry walked up slowly behind him, stooped to pick up his dropped gun, stood over him and said tonelessly:

"It's all over, Lew. That's all there is. You've gone as far as you're going."

Docilely, eyes blank, Lew let himself be jerked to his feet. He shambled ahead of Harry back up the path toward the house. Goff met them, holding his handkerchief to his cut forehead. He looked at Lew, at Harry.

"Grizzard?" he asked.

Harry said, "Dead."

"Vito?"

"Dead."

Harry looked straight ahead. Nellie was standing tensely in the wide front doorway. He quickened his steps and the dulling listlessness fell from him. He had been thinking heavily, "It's over, thank God it's over...."

But it was just the nightmare that was over. There was Nellie and in Nellie was reality, and reality was about to begin again....

THE END

I GET WHAT I WANT

LORENZ HELLER

writing as Larry Heller

CHAPTER ONE

It was a Monday that the commercial fisherman came in from the Gulf of Mexico and reported a new "red tide." By Wednesday the dead fish were drifting through the inlet and into the bays, and wherever you looked over the water you could see the white flash of their bloated bellies in the sunlight.

It's called a red tide because it's this red, marine germ that kills the fish by the ton. It gets in their gills and suffocates them, or something. Don't ask me what it is. I don't know. Nobody knows, exactly, where it really comes from or why. One day these big red "blooms" turn up in the Gulf, and right after that there are dead fish all over the place—even porpoise. And it takes a lot to kill a porpoise.

Hundreds and hundreds of fish—trout, redfish, snook, and almost every variety you could name—got caught under the Municipal Pier and in a day or two they stank to high heaven. But it didn't make much difference because it was the same from Clearwater to Fort Myers—dead fish by the million, cooking in the Florida sun.

It just about ruined the charter boat business for us. It knocked the bottom out of a lot of other businesses, too. The tourists didn't stop to take another sniff, but kept right on going down the old Tamiami Trail and didn't stop till they reached Miami on the east coast. The tourist dollar was a mighty important dollar, and when it by-passed us, it meant that the majority of us weren't going to get off the nut that season. There was over a hundred miles of dead fish out in the Gulf and no end in sight and nobody knew what to do about it. Things were just about as bad as they could be.

On the fourth day of it, old man Brady, who was captain of the *Gulf Girl*, said to me, "The hell with this, Jeff. I'm pulling out for Bimini. How about you?"

"I live here," I said.

"That won't get you any charters, boy. This might go on for a month."

"I know. I've been through it before."

"But this is the height of the season, Jeff. Now's the time to make your money, if you're going to make it at all. This place'll be a graveyard at the end of the month."

"Maybe, but I think I'll stick around anyway."

"Ah, hell!" he said, disgusted. "I should of known better than try to talk to a dumb cracker in the first place."

That's the way he was. It didn't mean anything to him one way or the other if I went down to Bimini with him, but he wanted everybody to agree with him all the time. He got sore when you didn't. I don't know why he even asked me to go along, because I have a mind of my own like all the Tuckers, and I practically never agreed with him. We tangled on everything from politics to the right kind of bait to use for tarpon. I don't like people like that.

That morning, three boats pulled out for Bimini, and in the afternoon six more went. By the end of the week almost the whole charter boat fleet had left for Key West, or Marathon on Vaca Key, Miami, Fort Lauderdale, or West Palm. The four of us left were all crackers who'd lived around Sanibar all our lives. When you live in a place you don't run out on it, anymore than you'd run out on a wife if she happened to catch pneumonia.

In the early mornings, after the mists had cleared, I went to the dock and cleaned up the *Skidoo* and ran the motors a little to keep them fresh. The rest of the day I worked on the beaches with the volunteer emergency crews, digging holes and burying rotten fish. It was kind of hopeless because every tide brought in another ten thousand. But you didn't think about that when you were slogging a heavy wheelbarrow of fish through the soft sand, dumping it in the pit, and going back for another load that somebody else—maybe the bank president or the Baptist minister—had raked together for you.

Everybody worked, and even if it did seem futile, at least you were trying to do something about it. There was nothing we could do about the fish that got caught in the mangrove roots in the bays. It would have been like trying to clean up a field of sandspurs with a hand comb. The smell was everywhere. When you stop to think, it was kind of awful how we got used to it and even made jokes about it.

All day, stripped to our shorts, we worked in the hammering sun. By evening our muscles jerked and quivered, our eyes watered, and we coughed from the gas that caught in our throats. Then we scattered into the gin mills and got drunk. Things were so bad that even the whores had packed up and left for the east coast.

In the beginning I had talked big about not running out and all that, but it got me down the same way it got everybody else down. I was bushed, but it wasn't only that. I wasn't making any money, and the bank account was getting smaller and smaller. I had a house out on Little Brother Key, but the smell was so bad I had to stay in town. The hotel bills alone were killing me, to say nothing of eating in restaurants three times a day.

So I was feeling pretty low this morning when I walked out to the dock. It was pretty dreary with all the boats gone. The kids' prams were racked up near the shore, but it had been over a week since anyone had gone sailing. The tide was slack and there was no wind. All around, the dead fish were motionless white blobs on the water, and I kept coughing and trying to clear my throat.

There were two people at the end of the dock. A man and a woman eating something out of a brown paper bag, and occasionally they threw bits of it into the water and leaned over to see if a fish would nibble. A lot of the tourists did that, even with cigarette butts. They must have thought a fish was some kind of freak to snap at anything. I didn't waste any time watching them. They weren't looking for a charter, and that was all I cared about.

The *Skidoo* was about halfway up the dock, and I usually got a big charge out of just looking at her. There was no doubt she was a pretty boat, slim and white and mahogany. She was lean and racy, like a thoroughbred, but she still had plenty of beam to steady her in a heavy sea. She was thirty-two feet long and was powered by a pair of twin Chrysler Crowns. There was a big cockpit aft with two fighting chairs, and she had an enclosed cabin and could sleep four. I had a ship-to-shore radio in her, a gas refrigerator, and I could just about take her anyplace I wanted.

She had cost me a big piece of property on the Tamiami Trail. At the time I had thought her well worth it, but, you know, you can't own things like that without winding up with them owning you. The *Skidoo* worked for me all right, but most of the time I worked for her—painting, polishing, scraping, fixing, and a lot of just plain fooling around that ate big chunks out of living. My house out on Little Brother Key was the same, always nagging to have things done for it. It's like buying a pretty piece of rope because you like the color, and then you hang yourself with it.

I went down into the cabin and started up the motors, let them warm up, then cut to idle so they were just about turning over with throaty little grunts coming out of the exhaust. I sat down at the dinette table with a tarpon reel, took it apart, oiled it, and put it back together again. It didn't have to be done—I always kept my tackle in good shape—but I wanted the feel of it in my hands again. I found an old boat rod that needed a new guide and I was pawing through my tackle box when I heard them up on the dock. The tourists, I mean. The man was reading the sign I had up in the cockpit.

"Hey, Letty, take a look at this. The *Skidoo*, it says. That means beat it, scram, drop dead. Don't you get a laugh out of it?"

"No-o-o, but it's a pretty boat, ain't it?"

"Look, the guy calls his boat the *Skidoo*. It's the same as though he called it the *Drop Dead*. You know the trouble with you, baby? No sense of humor."

"I don't think it's funny, that's all, Buster. You're always laughing at things."

"That's right. *I* got a sense of humor."

"But you laugh at things when they're not really funny, like you're making fun of them. I guess maybe I don't have a sense of humor. That kind anyway. What's them chairs for?"

"How do I know? They're chairs, you sit in them."

"Why're they screwed down to the floor?"

"So they don't fall overboard, I guess."

"They look like office chairs. Why don't they have something comfortable? Who wants to sit in an office chair?"

"Say, how'd you like to go for a boat ride, baby?"

"In them chairs?" She laughed.

"In the boat, in the boat. You don't have to sit in the chairs. Maybe this Captain Tucker's got a couch or something. How's about it?"

"You mean you'll take me, Buster?"

"Sure. What the hell, I got a couple bucks left. Hey, rube! Hey, you in there!"

I didn't look up. I didn't want any part of them. He yelled at me again and started kicking the side of the boat. I went out to the cockpit. He was sitting on the dock, kicking the side of the boat with his toe.

"Cut that out," I said.

He grinned and stopped. He was one of the biggest and solidest men I had ever seen. He must have been about six-foot-four, built square and massive, with a round, hard-looking head like a bowling ball. He had on combat boots, khaki pants, and a dirty blue sport shirt. His hair was blonde and crew-cut.

"How much for a boat ride, George?" he asked.

"This is a fishing boat," I said curtly. "I don't sell boat rides."

"Okay, we'll go fishing. How much?"

"Forty-five dollars a day."

He whistled. "Some fish! What do you get—whales?"

I still didn't want any part of them. "There's nothing much running right now."

"Who cares? Come on, baby, the man's going to take us for a boat ride."

I was just about to turn him down with the red tide as an excuse, but then I looked up and saw her. There was no question about it anymore. Something opened up inside me as if this was what I had been waiting for all along. She wasn't beautiful or anything like that, but there was something there and I can't tell you what it was.

She was a tall girl, about five-seven, and she must have weighed around a hundred and thirty. Her hair was the same blonde shade as his, cropped and untidy and curly, and her face was wide across the cheekbones. She had on shorts that had been clumsily made from a pair of blue jeans, men's jeans at that. Her legs were magnificent, but I had seen legs before (it's the one thing in Florida you see plenty of) so it wasn't that. I don't know what it was, but the impact of this girl was incredible.

She jumped down into the cockpit. She stumbled and I caught her, and at the feel of her bare arms, I held her tighter. I couldn't help myself. She looked up into my face, surprised.

Buster guffawed. "Well I'll be damned!" he said. "You're just about the fastest worker I ever saw, George."

I flushed and let her go. She laughed at him. "Drop dead," she said. And then to me, "Don't mind him. That's his sense of humor."

He grinned and lowered himself into the boat. He was a tremendous monolith of a man, as solid as a piece of sculpture. He looked absolutely impregnable, indestructible.

"This is Letty, George," he said, introducing me. "My brother's kid. He's dead. I'm Buster."

"That's him, all right," said Letty. "He busts everybody."

"The name's Jeff," I said.

"Yeah? Hey, Letty, don't he look just like George Daly, that mick from New York?"

She looked at me. Her face was young and serious. She shook her head. "Oh, a little maybe." She sat in one of the fighting chairs and swiveled. "What's these chairs for, Jeff?"

"Fishing. You get a tarpon on, you can't hold him standing up."

She laughed. "All the comforts of home."

Buster had his wallet open and was counting off forty-five dollars from a thin sheaf of bills inside. "Here you are, George. But let me tell you, you really got a racket, forty-five bucks a day. Better'n a plumber."

I couldn't take his money. I'd only set the price to get rid of him. "Forget it, I have to run the motors anyway."

"Don't be a dope, George. Take it and let's get going."

"Give me ten. That'll pay for the gas. And the name's Jeff."

"Uh-uh. I wouldn't feel right calling you Jeff, George. You look too much like that mick, George Daly. Here's your ten, but you're a dope to cut your rate. Hell," he winked at Letty, "I wouldn't even beat up a guy for less than twenty."

"Very funny," she said and peered into the cabin. "Hey, Buster, look how nice he's got it fixed up inside, just like a little house. A stove, a sink, a couch and chairs and everything, even a radio."

He wasn't interested. He sat down in the fighting chair she had just vacated, cocked his feet up on the rail, and lit a cigar.

"This is for me," he said. "Drive us around the lake, George."

I told him I had to stay in the channel because the bay was too shallow in other spots. Then I cast off and pointed the *Skidoo* toward the inlet and the Gulf beyond. I had made this trip so many times I didn't have to look at the markers. That gave me plenty of time to watch Letty prowl around, poking and peering into everything like a cat in a new house. She bounced on the forepeak berths, came out and looked into the refrigerator and all the lockers that happened to catch her eye, lit the stove and turned it off. She treated everything very carefully, as if this were a doll house and fragile. Her eyes were round with a childlike awe and delight.

"Gee," she said, "it sure is cute. Are all boats like this?"

"The charter boats, yes," I told her.

"I'll bet you can take some nice trips, huh?"

"I've been down to Cuba."

"How far's that?"

"Oh, that's only ninety miles off Key West."

"Oh." She was considerably less impressed. "How about South America?"

"I haven't tried it, but it's possible."

"What do you say, let's go?"

"Sure."

"Hey, Buster," she called, "we're going to South America."

"What?"

"Jeff's going to take us for a boat ride to South America."

"In this tub?" He laughed. "Don't let him kid you, baby."

"He's been to Cuba, he says."

"He's still kidding you. Once around the lake is just about his speed."

She looked at me, and her face was less friendly. She had a temper. "I don't like to be kidded."

"I wasn't kidding," I said. "I've been to Cuba."

"For real?"

"It felt real. It was a little rough."

She turned back toward the cockpit and hooted. "There you are, wise guy."

Buster came into the cabin and leaned against the wardrobe. "You really been to Cuba in this tub, George?" he asked with interest.

"Five or six times."

"Well I'll be damned. How fast can this thing go?"

"I can get her up to fifty. I did some special work on the engines."

"Is that good, fifty?"

"Damn good."

He looked at Letty. "Go outside and look at the fish for a minute, baby."

"Why?"

"Beat it."

"Drop dead," she said angrily, but went out to the cockpit.

Buster went over and closed the door. He winked at me. "What she don't hear won't hurt her."

"What's there to hear?"

He ignored that. He leaned against the wardrobe again, puffing slowly and thoughtfully at his cigar. "I never been to Cuba myself," he said finally, "but I heard a lot about it. It was a big place during Prohibition."

"Was it?" I said dryly. I had an idea what was coming.

"So they say. And they say it's a big place again, the way the government slapped the taxes on liquor. I heard of one guy took his boat down there, loaded up with Scotch, and tripled his dough in one run. Not bad."

"Where's he now?" I asked. "Leavenworth?"

"Hell, no. He's got guys working for him now. A friend of mine knows him good. Works for him, in fact."

"He won't be working long."

"What do you mean?"

"The Coast Guard works twenty-four hours a day in these waters."

"How fast can they go—forty?"

"They don't have to go that fast. When they start shooting, you just plain stop."

"Make the run at night. What they can't see, they can't hit."

I couldn't help laughing. He was big and tough and in earnest, but about this he was as naive as a schoolboy playing cops and robbers.

"In the first place, Buster," I said, "I'm not interested. But just so you don't waste anymore time thinking about it, if I took on a load of liquor big enough to pay, it'd cut my speed in half. Then if the Coast Guard came up, I'd be a sitting duck. They'd laugh themselves silly."

"Not at night."

"They've got radar and searchlights."

"You're not interested in making yourself a grand for a couple days' work? You wouldn't have to put up a cent. I'll get the dough."

"No."

"Forget the Coast Guard. We'll figure an angle. There's an angle for everything. I'll find out how this other guy does it. If he can get away with it, you can."

"I'm not interested!" I said, getting annoyed.

"Okay," he said easily, "it was just an idea. No hard feelings?"

I said, "No hard feelings," but I had a feeling that he was studying me for future reference. He had one of those round faces that looked tough but good-natured, like maybe a truck driver's. But there was something going on behind it all the time, and it was more than just an angle to be figured, or just another chance for a quick buck. Maybe that's the reason I didn't get really sore. He wasn't just another cheap crook.

He slapped me on the shoulder and said, "Take it easy, George," and walked out to the cockpit, humming through his cigar.

CHAPTER TWO

We were going through the inlet now. There was a heavy chop coming out of the northwest, and I quartered into it, giving all my attention to the wheel. It was pretty rough for a few minutes and the spray lashed the windscreen. We rolled and pitched and I heard Buster's heavy voice yell from the cockpit. I grinned, thinking how much worse it could be making the run to Cuba. Then we were out in the Gulf and it was much calmer.

The door slammed open and Buster roared, "Cut it out, dammit, we're soaked!"

Letty laughed, "Tell him to watch them bumps."

"That was just the inlet," I said. "It's always a little rougher. We're all right now."

"It put out my damned cigar."

"The sun'll dry you off."

He came down into the cabin, biting the end from a fresh cigar, spitting it on the deck. "Tell me something, George. Does it always stink like this around here?"

"That's the red tide. It'll be better out in the Gulf."

"Hell, I don't mind. I was raised on a pig farm in Secaucus up in Jersey. I just wondered, that's all."

"He used to reek," said Letty, laughing.

"So what? It was a good healthy stink. It put hair on your chest. We all stank."

"Not me."

"That's a fact, baby, you didn't. But you should of seen her, George. She drove a truck, a five-ton job, and she could handle it, too. She was a bitch on wheels. Remember the night you damn near killed old man Tutchek, baby? This guy, George, he was an old bastard, and all the time he was after Letty here. So this night he tries to make her ..."

"He did more than that. His hands was all over me."

"Okay, okay, who's telling it? Anyway, George, this night he goes after her but good, and she blows up. She jumps in her truck and drives straight at him and he's standing right there in front of the pens. He lets out a squawk and dives over the fence and there he is down in a foot of muck with the rest of the pigs. And stink! Hell, you could smell him clear to Hoboken. Laugh! I thought I'd split a gut. Remember that, baby?"

"He got me sore."

"He sure did, and man-o-man, George, if you'd ever hit him, he'd of gone through them bars like hamburger. He never fooled around with her after that."

"Lucky for him, too," said Letty.

"She's not kidding about that, George. She's a real pepper when she gets going." He chuckled and rolled his cigar in his mouth. "Is it safe for me to go out and sit on the tailboard again, George?"

"In a few minutes," I said. There was still some spray.

I turned southwest, running ahead of the chop. I knew they weren't interested in fishing, so I thought I'd take them down the coast, cut in through Coquina Pass, and come back up the bay. It was a nice trip with lots of tropical foliage and all kinds of birds. As we passed Little Brother Key, I pointed it out to Letty.

"That's where I live. The house is behind the sea grape. You can't see it from here."

She looked through the window. "It's a kind of island, huh?"

"That's right. It's a wonderful spot. There's no bridge over from the mainland, and the only way you can reach it is by boat."

"You live there all by yourself?"

"Yes. My grandfather built the house sixty years ago. It's made of cypress and it'll be there another two hundred years."

I don't know what I was trying to do—impress her probably, but she punctured that.

She gave me an odd glance and said, "Oh, brother!"

I felt flattened but at the same time a little sore. If anybody else had said "Oh, brother!" in just that tone, I'd have laughed and felt a little sorry for them because they didn't know what they were missing. But then I thought, oh, cut it out, you damn fool, she's nothing but a female truck driver. But who believes everything he tries to tell himself?

Then, unexpectedly, Buster put in, "It looks like a nice spot, George. You really live there all by yourself?"

"Most of the time."

"Don't it get a little lonesome?"

"Sometimes. But sometimes you get a little lonesome no matter where you are."

"I'm nuts about the seashore myself. So's Letty here. We used to go to Atlantic City all the time."

She said, "Ha, ha," and looked amused. "The last time you were in Atlantic City, they threw you in jail." She laughed.

He laughed with her, and I had the feeling that nothing could shake his self-assurance. "Just a little mistake, George. I beat up the wrong guy."

Letty looked even more amused. "You sure did. A cop."

They laughed again, but did not explain why Buster had beaten up a cop. I didn't like them. There was something destructive about the pair. If you got mixed up with them, you'd really be behind the eight-ball before you knew what was happening to you. They both had the same kind of self-assurance and vitality, and neither of them, so far as I could see, cared about anybody except themselves. I could hardly keep my eyes off Letty, but I made up my mind not to have anything to do with her.

Buster looked around, scattering cigar ashes on the deck. "Where's the can, George?"

I pointed out the head, told him how to work it, and he went in and left the door open. *The hell with this*, I thought to myself. The feeling lasted until Letty came over and leaned against my shoulder and looked down at the compass.

"What's that thing?" she asked.

"That's the compass."

"You mean, like a speedometer?"

"No. It tells you the direction you're going. There are no road signs out in the Gulf. When you get out of sight of land, you have to have a compass."

"Well, I'll be damned! Can I drive it for awhile?"

As I held the wheel, I was acutely aware of her standing over me. She didn't have on any perfume, and she was just like a cat—she had no odor. You know how it is when you smell a cat's fur, just clean and fresh and soft. Her thigh felt sinuous and deep against my arm, and when she moved, I could feel the division of her legs and her soft belly against my shoulder. I had to do something about it, but when I turned, she put her hand over my mouth and looked toward the head.

"You work fast, don't you?" she whispered.

I hated to hear those banal words come out of her, but there was nothing I could do about it. There was nothing banal about her body. That was the thing she was.

"Can I see you tonight?" I asked her,

"Why?"

"You know why."

"Don't be a jerk."

"Where can I pick you up?"

She hesitated. "Well, we're in that motel next to the electric works on the Tamiami Trail. What a lousy place! It buzzes like a hatful of bees all night. Know where I mean?"

"The Tami-Kota Motel?"

"Yeah, that's the place."

"I'll pick you up at seven. We'll go someplace and eat."

"Make it before six. I like to eat early."

"Five-thirty."

"Okay. But listen, I'm no nutsy fagin. So don't get any funny ideas and maybe we'll get along."

I didn't know what a "nutsy fagin" was, but I got the general idea, so I said, "Okay." But when I thought of seeing her alone that night, I was filled with the urgency of it and my hand went out by itself and dug into her thigh.

She slapped it away, but she wasn't sore. "Don't give me trouble."

She didn't smile, but she looked down into my face as if trying to find something there. There seemed to be a puzzlement in her eyes, and in an odd, tentative sort of way, she ran her hand across the back of my shoulder, touching the ridges of the wide muscle that padded it.

That was just about all I could stand, and I pulled her down to me.

Her mouth came twisting into mine, open but hard, pressing harshly and spreading the kiss until it became a grimace of raw emotion. Then she pushed herself away abruptly and straightened up, looking down at me with that same puzzlement in her eyes. She was breathing shallowly through her mouth.

"I don't get you," she muttered. "I don't get you at all."

"Because I kissed you, Letty?"

"I don't know. You're not the kind of guy that'd just grab a girl."

"I wanted to grab you the minute I saw you. I grabbed you when you jumped down into the boat and stumbled."

"That was different. You're no wolf. You don't go around making passes all the time. Why'd you make a pass at me just then? You think I'm a nutsy fagin?"

"No." But again I wondered what she meant.

"The hell you didn't!" she said angrily. "You meet me one minute, and the next minute you're making a pass, like I'm a tramp."

We heard Buster laugh, and we both turned sharply. He was sitting out in the cockpit with his feet up on the rail again, grinning at us.

"What're you two comedians battling about?"

"Nothing," Letty said quickly, digging her fingers into the muscle of my arm in a painful, warning squeeze.

"I'll bet!" he laughed. "It sure sounded like nothing. Why don't you clowns grow up or something? Don't mind her, George. I told you she was a pepper." He waved his cigar, "Come on, let's go for that drive around the ocean." He swiveled in the chair and turned his back to us.

"He saw us," I said to Letty in a low voice.

"Like hell he did. If he saw you making a pass at me, he'd beat your brains out."

"He must have seen us when he came out of the head."

"If he saw us, you'd know it. He don't let guys make passes at me."

"It wasn't that kind of pass, Letty."

"Nuts."

"Honestly. You were so close and, well, it was just something I couldn't help."

"Yeah, sure. You just washed your hands and couldn't do a thing with them. Drop dead."

"I'll see you tonight, Letty. We'll talk about it then."

"The hell you will. You're not seeing me tonight or any other night!"

She turned and walked back to the cockpit, and she stayed there, too. We were out another hour and a half, and from time to time I glanced over my shoulder, hoping to see her returning. But she just sat there smoking one cigarette after another, her long, wonderful legs stretched out in front of her.

When we got back to the basin, she jumped up on the dock and strode away without a word to either Buster or me. He stayed for another few minutes and helped me tie up. When we finished, he stuck a cigar in my shirt pocket and slapped me on the shoulder.

"It's a great life, George," he said, "but you got to take it easy."

I watched him walk down the dock and climb into a battered '39 Chevvy sedan. It had a broken muffler and it roared out of the parking lot amid a series of explosions like guns.

CHAPTER THREE

I had a date with another girl that night, but I called her up and broke it. I felt guilty doing it. Her name was Helen Anders, and we had been going around, on and off, for over a year. She was a small girl, a brunette. She had a slender face with a quiet, delicate mouth that was serene without being placid, as if she had discovered the secret of knowing where she was most of the time and didn't have to waste any vital energies running up and down looking for signposts.

I had never gone to bed with her or anything like that, but she had passion and when I kissed her, her lips were soft and generous and I could feel the deep burning. She was very lovely, and I knew that being married to her would be wonderful—when the time came. We Tuckers have never been quiet men. My father was thirty-seven when he married, and my grandfather was forty, and neither had been what you could call a family man, though both were good providers. They were always in fights, and my mother used to cry when my father came home all bloody, but laughing and having a wonderful time.

I wasn't in love with Helen, but I didn't feel right when I made excuses over the telephone.

"I can't see you tonight, honey. Something came up. I'll call you tomorrow."

"That's all right, Jeff." She had a light, sweet voice, like a good lyric soprano.

"You don't mind?"

"But I do! I just had my hair set, bought a blouse and a new pair of shoes with a handbag to match, and a very special lipstick."

"Well, in that case ..."

"Oh, Jeff. Of course I don't mind if there's something you have to do."

"I mean, if you bought all that stuff ..."

"I didn't buy anything. I was just joking. What's the matter, Jeff? You sound as if there's something bothering you."

"There's nothing bothering me."

"Are you sure?"

"Yes."

"Well ..." Then after awhile she said, "Why didn't you go down to Bimini or Marathon with the other boats, Jeff?"

"I like it here," I said, irritated with her for asking.

"Aren't you losing a lot of money by not going?"

"I'll make it when the kingfish start running. A lot of people come down for the kings. And I'll make it in the spring with the tarpon. I'm not worried about the money."

"You don't sound like yourself at all."

"I'm just restless, I guess."

"It's this awful red tide," she said, with conviction. "Everybody's coughing and there's that horrible smell all the time. You're tired. You've been working too hard on the beaches."

"Not any harder than anybody else."

"Still, I think you should rest."

"I don't need a rest," I said impatiently.

"Please don't be annoyed with me, Jeff."

There was such a warmth and contrition in her voice, as if she really had done something to annoy me, that I almost blurted that I *would* see her that night. And that we'd go to the Hofbrau and have *sauerbraten*, which she loved, and afterward go to the Colony and dance and listen to the calypso and walk on the beach at Lido and watch the porpoise feeding and snorting in the Gulf.

But I couldn't do it. I couldn't get the words out. I wanted Letty so bad that I couldn't think of anything else. But that didn't keep me from feeling lousy, the way I was treating Helen, snapping at her like that.

"I'm sorry, honey. I'm not annoyed with you. Maybe it is this damn red tide. I'll call you tomorrow."

"Get some sleep tonight, Jeff. Try to rest."

I said, "Sure," and hung up.

Outside on the sidewalk I knew I was really in a foul mood. I was all mixed up about Letty, and the worst of it was that I didn't actually have a date with her that night. It had been very definitely called off, I was still going to go up to the Tami-Kota Motel around six and see what I could do about it and maybe get her to change her mind. But the thing I couldn't understand was why I was going through all this. I've done the usual amount of playing around with women, but none of them had ever hit me like this, not even Helen. It didn't make me happy or give me a lift or any of those things. It just made me feel mean.

I drove cross-town to a beer joint where the commercial fishermen hung out. There were about a dozen of them in there, and they were all pretty quiet. The red tide had hit them as hard as everybody else. They couldn't spread their nets without getting loaded with dead and bloated carcasses, but they didn't go out at all because nobody was buying fish these days anyway. They were making a little money on clams, crabs, and oysters, but hardly enough to gas up their boats for the trip.

I ordered a beer and leaned against the bar by myself, though I knew all of them. I was a cracker, too. I'd been brought up with them. I said, "Hi, suckers," the way I always did—you know the kind of insult that passes for humor—but I stayed down the bar by myself.

I drank my beer and wondered if maybe I should have gone to Bimini with the others. Then I thought of old man Brady trying to boss everybody around down there, and I knew if I had gone, I'd have tangled with him sooner or later and we'd both have wound up in the jailhouse. They take a dim view of such things in Bimini. The English don't understand an honest fight. It doesn't fit in with their idea of law and order. It isn't neat or respectable.

Still, you couldn't beat the fishing in those waters. Nor the honesty in the hard strike of a marlin when he whipped himself at the end of your line like a tempered steel blade and you knew that it was just between the two of you unless you cheated.

But that was all spoiled, too. Once in awhile you got a real fisherman who'd fight for the truth there was in it, the proof and the decency, but most of them turned sour if they couldn't boat something over a thousand pounds. It wasn't the fish or the sport they were after; it was the record, the competition, and the rat-race—something to fill in place of the straw they were stuffed with.

I gradually became aware that the talk down the bar had become louder and that it was being directed at me. Most of it was being done by a loud-mouth named Floyd Hammond, a lanky redhead with pale blue eyes and leprous freckles. I'd known him all my life and we'd always gotten along, though I can't say I was fond of him. There was always an edge to everything he said, even when he was joking.

His cousin was a detective on the cops, and that was just about the only thing that had kept him out of real trouble. He'd been in a couple bad knife fights that I knew of, but it had all been hushed up. None of it had even gotten into the papers, or even on the police blotter, as far as that went.

He saw me look up and he said, "How's it feel to be a Yankee-lover, Jeff? Tell us. We'd like to know."

I thought he was kidding. This was the kind of talk that went on all the time, and none of it meant anything. Nobody got sore.

"Ah, go crawl back in the palmetto with the rest of the crackers." I could say that because I was just as much of a cracker as he was.

"That's right," he said. "I'm a cracker and I'm proud of it. But I was just saying there's only one thing lower'n a damnyankee and that's a Yankee-lover. A damnyankee, now, he can't help it. He was born that way, like a hog. A hog can't help it either. But a Yankee-lover, he does it because he wants to and because there's a buck in it. So that makes him just about as low as they come, except maybe a Republican. That's right, ain't it? I'm asking you because you'd know."

He was leaning over the bar, grinning at me, and I still thought he was kidding. "Go blow. You'll take a damnyankee buck as fast as the next."

"I sure will, and as many as I can get, but I won't suck around. I don't hang out a sign begging them to hire my boat like it was an old whore or something. I got more respect for my boat than that. A man's got to be a kind of pimp to hire out his boat to a damnyankee, and that's a fact."

There was nothing new in any of this. I'd taken a lot of kidding from them on account of running a charter boat, but today I didn't feel like it. I just shrugged and said, "So what?" and turned back to my beer.

Usually, that would have ended it, but he kept it up. "Come on, Jeff, come on. Let us in on this. You used to be a good man, but now you've got manure in your blood and it's a shame. What makes a good man go wrong? What made you a Yankee-loving son of a bitch? We'd like to know."

Some of them were laughing because this was the kind of thing Floyd did all the time. It was supposed to be funny, and sometimes maybe it was, but today I just couldn't take it. I knew if I had to listen to much more of this, I'd get up and take a swing at him.

"There's nothing dumber than a dumb cracker," I said, and walked out.

I heard him laugh just as the door was closing behind me. I felt like going back and taking a poke at him anyway, but it would have been wrong, and I wasn't that far gone—yet.

I had four hours to kill before I could go up the Trail and see Letty— if she'd see me—and the time stretched in front of me like a highway from here to forever. I didn't feel like going down to the beach and burying dead fish; so I drove over to the dock, warmed up the *Skidoo*, and took her out to my place on Little Brother Key.

There was a channel in the bay and a cypress dock. I went up the walk to the old house. It was on pilings, the way they used to build them in case of high water and hurricane. The main floor was about ten feet above the sand. The wind had swung around to the northeast, so the stink wasn't so bad. I opened all the doors and windows. I hadn't been there for over a week, and the inside was pretty musty.

I went down to the beach and there were dead fish heaped at the high water mark as far as you could see in either direction. Within two minutes, I was coughing like a consumptive. There had been a lot of talk about the Army dumping mustard gas out in the Gulf, but that was only because people liked to blame somebody for something they didn't understand. An act of God was too impersonal.

I went back to the house. There was a gallon jug of 'shine under the sink in the kitchen, and I had a few drinks out of it. 'Shine has a kind of oily taste. When you hold the jug up to the light, you can actually see the swirls of oil in it, wispy and coiling like smoke. You can get killing-mean on 'shine, but I was in the mood for it.

CHAPTER FOUR

I was fairly sober when I drove up to the Tami-Kota Motel at quarter of six. I was shaved and had on a shirt and tie, sport jacket and slacks. All the way over I kept telling myself that if she wasn't there, the hell with her. But when I turned into the shell driveway, my heart was churning like a cement mixer and I felt a little sick in my stomach. Of course, that might have been all the 'shine I had drunk and not having eaten any lunch. I stopped at the office, then I saw her sitting on a bench under a cluster of date palms at the opposite side.

I walked over, and Letty stood up. She was dressed all wrong. She was wearing a woolen plaid skirt that was too tight around the hips, a sweater that made her breasts look like fists, and high-heeled shoes with straps that criss-crossed high on her ankles. When I laid eyes on her, I felt like turning around and getting out of there. She looked like a two-buck pickup on the Tampa waterfront; at first glance she had nothing that same two bucks wouldn't buy any place in Florida from Jax to Miami. Her face was sullen.

"Hi," I said, wondering how soon I could get rid of her.

"Hi," she replied, and walked past me. She went over to the car and got in and sat there, looking straight ahead, her hands tight and set in her lap.

The minute I got in beside her, close to her, it hit me again, and it didn't make any difference what she wore. My tongue felt thick in my mouth and I wanted to reach out and pull her against me. Her skirt was tight across her thighs and her body seemed ready to burst out of her clothes. I had to grip the wheel to keep my hands off her.

"Any place you want to go to eat in particular?" I asked finally, just to say something.

She shrugged. "Anyplace."

"You like seafood?"

"Anything," she said indifferently.

"How about a Spanish restaurant, *arroz con pollo* and Spanish bean soup?"

"Suit yourself."

"How about the Hofbrau—*wiener schnitzel* and beer?"

"Look," she said stolidly, "I'm not here because I want to be. He made me, so let's go and get it over, or I'll never hear the end of it."

"Who made you?"

"Him. Buster."

"But ... why?"

"He said it's about time I went out with somebody that wasn't on the make." One corner of her mouth lifted humorlessly, "That's a laugh."

"Will you listen to me for a minute, Letty?" I asked and she shrugged again. "I didn't make a pass at you back there in the boat."

"Nuts."

"It's the truth. I was wrong and I admit it. I apologize."

She scowled and her hands moved in her lap, tightening. She kept staring straight ahead through the windshield. At length she said sullenly, "I'm not a tramp."

"I know you're not a tramp. Hell, if I wanted a tramp, I could go downtown and pick up a dozen of them in the first two blocks. And it wouldn't cost me a dinner either. But who wants a tramp?"

Her hands stirred now in the small, formless movements of indecision. She looked at me. "You're funny. I don't get you at all."

"Look, honey. I won't touch you tonight if you don't want me to. I won't lay a hand on you. Okay?"

I said this very earnestly because I wanted to impress her. Her mouth hung open, an incredulous sag, and she burst into a hoot of laughter.

"Oh brother! This I want to see. This'll be one for the book. What'll you do, wear boxing gloves?"

Coming from Letty, those banalities flattened me as nothing else could. Then she moved closer and I could feel her soft, sensual warmth. It spread over me like a double shot of strong whisky. I knew I wasn't going to be able to keep my hands off her.

I took her to the Bamboo Inn for dinner, out on La Concha Key. It was the most expensive place around and had lots of style. The music and lights were subdued, and the people at the other tables talked softly and intimately. That was chiefly the reason I had brought her there: for the intimacy you could develop. The waiter came over and set up a menu the size of a pillowcase on a little easel beside the table. It was handwritten. Some of it was in Spanish and hard to understand.

"Would you care for a cocktail before dinner, sir?" he asked.

"Martini?" I asked Letty.

She had her head down and was making crosses on the tablecloth with her fingernail. She nodded shortly without looking up. I ordered two extra-dry martinis, and the waiter walked away with that kind of placid dignity they have in the better restaurants where they know their tips will run at least twenty percent. He looked a little like Charles Boyer.

"He looks like Charles Boyer," I said to Letty.

"So what?" She kept making those crosses on the tablecloth.

"And that woman over there by the window, she looks like Greer Garson. If the bartender turns out to be Humphrey Bogart, we're in Key Largo."

"Very funny. Ha, ha."

I didn't know what to say. I didn't know how to talk to her. "Do you see anything you like?" I asked, pointing at the menu on the easel.

She gave it a very brief glance. "I don't like wop food," she muttered.

"You can have steak, veal cutlet, pork chops, stone crab ..."

"Steak."

It was a dead end every time I tried to say something. I couldn't figure it out. Letty was closed up and even antagonistic. She wouldn't look up and she kept marking the tablecloth with her fingernail.

"The food is very good here," I said inanely.

I saw her eyes shift from side to side, raking the room. "Kind of dead though, huh?"

"The music's good. Would you like to dance?"

"No!" Very short and hard.

Her left hand was working under the table and I saw that she was pulling her skirt down to cover her knees. Then I got it. All the other women were very well-dressed and as highly groomed as French poodles, and there she sat in that woolen skirt and sweater, looking like a Tampa waterfront tart. It was my fault. I should have known better. I should never have brought her to a place like this. I should have taken her to Mama Maria's on the Trail, where you could walk in in shorts and sit down and feel at home. Letty was sore at me, and I didn't blame her.

The waiter came back with our cocktails. While he was placing them, I caught his eye and raised two fingers and spread my thumb and forefinger to tell him I wanted two more right away, but doubles. He nodded slightly and moved away without saying a word. He was a smart waiter.

I knew that if I couldn't loosen her up, I'd never see her again after tonight. I had done something she wouldn't forgive. I had made her feel like a tramp on the boat when I kissed her, but this was worse because it was public. Letty sipped the first martini as if it were made of ammonia and Clorox, but the second one, the double, did the job. She loosened up and raised her head and became excessively ladylike.

She crooked her little finger while cutting her steak and she sat up very straight and raised her fork slowly to her mouth and chewed with her front teeth. Letty had a brandy with coffee because the waiter suggested it. When we finally walked out, after an eternity of overpolite conversation, she took very short steps and held her hands self-consciously at her waist.

Watching her as I walked behind her I decided she wasn't wearing a thing under that tight skirt. Almost every male head in the line of march turned to watch her go. I wanted to tell her about this later, but decided it would be poor policy. She was being a lady, and gentlemen don't turn to watch a lady from the rear. The water I was in was hot enough as it was, if she decided to remember it.

Still, there was a momentum to all this. So when we were out in the car, I asked her if she'd like to go someplace and dance.

"That would be very nice, I'm sure," she said mincingly.

I didn't know where to take her. I didn't want to pull another boner like the Bamboo Inn or I'd be all washed up with her. But on the other hand I had a feeling that she'd resent it if I took her to a joint after the Bamboo Inn.

"What're you waiting for?" she asked, "A green light?"

I started guiltily. "No, I was just trying ..."

She burst into a hoot of laughter. "Don't try too hard, Jeff-boy. All I ask is we don't go to another morgue like that one. Hell, they don't feed you in there, they embalm you. The cooks must all be undertakers. Now come clean, you really like this place, Jeffie?"

"I was trying to impress you." I grinned.

Letty made a jeering, amused sound in her throat. "You'd of done just as good taking me to a funeral. You can have fun at a funeral. Come on, let's get out of here before somebody sticks a lily in my hand."

I took her to Captain Ben's, a gin mill down on the bay near the Manana Key causeway. It had been a fishhouse before the Mid-Coast Fisheries went broke. Ben had had it deodorized and painted and had put in a bar, some tables, a shuffleboard, and a juke box. It couldn't be compared to the Siesta Lounge in the Hotel Marina, where the wealthier tourists went, but I'll say this much for it: there had never been a fight or a stabbing indoors while Ben was behind the bar. He had an eighteen-inch length of garden hose filled with sand and plugged at both ends. You paid attention when he roared, "Behave yourself, you sons of bitches, there's ladies present."

The juke box was hammering like a machine shop in full production when we walked in. The bar was packed solidly, and there were a half dozen mouth-fights going on, but they didn't mean anything. Ben kept things under control. Four couples were dancing down by the juke box. Three of them were all right, but the fourth was a little drunk.

I knew them, a commercial fisherman named Byrne and his girl friend. They weren't really dancing. They moved around the floor, swaying against each other, paying no attention to the beat of the music whatever. This would go on for a little while, and they'd disappear for a half hour or so. That would happen a couple times during the evening.

Shuffleboard was played savagely and stormily in Ben's, even though the stake was nothing more than a fifteen-cent beer. Floyd Hammond and two others made their own group at the end of the bar. They were all cousins. The Hammonds, the Burkitts, the Peckovers, and the Purcells were one big family in these parts. Floyd's cousin, the police detective, was a Burkitt, for instance. I waved at Floyd and he waved back limply.

Ben saw me and roared, "Jeff Tucker, you old louse! Where've you been, in jail again?" And then he spied Letty and his eyebrows went up and his lips formed a soundless whistle. He mitted me with both hands clasped over his head, and winked.

I looked at Letty. Her eyes were shining.

"You know something?" she said, as we took a table at the side of the room. "We got a place something like this in Secaucus, always something goin' on. Salaski. That was the guy that ran it, a hunky. The times we had there. Brother!"

This was her element, all right. This was what she liked: the raw hammering of the juke box, the racketing voices, the hint or promise of violence—most of which, she knew as well as I did, was just another form of entertainment.

The waitress, who was another of Floyd's cousins by the way, took our order and brought us rye and soda. In Ben's this was the equivalent of two drinks anywhere else. He wasn't stingy. Letty took a deep swallow and leaned her forearms on the table.

"You know something else, Jeffie," she said happily, "I'm glad Buster made me come. I wasn't gonna, but he made me."

I had passed that over the first time she told me, back at the motel, but now it rang a bell. "Why'd he make you?"

"I told you. He said it was about time I went out with a guy that had some class."

"That was the only reason?"

"Well, sure."

"He didn't say anything about a little proposition he made to me in the boat this morning, did he?"

"Proposition?" She tried to look surprised, but she wasn't very good at it. "What kind of proposition?"

"The one he told you about," I said dryly.

"Oh, that." Her sudden remembrance was just as false as her surprise had been. "He kind of mentioned it, that's all. We were just talking. He said you didn't go for it. So what?"

"But he has hopes."

"Hopes? I don't get it."

"You're supposed to work on me, aren't you? That's why he made you come with me tonight, isn't it? You're supposed to soften me up."

"Me? Soften you up? Why?"

"Oh, hell, Letty." I wasn't angry with her, but angry that she was being used in this shabby manner. "Don't sit there giving me the big-eyes. You know what it's all about, so let's go. Work on me, soften me up, give me the pitch."

Temper flamed in her cheeks, but it left her lips white and rigid. Her throat swelled with the fury of words dammed inside it. She jumped to her feet.

"Where's the john?" she demanded harshly.

I pointed. "Over in the corner."

Her heels stabbed the floor as she walked away. I drank my rye and soda and lit a cigarette. I was a damn fool and there was no doubt about it. There had been no reason for me to sound off at Letty like that. It hadn't served any useful purpose, and I didn't feel any better for having done it. I felt worse. And it didn't change the fact that Buster had put her up to this. The only thing it had done was make a mess out of the evening.

I finished my drink and the waitress brought me another. I was on my third cigarette when I glanced down the room and saw Letty dancing in front of the juke box with Floyd Hammond. He was pretty drunk and hanging on her like an old overcoat. His right hand was in the small of her back, and he must have been trying to pull her in close because she arched away from him and turned a little, evading the knee he sought to push between her legs.

I pushed back my chair, but it was all over before I could get to my feet. Letty reached out, picked up an empty beer mug from the top of the juke box, and rapped him on the back of the head with it. She turned and walked away from him while he was still staggering in dazed circles. She came back to the table and sat down.

"If there's anything I can't stand," she said calmly, "it's a jerk." She turned her head and watched Floyd's two cousins lead him back to the end of the bar and hold a glass of whiskey to his mouth. "He'll know better the next time."

"He knows better this time."

"What's he think I am anyway, a nutsy fagin?"

Here we go again, I thought. "He was drunk, Letty."

"Well, now he'll have a double hangover in the morning, and I hope he does, the jerk. I'm no cheap broad."

I said, "Uh huh," but I wasn't paying much attention because I had my eye on Floyd. The cousins were having a little trouble with him. He shoved them away and came weaving across the floor toward our table, his lip pushed out and his eyes mean and little. I got up and stopped him before he reached us.

"You asked for it, Floyd. Now forget it."

"Get out of my way, you Yankee-loving son of a bitch," he said, in a clotted voice.

"I said, forget it. Go back to the bar and drink your drink. Don't make things worse."

"No two-buck whore's gonna smack me with a beer glass, dammit!"

He tried to bull his way past me, and I hit him sharply on the chin. I caught him as he was falling, dragged him out the front door, and sat him in one of the cypress chairs against the wall. I felt his jaw and listened to his breathing to make sure I hadn't hurt him, then went back inside. The two cousins were in the middle of the floor halfway down the room, and Ben was standing in front of them. He had that eighteen-inch length of garden hose in his hand.

"And on top of that," he was telling them belligerently, "you keep Floyd the hell out of here from now on. He insulted the lady and I seen him do it. Jeff should of mopped up the floor with him. Now if you still want trouble, okay, let's go."

I walked over to them and said, "Trouble?" and looked at the cousins.

They were lean, stringy men with faded blue eyes and rope-colored hair. They looked back at me without any expression, then walked around Ben and out the front door.

"That Floyd's getting meaner all the time," Ben said, flexing his short, thick arms as if sorry the cousins hadn't pressed the issue. "He's getting too mean for his own good. One of these days he's gonna do something even Burkitt can't get him out of. If he tries to come back in here, I'll clobber him, so help me."

"I hope I'm here to give you a hand."

"I won't need a hand. And look Jeff, tell the lady I run a decent place here. I don't want her to get any bad ideas."

"Don't worry about that, Ben."

He slapped me on the shoulder and said, "Have a good time, sonny boy," and went back to the bar.

Letty was sitting up very straight in her chair. There were dancing flecks of excitement in her eyes.

"Ben said to tell you he runs a decent place here," I said gravely. "He doesn't want you to get any bad ideas."

She laughed and looked toward the bar. She smiled and he mitted her, grinning widely. He liked a girl who could take care of herself without screeching or making a fuss.

She reached across the table and put her hand on my arm. "I'm not sore at you anymore, Jeff."

"I shouldn't have shot off my big mouth."

"But Buster did tell me to work on you."

"That's what I thought."

"He says it's a good deal, Jeff. Why don't you go in on it with him?"

"It's a lousy deal, Letty."

"But you don't know Buster. He's very smart."

"Not in this. Did he tell you the proposition he made me?"

"Something about liquor."

"He wants me to run in a load of liquor from Cuba on the boat."

"Is there money in it?"

"If you can stay out of jail."

"But you won't have to worry about that, Jeff," she said earnestly. "If Buster's in on it, he'll have it all figured out. He's very smart."

"There's a law against it, honey."

"I know, but Buster says that law's almost as bad as Prohibition. There's such high taxes on liquor that a guy can't afford to buy a bottle anymore, if he's got a wife and kids and the rent to pay. He's got to buy bootleg stuff. Laws like that, Buster says, are made to be broken. Nobody gives the little guy a break these days. Somebody's got to give him a break. Know what I mean?"

She was still very earnest and she may even have believed all that because she had been persuaded. But all the same she was doing nothing more than parroting what Buster had told her, and I knew how much he cared about giving the little guy a break.

There would be no sense in arguing it out with her, so I said, "My boat just isn't big enough and with a load like that, it wouldn't be fast enough. That's all there's to it."

She had been coached pretty well, but she had no answer to that one. "Honest?" she asked finally. "You're not kidding me?"

"It's the truth."

"Did you tell Buster that?"

"Yes. He doesn't know very much about boats, does he?"

"Well, no, he never ..."

"I know all about boats." That was stretching it, but I did know all about the *Skidoo*. "It's my business. I know the kind of boat he needs for the job, something big and fast, like a PT boat, not a little fishing boat like mine. Why, I wouldn't even be able to make the crossing at all if there was any kind of sea running. And if we hit a squall, it'd be murder."

That impressed her. "I'll tell him," she said. "Maybe he didn't understand you the first time. But he's very smart, Jeff. He could figure it out if there was a way to do it."

Oh sure, I thought, given time he'd figure it out—probably by smuggling her aboard the Coast Guard boat to entertain the boys while we slipped by with our load of liquor. Judging from the way he sicked her on me, that would just about be what he'd come up with.

"There's no way, honey. My boat isn't big enough and it can't be stretched."

"I'll tell him," she repeated. Then, regretfully, "But he's gonna be disappointed."

I thought that as good a time as any to cut it short, so I asked her to dance with me. Letty was very good. She had an animal grace that went beyond the mere rhythm of the music. Her breasts were soft against me, and I put my face down close to her hair and sniffed the clean odorlessness of her. She did not use perfume. I was very conscious of her body against mine, and it got so that on the turns I felt as if I were merging with her.

Byrne and his girl friend left the floor in the middle of the dance and went out the back door, their arms around each other's waist. They stopped for a swaying kiss just outside the door, then staggered off into the darkness. They were going to his car. I tried not to think about them while I was dancing with Letty, although I could feel the moving softness of her under my hand. But she came so readily at the slightest touch that it was almost like surrender; actually it was only because she was such a fine dancer.

I tightened my arm around her, but she stiffened immediately and I let her go. When the record finished, I took her over to the bar. There was room there, now that Floyd and his cousins had gone. I didn't like sitting at a table in Ben's place. It made me feel like a stranger.

"You think a lot of Buster, don't you?" I said.

"You're not kidding. He took care of me since I was nine when my father was shot."

"Shot!"

"Yeah. He was shot down Hoboken. Buster told me it was an accident but I found out it was the cops. He was holding up a gas station." She spoke defiantly and gave me an appraising sideways look. "My mother died when I was only a little kid, so if it wasn't for Buster I'd of been an orphan. No kidding, he's one swell guy. Anything I want, I can have it if he isn't broke, and he takes me all over with him."

"Are you down here on vacation?"

Letty laughed as if there were something funny about the idea of taking a vacation. "I don't know what you call it. We just go from one place to another. Miami was the last place. He was running a crap game but they made him bust it up. You had to belong to the organization or something. They sent two guys around to beat him up, but did they get the surprise of their life."

She laughed again, then added ruefully, "But we had to get out of town right away even though there was another guy that owed Buster two hundred. We stopped in Fort Myers and Buster worked in a garage for a couple weeks. He can fix anything, Buster can. And now we're here, but I don't know how long. Here today, gone tomorrow, know what I mean?"

I said I knew what she meant, but I didn't. My roots were here in Florida, in Sanibar, in the *Skidoo*, and I just couldn't understand the amoral kind of life they were leading. I don't think Letty understood it either, or was aware of it, because there was actually a kind of innocence in her acceptance of it. I wondered how many times Buster had used her to work on somebody, the way he was using her to work on me, but I didn't probe. I didn't want to know.

We danced again and had some drinks. She told me more about Buster, but it was all more or less the same kind of thing. At times she sounded cynical and hardboiled, especially when she talked about the police, who had to be paid off when Buster was running one of his crap or poker games. But most of the time she seemed incredibly naive, as if she didn't realize that they were living on the fringe of a kind of underworld. Her face became very animated when she talked about Buster. It was obvious that Letty was very fond of him.

"Once in awhile I get down in the dumps, but he can always snap me out of it with funny sayings or something. He never gets down in the dumps. There's always something going on with Buster, and honest to God, we've had the time of our life since we left Secaucus. Secaucus was the worst hole in the world, and, brother, did it stink! The pigs. It's really been living since we got out of there, the time of our life."

Still, she must have had some vague longing for something more settled. She must or she wouldn't have reacted so violently when she thought somebody was taking her for a "nutsy fagin." Which I finally gathered was a sort of disreputable pushover, a round-heel, a mud-kicker.

I couldn't figure Letty out. I was all mixed up about her, both repelled and urgently attracted. I mean, when I was sitting there listening to her tell a supposedly hilarious story about how they had scooted out of Atlanta one jump ahead of the police, or how Buster had been thrown in jail in Atlantic City for beating up a cop, I wasn't sure. But when I was dancing with Letty and the full rhythm of her body was alive against mine, it was something quite different.

Once we went outside for a breath of air. Behind Ben's was a long broad platform that overhung the darkly moving water. That was where the commercial fishermen had unloaded their catches when the Mid-Coast Fisheries owned the place. We walked down to the end of it and stood looking out at the water. There was a thin shaving of moon curled in the sky, and there was just enough light to spark the ripples. Before the red tide, the bay would have been alive with leaping mullet, the darting splash of skimming houndfish, or the savage flurry of a snook striking into a school of minnows. But tonight it was very quiet except for the dry rattle of the breeze in the fronds of the cabbage palms.

I put my arm around her and Letty was turning to me even before I started tightening my grip. Her lips came thrusting up to mine, moving and molding the kiss. Her hand slid lip from my shoulder and cupped-the back of my head, pulling me down deeper into it. Her breasts were hard against me and her hips moved and came forward, twisting. For a roaring moment we stood suspended in the embrace like the overhang of a breaking wave.

Then suddenly Letty's hands were between us. Her palms were flat against my chest, not pushing me away, but checking the momentum like a gradually applied brake, so that the kiss slowly came to a stop without developing. In the end we were standing there as we had in the beginning, my arm loosely around her waist, side by side looking out at the water. I heard her draw a deep breath, but there was nothing in her expressionless face to show what it meant.

"You know something," she said after awhile. "I'm really glad Buster made me come. Honest, Jeff. You're a nice guy."

But there was something missing in her voice. I was a nice guy, but not particularly interesting. She was glad to be there with me; it was nice to be treated as a lady, pleasant not to be pawed or clutched—but as a steady diet it could become dull. In the meantime, Letty was willing to accept it for what it was, an agreeable interlude. And not having the background of restless wandering she and Buster had, there was nothing I could do about it. I'd had my date with her, it would dribble out in polite good-nights and I'd probably never see her again. She was restless even now, and finally she asked what time it was.

I looked at my watch and said, "One-fifteen."

"Oh-oh!" she said. "End of the line, all out, set 'em up in the other alley. I got to get home and get my beauty sleep."

"One more drink before we go?"

"Not for me. I'm up to here." Letty pulled her forefinger across her throat. "Let's go. Okay?"

And so it was dribbling out.

We walked back toward the car in the dark parking lot in the shadows of the cabbage palms and sea grape. We walked apart, not touching. The moon shed a faint light, and I saw her yawn. My car was parked at the end of the lot beside a wind-breaking row of punk trees, and I didn't see the three men until Floyd Hammond stepped out in front of me.

"I been waiting for you, Tucker," he said. And before I could do anything, his fist came whipping up and caught me flush on the jaw.

I went sprawling backward on the grass. It was a hard blow and it hurt. I got dizzily to my feet and he hit me again. The cabbage palm silhouettes wheeled against the sky, and Floyd's white shirt was a floating blob above me. My mouth felt numb. I kept falling on my side when I tried to raise myself to my hands and knees, and the coarse grass blades only an inch from my eyes kept shifting and blurring. But I still clung to a thin edge of consciousness. Finally things steadied and I was on my hands and knees, looking at the frayed tips of Floyd's canvas shoes three feet in front of me.

"Come on, get up, Tucker," he sneered. "You did fine when I was drunk. Let's see how you can do when I'm sober. What do you want me to do, help you up?"

His feet came toward me and his right leg swung back for a kick. I rolled desperately and stood up shakily to my feet about six feet from him. Floyd sidled toward me, hunched over his fists. His left hand came out, hooking for my face, and he swung with his right when I ducked. He missed, then rushed, flailing at me with both hands. I had all I could do to back-pedal away from him till my head cleared.

The two cousins were leaning against my car, grinning. Floyd kept taunting me to "Come on. Come on," and laughing. I let him chase me till I could trust my legs. When he rushed, impatient now to get it over, I let him have it on the hinge of the jaw just under his left ear. His legs twisted and he went down, but jumped up right away, swearing. He drove straight at me, hooking. I gave him everything I had right on the point of his long chin, and it was like putting my fist through the thin wood of an orange crate. Floyd went down and didn't move.

This happened so fast that when I turned, the two cousins were still leaning against my car, their grins frozen incredulously on their slack faces.

"Who's next?" I said, breathing hard. They looked at each other but didn't move. It was all over. "Then get him out of here."

They moved reluctantly as if afraid I'd start on them next. They carried Floyd over to their old Chevvy pickup and drove away. I looked around for Letty. There hadn't been a sound out of her all this time. She was standing beside one of the cabbage palms. I could see her breasts lift and fall with her rapid breathing. Her mouth hung open a little, whether from fright or what I didn't know.

"Let's us get out of here too," I growled, and walked over to my car and slid in under the wheel.

She slid in from the other side. I pulled her to me so hard that she gasped. I kissed her roughly and for a moment she was limp in my arms, her lips too soft and surprised under my mouth. Then her body galvanized with a suddenness that was as sharp as a scream, and I held her tighter to prevent her from breaking away. I ground my mouth into her, pushing her head against the back of the seat and locking it there with the force of the kiss. Her fingers dug into my back and, twisting in the seat, she thrust against me.

In the flash of an instant, we were beyond thought or coherence or awareness of anything but the flaming emotion that fused us. Nothing existed but the hard-clashing consuming fury of our togetherness.

Afterward I lit two cigarettes and she smoked languidly. I remember thinking with some surprise (though it had been evident all the time) that that was the key to her—violence. I remembered, too, how excited she had looked after I clipped Floyd the first time back in the tavern. Violence was the trigger that fired Letty.

I looked at her. Her mouth was heavy and sensual, her eyes dark. I threw my cigarette out the window and reached for her, and she came to me with a cry that was savage and exultant.

It was four A.M. when I turned the car into the driveway of the Tami-Kota Motel. Letty was curled against me, holding my arm, not sleeping but quiet.

"Which cabin, honey?"

And she murmured drowsily, "Twelve."

I stopped in front of Number Twelve, facing a large banyan tree at the rear of the court. I put my arms around her and kissed her a number of times. Letty nuzzled her lips against my cheek and chin and nose, making small contented sounds in her throat.

"Would four hours sleep be enough for you, honey?"

"Sure, Jeff. Why?"

"I could pick you up at eight and we could go out in the boat. We could go out to the grouper banks and maybe do some fishing."

"You mean I could catch a fish!"

I grinned. "Anybody can catch a fish. Would you like to go? I'll get the diner to pack us a box lunch."

"Sure! Can Buster come too?"

I hadn't planned it that way, but I said, "Why not ...?"

She hesitated. "Jeff?"

"What, honey?"

"What we talked about back there in the tavern, you and Buster going in together on that proposition, you'll think it over?"

"But there's nothing to think over, Letty. I told you that."

"I know, but you might think of something, some way of doing it."

"Okay," I said, "I'll think it over."

Her asking that for Buster's sake didn't bother me now because I knew how it was. I kissed her again lingeringly. When she got out of the car, I told her I'd pick her up at eight sharp. I waited until she was inside the cabin before turning on the ignition.

A car turned into the driveway behind me. In the sweep of headlights, I saw Buster standing under the banyan tree, not twenty feet away. His cigar was half-raised to his mouth, and he was grinning widely. He had been watching and probably listening. I felt a flush of anger and drove out, giving him only a brief wave of my hand in passing.

CHAPTER FIVE

It was too late to go to a hotel or back to my place on the Key, so I slept aboard the *Skidoo*—if you could call it sleeping. Letty was so much with me that I could close my eyes and feel the warmth of her, and taste her and smell her and feel her arms about me. Nothing like that had ever happened to me before. I had had affairs before and there had usually been a pleasant carry-over, but nothing like this. Something really had fused between us back there in the car.

I'd doze off and wake up almost immediately, thinking about her and how wonderful it was going to be with us. I finally got up and dressed at quarter of seven. I hadn't had an hour's sleep in all, but I felt fine, full of energy and eager. I was coughing and the cabin smelled of dead fish, but that would clear up once we were out in the Gulf.

I drove over to the all-night diner on the Trail and had a rasher of ham with fried eggs, orange juice and coffee. While the counterman was fixing up a box lunch of pickles, sandwiches, and pie, I picked up a case of beer and a chunk of ice. I took them back to the *Skidoo* and packed them into the ice chest.

It was five of eight when I turned into the Tami-Kota Motel and stopped in front of Number Twelve. The shades were still drawn. Thinking that Letty was probably dressing, I gave the horn the old, shave-and-a-haircut-bayrum beat. I sat back and lighted a cigarette, not thinking of anything really, just letting myself float in a pleasant wash of anticipation. It wasn't till I finished my cigarette that I realized that Letty hadn't even shown at the window. I didn't want to sound the horn again, so I got out and knocked on the door.

For some reason or other, an empty house has a different sound, a loneliness and a deadness, and I knew even while I was knocking that there was no one inside. It was then that I noticed for the first time that Buster's old '39 Chevvy was gone from the carport beside the cottage. I heard footsteps on the shell drive behind me. I turned and there was a tall, angular woman with rusty blonde hair done in a pony tail that looked as if it had been plugged into the back of her head.

"If you're looking for the folks in Twelve," she said, "they went."

"Went?" I said blankly. "To breakfast?"

"No, just went. They left a little after four this morning. I checked them out."

"B-but I was supposed to meet them here at eight," I stammered, unable to believe that they had really gone.

The woman sensed that something was wrong and she gave me a sympathetic look with a touch of pity in it. "They must have forgot. They were talking about being in Atlanta before evening."

"Didn't she ... they leave me a note or a message or something?"

She shook her head. "Not with me. Maybe they left it inside."

She took a key from her pocket and unlocked the door. You know these motel cottages, there's not much to them—a small room with twin beds, a chair, and a dresser, and off to one side a tiny bathroom. The beds were made and there were clean, fresh towels in the bathroom.

"I always clean up right away," the woman explained. "Some folks like to drive all night and stop off in the morning. I didn't notice anything around."

There wasn't any note. There wasn't anything at all to show that they had been there, not even a bit of Kleenex with a lipstick smear in the waste basket, or a used razor blade in the bathroom, nor a lingering trace of perfume. I remember thinking a little dully that that was how it would be with them, no matter where they went. I gave the room a futile last glance.

"Well, thanks anyway."

She walked outside with me and relocked the door. "I'm sorry."

"Oh, I'll probably hear from them."

"That's right. Folks forget things when they're in a hurry."

On the way out, I saw a tall waste can beside the office, and I threw the box lunch into it. The woman was still standing in front of Number Twelve, watching me. I drove out to Ben's place on the Bay. He opened at seven every morning. I don't think he ever got more than four hours sleep a night, but he always looked the same—tough and contented, but ready for anything from a gag to a fight. There was one other customer at the bar, a sick-looking cracker, hunched over a beer, probably trying to drink his way out of a hangover.

"Give me a glass of 'shine," I said brusquely.

Ben lifted his eyebrows and made a face. "Like that, eh?"

"Just like that."

He shrugged. "It's your gut, but why don't you try a beer first?"

"'Shine."

He brought me a wine glass of 'shine. It looked like sauterne. He leaned against the bar and watched me drink it down. I set the empty glass in front of him and he refilled it without comment. Neither of us said a word while I was drinking that one. Ben refilled it again.

"You know," he said, "I've seen men drink as many as eight of these at a sitting before it went to their brains. Like to try for nine?"

"Go to hell, Ben."

"I liked that bim you brought in last night, sonny boy. It was a joy and a pleasure to see the way she bounced that beer mug off Floyd, but just between you and me, I was just as glad she was yours and not mine. A bim like that, she's fine for a one-night stand, but I got an idea you'd flip your lid if you tried to stay with it too long. She's what you'd call a real wildcat, and I don't mean the bobtail kind."

His face and voice were bland and a little vague, but I knew he was giving me the needle just to hear what I'd say. And if I got sore, so much the better. That was one thing about Ben, he was nosy. He wanted to know everything about everybody, but I'll say this for him: no matter what he found out, he never blabbed. Still, I wasn't going to let him know how it was with Letty and me, or the way it wound up.

"She was okay," I said.

"She live around here?"

He knew damn well she didn't.

"She was just passing through."

"Where's she from, Jeff?"

"Points north, east, south, and west."

"That's what I kind of figured. Not that she was a tramp or anything like that, mind you, but she didn't look like anything you could settle down with."

Maybe this was his idea of warning me. He was pretty smart about people most of the time.

I didn't answer and he asked, "Seeing much of Helen these days?"

"Why don't you hire a detective? Then you wouldn't have to ask so many questions."

"She's a nice kid. You could do worse."

"Shove off, will you?"

"Okay. Take it easy, sonny boy."

He walked down the bar to the hungover cracker and I heard him say, "Well, how's it going, Creeping Moses? The snakes still churning up your brains?"

A hangover never got any sympathy from Ben. He thought it was comic. If he knew I was feeling lousy because of Letty, he'd think that comic, too. But I was as far from understanding Buster and Letty as I had been in the beginning. They must have pulled out of that motel five minutes after I drove away. I thought I could see Buster's point of view. He knew he couldn't make a deal with me on the boat, so there was no sense in hanging around. Sanibar wasn't a place you could promote a profitable crap game, and with business so bad on account of the red tide, there weren't any jobs around. It was Letty I didn't get, how she could have gone so abruptly without even a word. Then I thought the hell with it.

Ben was right. She and Buster were as alien as men from Mars and poison to anyone but their own kind. I could see it very clearly and objectively. I was better off no matter how you looked at it. They were the kind of people you couldn't scrub off with sulfuric acid once they got on you. The bitterness I felt now was only a small indication of the harm they could have done me. I was lucky to be rid of them.

The only trouble with this reasoning was that I didn't believe a word of it, even though I knew it was true.

Ben abruptly stopped talking to the cracker, picked up a glass, and began polishing it with his towel. The next moment somebody rapped me on the shoulder. I looked around and it was Floyd's cousin, Matt Burkitt, who was a detective on the cops.

"I want to talk to you." He turned and walked out, expecting me to follow him.

I didn't follow him. I sat there, mad and stubborn. In a few minutes, he was back again. "I said I want to talk to you."

"Go ahead," I said.

"Outside."

His voice was dull and monotonous as if he were bone-tired, but that was the way he talked all the time. Burkitt was a big, shambling man with a jaw that ran straight across his face. He was said to have immense strength in his loose-hung arms.

"You can talk here just as easy," I said.

"You want to be invited, is that the idea?"

"I don't like being *told*."

"All right," he said in that wooden voice, "I'll invite you. Let's go outside. I want to talk to you."

This time I went outside with him. We walked over to the shade of the Poinciana tree and he took out a package of cigarettes and offered me one.

While he was holding a light for me, he said, "You busted Floyd's jaw in two places last night."

"I thought so," I said without any inflection. "I felt it go when I hit him."

He lighted his own cigarette and flipped the match away. "You must have quite a wallop. Or did you have a lead sinker in your hand?"

"I didn't need a lead sinker."

"Did you have to smack him that hard?"

"Floyd asked for it. He's been asking for it for a long time, and last night he made a point of asking for it."

"I know all about it. The girl too. That wasn't why she left town, was it?"

I was surprised that he knew about Letty. "That wasn't the reason."

"I didn't think so. Floyd's in pretty bad shape. He's in the hospital. That smack with the beer mug didn't do him any good either."

"He practically begged for that."

"I know."

This was all so casual that you'd have thought we were talking about the mackerel run or a game of horseshoes. They said Matt Burkitt never got excited, and I could believe it.

"What'd you want to talk to me about?" The way the conversation was going, it could drift on forever, and I didn't feel like talking to him or anybody else.

"I'm coming to that. Floyd'll be in the hospital for another few days.

When they let him go, I want you to keep out of his way."

"The hell with that!"

Burkitt took a deep drag on his cigarette. "He's going to be feeling pretty mean and he'll probably go looking for trouble. I don't want any trouble. There's been enough trouble."

"That's your job, not mine. You've been *getting* him out of trouble all this time, so suppose you try *keeping* him out for a change."

He looked at me. "What's the matter with you? Don't you have no sense?"

"Hell, what do you expect me to do, duck up a side street every time I see him coming?"

"What's eating you, Tucker? You used to listen when somebody tried to talk to you. You got a bellyache or something? A hangover? I'm only telling you this for your own good."

"Tell it to Floyd."

Burkitt didn't get sore. His expression didn't even change. He just stood there, thinking it over. "Well," he said finally, "I can always throw one of you in the stockade, if it comes to that."

"Is that a threat, Burkitt?"

"A threat? I don't make threats. I'm just telling you." He dropped his cigarette and ground it out with his heel. "Use your head and there won't be any trouble. And don't think I won't throw you in the stockade if I have to. I will."

"The hell you will!"

"Be as tough as you want, Tucker. It don't make no difference to me." He walked to his car, got in, and drove away without looking back.

I was sore. Childishly, I felt like skimming an oyster shell after him from the driveway or yelling, "Go to hell!" or something equally intelligent. Matt Burkitt affected everybody that way when they had any dealings with him. You just couldn't talk to him. He told you what he wanted you to do, and that was all there was to it. He had the kind of mind you couldn't dent even with a diamond drill.

I went back into the bar. My last glass of 'shine was still there, nearly full. I downed it at a gulp and called to Ben for another. He poured it for me, bunching up his mouth in disapproval.

"Just this once, Jeff. I'm going to bust a rule and give you a hunk of advice. Don't fool around with Matt Burkitt."

"When you make a rule, stick to it."

"Okay, but I'll give you another hunk of the same advice. If you do fool around with Matt Burkitt, keep your mind on it. Don't fool around with 'shine first. Matt Burkitt'll walk right over you and never know he even stepped on something."

"Nuts!"

Ben looked patient, which meant that he was boiling mad. He was as nosy as hell about everybody else, but he never liked to let you know what was going on inside him.

"I don't know why I waste time on you, boy. Except I know you ain't very bright. I don't know what you and Burkitt talked about out there ..."

"You know damn well what we talked about."

"Okay, so I got an idea. But what I'm leading up to is this—Burkitt's a guy he always means just what he says. He don't mean no more, and he don't mean no less. If he says he'll smack you in the snoot, you can bet your bottom buck, he won't smack you in the belly. Right in the snoot is where you'll get it. And you want me to tell you something else about him?"

I was still sore, but the 'shine had taken the edge off it. Anyway, Ben was so serious, I couldn't help laughing at him.

"Go right ahead, but don't try to tell me he's human. He's one of those robots they operate by remote control."

"He'll operate you by remote control, sonny boy. He'll operate you right into the state pen at Raiford. Look, in this county the Hammonds, the Burkitts, the Peckovers, and the Purcells all stick together like tar to a fender. They got enough votes so they could elect Russia king of the county if they wanted. They're the ones that put Matt on the cops, and he's the one that'll put you on the spot unless you use some sense. And he'll get away with it too, and don't think he won't!"

He brought his fist down on the bar and knocked over my glass and the 'shine spilled all over the front of his pants. He looked down at himself with disgust.

"Damn, that's what I get for fooling around with a lame-brain like you."

"You knocked over my drink," I said innocently. "Now you'll have to buy me another one."

"Pour it yourself, jerk!" He began mopping off his trousers with a bar towel.

I poured myself a drink and grinned at him over the rim of the glass. After awhile he began grinning a little, too, but in a troubled way.

"Ah, look, Jeff, if I didn't like you, I wouldn't waste my time. But I got a pretty fair idea what Matt Burkitt wants you to do. He wants you to stay out of Floyd's way for awhile. Right? Okay. So stay out of Floyd's way for awhile. It won't hurt you, and you can save yourself a lot of grief. Nobody'll think you're yellow. They'll just think you're smart. And they'll be right, too. Matt's a tough man, but he's honest, Jeff. You got to hand it to him; he's honest and he'll do what he thinks is right, no matter what you think about it. So go along with him, boy, and don't forget I'm only telling you this for your own good. Now what do you say?"

He smiled encouragingly, and I smiled back.

"The hell with Matt Burkitt, Ben," I said pleasantly. "And the hell with Floyd, too."

His smiled faded. He picked up the bottle of 'shine and put it under the bar.

"So long, Jeff," he said heavily. "Nice to have known you. But as a special favor, do your drinking someplace else from now on. When the mess comes, I don't want it in my place."

"Okay, if that's the way you feel about it."

I finished my drink and walked out. I said, "So long, Ben," and he said, "Goodbye, Jeff." He sounded as if he meant it.

CHAPTER SIX

I climbed in the car and in an aimless sort of way started for town, not even thinking about what I was going to do when I got there. Then I started thinking about Letty again. How incredibly wonderful it had been with her and how, really for the first time with a woman, it had been everything. And then I thought of that son of a bitch Buster, and how he had taken her away so casually just because there wasn't anything in it here for him anymore. And how at the next stop he'd probably try to put her through the same thing again.

It got pretty bad, because there wasn't a damn thing I could do about it one way or the other. Furthermore, it was obvious that Letty didn't want anything done about it or she wouldn't have gone away with him. *In the first place*, I thought. And there weren't any places after the first place.

As I rolled into town, I glanced up at the big bronze clock that hung on the side of the Sanibar National Bank. I don't know why. I wasn't going anyplace and I didn't have to be there at any special time. It was eleven o'clock, which, when you thought about it, was a pretty static time of day, too late for one thing and too early for another. All you could do at eleven o'clock was stall around and wait for lunch time. I wasn't interested in lunch.

I parked the car and stuck a nickel in the parking meter. A nickel bought you an hour. For a dollar twenty you could buy yourself a whole day. Time is a wonderful thing, and when you really consider it, a nickel an hour is pretty cheap. What I needed was about a week, and here was the town of Sanibar ready and willing to sell it to me for only eight dollars and forty cents. A bargain. A man couldn't afford to pass up a chance like that.

Damn it to hell, I thought. Much more of this and I'd be talking to myself.

I turned around and there I was, parked smack in front of the Tropical Liquor Store. Things like that are never accidental. I went inside and asked for a bottle of bourbon. But on second thought, I told the clerk to make it two.

"One might get lonesome all by itself," I told him.

"That's right," he said, with a hearty commercial chuckle. "How're you fixed for soda, ginger ale, 7-Up, Tom Collins Mix, quinine water ... We got a special on rum today, two-ninety-nine, Ron Grande." He pointed at the shelves back of him.

"I'm nuts about rum, but it makes me puke. How much do I owe you?"

"Nine hundred dollars." He chuckled again.

That clerk was almost as much of a comedian as I was, but on the other hand, maybe all he needed was experience. Like Letty, for instance. There was a real experience, Letty. One experience like Letty and you could be right up there with Bob Hope, Red Skelton, and the biggest clown of them all, Jack the Ripper.

He started to put the bottles in a bag and I said, "Don't bother wrapping them up. I'll drink them right here."

I walked out to the car with a bottle in each hand. I reached through the window and put them on the front seat, and then I looked at the parking meter. I still had fifty minutes left, four cents worth of precious time. Being in a generous mood, I donated it to the town of Sanibar as a public service. I walked around the end of the car and as I did, I happened to glance across the street. There was Matt Burkitt, parked in his car, watching me. I gave him a lopsided grin and tipped my hand from my forehead.

"The next time you see the dog catcher, Matt," I called out, "tell him to remember me to your mother."

He heard me all right, but all he did was glance indifferently up and down the street as if making a routine check on traffic conditions. You couldn't make a dent in him. Maybe he didn't exist personally. I don't think he did. I happened to know that he didn't go home or to the movies or go bowling the way other cops did after their eight hour tour of duty. He kept right on working. If there was a raid on some two bit juke-joint at four in the morning, Matt Burkitt would be right there with the rest of the squad, even if he had worked the whole day before. He turned up at almost every fire, accident, or disturbance we had in town, day or night. And if some ambitious Cuban from Tampa turned up in town at noon selling *bolita* numbers, it was Matt Burkitt who had the cuffs on him before the guy had a chance to have lunch.

Some of the boys swore that he never slept, and maybe he didn't. Maybe he didn't need sleep or friends or any of the ordinary human things that keep the rest, of us from going crazy. He was the Law, and that's all he cared about. You can't insult the Law. You can break it and be punished, but you can't insult it. The Law doesn't care what you think about it or know about it or say about it, just as long as you don't break it.

I was probably off the beam, but that's the way I felt about Matt Burkitt. He didn't care if I stood there all day and called him the lowest son of a bitch in the tail end of the world, as long as I didn't obstruct traffic, incite to riot, or spit on the sidewalk. That was the only way you could get a reaction out of him.

I got in my car and drove down to the docks. There was nothing like a few glasses of Captain Ben's good old 'shine to help you figure out things intelligently. I went down into the cabin of the *Skidoo* and opened one of the bottles of bourbon. Bourbon is corn liquor too, like 'shine only better. If 'shine could make me intelligent, bourbon would make me a genius.

Everybody knows that eight drinks make you smarter than four drinks, and if you keep it up long enough, people like Einstein will come around on their hands and knees begging you to solve all their problems for them. If you're in a good mood, you'll feel sorry for them and maybe let them have a drink or two out of your bottle. Though as a matter of reciprocal justice you really should boot them the hell-and-gone out of there because nobody ever did anything for you, did they? Damn right they didn't, and that included Ben, that nosy old he-tit, Matt Burkitt, Letty, and all the rest. The hell with them. Why should I worry about them anyway? When you came right down to it, there wasn't a one of them who wouldn't puke if you stuck your finger down his throat. Damn right they would.

And furthermore, they weren't going to push me around. I'd had some pretty damn good workouts in my life and I could push just as hard as they could. Maybe harder, because I didn't give a damn. That's the secret. When you don't give a damn, you can push twice as hard and there's nothing they can do about it, because you don't give a damn about them. One shove and down they go, and it's enough to make you laugh right out loud at the surprise in their faces because they were the ones who thought they were going to push you around.

All you had to do was figure it for yourself and you soon found out you didn't need any of them. Hell, if you wanted to take twenty or thirty bucks and go up to Tampa, you could get yourself some of the best Spanish loving in the world, and there wasn't a soul who could stop you. Not Matt Burkitt, Ben, Letty, or anybody. All you had to do was get in your car and go, and what could they do about it? Not a damn thing. Nobody could do anything about it, not a single one of them. They couldn't even lift a finger to stop you. That's where you had them. Thumb your nose, say so long, sucker, and take off.

I poured myself another drink. It was damn fine bourbon. I put on a pair of slacks I gave thirty bucks for the time I was up New York, a nylon sport shirt, socks, and a pair of English-made sport shoes I got in the Bahamas, the time I was down there with a party on the *Skidoo* for marlin. The English might be snooty bastards and all that, but let me tell you this, they're damn good shoemakers. And don't think different, because if you take care of a pair of English shoes, you can hand them down to your grandchildren. But as far as their lousy Scotch is concerned, they can shove it. They don't know a damn thing about making an honest drink like bourbon.

I had another drink out of the bottle and took it along with me when I stepped off the *Skidoo* and onto the dock. I guess I was really looping by that time. I hadn't had any breakfast. I'd put down quite a load of 'shine out at Captain Ben's and topped it off here on the *Skidoo* with a half bottle of hundred-proof bonded bourbon. So things became a little shrouded in mystery after I fumbled my way into my car at the end of the dock and took off down the road, but whether north or south, I'll never know.

There were little snatches of memory, fragmentary and frustrating, like odd pages torn from a book, or more aptly, a few feet of film cut from a full-length movie.

There was this girl, a blonde, and she was walking across the room toward me. Her breasts were very large and round and they quivered when she walked. She had slender calves, but her thighs were full and cushiony and she had a mocking smile. I don't know what had gone on before, but when I reached for her, she pushed me away.

"You've had, it, boy," she said, and began to put on her clothes.

I'd had what? I just gaped at her, then called her a whore.

She laughed. "Well what the hell did you think I was?"

That's all I can remember about that.

And then there was another girl, a big girl, also a blonde. She had her arms around me and kept saying, "What's the matter, big boy, what's the matter?"

"Keep away from me, you bitch," I said, pushing her away. "I don't like blondes and never did."

"Well this is a helluva time to find that out!" She picked up a pair of pants from the chair, and threw them at me. "Beat it!" she said angrily.

"You're damn right. I wouldn't have anything to do with a blonde if they served you with mushrooms and artichokes."

"You poor dumb son of a bitch." She kept shaking her head slowly from side to side ...

And that's all I can remember of that, her standing there, voluptuously beautiful and blonde, and slowly shaking her head as if I'd gone out of my mind.

As for the rest, I can't remember anything but clash, chaos, and violence—and a great dark segment of wheeling sky in which the stars glittered like crushed glass.

When I woke up, I was in jail in Donaldston, a tough cattletown about thirty miles inland. There was a scrap of mirror over the washbowl in the corner of the cell. I stared at myself in amazement. I had a black eye, a swollen cheekbone, and a split lip. It was the kind of face to which the most lenient judge in the world would give thirty days on the road gang, without having to think twice about it. A dirty, unshaven, bloody face, anyone could see with half-an-eye was guilty of everything in the book. You don't stand a chance with a face like that.

I was pretty glum when the police prowl car picked me up (the jail was in the firehouse) and took me down to the town hall. It was a wooden barracks kind of building with the municipal offices at one end, the civic auditorium in the middle, and the police station and chamber of commerce at the other end. Court was held in the auditorium.

I was the only prisoner. I stood up in front of the judge, a bald man who sat behind a small, rickety table and looked at the ceiling while the town clerk mumbled the charge against me. On the night before in Roy's Tavern at one-thirty A.M., I had assaulted or had attempted to assault several citizens named Howie Peters, Marty Branigan, Joe Connors, Tex McMahon, and Paul Lindstrom.

The judge concealed a grin behind his hand and, still looking at the ceiling, said, "All together or one at a time?"

He was answered by the cop who stood beside me, holding his hat in front of him with both hands. "All together, your honor. He plowed right into them."

The judge's shoulders shook with silent laughter for a moment. "Guilty or not guilty, Tucker?"

I touched my eye. "I don't know, your honor, but it sure feels guilty."

They were all grinning openly by this time. Finally the judge said, "Well, I've got to fine you something, Tucker. You just can't go around assaulting large bodies of the population, and I might add that you picked five of the largest bodies in town. Ten dollars and costs. But the next time you feel like committing suicide, please do it someplace else. Inquests cost money."

The clerk had my wallet and wrist watch in an envelope. I had twenty-three dollars, and after I paid my fine, the cop took me back to the firehouse where my car was parked.

"You were something," he told me. "You had them going when I broke it up. You were really giving them a hard time, even if there was five of them."

"What was it all about?"

"I couldn't make head or tail out of it. When I walked in, you had them backed off for a minute and you were yelling that you could lick any blonde son of a bitch in the world, or something like that. I don't know. Lindstrom, he's kind of blonde, says you just up and took a swing at him."

I said, "Oh," and didn't ask any more questions.

Letty and Buster were both blonde.

I drove back to Sanibar and got there about five-thirty in the afternoon. I didn't have the faintest idea what date it was until I picked up a newspaper. I had been gone two and a half days.

CHAPTER SEVEN

I had done a lot of thinking driving those thirty miles across the state from Donaldston, and I was sure that I had gotten Letty out of my system. I had done it the hard way, something like pulling a tooth with a Stillson wrench, but it was out and the poison was gone. I was certain I wouldn't go around fighting people anymore just because they were blonde. In fact, when a tall blonde girl passed me on the sidewalk, I deliberately turned my head and watched her walk away from me. It didn't bother me a bit.

Suddenly I thought of Helen and her light, sweet, clear voice. The warmth and serenity of the way it had always been with us, and her calm intimacy and well-ordered friendliness. With all this in my mind, I found that I couldn't think of anything more desirable. I wanted to talk to her.

As I started down the street toward the phone booth in the drugstore on the corner, Floyd Hammond came out of the Oasis Bar. He was staggering a little and almost ran into me. His jaw was in an aluminum brace and his face had the dead opacity of lard.

He reeled back, his eyes vacant with non-recognition. "Watch where you're goin', dammit!" he said nastily.

I didn't want to bother with him. You could see the small, rodent viciousness of him in the way his pointed features were spitefully bunched together in the middle of his face. It would have been a stupid waste of time even to answer him. I started to walk around him, but he must suddenly have brought me into focus. He lurched in front of me, brought up his arm, and shoved me on the chest with the heel of his hand.

"Wa-a-a-ait a minute, you!" he said. "Wa-a-a-ait a minute."

"Forget it, Floyd."

"Forget it! Why you Yankee-loving son of a bitch, who the hell do you think you are anyway?"

I still didn't want anything to do with him, but when I tried to walk around him again, he blocked my way. He stood there wide-legged, his braced jaw thrust out, eying me with his meager belligerence.

"Get out of my way, Floyd. I don't want any trouble with you."

A laugh rattled emptily in his throat. "What you want and what you get are two different things, you bastard." He butted my chest with the heel of his hand again. "If you know what's good for you, you'll stay out of my way, understand? Just stay out of my way or you'll be sorry!"

People were beginning to turn their heads and look at us. I felt my face getting hot, but I held my temper down.

"Okay, Floyd," I said as quietly as I could. "Let's let it go at that."

He let out a great braying blat of a laugh and seemed convulsed with merriment. "I knew you'd crawl," he jeered, and then contemptuously, "But maybe you're smart. Maybe you know what's good for you. Why, you dumb clunk, if you don't stay out of my way ..."

He butted his hand at my face, and that was too much. I grabbed him by the shirt front and pulled him to me.

"If I don't stay out of your way, what?" I said furiously. "What would you do, burn my boat some night when nobody was looking? Or jump me from behind in the dark, or what? Now listen to *me*. You stay out of *my* way or the next time it'll be your neck that gets broken!"

He hadn't expected me to attack him. His eyes rolled with sudden terror and his hands fluttered at his face. "My jaw ..." he bleated, "my jaw ... my jaw ..."

I let him go. Disgusted with myself, I walked down the street toward the phone in the drugstore. After about twenty steps, I looked back and saw Matt Burkitt take him by the arm and lead him quietly across the street to the police car that was parked in front of the bank. Floyd walked jerkily as if he had locomotor ataxia, and Matt was talking to him and patting him, soothingly on the shoulder. As I watched them drive away in the direction of Floyd's place on the bay, I had the uneasy feeling there was something in Matt Burkitt that I had missed entirely. But I put both of them out of my mind when I stepped into the phone booth, closed the door, and dialed Helen's number.

I brightened when I heard the rattle as she picked up her phone and said, "Hello?" It was really good to hear the limpid sweetness of her voice again. It was like a sun-shiny afternoon at the beach with the Gulf so calm that it barely creamed on the white sand, as the swells rose and fell in drowsy breathing and overhead the cleanness of the wheeling gulls against the blue sky.

"Hello, Helen. This is Jeff."

"Oh."

"What's the matter, honey?"

"I'm surprised you called me, that's all," she said coolly.

"Well, I wanted to apologize about the other night. I'm sorry I broke the date, Helen, but ..."

"Your breaking the date has nothing to do with it."

"Then what is it, Helen?"

"Oh for heaven's sake, Jeff, don't pretend. You know very well what it is. You couldn't have been that drunk," she added coldly.

I thought she was talking about my being arrested over in Donaldston. I laughed. "Ah, Helen, that wasn't anything …"

"Please, Jeff, for heaven's sake! I'm not a complete fool. If it wasn't anything, why is the whole town talking about it?"

"Hell," I said cheerfully, "that little trouble I had in Donaldston wasn't anything. All I did was get in a little fight. Even the judge had to laugh about it."

"I'm afraid we're talking about two different things," she said in that same icy, forbidding voice. "I certainly didn't know about this new trouble you had in Donaldston, though it doesn't surprise me."

"Then what are you talking about?"

"I'm talking about the fight you had with Floyd Hammond over that prostitute you picked up someplace. Don't bother denying it because everybody's been talking about it for days. You fought like animals while this—" her anger seemed to choke her—"this *whore* stood on the sidelines laughing and egging you on and Floyd wound up in the hospital. And if it hadn't been that Matt Burkitt was fair-minded enough to go around and get both sides of the story, you'd have had some pretty serious charges pressed against you. And your cheap girl friend, too, seeing how she hit him with a beer bottle during the fight. Frankly, I'm disgusted with you!"

I was so flabbergasted that I could hardly think of a word to say. "But—but it wasn't anything like that …"

"Please, Jeff, I don't want to discuss it. It's over and done with, and you can count yourself lucky that it didn't have more serious consequences."

"But let me explain …"

"There's nothing to explain. I'm sorry, Jeff, but I'm *very* tired and I don't want to argue over the telephone. There's nothing more to say, and frankly I'm not interested in your excuses."

"Let me come over and see you …"

"See me! Do you think I'd be seen with you after the disgusting way you've acted? If you think so, get that idea out of your head right away. If I were seen with you, people would consider me no better than that prostitute about whom you and Floyd were fighting in the gutter!"

She had me so thoroughly in the wrong and was yet so close to the truth of the matter that I felt choked and shamed and floundering that I could only stammer, "I'll—I'll call you tomorrow, Helen. I want to tell you ..."

She broke in impatiently, "Can't you understand that I'm simply not interested in your excuses, Jeff? I don't want to discuss it any further. The whole thing has been a nightmare for me, and the sooner I can forget it, the better. So please don't call me! If you do, I'll hang up."

"Helen ..."

"And while we're on the subject," she went on inexorably, "don't you think it's about time you sat down and took stock of yourself? You're thoroughly irresponsible, you know. This red tide thing, for instance. With all the dead fish and the smell, everybody knows you can't even *attempt* to make a living taking out fishing parties on your boat. Yet you insisted upon staying here while every sensible boat captain took his boat elsewhere, to the Keys or to Bimini or up to Jersey. Everyone except *you*. No, you had to stay."

"I was born here, Helen," I said lamely.

"So were a lot of other people, but I notice they took their boats out when the red tide came in. All I hope, Jeff," she said crisply, "is that you can pull yourself together before you harm yourself and those who might just happen to love you!" Then she hung up.

My hand went out and put up the receiver, but I stood there not believing what I'd heard. That hadn't been Helen. That had been someone else. That couldn't *possibly* have been Helen. I pulled open the door of the booth and went outside. On the sidewalk, I was vaguely surprised that the sun was shining. It should have been night.

I didn't try to tell myself that she'd get over it because I didn't think she would. I remembered how implacable she'd been when Herb Stokely ran away from his wife. "A man like that should be horsewhipped!" Helen had said. And how disgusted when she heard that Herb and his wife were together again. "I don't see how she can possibly face her friends again after a thing like that. If she had an ounce of pride, she'd have put that man out of her life forever ... She's cheapened herself, that's all. I have absolutely no respect for her." And I knew for a fact that she'd never spoken to Muriel Stokely again.

I didn't think anything of it at the time because the Stokelys didn't mean a thing to me, but here I was in the same category as Herb. Helen would never think of me again except with bitterness. I had been involved in a public scandal and, by association, I had involved her. Furthermore, the things I had done were a threat to decency, as they had always been. Seducers, drunkards, and law-breakers stand condemned. She was my enemy.

It made me sore and I thought, the hell with her. I started to walk back to the car and halfway down the street I got some more of the same. I met Henny Gant and his wife Amy coming out of the Sand-'N-Surf Toggery Shop. "Hi, Mrs. Grant," I said. "Hi, Henny."

Amy set her face straight ahead and didn't answer. "Hi, Tucker," said Henny curtly, and the pair of them walked on.

I was on the blacklist, and there was no doubt about it.

I should have been amused, I suppose, because when Henny was drinking he had just about the foulest mouth in town and Amy was the hatchet woman for the gossip brigade. They were a joyless lot, but I wasn't in the mood to be amused. I felt sour about the whole thing.

I drove around to the supermarket, picked up a load of groceries and took it down to the *Skidoo*. I had a lot of cleaning up to do at my place out on Little Brother Key, and I had neglected it long enough. I ran the motors for a few minutes to get them warmed up, then cast off. It was quite dark. I took it easy, sweeping the channel every once in awhile with the searchlight just in case some idiot was out there fishing without a lantern. I lounged at the wheel listening to the quiet slap-slap of the water against the hull and every now and then glancing back at the tumble of phosphorus in the wake.

Pretty soon I began to think that maybe it would be a good idea to make the run down to Marathon or even over to Bimini. I was done with Sanibar. I'd never feel the same about the place again. I didn't care what they thought about me, but I did care what I thought about them. And, too, it would be wonderful to be out on the *Skidoo* again. There's a cleanness and decency about a boat in the open water. On land everything is so close and immediate that there's an urgency involved even in the simple act of getting a cup of coffee at noon in the local lunchroom.

I turned on the searchlight again as I approached my dock on the Key. As I did I saw the white stern of a dinghy bobbing beside it. I didn't like that. I didn't mind people fishing from the Key when I was there, but I didn't like it when I wasn't there, because three or four times they had broken into the house and I had lost some pretty expensive fishing tackle. That's why I had put up a sign on the end of the dock saying Private, Keep Off.

I turned the searchlight toward the house and there, striding down the path, was Buster. He dodged the moment the light struck him. He disappeared into the sea-grape beside the path, but not so quickly that I missed the gun in his hand.

CHAPTER EIGHT

Angrily, I cut the motors to neutral and slid in toward the end of the dock.

"Hey, you!" Buster yelled at me. "Beat it. This is private property. What's the matter with you, lame brains, cancha read?"

"You're damn right it's private property," I yelled back. "What the hell are you doing here?"

"What?" He sounded confused, and I could feel him peering through the bushes at me as I jumped down to the dock and threw the stern line over the bit. "Well, dammit, it's George. Hiya, George! I didn't recognize your scow for a minute."

Buster walked out on the dock, grinning amiably at me. He had on the same khaki pants and dirty blue sport shirt. He looked bigger than I remembered him. He was immense; his thick neck seemed to bulge with muscle like that of a great bull. He wasn't carrying the gun now, but there was a telltale bulge under his shirt at the waistband of his pants.

"Well, how's George?" he asked, looking guileless, good-natured, and very pleased to see me. It was as if this were his place and I had just dropped in for a short visit.

"All right! Now tell me what you're doing here?"

He shook his round, hard head and his face was humorously rueful. "It's a long story, George. You don't mind, do you?"

"Yes, I mind."

"Now what kind of way is that, George? We thought you'd be glad to see us." Then, slyly, he added, "Letty's up the house."

I knew that if he was there Letty would be there, too. That's the reason my pulses were hammering the way they were and my throat was tight and constricted.

"You didn't answer my question," I said.

"I'll tell you all about it, but first come up the house and say hello to Letty."

"You're in trouble?"

"Trouble?" Buster's face was open and innocent. "Why, I'm not in any trouble, George. What kind of trouble would I be in? Don't be a guy like that."

"Nuts!" I said, and walked past him and up the path toward the house.

He strode along behind me. "Nice place you got here, George, real nice. Like a desert island. A guy could have some real times for himself on a place like this, nobody around to worry about, or nothing. I'll bet you had some wild times here, hey, George?" He chuckled. "You don't have to worry about neighbors on a place like this, right, George?"

I didn't answer. Something had happened, all right, or they wouldn't be here. I wanted to see Letty. I ached to see her, but at the same time I dreaded meeting her again because I was sure Buster had gotten them in trouble. Not trouble like the trouble I had in Sanibar, but bad trouble. And there was something menacing in the way Buster kept talking, as if he were laughing at me, as if it didn't make any difference what I thought about their being here. They were here and they were going to stay.

The hell they are, I thought grimly.

I went up the steps. When I walked into the house, Letty was standing in the middle of the room, facing me. She looked sullen and hostile.

"What do you think, baby," Buster rumbled behind me, "George here ain't glad to see us at all. Now ain't that the ..."

She looked past me. "Shut your trap!"

Buster's booming laugh rolled out. "Well, I'll be go to hell! Nobody loves me." And, still laughing, he backed out on the porch and closed the door.

Letty looked at me with eyes that were as hard and direct as a flung stone. "I didn't want to come here," she said truculently. "It was one of *his* bright ideas."

In spite of myself, the impact of her full-bodied sensuality was even more terrific than it had been in the first place. It was an assault on all my senses. She had on a cheap, skimpy cotton dress. She seemed to be wearing it angrily, as if her breasts and thighs and hips were trying to force their way out of it.

"Are you in trouble, Letty?" I asked in a muffled voice.

She plunged on angrily, ignoring the question. "I told him I didn't want to come here. I told him. 'Don't be a jerk,' I said. But you can't tell *him* nothin'."

"What trouble are you in, Letty?"

"If you don't want us here, just say so and we'll go. Nobody's gonna beg you!"

"Damn it, are you in trouble or aren't you!"

She glowered at me, clenching her hands, and then tilted her chin toward the porch.

"Didn't *he* tell you?"

"No."

"Then let him tell you himself. It was *his* bright idea. Don't think *I* wanted to come here. It was *him*."

I walked toward her. "Damn you, will you listen to me for a minute, Letty ..."

There was a cypress table in the middle of the room. She quickly stepped to the side of it, putting it between us and never taking her angry eyes from me for an instant.

"I'm not going down on my knees for nothin' or nobody," she said. "And if you think I am, you can stick it!"

"Damn it!" I yelled at her. "Just tell me what it's all about, that's all. All you've been doing is standing there and telling me to stick it. Stick *what?*"

"Don't shout at me. I don't have to take that from anybody!"

"Oh, hell!"

There was a bottle of two-fifty rum on the table. Letty backed away as I walked over and poured myself a drink in the water tumbler that stood beside it. I threw it down and slapped the cork back into the bottle. I stared at her. Letty was standing near the kitchen door, as wary and snarling as a cornered animal. Her hands were shaking, but the moment she saw me glance at them, she put them behind her back.

"Nobody's askin' you no favors," she spat at me.

I turned my back and walked to the window that overlooked the beach. The light surf muttered along the shore. The windows were closed, but the oily odor of rotting fish was heavy. I lighted a cigarette.

"When did you get here?"

"Last night," she said sullenly.

"Have you had anything to eat?"

She hesitated. "There was some bread and a can of stuff in the kitchen. But we'll pay you for it!"

"Is that all you've had to eat?"

"I just told you, didn't I?"

"Then you're hungry. There was only a can of okra. Don't tell me you ate it on bread!"

I wanted to soften her up. I had a feeling that she was frightened, and I had to find out what kind of trouble Buster had gotten her into.

"We ate it with a spoon. It was slimy."

"I imagine. Well, you need something to eat, if that's all you've had.

I've got some groceries down in the boat. I'll bring them up and you can make yourself some dinner."

"Suit yourself," she said in that angry, hectoring voice. "But just keep it in mind nobody asked you for nothin'."

"Get some water heated and you can have a cup of coffee when I come back."

She glared at me for a moment, then turned her back and went into the kitchen. When I left, I heard her angrily rattling among the pans in the closet. Buster was leaning against the wall just outside the door, smoking a cigarette from his cupped hand. I passed him without a word, and he clattered hurriedly down the steps after me.

"Where you goin', George?" he asked, falling in step beside me.

"Worried?" I snapped.

"Ah, now don't be a guy like that, George." He squeezed my arm in what I was supposed to take as a friendly gesture, but he squeezed hard enough to hurt. "What'd she tell you, sport?"

"She said you'd tell me, so go ahead."

"Well, she'll tell you in her own good time, George. That's the way she is. You know how dames are. They get their kicks out of giving you the runaround. You kickin' us out, George?"

It was asked in his ostensibly good-natured, offhand way, but again I could feel the menace under his rumbling voice. And I remembered the gun he had concealed under his shirt.

"I haven't made up my mind," I said deliberately.

"Well, don't let it worry you, George," Buster squeezed my arm again, a little harder this time. "You'll do the right thing when the time comes. It's just like I always say, you ain't the kind of guy that lets your friends down. Hell, I was telling Letty only this afternoon. 'Hell, I said, you take George now, he's a guy you can trust, know what I mean?'" He grinned and gave my arm another squeeze.

I pulled away and faced him. "Listen, Buster, let me tell you something straight. I don't like you. In the first place, you're a small-time crook; and in the second place, you don't have the conscience of a rat trap. You're nothing but a damned pimp the way you peddle Letty around. So if you're in trouble, you bastard, I wouldn't give you the time of day to help you out of it."

His mouth hung open and he kept nodding his head. When I finished, he broke into an immense roar of laughter and slapped me on the shoulder.

"Well, poke my snoot!" he cried with gargantuan delight. "You're okay, George. 'In the first place, I don't like you, Buster!'" he mimicked me gleefully. "Why, you gutty little runt! But just between the two of us, sport," he gave me an enormous, confidential wink and nudged me with his elbow, "what would you do if I got sore and took a swing at you? Ever think of that?"

"Go ahead."

He fairly shook with vast peals of Olympian joy and threw his tremendous arms around me. I wriggled loose and hit him furiously in the ribs, but all he did was ruffle my hair and grin at me.

"Why you peppery, red-headed runt," he said. "I'm nuts about you."

"Go to hell," I said, and walked down the dock to the boat.

Buster ambled after me, singing contentedly to himself, "Get that ti-*guh!* Get that ti-*guh!*" That was the only song I was ever to hear him sing, the only words he ever used. He loved the guttural slam of it, and every once in awhile he would let out a great bellowing laugh and yell, "Yeah-yeah, *get* the lousy runt!"

I had three cartons of meat, vegetables, canned goods and other groceries, all heavy. I piled them one at a time on the dock and went into the cabin to turn off the stern light. When I came out, Buster had picked up all three cartons and was walking easily up the path to the house, howling, "Get that ti-*guh!* Get that ti-*guh! Wow!*"

I let him carry them all the way into the house. If he wanted to show off, let him. He wasn't even breathing hard when he set them down on the kitchen table. The water was boiling furiously on the oil range. I looked around for Letty and Buster said quickly, "She'll be right back, sport." But he wasn't quick enough to cover the groan that came from the bedroom.

He began to talk very fast and lift things out of the cartons and slam them down noisily on the table. "Hell, George, you got enough stuff here for a regular banquet. Just look at the stuff you got, potatoes, chicken, canned pears, soap, pepper 'n' salt ..."

Ignoring him, I walked toward the bedroom. Buster stopped in mid-sentence and followed me silently. Letty was bent over a man on my bed, clumsily trying to wind a bloody bandage around his left shoulder. He moved restlessly, moaning. His face was flushed and his eyes were bright with fever. She didn't know how to handle him, and she must have been hurting him because he pushed weakly at her arm with his right hand and whimpered. This was what they had been concealing from me.

"Let me do that," I said abruptly.

Letty gasped, but immediately set her mouth in a thin line and stepped away from the bed. I unwound the bandage she had tied around him and examined the wound. Just under the shoulder, the fleshy flanges of the armpit were perforated, front and back. It was a bullet hole. Buster and Letty watched me silently as I walked out of the room and went to the kitchen for the hot water and the first aid kit.

When I came back, they were standing exactly where I had left them. I could see that they hadn't said a word to each other. Letty's face was pale and angry, and Buster was expressionless.

I washed the wound. It was clean and there seemed to be no infection. Nevertheless, I sprinkled it with sulfa powder, put a clean dressing on it, and wound it with a fresh bandage.

The man was about as tall as I am and built along the same lean lines. But his hair was more cinnamon than red, his eyes green and close-set where mine were gray, and his mouth thick and heavy. He was breathing shallowly when I finished, and he lay back on his pillow, exhausted. His face was waxy. I straightened up and closed the first aid kit.

"He needs a doctor."

Buster shook his head. "Uh-uh. No can do, George."

"I'm sorry, but I'm going to get a doctor for him. He's lost too much blood."

"He'll get it back."

"Don't be a damn fool! All he has to do is catch a cold and it'll turn into pneumonia in an hour."

"No doctors, George," said Buster flatly. "He ain't gonna catch no cold. We'll keep him covered up. Anyway, Daly's a tough monkey. You couldn't kill that bum with a sixteen-pound sledge." He grinned. "Right, Letty?"

She didn't answer. She looked at me and she looked at Daly and her mouth set more tightly. Letty wasn't going to ask anything of me.

"I'm getting a doctor."

Buster let me get as far as the door. "Go right ahead, George," he drawled. "And while you're at it, get the cops too. Daly's been shot, and the law says the doc has to report all gunshots. So get the doc. It's okay. It's your fun. But just remember, sport, when they stick Daly and Letty in the clink, it's your doings."

He didn't include himself, and that's what stopped me. He had said Letty and Daly, leaving himself out. It caught me off-balance. I had been so sure that he was the one who was in trouble. He knew what I was thinking, too. There was a hard core of shrewdness inside that thick envelope of muscle.

"I'm not the one that's in trouble, George." A laugh insinuated itself into the statement. "That's what you thought, ain't it? But I ain't in no trouble. I'm free as a bird as far as this is concerned. I didn't have nothin' to do with it. Ask Letty if you don't believe me. Go ahead, ask her."

I hesitated, and turned slowly. His face was bland. "Is that the truth, Letty?" I asked.

"He ain't in no trouble." Her voice was stony and uncompromising.

"And on top of that, George," Buster smiled benevolently, "Letty might be in trouble and all that, but it ain't no fault of hers either. That's the honest truth. She was just dumb, that's all."

I looked at Daly. I didn't dare look at Letty. If I had looked at her then, I wouldn't have been able to make any sort of decent decision. I went over to the bed and picked up Daly's right arm. His pulse was steady and not too weak. There wasn't any of the flutter and dying-away that it would have had if he were in a really bad way. I knew the wound was clean. And I'd learned that bullet punctures seldom get infected if no outside dirt gets in. He had lost blood, sure, but if we kept him covered and fed him, he'd come out of it without any trouble. He looked strong and tough enough.

Anyway, that's what I told myself.

I was ready to do what they wanted, but still I wanted one word, just one word of reassurance that this wasn't worse than it seemed.

"What happened?" I asked.

Buster knew he had me then. He had seemed relaxed enough, but he must have been keyed up, because I could see the difference immediately. He seemed to get bigger; he expanded. He leaned against the door frame and lighted a cigarette. He blew out a plume of smoke and waved it away from his face with the palm of his hand. He grinned ingenuously, as if he were just a little surprised and really couldn't figure out what the fuss was all about, but was willing to explain, if only to indulge my whim.

"When you get right down to it, George," he said, "it really ain't nothin' at all. Daly was a damn fool and got himself shot. I ain't got no sympathy for him."

Now Buster was putting himself on my side. Daly was the real culprit. He had gotten himself shot and it served him right. The suggestion was that if Letty were not involved, Buster would have been more than willing to turn him over to the police and let him take his medicine. I was perfectly right in wanting to call in the cops, and Buster wanted to be the first to admit it. Maybe I was reading something into his attitude that wasn't there, but I don't think so. He was crafty and smart, and he concealed it well behind that good-natured, happy-go-lucky front he had.

"Honest, George," he said, "I could have wrung his neck."

The story was just about what I expected. Buster and Letty had gone to Tampa to meet Daly. They had a fair bankroll, but a run of bad luck in a crap game took all but about sixty dollars. That night Letty was out in the car with Daly while Buster stayed in the hotel room. Daly was in a bad humor because Buster had given him only five of the sixty dollars. He stopped at a gin mill and told Letty he was going in for a bottle of rum. She got out of the car to stretch.

Then she heard a shot and Daly came running from the gin mill, panting, "Get us the hell out of here!" He was bleeding from the left shoulder and she thought he had gotten into a fight. He was always getting into fights. She jumped into the driver's seat and gunned the car. Then they picked up Buster and got out of town and fled to my place on Little Brother Key. They hid the car in the palmetto, and Buster walked out to Rossiter's Bait & Boats dock and bought the dinghy for thirty dollars. After it got dark, they rowed out to the Key.

"The damn fool," said Buster, "he was half soused and tried to hold up that gin mill. If he wasn't half dead, I'd kick his ass from here to Hoboken for getting Letty mixed up in it. Here, read this yourself if you don't believe me."

He took his wallet from his hip pocket, plucked a newspaper clipping from it and handed it to me with the reproachful air of a man who had been wrongfully accused of rape, rapine, and murder. It had been torn from the Sanibar *Herald*. I recognized the type-face they used in their heads, a bold, modern letter.

BARKEEP STYMIES
HOLDUP ATTEMPT

TAMPA, Feb. 5—A fast-thinking, fast-acting Tampa bartender last night foiled a holdup try by a red-headed gunman and his blonde moll.

Joe Caputo was quietly tending bar in Joe's Tavern, 779 Palmero St. last night at approximately 9:30 p.m. when a tall, spare, red-headed man walked in, waved a revolver and announced, "This is a holdup."

The customers froze with their hands on their beer glasses, but not Joe. Uttering an outraged roar, he scooped a gun from the cash register, a Colt .38 Bankers Special, and, closing his eyes, turned loose a volley of hot lead, putting three holes in the ceiling and smashing the glass in the front door.

The amazed bandit fled, but not before bystanders were able to obtain a full description of both him and his tall, good-looking, blonde girl friend. According to Detective Lieutenant James P. Helm, who was assigned to the case, the distinctive pair, believed to be fleeing for the Georgia line, will not get out of Florida.

Joe swears that every shot took effect, wounding the gunman several times in the chest and abdomen, but Lt. Helm was less optimistic.

"He was probably unhurt," he said, "but state and county police have been alerted, and it is unlikely that they will be able to get through the road blocks."

An early arrest, he said, is expected.

Today, Joe is serving beer as fast as he can pull the taps, and is proudly exhibiting the gun with which he routed the dangerous pair.

The reporter had treated the holdup attempt with cynical levity, but the fact remained that if the police caught up with Letty and Daly, there wouldn't be anything funny about the state prison at Raiford.

"There it is in black and white, George," said Buster, "just like I told you."

"Tell him the rest of it," said Letty stolidly.

"The rest of what, baby?"

"How you and Daly had it all made up to turn Jeff here over to the cops to take the heat off Daly. Go ahead, tell him about that."

"She's talking through her hat, George," said Buster easily.

"Am I, am I?" She looked angrily at me. "That's what they had all made up. When Daly got better they were gonna scram out of here and turn you in to the cops on account of you look like Daly, red hair and all. And that dumb bartender wouldn't know the difference and you'd take the rap and Daly wouldn't have nothin' to worry about."

"She's kidding you, George," Buster laughed. "She's taking you for a ride. Nobody could get away with nothin' like that, and you know that as much as I do. Hell, you don't look nothin' like Daly."

But I did look like Daly, in a way, and they could get away with it.

"I don't care what you do," Letty told me indifferently. "I just wanted to let you know, that's all. Now you know the score and if you let us stay, I don't want no kickbacks later."

"You can stay," I said.

Her eyes blazed. "Oh, hell," she snapped, "you're dumber than I thought!" Then she turned and walked out of the room.

Buster stared after her and then looked at me, his round blue eyes like cornflowers, the picture of innocent astonishment. He threw up his hands and shook his head helplessly. It was just too much for him. He couldn't cope with it. He was just a poor, benighted male, and it was all beyond him.

"That's the way it goes, George," he said sympathetically. "You can't live with 'em and you can't live without 'em, and ain't it the truth?"

I was sick of him. "Beat it."

"Huh?"

"Beat it. I'm going to stay with Daly. If he gets worse, I'm going for a doctor."

"Oh sure, George, sure." He stopped in the doorway and looked back slyly over his shoulder. "Anything you say. You're the doctor, sport."

I stayed with Daly until about three in the morning. He'd had a terrific sweat, I'd kept him bundled in blankets, and suddenly it was all over. He sighed, turned over, buried the side of his face in the pillow and began to breathe evenly and slowly, stretching out comfortably. I felt his forehead. It was cool and normal. He was all right, but I felt like a rag. I went out into the living room. Buster was lying on his back snoring on the sofa. I poured myself a drink from the rum bottle on the cypress table and looked down at him. Even asleep, he looked powerful and impregnable, carved from a granite that resembled flesh, and not at all defenseless, the way most people look when they're asleep.

"But you're not fooling me ... sport," I said heavily. "You're not getting away with a thing."

I looked in the other bedroom and Letty was curled up with the blanket pulled to her chin, but her magnificent, full-thighed legs were uncovered. There was a hot, acrid tightness in my throat when I backed out of the room.

I went down to the beach and stripped off my clothes. I swam in the somnolent water of the Gulf for about a half-hour before I walked to the boat, opened the bunk in the cabin, and lay down. Dawn was seeping into the sky before I fell asleep.

CHAPTER NINE

I awakened the next morning about eleven o'clock with a vague feeling of apprehension. Just as if I had done something reprehensible the night before and was about to be punished for it, though I couldn't quite remember what it was I had done. At some time or other, everybody wakes up with a feeling like that, of something dire impending, but I've found that it usually goes away after a bromo, a tomato juice and tabasco or some other hangover remedy.

Of course I wasn't fully awake, so I lay there in the bunk worrying about it. It was several minutes before it came to me that I was doing nothing more or less than feeling sore about Letty, Buster and Daly being up at the house—and feeling guilty about it, too.

I should have kicked them out. I know that. They were the kind of people who'd mess up the lives of everybody with whom they came in contact. This amoral, rootless, violent existence they led, without conscience or regret, was corrosive; the whole thing would wind up with their destroying themselves. I don't mean crime doesn't pay or anything like that—that's for the women's clubs, editorial writers, and other unenlightened cynics. Maybe I don't know what I mean, exactly, but I had a feeling and when you aren't very bright, feelings are very important.

I made my own breakfast on the *Skidoo* and spent the rest of the morning cleaning the boat, tuning the motors, fussing around—and thinking. Thinking about how I ever let myself get mixed up with this bunch of crooks. I had better sense than to let myself be played for a fool. I knew that and a lot of other things, but I was confused.

I couldn't think straight even about Letty. I had never felt about any other woman the way I felt about her. All I had to do was just say "Letty" to myself, and a terrific charge went through me. So as long as she was there, I knew I wasn't going to kick anybody out.

I had lunch, washed up, and it was a little after one o'clock when I walked up the path to the house, high on the rocky spine of the Key. There was a cluster of cabbage palms at the foot of the porch steps and in the shade of these, Daly was sitting in a canvas sling chair. He was wearing a pair of my sun glasses and he looked very pale and tired. Buster was sitting cross-legged in the sand with my underwater spear gun in his lap. Letty wasn't anywhere to be seen. I felt both glad and disappointed, because I was in bad humor. Buster heard my footsteps crunch on the shell walk, and he looked up with a grin splitting his round, hard face.

"Hi, George." He held up the spear gun. "What's this gizmo for?"

"Fish," I said curtly.

Daly took off my dark glasses. He turned painfully in the chair, stared at me, and addressed Buster in a weak but malevolent voice. "Who's this joker?"

"Ain't you got no manners, Daly?" Buster said reproachfully. "Were you brung up or dragged up? This is the guy that owns the place. He's the landlord. George meet George. This is George, George, George— George." He guffawed, enjoying himself hugely and watching slyly to see what we were going to do.

"The name's Jeff, not George," I said angrily.

And Daly glowered at Buster and snarled, "What the hell are you talking about?"

Buster grinned and waved his hand at us. "You look alike. Mike and Ike, they look alike. Ham and eggs, bread and butter, Georgie-Schmorgie." He beamed happily upon us. "The Gold Dust Twins." He was very pleased with himself.

The effect of this was that Daly and I glared at each other like enemies, opposite sides of the same coin. Maybe we did look somewhat alike, but I didn't think so and neither did Daly. And both of us were infuriated by the comparison. Daly turned on Buster, showing his teeth in the most animal-like snarl I have ever seen on a human face.

"Aaah, the hell with that!" he said viciously.

"When did you break your glasses, grandpa?" I used the same tone.

As far as I was concerned, Daly was a rat-faced, smalltime chiseler, with a big idea of himself. I had a fair idea what he thought about me; in his own eyes, he was a very tough monkey and I was a hick and looked like a hick. We were never going to get along with each other no matter what happened. It was a case of hate at first sight—two hump-backed tom cats with their tails up like flagpoles and growling in their throats.

Then I saw Buster grinning and I knew that this was exactly what he wanted. I couldn't imagine why, but he was very pleased with the mutual enmity he had promoted. Then it came to me that he had a use for both of us, but separately; he didn't want us to get together to compare notes and talk things over. If there was any talking over, he wanted it to be done with him. No matter how much Daly and I disliked each other, he was very sure he could keep us tame enough for his purposes. He was a crafty son of a bitch.

And then, too, I remembered what Letty had blurted the night before. About Buster and Daly making it up between them that when Daly was well enough to travel, they were going to turn me in. I was to take the rap for Daly's attempted holdup of that gin mill in Tampa, so that Daly could run free.

I didn't think Letty was lying, but I didn't entirely believe it either. There were too many factors involved. How, for instance, did Buster know that I didn't have a shock-proof alibi for that night? As a matter of fact, I did. I had been in jail in Donaldston on a charge of being drunk and disorderly. So Buster wouldn't have promoted a scheme like that unless he had something else in mind—something that had nothing to do with framing me. What it came down to then was that, for some reason or other, he had wanted to keep Daly happy. He had a use for Daly and wanted to keep him in line.

I didn't like Daly and I never would (no real reason, just one of those things), but I put on a grin. "Sure, I look like Daly and you look like Lana Q. Turner. So what?"

"Now, George..." Buster began.

"The name is Jeff from now on."

"Well sure, sport. Anything you say. You're the landlord." His face was a mask of innocent contrition. He lifted the spear gun. "Just what the hell is this thing, sport?"

"It's an underwater gun."

"Well I'll be damned. I been trying to figure it out for an hour. Underwater, eh? For fish you said?"

"That's right."

"You dive down and shoot 'em?"

"Yes."

Daly looked at the gun, sneering, his eyes were thinly contemptuous. "Aaah, hell," he said with disgust, "why don't you clowns grow up?"

Buster pulled back the live rubber tubing, notched the spear and, grinning, shot it into the sand at Daly's feet. The shaft sank in over fifteen inches and quivered from the lethal propulsive force.

Daly jumped in alarm. "Don't point that damn thing at me, you jerk!"

Buster reached out and pulled the spear from the sand. He looked at the razor-sharp barb and smiled. "This'd go right through a guy, would it, George? I mean Jeff."

"It's not a toy," I spoke sharply. "Don't aim it at people!"

"Jerk!" Daly glared, looking uneasily at the spear in Buster's huge hands. "You damn fool, cancha see I'm sick? What's the matter with you? I'm sick, so cut it out!" There was a whine in his voice and he huddled in his chair, looking a little sicker than he had a few minutes ago. "If you think it's a joke getting a bullet in you, go out and try it yourself sometime. Hell, Bus, with you around, a guy can't even die in peace."

Buster didn't laugh, but he was close to it. There was no sympathy for Daly in his eyes. "When you kick off, sport, I'll send you a wreath." He stood up, stretched, and gazed out at the placid water of the Gulf. "I think I'll take a swim in the ocean and shoot me some fish."

He ambled down the beach. Daly swore after him.

"Who the hell's gonna help me if I gotta go to the john?" he called. "Dammit, Bus, I'm sick. You can't leave me like this. Suppose I start to bleed or something. What're you tryin' to do, kill me? You don't leave a guy alone with a bullet in him."

He was really frightened. He didn't want Buster to leave him, but there was more to it than that. The fact that a man could fire a gun and actually shoot him seemed to have scared the pants off him. He was cocky and had never believed that anything could ever happen to him. To other men, yes, but not to Daly. He probably had his own kind of toughness, but he wasn't bone-tough or marrow-tough; he was just skin-tough.

Buster continued to walk down the beach, not even looking back, and Daly cursed him wildly.

"You don't have a bullet in you," I said finally. He looked at me stupidly. "It went right through. All you have is a flesh wound, and not a very bad one at that."

"What the hell do you know about it? I could bleed to death."

"I bandaged you up last night. The wound's all right. You don't have anything to worry about unless you keep jumping around like a damn fool and tear the wound open."

Daly was visibly relieved. He sat back carefully in his chair as if he were very precious and fragile, but wouldn't break if he treated himself with tender solicitude.

He had found his voice. "Hell, if you bandaged me, they can start sendin' flowers right now." He had recovered enough to sneer, "Beat it! Go on, scram. Every time I look at you I wanna puke!"

I thought it about time I set him straight. "Listen, this is my place. I own it, and the minute I think you're able to travel, I'm kicking you off. Or maybe sooner. Understand?"

"Don't make me laugh, jerk," said Daly nastily. "I told you to beat it."

I didn't bother answering him. Sooner or later we were going to have trouble, but not until his wound got better. And, I thought, that wouldn't be for awhile yet. I looked down the beach. Buster had taken off his clothes and was wading, naked, into the water. Man, he was big. He looked bigger without his clothes than he did with them on. He was massive.

He didn't have the build of an athlete nor the obvious, knotty muscles of a professional weight-lifter, but he was thick, solid, and heavy. I had the impression that nothing could ever hurt him. He plunged into the water and swam out into the Gulf with a clumsy side stroke. He didn't swim very fast, but with his strength, he could swim forever.

Letty came out of the house, but stopped on the porch when she saw me standing below. Then she walked steadily down the steps, her lips thin and pressed together. There was something eating her, and I thought it about time I found out what it was. Her mouth was surly, but this was my day for taking the bull by the horns or whatever you want to call it.

"Did you have a good sleep, Letty?" I asked, friendlily.

"All right," she said and looked at Daly. "How you feelin'?"

"How do you think?" he snapped.

"It hurt?"

"Don't ask dumb questions!"

"Anything you want me to get you?"

"Get me a shot of rum."

She turned and walked up the stairs. Daly looked at me. "When I get better, jerk," he promised, "and I tell you to beat it, you'll beat it."

"Or else?" I said sarcastically.

"Yeah, or else."

"Says you?"

"Yeah, says me."

"That's what I thought," I smiled.

The whole thing was worse than silly because I kept underestimating him, forgetting that he was also underestimating me. Also I had the idea that just because I happened to own the house and the Key, they were going to play this my way.

Letty came down from the house with the rum bottle and a water tumbler. "Now go ahead and get yourself stinko again," she said, handing them to Daly. "Maybe this time you'll get your head shot off."

"Drop dead."

He poured an extra large dollop of rum into the glass, just to show her he was his own boss. He drank it down and sneered at her over the rim of the glass.

"Take another one," she said. "Get good and stinko. Jeez, if I fed your brains to the birds they'd starve to death."

He cursed her obscenely. This time it was she who said, "Drop dead," but otherwise Letty didn't seem to mind being talked to like that. I found out later that this was the way they talked to each other all the time. I never got used to it or the fact that they didn't seem to mind the most violent insults. That's where they had the advantage over me. They understood me after a fashion, but I didn't understand them at all.

I wanted to take Daly by the shirtfront and stuff his foul mouth with sandspurs, but something told me to stay out of it. For once I was right. After a few more insults, the whole thing petered out and Letty started down the beach.

"I think I'll take a walk."

I wanted to talk to her alone. "I'll go with you."

"I can't stop you," she said indifferently.

As we scuffed through the fine white sand, she muttered, mostly to herself, "I shouldn't of given him the bottle. He gets mean when he's stinko."

I glanced back. Daly was watching me with quivering, vicious hatred.

CHAPTER TEN

We walked in silence on the firm sand near the water's edge, and the little sandpipers ran ahead of us like mechanical toys. Letty kept her eyes straight front and didn't look at me or acknowledge in any way that I was walking beside her.

"So that's George Daly," I said after a while. "The guy I'm supposed to look like."

"You do."

"I never looked like that in my life. He looks like a fox terrier with a toothache. His face comes to a point."

Her eyes glinted sideways at me, but her expression didn't change. "That's the way you look when you're sore."

"You're thinking of two other guys."

"You look *exactly* like him."

Letty meant it, and I thought, dammit, I don't have any more vanity than anybody else, but the last person in the world I wanted to look like was George Daly.

"What do you think you are, too good, or somethin'?" she burst out resentfully.

I stopped, took her arm, and turned her so that she faced me. "What are we fighting about, Letty?"

"I'm not fighting. Maybe you are, but I'm not."

"You've been standing me off ever since last night, Letty. What's the matter?"

"Let's not go into *that!*" she said flatly.

"I want to go into it. I want to find out what's the matter. That night when we—"

"I must of been nuts that night," she said angrily. "I must of been stinko. I'm nobody's pushover, brother!"

"I know you're not, Letty."

"And if you must know, I'm the one that made Buster pull up his socks and get out of the motel that night. And I didn't leave you a note either. I didn't want to see you ever again."

"Why not, honey?"

I tried to tilt her chin to me with my hand, but she pulled away with a jerk of her head. The whole thing was in her face now—angry pride, resentment, shame.

"That was only the second time I ever made love with a guy in my whole life," she said bitterly, "and believe me, brother, it's the last till I see it signed on the dotted line!"

I suddenly wanted her so fiercely and completely. "All right, honey. Let's get married then."

She stared at me incredulously. "You're nuts!"

Letty looked completely confused. I don't think she'd ever had an offer of marriage in her life. It was the last thing she expected from me.

"I really mean it, honey." And I did. I wanted her wholly, and nothing less would be enough anymore.

She stared long and hard into my face. Slowly the suspicion and resentment drained out of hers, still leaving the incredulity.

"You—you mean it?" she stammered.

"I mean it, honey."

She looked first to one side and then to the other. Her hands made small, formless gestures of bewilderment. Finally she mumbled, "I can't leave Buster now. He's broke." Then she added quickly, "But he didn't bring me here to work on you this time, honest, Jeff."

"Will you marry me, honey?"

Letty pulled back into her shell. "I don't know. I never thought much about getting married. Seen too much of it. Guys cheatin' every chance they get, the wife gettin' hers on the side, too, and a mess of kids rollin' around on the floor. Nuts."

"Think it over, honey. It doesn't have to be like that."

"Okay. I'll think it over." Then she went on defensively, "But this isn't buying you a thing, remember that. This wouldn't be the first time a guy used that line to get in."

Dammit, I wanted to take her in my arms and soothe the years of accumulated resentment and suspicion out of her. But it wasn't the right time for that; it wouldn't have helped.

"It isn't a line. I'll ask you again, later on." It was hard to keep my hands off her. Hard not to kiss her, remembering the passionate pressure of her lips against mine, the violence and completeness of her magnificent body and—oh, the terror and the winging infinity that was in it, too! "Let's just walk, Letty," I said.

We walked. A stately echelon of serious pelicans swept by overhead. The feeding gulls on the sand waddled away like fussy old men as we approached, breaking into flight and uttering hoarse, exasperated cries when we got too close. The sky was blue and faraway and white crabs scuttled out from underfoot, their legs going so fast they looked like sewing machines. Letty walked closer to me. She felt soft and I knew the stiff hostility had gone out of her.

I felt fine, peaceful, and alive until we came upon the carcasses of five dead grouper rotting on the sand. For some reason or other, I started thinking about George Daly. It bothered me because I had the feeling that there was something about him that I had missed; something that didn't quite square up, and I couldn't figure out what it was. I didn't give a damn about him personally.

As far as I was concerned, he was one of the lesser rodents (this was a mistake) and was more mouse than rat. I knew he couldn't be trusted around the corner with the right time, but that wasn't what bothered me. There was something out of focus and the outlines were blurred. He was in the picture, all right, but there was something else in the picture, too. I couldn't see what it was, and it really bothered me. I don't know why I went off on a tangent like that, walking with Letty, but maybe it was because she was part of the picture too.

I was trying to get it clear when she said anxiously, "What you makin' such a face about, Jeff?"

I didn't quite snap all the way back. "A face?" I said stupidly.

"Yeah. Like it was somethin' you et. What's the matter?"

"There's nothing the matter. I was just thinking about Daly, that's all."

"Him!" she said scornfully.

Something began to tick in the back of my mind. "You don't think much of him, do you?"

Letty moved her shoulders in a slight shrug that might have meant almost anything. "Aaah, he's okay. It's just that he's a jerk when he gets stinko, that's all. You don't wanna pay attention to him. He's all right if you don't take him serious. We been scrappin' for years. We were kids together."

I felt a stab of jealousy. "How long have you known him?"

"Mmm, ten, fifteen years. We lived next door up Secaucus. What a guy, always in trouble. Then one night he busted into the lumber yard and the burglar alarm went off and the cops almost got him. That was when he came down to Tampa." Her smile was fond and she seemed a little amused. "He was always up to somethin'. You never knew what he was gonna do next. What a guy. And Buster's worse."

I looked at her. She was smiling and I knew that her smile enveloped both Buster and Daly. That made two hurdles I had to get over—if I wanted Letty. To make it worse, they were three of a kind and I was the outsider. If there were any kind of showdown now, I knew where her loyalties would be. But I had this on my mind, and I wanted to find out.

"How does Buster feel about him?"

"Buster? I dunno. Okay, I guess. Why?"

"The way he treats Daly, the way he talks to him. I don't think he gives a damn about Daly."

She nodded. "I know what you mean." Letty glanced at me and saw that I was waiting for her to go on. She frowned. "What's this all about anyway?" she demanded. "What're you trying to do, get me to rat on Daly or somethin'? What's goin' on?"

"I'm trying to figure out why Buster brought him here."

"He was shot."

"It's a hell of a long way from here to Tampa."

"The cops were after him, dope."

She was getting angry, but so was I. "If he doesn't give a damn about Daly, why did he take such a chance and drive all the way down here, when Daly could have been hidden out in Tampa much more easily? Hell, the county and state police patrol that highway twenty-four hours a day, so why did Buster stick his neck out like that? If you can make sense out of that, come ahead and let me know."

We faced each other, ready to flare into a knock-down-drag-out fight. A puzzled pucker began to knot up between her brows. Letty looked away and took her full, ripe under-lip between her teeth, her eyes clouding.

"If you think Buster brought me down here to work on you again, well, he didn't say nothin' to me about it, honest, Jeff."

"I think he's got something on his mind."

"I told you they were talking about turning you in for what Daly did …"

"I didn't buy that one."

"I wasn't lying to you!" Her eyes blazed.

Letty was startlingly beautiful when she was angry. It brought out all her primitive, animal force. Her breasts swelled and her full mouth spread with the passion that was in her. There was a crimson, flowering burst inside of me and the next thing I knew, we were wrestling on the sand.

She writhed savagely in my arms, biting and kicking and scratching, and then without any seeming transition it became something else. Though briefly the violence was intensified, that passed too and with it the convulsion of struggle. There weren't two of us anymore.

CHAPTER ELEVEN

After a long interval I became conscious first of blue distance and a whiteness dissolving—a cloud. Of an intimate sound—the Gulf breathing on the gentle sand. Of a caress —Letty breathing beside me, her breasts rising and falling against my side. Of a tenderness—her face soft and defenseless.

I leaned over and kissed her on the corner of the mouth. She stirred and her eyes opened. They were vague and she looked at me for a moment without recognition. Her lips were slightly parted and there was a very young and unformed wonder in her face. I smiled and laid the back of my hand against her cheek. "Hello, darling," I said softly.

Letty stared at me, still uncomprehending. Her lips moved as if framing an uncertain question. Then I saw understanding spread into her face. She gave an inarticulate cry and, in a single steely spring, leaped to her feet. She uttered that wild, lost cry again and, with a full-arm swing, hit me across the face as hard as she could with her open palm. She whirled and ran up the beach with the fleeing speed and lightness of a whippet. I jumped up and pounded after her.

"Letty. Letty, honey!" I called after her.

She plunged into the tangle of sea grape, palmetto, and cabbage palms that crested the Key. I searched for her, calling her name over and over, but she could have been only three feet away from me in that green, leafy maze and I would never have seen her. I gave up and walked heavily back to the beach. There was nothing I could do now except wait.

I plodded gloomily along the shore. The red tide had brought in heaps of dead fish of all kinds at the southern end of the Key. The smell was pretty bad. My eyes watered from it and I began to cough. The fish lay in a wavering row at the high tide mark. I couldn't leave them there. The smell would get worse every day; unless I did something about it, we'd have a plague of carrion flies.

It was horrible, this wanton, senseless destruction, and there was nothing you could do to stop it. The red tide killed everything it touched. It dirtied and spoiled the beaches and drove you back with its stench. All you could do was bury the dead. I turned around and went back to the house for a spade.

Buster and Daly were deep in a wrangling conversation when I walked up, but they broke it off immediately when they saw me. Daly's face was sullen and stubborn, but Buster broke into that big grin of his. He leaped to his feet, holding up a three-foot sand shark by the tail. "Whattaya think of that, sport?" he asked, looking down at it with happy pride. "I shot it with the bow and arrow." The spear gun was leaning against the cabbage palm beside him. "What kind of a fish would you call it anyway?"

"Shark."

He looked astounded. "This little thing? Aaah, you're kiddin'. Sharks're big. They go after people."

"Not very often."

"Well I'll be damned." He shook his head and seemed lost in ingenuous wonderment. "Whattaya think of that, Daly?"

Daly didn't answer as he turned his head away. He looked peevishly stubborn, as if Buster had been trying to make him do something against his will. And he was definitely uneasy, too. I had the feeling that Buster had said something that had really frightened him. He had a cornered expression.

More than ever now, I was sure that Buster had brought Daly to the Key for a reason that had nothing to do with keeping Daly under cover because of that abortive holdup. Buster had something cooking; both Daly and I were ingredients—and probably Letty. I glanced at Daly again. This time I could see that he was really frightened, for he had the desperate look of a man who wanted to flee but couldn't.

"You two have a fight about something?" I asked.

Daly started, but Buster said innocently, "A fight? Where'd you get that idea, sport? I wouldn't fight with a dear old pal like Daly here."

"You were having some kind of scrap when I walked up."

"Not us, sport. Hell, we get along like ham and eggs, don't we, Daly? Tell the man."

"I wouldn't tell that clown what way was up," Daly snapped.

"Listen to me," I said sharply to Buster. "This man's been hurt and he's a long way from being over it. I don't give a damn about him personally, but as long as he's in this house and sick, I want you to leave him alone. He needs rest and quiet. Understand?"

Buster's eyes narrowed and he looked quickly from me to Daly. "Buddies, eh? Pals. Since when is this?"

"Since no time. I'd do as much for a sick goat. If you feel like scrapping with somebody, scrap with me and not with a man who's too sick to take it."

"Aaah, the hell with both of you!" Daly jeered, but his eyebrows settled more stubbornly.

I was satisfied with that. If I could make it a little tougher for Buster, maybe I could break up his scheme before he got it started. Now I went over and got the spade out from under the porch steps.

"I have to bury a mess of dead fish," I told Buster. "Come along and give me a hand."

"Some other time, sport. I feel a nap coming on."

He knew what I had done with Daly all right, and he didn't like it. He was grinning lazily, but his eyes were cold. He didn't like opposition.

"Well, tomorrow you're getting out there with a shovel. If you're going to stay here, you're going to do some of the work, too." I walked away.

I hadn't gone fifty feet when Daly's voice rose querulously, "Now cut it out, damn it. I'm sick. I ain't got nothin' to say, so forget about it!"

I grinned to myself, turned, and yelled back, "That's all, Buster. Come on, on your feet! We got work to do. Your nap'll have to wait till tonight."

To my surprise, he came shambling down the incline, shaking his head with mock reproach at my inhumanity.

"Ain't you got no mercy, George?" he grumbled. "Ain't you got no feelings?"

"The name's Jeff, remember?"

"Sure I do. I'm sorry, sport. Sometimes I think I got a brain like a sieve. But I won't forget it again—Jeff. I got it straight now. It's Jeff, like in the Jefferson Reform School in Newark. Right, sport?"

"Is that where you graduated from?"

"Nope. I never got reformed." He laughed and was the big, bumbling happy-go-lucky, All-American boy again, his favorite role. "But you know something, sport? I'd watch that mutt Daly, if I was you. He's got his eye on Letty."

"So what?"

"W-e-l-l, he's not a guy you'd trust with a dame, know what I mean? He's got a bad name." He watched me slyly. "And on top of that, he's got a way with dames, too. They go for him."

"Well, well."

"And he don't like it that you're going around with Letty. He's jealous as hell. But don't worry about it. The next time he gets snotty, just tell him off. Don't let him talk to you like he does, Jeff boy. You let him get away with too much, and you can't do that with a guy like Daly or he'll walk all over you. He's just a mutt and you got to slap him down once in awhile."

"Okay. I'll go right back and give him a poke in the snoot."

"You think I'm lying?"

"You're damn right I do."

He sighed. "You're a hard man, Jeff, but I love you."

"I'll bet. You wouldn't still be thinking about running liquor up from Cuba in my boat, would you?"

"Nope. That's dead and done for. I figured it out for myself. No percentage in it."

"It's something new, then."

He stopped and folded his arms across his great chest and there was something hard and cold and deadly about him. "Look, sport, you keep your nose out of my business and I'll keep mine out of yours. Okay?"

"This place is mine. Everything that goes on here is my business."

"This is something that ain't got nothin' to do with you. It's just between me and Daly."

"Then let it wait till you get off the Key, or I'll kick the whole lot of you off right now."

His neck swelled, and I gripped the shovel, ready to lay it on the side of his head if he came at me. It was close, very close, for I could see the fury pulse in his throat. I felt suddenly breathless and the shovel seemed as flimsy as a violin bow in my hands. It would have taken a crowbar to stop a mountain of muscle like Buster, once it moved. Fear shriveled my mouth. I stepped back, but he burst into a ragged, jarring laugh and threw up his hands in a short, hard gesture that broke the tension.

"Aaah, what the hell! This is dumb. Let's go bury them dead fish of yours."

"All right, but remember what I said."

"Okay, sport, okay."

Nothing had been settled, and nobody had capitulated. It was a momentary truce, and that was all. But we walked up the beach, and in a little while he was singing. "Get that ti-*guh!* Get that ti-*guh!*" Everything was fine. Nothing had happened. We were just taking a stroll at the seashore in the sunshine.

We worked all afternoon. I dug a long trench in the sand above the high water mark, and he shoveled the dead fish into it with a six-foot plank of driftwood that he had found. He worked hard and cheerfully, and we got three times as much done as if I had worked alone. It was sundown when we walked back to the house. As we climbed the porch steps, Buster raised his head and sniffed. There was the rich odor of roasting pork in the air.

"That's for me," he said with satisfaction. "Nothing like a little work to give you an appetite, right, Jeff boy?" He slapped me heartily on the shoulder. "Letty now, she's a dame she can really cook that meat."

He went into the bathroom and I walked to the kitchen. Letty was standing at the sink, peeling potatoes. She knew I was there, but she didn't turn around.

"I looked for you," I said.

She turned on the faucet and washed the potatoes. "You better change your clothes. You stink like dead fish." Her voice was stolid, neither friendly nor hostile—the voice of a busy housewife who didn't want to be bothered with casual visitors in her kitchen.

"About this afternoon, honey," I started. "Please, don't think I ..."

"Will you please do me the favor of getting out of here in those clothes? You're stinking up the whole supper!" Irritably, she cut the potatoes in halves and threw them into a pot.

"I'll talk to you later then," I went on, trying to get a positive reaction from her.

"And wash yourself, too. You ain't sittin' at the same table with me, smellin' like that. It makes me sick to my stomach!"

"Don't forget to mash the potatoes, honey. I'm crazy about mashed potatoes and gravy."

"Oh, damn you!" Letty hurled a potato at me.

I caught it, grinning, and tossed it back to her, underhand. "And I'm crazy about you, too." But this time I got out of there, leaving on a friendly note. *Mine.*

The shower was roaring in the bathroom and Buster was bellowing to the world at large to "Get that ti-*guh!*" Reflecting that he was probably the last person on earth who would need help in getting that ti-*guh*, I went into my bedroom for a change of clothes.

Daly was lying on my bed, smoking. He had on all his clothes, including his shoes, and there were cigarette ashes all over the blanket, sheet and pillowcase, and down the front of his shirt. The rum bottle was on the night stand beside the bed, but there wasn't much gone out of it. He looked sick, but that was his own fault. He should have spent the whole day in bed.

"How do you feel?" I asked, going to the clothes closet.

"Who cares?" he snarled, but the snarl was feeble. He was feeling sorry for himself.

I laid out a change of underwear, a fresh shirt and slacks. "I want to take another look at that bullet hole after dinner." I shook my head. "You don't look so good. Here, let me take your pulse."

"Drop dead, willya?" he snapped, but held up his arm.

I felt the pulse in his wrist. It was a little fast, but that was natural at the end of a day. It was strong enough. I gave my head a little shake, however, and went to the chest of drawers for a pair of socks.

"Well, what about it?" Daly asked anxiously, sitting up.

"I'm going to speak frankly, but I don't want you to worry." I cleared my throat. "You're not doing so well."

I wanted to needle him. I wanted him to get good and worried about himself so that he'd scream every time Buster got within six feet of him. In a few days he'd be well enough to leave the Key, and I was damn well going to speed him on his way. But in the meanwhile I was going to fix it so he and Buster didn't hatch any vulture eggs on my property.

He licked his pale lips. "What the hell you talkin' about, jerk?"

"I can't help you, Daly, if you won't help yourself. Neither could the best doctor in the country. For one thing, you let yourself get too excited."

"Who's excited!" He tried to sneer, but it didn't come off.

"You are. Right this minute. And do you know what excitement does? It sends your pulse rate up and, in your case, that could be fatal." I shook my head. "You've got to take care of yourself, Daly."

"I am. What the hell do you think I'm doing?"

"Good. Just don't let anything excite you, that's all. I'll give that wound another examination after dinner." As I gathered up my clothes, he lay back on the bed and was anxiously trying to find his pulse with his thumb. I knew he had been feeling low before, but now he obviously felt twice as low. Buster ambled in just before I left.

"Now don't excite him, Buster," I said solemnly. "He's really in a bad way."

He grinned. "Ah, you're a cute son of a bitch, Jeff boy," he said without rancor. "But don't worry, sport. I wouldn't think of exciting the poor mutt. All you got to do is look at him to see he's on his last legs. But tell me somethin', pal. What'd you stick on that wound of his last night—arsenic?"

Daly looked startled.

"Sulfa," I said. "He's healing fine, but he has to take care of himself."

I walked off to the bathroom and heard Daly say feebly, "Leave me alone for once, willya, Bus?" Then Buster's reassuring answer, "Sure, Daly boy, but where's it hurt the most?"

I took a shower and dressed. When I came out, Letty had the table set in the alcove that over-looked the beach. Daly joined us for dinner, which surprised me until Buster murmured something about his having to keep up his strength. Daly was the perfect invalid. He had a talent for it. He limped across the room, sat down weakly and slumped in his chair. I think he was tough enough in a wolfish way when he was well, but physical ills and pains scared him because it shook his faith in his own invincibility.

I wanted to sit next to Letty, but she brusquely ordered Buster and Daly into the chairs at opposite sides of the table, which left me at one end and her at the other. Nobody said very much during the meal. The food was excellent. Letty was a good cook on the plain and hearty side. Buster ate noisily and with gusto, scooping great forkfuls of potatoes, meat and string beans into his mouth, but somehow or other the method suited him. He was a powerful animal, and you'd sooner have expected a bear to eat with politesse.

Daly was something different. He hunched over the table, his left arm out of its sling and curled around his plate greedily on guard. He shoveled the food into his mouth as fast as he could go, snapping at each fork load as it came up from his plate.

Letty kept her eyes on her plate and barely picked at her food. It was a long while before I realized that she was very self-conscious and was trying to use her knife and fork with painful correctness. Her face was pinched and strained. With a start I saw that there was a terrible struggle going on inside her. Part of her belonged to the feral, animal world of Buster and Daly, but the other part wanted to be free of it.

She was on the balance between the two, and at this point it would take no more than a nudge to tip her one way or the other.

I caught Buster staring at her for a second. "Hey, you ain't eatin' nothin', baby," he said. "Got a gut ache or somethin'?"

"Mind your own business for once, will you?" she snapped back at him.

A little later on, when I asked her to pass the bread, her eyes flashed at me. "Are you a cripple? You can reach it."

Daly got his, too. He splashed gravy on the table cloth, and she looked at him with disgust. "Dammit, I can't eat with slobs!" She jumped up and strode into the kitchen, and Daly yelled after her, "Slob yourself!" I kept my mouth shut.

After dinner, I cleared off the dishes and took them out to the kitchen, but she wasn't there. I glanced through the window and saw her sitting in the darkness on the railing of the back porch, smoking a cigarette. While I washed the dishes and put them away, a match flared three times as she lit one cigarette after another.

I went back into the living room. Daly was still sitting at the table. His face was sick, but he managed to give me a venomous glance.

"I'll look at that shoulder of yours now, Daly."

He showed his teeth. "The hell you will!"

"I have to change the band—"

"I'll change it myself!"

I didn't get it till I remembered what Buster had said about putting arsenic in his wound. Oh, hell, I thought, the damn fool can't believe that. But evidently he did.

"Listen, Daly, if I tampered with that hole in your shoulder last night, you'd have been flat on your back by this time. Use your head ..."

"Nuts!"

Buster came in from the front porch with the spear gun, which he leaned against the wall beside the door.

"Hey, remember what the doc here said," he grinned at Daly. "You gotta watch that excitement. Now if I was you ..."

"And you can shove it, too!" Daly yelled at him.

Buster clucked his tongue and shook his head. "Calm yourself, Daly. You don't wanna die young, do you? Say, Jeff boy, how's about a game of rummy? That hadn't ought to be too exciting for the patient."

"Some other time. I'm going down to the boat."

"So early, sport? How come?"

"See you in the morning."

I got as far as the door when Daly's voice stopped me. He didn't yell or snarl. His voice was just edged and thin. "You ain't goin' noplace, jerk."

I turned. He was crouched in his chair and in his hand was a gun. His arm rested on his knee and the gun was very steady. I started to say something—I don't know what—and, incredulously, I saw the mad gleam of murder in his eyes. I stood there with my mouth open.

"You ain't goin' no place," he repeated a little wildly. "And 'specially you ain't goin' to the cops. Shut that door."

Very carefully, I shut the door. I glanced at Buster, and he looked as incredulous as I was. But Daly went on snarling at me.

"And you been tryin' to make time with Letty, and that's done, too. You, Bus, get somethin' to tie him up. From now on he ain't movin' out of my sight." He swung the gun toward Buster. "*Move!*"

When Daly turned on Buster, he gave me the fraction of a second in which to snatch up the spear gun from beside the door. I didn't have time to cock it, and I prayed that he wouldn't notice.

"Now what?" I said with a confidence I didn't feel. "Who's got who covered?"

Daly's jaw dropped and he shrank back into his chair.

Buster jumped between us. "Get out!" he said sharply to me. "Go on, Jeff!"

I opened the door and stepped out to the porch. I was shaking when I got to the bottom of the steps. It takes something out of you to face a sick, half-mad, frightened man with nothing but an uncocked spear gun in your hands. And I've never been much of a hero.

I walked over to the dense shadows of the cabbage palm cluster, sat down, and lighted a cigarette. In about ten minutes, the door opened behind me and Buster came down the steps. He saw the gleam of my cigarette. He put a match to one of his own and hunkered down in the sand beside me.

"You did a good job on him," I said. "What'd you tell him back there in the bedroom—that I was going to poison him and then call out the state guard?"

"You didn't do such a bad job yourself. He's got so, now, that he don't trust nobody, not even Letty. How's that hole in his shoulder, bad?"

"He'll live, worse luck."

"But you said somethin' about having to change the bandage."

"He'll get along."

"Good." He sounded relieved. "I got him calmed down for now anyway. I told him you couldn't turn him in to the cops without turning Letty in, too. And that's a fact, sport. Keep it in mind."

"I've kept it in mind. That's the only reason I haven't kicked you and him off this Key."

"And here's something else to keep in mind, sport. We've let it go so long now that, if you do run to the cops, we're all in the soup—me and you, too."

"Nuts."

I half rose, and he put out his hand and pushed me back against the tree.

"Wait a minute, sport. We're still friends, understand? But I been thinking, too. Hell," he went on irritably, "there's so damn much thinking goin' on around here, you'd think it was a book factory. Daly sits around thinking, you sit around thinking, Letty's moping on the back stoop, and now I've started it. But in my case, I got somewhere. That's the difference."

"Tell me all about it, Buster."

"Sure. But we're still friends, remember. Now here's the way it figures out. If it comes to a showdown, it's just your word against the three of us, and don't think Letty won't play along with me. She will. We could say we had this hideout all set with you beforehand; and on top of that, we could say this isn't the first time. We could say you turned us in because you got sore about your split. There are a couple jobs the cops're just aching to get their hands on Daly for. Now I ain't saying any of this is gonna happen, sport, but you can see for yourself how it might figure out."

"Man," I said, "that wouldn't stop me for a minute."

He flipped his cigarette out over the beach and watched the tip explode in a flurry of sparks. "You sure like to make it tough for yourself," he said thoughtfully. "In more ways than one."

I pushed myself to my feet, and this time he didn't try to stop me. "The next time ..." I started to say, but he broke in with, "There won't be any *next* time, sport. That's all there is, there ain't no more. You're in and there ain't no back doors out."

"Don't scare me," I said, and walked up the beach. He didn't call after me.

It wasn't until I was about two hundred yards away that I remembered the spear gun. I wanted it. It wasn't the most effective weapon in the world, but at short range it could be pretty deadly. I walked back to the group of cabbage palms at the foot of the porch steps, but when I got there, the spear gun was gone and so was Buster. The lights were still on in the house and I could hear voices,

Buster's and Daly's. I listened but couldn't hear Letty's.

"And I don't want to hear no more about it, Bus," Daly was saying with shrill finality. "All you wanna do is get your ass in a sling and mine, too, so forget it!"

Buster's voice rumbled calmly, and Daly answered, "Aaah, shove it. I'm goin' to bed."

I saw him limp past the lighted living room window, stoop-shouldered, holding his left arm to his chest with his right. There was a sick stubbornness in him, yes, but what chance did he have against the inexorable strength of Buster?

But Buster didn't have me on the run. I wasn't sick; I could take care of myself. I knew the score, and I wasn't kidding myself, either.

But, damn it, no matter what you did, he just kept coming at you!

CHAPTER TWELVE

As I walked to the path that led to the dock I could hear the thieving raccoons that lived on the Key scrabbling at the garbage can at the rear of the house. I felt restless. I wanted to go into town and have a few beers with the boys, but after I thought it over for about ten seconds I knew that when I got there it would be the same old thing and not what I wanted at all.

I knew just what would happen. I'd go in for a beer and next to me would be standing some guy who'd been hanging around all evening waiting for somebody to pass a remark. And the next thing you know we'd be swinging at each other like a pair of punch-drunk twelve-year-olds. Tomorrow morning we'd both wake up with a black eye, a fat lip, and a hangover, or maybe I'd even try to fight a half-dozen of them the way I did up in Donaldston.

I was really in a mood, and I figured the best thing for me to do was go to bed and sleep it off. Why go into town and get in any more fights, when I had all the fights I could use right here on the Key. I went aboard the *Skidoo* and made up the bunk in the cabin. As I was undressing, I happened to glance at the window.

With a shock I realized that, with the light on in the cabin, I'd make a beautiful target for anybody out there with a gun. For a minute I was mad enough to go up to the house and have it out with Buster and Daly there and then, but it wouldn't have been very smart. They had guns and I didn't. I let down the venetian blinds over the windows and rocked the cabin door. I went to bed and after awhile I fell asleep.

Then, suddenly, I was wide awake, sitting up in the bunk, holding my breath and listening. I didn't know what had awakened me, but then a board creaked on the dock outside, then another creaked, and another. It was not an illusion. Somebody was walking on the dock right beside the *Skidoo*. I couldn't see through the venetian blinds because the slats were tilted. I waited.

The creaks receded, then came back again. Someone had walked the length of the dock and was returning. I pulled up the blind about an inch and peered out, but it was too dark and shadowed by the massy sea grape and mangrove to see anything. Very quietly, I cranked the big bow light around so that when I switched it on, it would flood the dock. I waited until I heard the boards creak again, then flipped the switch and sprang to the window.

The beam of light shot straight up into the air, lighting nothing. In the dark I had turned the wrong crank. I heard running footsteps, and by the time I got the light turned in the right direction, there was nothing to see. I turned it to and fro, sweeping the path all the way up to the house, but whoever had been out there had probably dived out of sight into the bushes.

A window was raised in the house. "What's goin' on down there?" Buster called.

"I had visitors but they didn't stay for coffee," I called back grimly. "And the next time they come calling, I'll pin a rose on them."

"Are you nuts?"

I turned off the light and went back to my bunk, taking a short-handled gaff with me. It was the only thing I had, but at close quarters I could make it damned unpleasant for anybody who tried to get in the window. I lay there for a long time. The last thing I remember before falling asleep again was a pair of hoot owls telling each other of a doom to come.

I was awake a little after eight the next morning. Without waiting for breakfast, I cast off from the dock, turned the *Skidoo* and headed diagonally across the bay for Sanibar. I couldn't stop myself from glancing back over my shoulder every few minutes.

I was about three hundred yards offshore when Buster came bounding down the path and ran to the edge of the dock. He waved his arms, and something that could have been a gun glinted in his hand. He was bellowing at me, but there was a stiff breeze from the northeast, and it blew the sound of his voice away. I didn't have to hear him, though, to know what he was yelling.

He gestured peremptorily, but I kept right on course. Then he held out his right arm straight in front of him and the sun glinted again on the gun in his hand. I watched for the puff of smoke from the shot, but it didn't come. I watched and he stuck the gun into his waistband and strode angrily up the path. There was going to be some fast talking in the house back there pretty soon.

Twenty minutes later I tied up to the Sanibar municipal dock and walked into town. I had something definite in mind, and the closest place was the Sunshine Loan Company, a hock shop. There were several hand guns displayed in the window, ranging from a pearl-handled .22 to a Colt .45 with a barrel not quite as long as a billiard cue. I looked them over and spotted the one I wanted, a snub-nosed .38, a handy gun that you could get into action without any waste motions.

I went into the shop. Herman Benz, the owner, was arranging a tray of secondhand watches in the showcase. He looked up with a smile. Herman always had a smile, and for the best reason in the world, I suppose. He was on the right side of the counter.

"Good morning, Jeff," he said cordially.

"Hi, Herm. Let's see that .38 you got in the window."

His smile disappeared. "The .38?"

"That's right. It's for sale, isn't it?"

"Everything I got's for sale—including my wife." He chuckled.

But he didn't go to the window for the gun, and his eyes darted uneasily toward the door. This wasn't like Herman at all. Usually, if he thought you a customer, he did everything but tie you hand and foot until you bought something. And he wasn't smiling now.

"What's the matter?" I asked, baffled at the change in him. "Don't you want to sell it to me?"

"No no, I can't refuse to sell it to you but, well, I thought you had a gun."

"Don't give me that, Herman. You'd sell a gun to the Fort Dix arsenal if you could talk them into it. Now what's the matter?"

He looked unhappy and worried without his smile. "You know."

"No, I don't know." He was beginning to bother me. "It's not against the law to buy a gun in this state, or did they just pass one last night?"

"But it's against the law to shoot somebody, Jeff, and I don't like to see you getting into trouble. I could sell you the gun, but it would be on my conscience."

"Just who am I going to shoot? If you don't mind telling me."

"You know who. Floyd Hammond." I laughed and he didn't like it.

"It's all over town, the names he called you and how he's going to get even with you, and all."

This was ridiculous, and I said solemnly, "Herman, I swear to you by my father's beard that I will positively not shoot Floyd Hammond even once. I'll give you a guarantee in writing. Now get me that gun," I reached for my wallet. "How much is it?"

"Twenty-five dollars, but I don't like ..."

"Here's five. It's all I've got with me. I'll drop off the other twenty the next time I come by."

He brightened and his smile came back as if he had pulled a string. "I'm sorry, Jeff. I don't like to turn you down, but you know my policy. This isn't a business I can give credit."

I put the five dollar bill on the counter and grinned. "Here's a deposit. The bank opens in fifteen minutes. I'll be right back." Then I waved and walked out.

The bank was only three blocks away. At the exact moment I arrived there, Helen Anders's neat little Chevvy sedan drew up to the curb. She worked in the insurance company on the second floor. She got out of the car, gave me a stiff nod and walked toward the doorway.

"Wait a minute, Helen," I said and fell in step beside her. "I'd like to talk to you."

"Please, Jeff, I'm not interested in anything you have to say."

"Ah, listen—"

"No, I won't listen. Can't you understand that I don't want anything to do with you any longer? If you want to talk to someone, I'd suggest you go back and talk to that woman you've got out there on your island."

I was so astonished that all I could do was stammer, "Woman?"

"Don't bother denying it." She was coldly contemptuous. "You were *seen*."

"Who told you—Floyd Hammond?"

"What difference does that make? You were seen chasing her up and down the beach. It's all over town. Excuse me, please, I have to go to work." Her heels clicked primly on the sidewalk as she moved away.

A flash of anger flamed inside me, and burned itself out at almost the same instant. What difference did it make if Floyd Hammond had seen us on the Key? It had been Floyd, all right. He'd probably been out in the Gulf in his boat and had turned his glasses on us. But he hadn't seen what had gone on before. I chased Letty, or he would have told Helen that, too. And she would have let me know. She would have called it disgusting. So what difference did it make, and why get excited?

I drew a hundred dollars from the bank and went back to the Sunshine Loan Company. Matt Burkitt was parked at the curb in his car, and I went over and leaned in the open window. The sight of him didn't bother me today.

"I hear you're buying a gun," he said impassively.

I nodded. "But not," I said evenly, "to shoot Floyd, if that's what's on your mind."

He looked vaguely in my direction, but I knew his vague glances; they didn't miss a thing. Then he turned his head and studied the dashboard. "You know he's been shooting off his mouth, don't you?"

"I've heard."

"About a woman you got out there on your place. Same woman you had the fight over, ain't it?"

"Similar," I admitted.

"Well, I told him to keep his trap shut. What you do out there is your business."

"I'm not doing anything out there. She's visiting me with her brother—" I thought of Daly—"and her cousin. If you want the straight story instead of Floyd's version."

"In some ways," Burkitt went on, "Floyd goes out of his way to make trouble."

"He doesn't bother me."

I must have passed some sort of test because he reached out and turned the ignition key. He stepped on the starter. "Take care of yourself," he said, and drove slowly down the street.

I went into the shop. Herman had the gun on the counter, ready for me. He was smiling, and the smile stayed on when I also bought a box of cartridges.

"No hard feelings, Jeff? A man in my business, he can't be too careful."

On the way back to the *Skidoo*, I stopped at the hardware store and bought another spade and a heavy rake. The morning breeze had died down, and the bay had scarcely a ripple in it. The dead fish floated soddenly with the tide. As I approached the Key, I saw a figure sitting on the dock. I took down the glasses from the hook over the wheel.

It was Buster. He must have seen the *Skidoo*, for he stared out over the bay, shielding his eyes with his hand. Then he stood up and walked to the edge of the dock. He watched narrowly as I came closer, but if he thought I had brought the police with me, you'd never have known it from his easy grin.

"Throw me the rope, sport," he called. "I'll help you park it." I threw him the lines, and after he tied up, he jumped down into the cockpit. "I want you to forget what I said last night, Jeff," he said. "I was outta line." He made an apologetic motion with his hand.

I was in the cabin, and he didn't try to come in. He stood outside in the cockpit, looking contrite.

This is just another angle, I warned myself. "So?" I said.

"Just forget it, that's all. And Daly won't bother you no more neither. I talked turkey to him this morning."

"That's fine," I took the gun from my pocket and bounced it in my palm. "Then maybe I ought to return this and get my money back."

His eyes sparkled with delight. "You're a card, sport, and that's the truth. A gun, he gets! And Daly thought you went for the cops. He's hiding in the bushes like a moose. Whattaya think of that?"

"I think he's smart."

"Sure he's smart, but not so's you'd notice it. He's a clunk, and he'll keep his nose clean from here on in."

There was no doubt at all in my mind that he had something brand new up his sleeve; or at the very least, a new approach to the thing that had been up his sleeve all along—whatever that was. He had gone (and was still going) to an awful lot of trouble to keep me in line and happy, though the "happy" part of it, I was sure, was purely incidental. He needed me—and the *Skidoo*, I suspected—for something undoubtedly illegal and probably criminal. And he'd use any means he could to get me. Last night he had tried threats, and that hadn't worked. Today he was using sweetness and light.

"You're so good to me," I said sarcastically, "and I'm so mean to you. If you say you'll forgive and forget, I'll let you wear my fraternity pin."

"You don't believe me, sport? Okay, take a look at this." He took a gun from his hip pocket and reached into his shirt and took out another. "This is my gun, and this is Daly's. I took it away from him. Okay now?"

Just what did he think, anyway? That I'd be overjoyed that he had two guns instead of one? It didn't mean that he had taken a gun away from Daly. They could have had a half-dozen guns between them for all I knew. They could have had a whole arsenal hidden away in the house, not counting brass knuckles and blackjacks.

But he was cute. I had to hand him that. Even standing there with two guns in his hands, he contrived to look like a mild, husky guy whose only aim in life was to make me happy.

"You're a good boy, junior," I told him. "And just as soon as you wash the car and mow the lawn and practice your violin, you can go out and play cops and robbers."

"Ah, go to hell," he said affectionately. "But listen, I got a yen to go for a boat ride. How's about it? I'll pay ten bucks worth."

"Ten bucks will buy you two and a half hours."

Buster made a great show of taking two bills from his pocket. They were both tens. He separated them slowly and reluctantly and gave me one. I put it in my pocket. He looked out over the rail and sighed. When he looked back at me, he was wearing a small, reproachful smile. All in all, it was quite a performance.

I went out to the Gulf through Hermano Grande Pass at the northern end of the Key. I was glad of the chance to take the *Skidoo* out and open her up. I know I could have done it any time at all by myself, but I'm a professional boatman and I have a professional dislike of burning gas without a payload aboard. Buster's ten dollars would buy the gas.

The day was all blue and gold and green and white. The Gulf was so smooth that when the mullet jumped the ripples seemed to spread forever, building one circle after another across the surface. Pelicans, swooping for fish, hit the water in their twisting, neck-breaking dive, and high, high overhead were the swift flying frigate birds, looking like jet planes with their backswept wings. There were a lot of dead fish floating from the red tide, but they didn't seem very important right now. It was good to be out in open water with the *Skidoo* again. I felt the way I did sometimes when was feeling very good: that I was about to discover the truth about something important and beautiful.

But the feeling passed very quickly when I realized that Buster had been hovering at my left shoulder ever since we left the dock.

"Mind if I steer this tub of yours for awhile, sport?" he asked. "Looks like a pushover, after a truck."

Normally I don't mind letting an interested customer take the wheel out in the Gulf, where he can't run down the pedestrians, but this wasn't normally.

I shook my head. "Ever run a boat before?"

"Sure. A rowboat on the Hackensack River. Nothin' to it."

"This isn't a rowboat. You'd be in trouble in two minutes."

"What's that gizmo?" he asked, pointing at the RPM dial.

"That's the strobostat. It governs the ratio of the gyro-flex. You have to keep your eye on it, especially when you have a three-bladed prop or twin screws. This is a twin screw job with a radial pitch and *no* universals. Know anything about hydronautic pilotry?"

"What's that?"

"I'll lend you a book when we get back to the house. It's the first thing you have to learn before you can run a boat this size."

"You gotta study?"

"My God, when you've got a mile of water under your hull, it's a little different than driving on a concrete highway only three inches thick."

"A mile?" He stared out the port. "That how deep it is?"

"Deeper in spots, especially around the shoals, and you have to take soundings. A boat doesn't just float on top of the water, you know. Water doesn't stand still like Fifth Avenue. It's always moving and your boat moves with it, and that's when you have to re-stow your ballast. Or else. Anybody can take a boat away from a dock. It's bringing it back alive that counts. And a boat isn't a submarine. When it goes down, it stays down. I'll lend you that book on hydronautic pilotry when we get back to the house."

Buster eyed me fondly. "Between me, you, and the lamppost, sport, how much of what you said then is just plain horse manure?"

That was a jolt! But it did pull me up sharply. There might come a time when it would be really dangerous to low-rate him. I smiled. "I'll put it this way, Buster. Don't fool with a boat unless you know what you're doing."

"I know. I ain't no dummy. Take that thing there. The compass. It tells you where you're goin', don't it?"

"Yes."

"Well, it don't tell me nothin'. It could turn on the television, for all I know about it. It's a hell of a big ocean out here, and a guy could really get himself lost. Me, I like a place where you can look up and see a street sign and know where you are. Okay, let's go home."

He fished a cigar stub from his shirt pocket and stretched himself out on the bunk at the opposite side of the cabin. He lighted the cigar and lazily watched the smoke stream toward the open door to the stern cockpit. Buster had no further interest in navigation. I cut to half speed and turned the *Skidoo* in a tight semi-circle.

There was quite a ground swell out here, and the *Skidoo* rolled heavily when I took her around. Buster grabbed the edge of the bunk to keep from sliding off. He raised his head and looked out the window. He didn't say anything, but he nodded to himself, and I knew what he was thinking. If the *Skidoo* would roll that heavily in a calm sea, she'd really cut up if she got caught in a storm. Now he was convinced.

"Tell me something, Buster," I said, knowing it was a dumb question, "why did you want to learn how to run the boat?"

"Me? I don't wanna run no boat, sport. That's your racket." He waved his cigar and laughed.

CHAPTER THIRTEEN

That was the morning. The afternoon was a little different.

When we went up to the house, Daly was sitting in the shade of the cabbage palms in the canvas sling chair at the foot of the porch steps. He looked pinched and gray, as if he hadn't had a wink of sleep all night. His face closed stubbornly at the sight of us, but there was a twitch in his left cheek. He looked like a man who'd scream if you touched him unexpectedly in the dark. He didn't say a word to either of us.

I didn't see Letty at all. She was in her room (the guest bedroom) and the door was closed. Buster tried to get her to come out, but all he got from her was a terse, "Beat it!" He winked at me, as if this were something personal between the two of us. "You know how it is," he said confidentially. "They get that way every so often."

The rest of the afternoon we worked on the beach, digging trenches, raking dead fish into them, and covering them up. And I didn't have to ask Buster to help me, either. He just shouldered the new rake and shovel and came along, and he really moved a couple tons of dead fish all by himself. I didn't try to keep up with him. I'd have killed myself if I'd tried.

We worked until the fat sun squatted on the rim of the Gulf and flamed the sky with blood-red streamers. Then we left the shovels sticking in the sand and walked slowly up the beach. Buster sniffed the air as we approached the house.

"Sauerkraut! There's somethin' that'll stick to your ribs, sport. And that Letty, she can really dish it up. You can have first shot at the shower. I had it first yesterday."

"I'm going down to the boat."

"You got a shower down there?"

"Yes."

"Well make it snappy. Dinner smells almost ready."

"I'll eat on the boat."

"What the hell, sport? Don't you like sauerkraut?"

"I like it all right, but I'm going down to the boat."

"Come on, don't be a guy like that." He took my arm and tried to steer me toward the porch steps. "There'll be plenty for everybody. You know Letty, there's nothin' she likes better'n see a guy eat."

It was a very affable and cordial invitation, considering the fact that he was inviting me into my own house to eat my own food at my own table.

All day Buster had been trying to suck me in with this buddy-buddy pitch of his, and I'd had enough of it.

"Come on," he urged. "Who wants to eat by theirself? Guys get sick that way. Letty's countin' on you. I know."

That was another thing he'd been doing all afternoon, bringing Letty into the conversation every chance he got, crowding me every minute. I wanted to get away from him for awhile.

"I'll see you in the morning." I started down the path to the boat.

"Okay, sport, but Letty'll be sore. Hey, look, if you really like kraut, kid, send her down with a bowl of it. How's that?"

"Nuts."

He called something after me, but it was lost in the crunch of my feet on the shell walk and the dry, windy rattle of the cabbage palm fronds overhead. I had the feeling that he was following, coming right down the path at my heels, but when I looked over my shoulder, he was still standing at the foot of the porch steps.

I took a swim in the bay, fried up a pan of scrambled eggs and bacon, and sat down on the bunk to listen to the boys talk to each other on the ship-to-shore radio while I ate.

"... Got a good catch of grouper and red snapper and Burl snagged a green turtle today that ought to go about four, five hundred pounds. How you doing?"

"'Bout the same. I'm about fished out here and I think I'll move on to a hundred fathoms in the morning. Seen any kings yet?"

"Not much. Got about fifty pounds. The run ain't started yet and maybe with this damn red tide it ain't gonna start. Saw Captain Raisch on the *Floradora* yesterday. Was shrimpin' off Mexico. Said the greasers were actin' up again. You gotta stay fifteen, twenty mile offshore or they tow you into Vera Cruz, grab all your shrimp and fine you on top of bustin' up all your gear. That Mexico ..."

It was about there that I dozed off. I was more tired than I realized. For almost a week now, I had been whirling like a runaway merry-go-round and the gears were beginning to slip. You can give the human body an awful beating, but you have to put it to bed once in awhile.

Somebody was playing a banjo on the ship-to-shore. They do that to entertain each other when there isn't much else on the air. It sounded terrible, and I turned it off. I looked at my watch and was shocked to see that it was almost midnight. I had really dozed off, but I wanted more sleep. So I locked up, stuck my gun down between the edge of the mattress and the frame of the bunk, and turned in.

I was tired and went to sleep right away. Then, just like the night before, I was suddenly awake. My senses told me I'd heard something, but I didn't know what. I listened, alert and suspicious, and then I heard it. A creaking. Somebody was walking on the dock just outside the cabin.

I pulled my gun from between the mattress and the bunk frame and crept to the door that led to the stern cockpit. If this was my mysterious visitor of last night, he was due for a surprise. It was a dark night and against the deeper blackness of the dense foliage ashore, I couldn't see a thing. I opened the door and slipped out into the cockpit. It was dead low tide and when I crouched, I was below the level of the dock. I listened. There wasn't a sound now and I felt angrily disappointed.

Then—*creak*—and the prowler was coming slowly and cautiously toward me from the long end of the dock. I could barely see his moving bulk in the darkness. I kept myself low so I wouldn't show any silhouette against the bay behind me. When he came almost abreast, I lunged up and over the edge of the dock and hit him hard just above the knees. He went down with a shrill cry. I sprawled across him.

I drew back my right fist and he screamed, and it wasn't until then that I realized that the figure bucking under me was too soft to be male, too curved, too definitely feminine, and under my left hand was the deep, rich swell of a full breast.

It was Letty. I said, "Oh, hell!" and pushed hastily to my knees beside her. She moaned. I had hurt her. I knew I had hurt her because I had really rammed her with a hundred and ninety pounds of damn fool. I lifted her gently in my arms, and she moved and made a painful, strangled noise in her throat. All I could think of was the death rattle, but then she gasped.

"You knocked the wind out of me," she said breathlessly.

"I'm sorry, honey. I didn't know who it was. I thought—"

"It isn't your fault. I should have called out. I'm all right." I helped her to her feet and Letty leaned dizzily against me. "It's me that should say I'm sorry," she whispered. "I shouldn't have come creepin' around like that. Let's sit down for a minute."

"Come in the boat then."

Letty hesitated. "I'd rather sit down out here, if you don't mind. I want to talk to you. If we go on the boat—"

She let it hang, but it was plain what she meant. If we went on the boat, there wouldn't be much talking. If we went on the boat, I'd make love to her and she'd *want* me to make love to her. This was the first time she'd said anything that even remotely resembled an acceptance of me. I felt a wild exultation, but the next moment I was floundering in suspicion again. Was there a wily touch of Buster in this? Had she come, or had she been sent? Earlier, he had wanted to send her to the boat with a plate of dinner for me, but I had turned that down. Yet, a man's resistance lowers as the night grows heavier, and that was something Buster would know. It is in the night that a man wants a woman most. He'd know that and he'd use it. Buster would use your own quivering flesh against you.

She must have felt the change in me. "Don't you wanna talk to me, Jeff?" she said anxiously.

"Did Buster send you down here?"

"He doesn't know I'm here, Jeff, honest. I waited till he was sleepin'. He wanted me to come with a plate of kraut at dinnertime, but I wouldn't go."

"What does he want? Why has he been trying to butter me up all day?"

"I don't know, Jeff."

"Didn't he tell you what a fine, loyal, trustworthy, generous, wholesome, respectable, up-and-coming guy I am? Didn't he praise my sterling character and point out that I'm a young man to keep an eye on? Didn't he mention that I've got my shoulder to the wheel, my nose to the grindstone, my foot on the right path, and my eye on the future? Didn't he even drop a hint?"

She began to cry, and nothing she could have done could more effectively have brought me up short. Not that I was a sucker for tears, but Letty just wasn't the kind who could turn them on or off. It wasn't something Buster could order her to do. She should have fought back furiously, cursed me out and given me a backhander across the face. That was what I would have expected, not these vulnerable, naked, defenseless tears. I held her tightly. I couldn't think of anything to say. All the words were phony. I just held her and rubbed my cheek against her hair.

"I don't blame you for thinkin' we're a pretty crummy bunch," she said dully. "We've given you nothin' but a bad time ever since the first day. Why'd you put up with it? Why didn't you just kick us out like we deserve?"

"I love you, honey."

"Let me go, Jeff. I want to go back to the house."

"You came down here to talk, honey. What did you want to talk about?"

"I said let me go!"

I had to wrestle to keep her from twisting free and darting away from me up the path. She fought me, not with anger or fury, but with despair. I knew that. Letty had fought me before, but always aggressively. There was none of that this time as she strained away from me. All she wanted to do was break free and run away, but that wouldn't be good. It would be the worst thing I could let her do. For her—and me, too.

I knew now why she had come down to the boat; I knew why she wanted to run back to the house and into the dark little cave of her room and lock the door behind her. I knew the reason. *Me.* If I had wanted to drive her away from me, I couldn't have done a better job with a knout. I had lashed her raw and bleeding, and she wanted to crawl away and heal.

I couldn't let her go now. I would have kept her there if I had to slug her. It almost came to that. Letty had a despairing, frantic strength, and she fought me with all her body, but never attacking—trying only to get away. It was a travesty of a lover's embrace, she straining away and I straining toward her.

"Stop it, honey," I panted. "I want to marry you. Don't you understand? *I want to marry you!*"

"No you don't."

"Damn it, I do! Now stop it or I *will* smack you."

She stopped struggling, but still held herself away from me. "But we been so rotten to you, Jeff."

"Let me worry about that. You came down here to say you would marry me, didn't you?"

Letty was in my arms now with her face against my chest and her voice was muffled. "I thought I was kidding myself."

"I know. You've been trying to make up your mind, and you came down to tell me. Then I shot off my big mouth, and all you wanted to do was get away from me. I can't tell you how sorry I am, honey ..."

"*You're* sorry!"

She began to laugh, a little wildly. "You're sorry, I'm sorry, we're both sorry. We sure got into a big wrestling match for nothin' didn't we, darling? Kiss me now, kiss me, please!"

I kissed her. Letty put both arms around my neck. Her lips were soft, very young and hesitant, and she broke it off and hid her face in the hollow of my shoulder.

"Now will you marry me, goon girl?" I whispered.

"That's what I came down to talk to you about, but—"

"But what, Letty?"

"I want to marry you. Jeff. Honest. More than anything in the world. But I can't. Yet."

"What do you mean, you can't—yet?"

"I have to wait till Buster gets himself a stake. I can't leave him broke like this."

"What do you mean by a stake?"

"Five hundred, a thousand bucks. Somethin' he can get started on."

"I'll lend it to him."

"No!"

"I've got it, Letty."

"No. He won't pay it back. I know him, darling. He means well, but he forgets. He isn't bad, honest, Jeff." She looked earnestly into my face, a little anxiously, wanting to convince me. "He's not like Daly. Daly's no good. Buster's got a lot of good in him, and all he needs is a stake. All he wants is a chance. I know him."

I didn't say anything. I knew Buster, too. He was a dangerous animal, shrewd and crafty, and probably a lot smarter than I was, in his way. But he had brought her up and Letty was remembering that: remembering other things about him, the sentimental things, the small and intimate and wonderful things that occur within a family, the laughter, the little surprise gifts at Christmas, the treat of being taken out unexpectedly for dinner in a restaurant, and the warmth and understanding, the laughs.

Buster meant all those things. I could see how she felt. He was—well, tremendous. I can say that for myself, too. He was probably the most tremendous person I had ever met. But he was twisted. He was as twisted and tough as an old cypress root, but that was the side of him Letty couldn't see, and possibly would never be able to see. There was that about him. If you closed your eyes, you could remember the glow you got when that great, rumbling, Olympian laugh thundered out of him.

"Don't you see, Jeff?" she went on. "I have to stick with him till he gets his stake. Buster needs me to keep him out of trouble. Buster just won't take care of the little things, that's all. I got to keep after him. Why, if it wasn't for me, he'd have been in trouble time and time again with the cops and with guys like Daly. And just because he doesn't know how they feel about things, the little things.

"You and me, the little things're important, but Buster doesn't realize. You know what I mean, darling?" Letty grasped my arms fiercely. "I'd do the same for you. When we're married, I'll stick to you no matter what. If anybody so much as opens his mouth about you, I'll knock his teeth in. But right now I have to stick with Buster. I just have to, darling, I just have to!"

"Sure. Sure you do, honey," I said, but I felt sick about it.

"I love you, darling," she said timidly. Then she gave an odd, embarrassed laugh. "You know something. I never called anybody darling before. Never. Nobody—even Daly."

I felt a stab of jealousy. "Daly?"

"I almost married him once. He asked me and I almost did, but what kind of life would I have with him. He'd be tom-cattin' around the back alleys the next day and in the clink the day after ..."

"Was it Daly you went to bed with before me?" I asked harshly, stupidly, insanely. I couldn't stand the thought of. Daly in bed with her. "Was it Daly?"

Letty brought me back to my senses with her firm answer. "Would it make a difference?"

I had to separate the past from the present. "No, Letty. No, it wouldn't make a bit of difference." I meant it.

She kissed me swiftly. "It wasn't Daly," she whispered. "It was when I was in high school. This guy, he was the big football hero, a jerk, he was always after me. I want to tell you about it now, and if you don't want me afterwards, well, it's better I tell you now. He was always tryin' to make me and I didn't want any part of him.

"Anyway, the night of this dance I went with this guy. They had a bottle. You know the Polacks out Secaucus, they make their own liquor out of potatoes or somethin'. Boy, what a kick to that stuff. It's like you get hit on the head with a club, as bad.

"So he gives me a drink out in the car and I have a couple. You know kids—they don't know any better and they want to be smart. So I drink every time they hand me the bottle, and the next thing I know I'm in the back seat. It's only the next day I know what's happened to me. If I told Buster, he'd have killed the jerk. You're the only one I ever told ..."

"Oh, honey!" I gripped her hand.

"If you don't want me now, just say so, but I had to tell you, and that's the way it was. It wasn't Daly."

"Honey, I love you. I don't care and—"

The scream split the air like an ax in your skull. There was pure terror in it, and it cut off as sharply as if you'd smothered it in a blanket. It came from the direction of the house. Letty went rigid against me, and my arms must have constricted because she gasped.

"Jeff! What was that?"

My only thought was that Buster had killed Daly. It was the kind of scream Daly would have let out. "Stay here!" I snapped, and ran down the dock.

She was right behind me, running. We ran up the long path to the house. I could see the hosing beam of a flashlight ahead, up there on the crest of the Key, and I ran toward it, falling twice in the shifting footholds on the shell walk. I swore each time, scrambled, and ran on from a half-risen crouch.

When I got to the house, Buster was standing there with the flashlight. He was holding the beam steadily on a figure that lay crumpled in the ruins of the long cypress ladder I had used to paint the house last year. The man was lying between two cabbage palms, and the ladder had broken. Even without looking twice, I could see that he was dead.

His head was at an angle that no head could be with the backbone still in one piece. It was twisted back half over his shoulder. And down the side of the house was a long, freshly scarred scrape mark that showed how the ladder had slipped in falling. The scrape led from my bedroom window (Daly's now) and off the side of the house.

"What happened?" I flung at Buster.

He shook his head and made a half motion toward the figure lying on the ground. "Why, hell, George, I—"

"Jeff, damn it!"

"Hell, Jeff, I don't know. All of a sudden I hear this awful scrape down the side of the house. I come out, and here's what I find."

I tried to see his face above the flashlight, but he was just a silhouette. I went over to the figure on the ground and knelt down beside it. It was Floyd, not Daly, and he was dead. I didn't touch him. He was very dead. His face was hideously twisted and the flaccid lips had fallen limply back from his long, yellowed horse-teeth. It was still the same rat-face, the long nose and the weak, retreating chin, but looking back so *finally* over his left shoulder, it was piteous.

I felt sorry for the son of a bitch. It was easy to see what he was trying to do. He thought that was my bedroom up there, and he put the ladder up against the window sill and tried to peek in. He wanted to catch me in bed with Letty, so he could spread the story around town. What other reason would he have to peek into my bedroom? He wanted to smear me. It was plain to see. The skunk, the louse, the poor bastard. And the ladder had collapsed under him and he had broken his neck. It was a mean, despicable, shaming way to die.

"He's dead?" Letty asked in a small voice. I nodded and stood up. She looked at Buster. "You had nothin' to do with it, did you, Bus?"

"Me?" His jaw dropped. "Hell, I was in the parlor listening to the radio, and all of a sudden I hear this noise like somebody pulled a dragline across the side of the house, and I come runnin' out and I see him. You know the guy, Jeff?"

"I know him."

"Friend of yours?" Buster went on.

"Not exactly."

"What was he trying to do, bust in or somethin'?"

"Just looking for trouble," I said.

"He sure found it," said Buster.

The porch light went on and Daly came out in his underwear. He looked terrible, gaunt and sick and scared. His legs were very thin and bony, and his drawers flapped around his skinny thighs. He held on to the corner post and leaned over the railing, staring down at the body with hollow eyes.

"Is he alive?" he asked shrilly, "Is he alive?"

"He's dead," said Buster.

"The son of a bitch! What was he tryin' to climb in my room for?"

"Shut up and go back to bed!" Buster told him.

"What are you going to do with him?" Daly asked.

I took a deep breath. "We're not going to do anything with him. We're going to let the police do it."

"Oh sure, sure," said Daly scathingly. "That's all we need is a bunch of cops crawlin' around here. Well, get that idea out of your head right away, jerk. We don't want no cops."

"I'm still going for the police."

I expected Buster to back him up on that, but he surprised me. "I guess you have to," 'he agreed reluctantly. "Though maybe—"

"There ain't no maybes about it," snapped Letty. "This ain't somethin' you can finagle around with. If Jeff says he's got to go for the cops, he's got to go for the cops. This is something, he knows more about than you guys do."

Buster looked at her reproachfully. "That's exactly what I said, baby." He grinned at me. "When you gotta go, you gotta go, right?"

Then Daly screeched inarticulately, and all three of us turned and stared up at him. He had a gun in his shaking, skinny hand. His face was congested and dark with fury.

"I've had just about all I can stand outta the whole damn bunch of you," he screamed. "This time you're gonna do what I say. No cops, and that's final!"

The way he was waving that gun, I was sure it was going to go off. I jumped quickly in front of Letty and Buster seemed to swell. Never taking his eyes off Daly, his neck thickened, his shoulders rounded, and his chest expanded. Suddenly there was a loud crack as the long, heavy flashlight broke in half in his hands. The surge of strength that it must have taken was almost unbelievable because the casing was of heavy gauge brass. He threw out his hands and flung the two pieces in opposite directions.

"If you ain't in that house in exactly two seconds," he said thickly, "I'm comin' up there."

Daly yammered and backed toward the door, one hand to the wall for support, reaching behind him for the doorknob.

"*Get!*" roared Buster.

Daly whirled, tripping over the sill as he plunged frantically into the house. It seemed to take Buster forever to compose himself, and it was an awful thing to watch. You could see the fury and murder that raged in him like hurricane winds raging over a torn sea. His hands were knotted, and the muscles in his great arms hardened until they seemed ready to burst. Even the muscles at the hinges of his jaws were like clenched fists, and there was violent death in his face.

"*Buster!*" Letty cried. "Buster, snap out of it!"

He turned ponderously, but his eyes were vague as if he were trying to focus on her through a red mist. His massive head swung to and fro like a bear's. Then he opened his mouth and let the deadly, compressed breath hiss out of him.

"Sometimes that guy gets me mad," he said in a surprisingly mild voice. "One of these days I'm gonna get sore and take a poke at him. But I shouldn't of lost my temper; he ain't worth it."

"It wasn't your fault, Bus," Letty said quickly. "But I thought you took his gun."

"I did." He patted both hip pockets. "Guess he must of had another one."

"You'd better make sure the next time," I said drily.

"There won't be no next time, sport. You better call the cops now."

"I can't call them. There's no phone. We'll have to go over to the mainland in the boat."

"I'll go with you."

I didn't want to leave Letty alone with Daly, but on the other hand I didn't want either Buster and/or Daly alone with Floyd's body.

I gave Letty my gun. "If Daly as much as sticks his head out of that house, just shoot this thing off in the air."

Letty took the gun gingerly. "I don't like guns." She looked at Buster. "And I don't like you to carry them either, specially when you're goin' to see cops. Give me yours."

Buster's glance flickered toward the house, then slowly he took the guns from his hip pockets and gave them to her.

"But watch it," he said uneasily. "Don't shoot that clown unless he absolutely blows his stack."

"I can handle Daly," said Letty.

"I don't know. Maybe I better stay here and you go with Jeff."

"*I'll* stay here, Buster, and *you* go with Jeff. That's the best."

"Sure, sure." I don't know what he'd had in mind, maybe an 'accident' for me on the way to the mainland, but he sure looked like a man on an unwelcome spot. "Just don't put any more holes in Daly, that's all. He's nothin' but a windbag. But maybe I better stay here with you ..."

"And maybe you better not. Jeff doesn't know anything about this and you do. You go with him. I'm not lettin' Jeff get in dutch with the cops."

"Sure, sis." His eyes darted from Letty to me in spreading surprise. "Let's go, sport."

We went down the path to the boat. He was very thoughtful when we were chugging across the bay.

"I guess this is gonna be a little rough, eh, sport?" he ventured finally.

"Yes," I said.

CHAPTER FOURTEEN

Old Walt Bivens was on the desk when we walked into the Sanibar police headquarters. I'd known Walt all my life. He'd always been friendly in an offhand way, but when I told him what had happened to Floyd, his face closed like a wooden box. He reached for the phone.

"I better call the chief on this," he said in a voice that warned me not to expect any favors. Then he mumbled into the phone so I couldn't hear what he was saying. After he hung up, he looked down at me expressionlessly. "They tell me you were in some kind of trouble over in Donaldston the other night."

"Nothing to speak of, Walt."

"They fined you ten bucks. You Tuckers were always in hot water, one way or the other. The chief said to wait in his office. He don't want Matt Burkitt to run into you just yet."

"Sure, Walt." I led Buster into the chief's office, closing the door behind us. Buster leaned against the wall and took a cigar stub from his shirt pocket. His eyes were narrow and thoughtful.

"Well, you sure got the brush-off that time, sport. The sergeant a friend of yours?"

"I know him."

"Well, he don't know you. Not tonight he don't. Who's this Matt Burkitt he didn't want to run into you?"

"A detective, cousin of the fellow who was killed."

His hand stopped half way to his cigar with a lighted match. "You stupid clunk. They'll crucify you. Didn't you think of that?"

I shrugged and went to the window. There was no point in explaining my reasons. Buster wouldn't know what I was talking about. The chief strode in fifteen minutes later with two detectives, Hart and Gilmartin. I tried desperately to think of Buster's name, but he had never told me. I had a very bad moment when the chief looked at him and demanded, "Who's this?"

But Buster said quickly, "The name's Sturgis, Chief, and I—"

The chief silenced him with a gesture. "Take his statement in the other office," he ordered Gilmartin.

He was hustled out roughly. The chief leaned against the corner of the green, steel desk. Hart put a toothpick between his teeth and chewed it slowly. His expression was entirely noncommittal, but from the way he watched the chief, I could see that he was waiting for a cue. Here's another boy who doesn't know me tonight, I thought. I remembered Buster's, "They'll crucify you," and it was a chilly feeling. They weren't men I had known for years; they were doors, and they were closed against me. The chief studied me as if he had never seen me before. I felt my ears get red.

"Let's hear it, Tucker," he said finally.

I started off resentfully, but I knew that was the wrong way to do it; so I calmed down and gave it to him without any color. He listened impassively. When I finished, he and Hart exchanged a stolid glance. He didn't want to believe me, but he had nothing to go on except the fight I'd had with Floyd. He pushed away from the desk.

"I'll be back in a minute," he told Hart, and went into the other office where Gilmartin had taken Buster.

"Can I smoke?" I asked Hart with heavy irony.

"Go ahead."

But when I put the cigarette in my mouth, I had the feeling that he was watching to see if my hands were shaking when I lit up. Buster was right, and I was wrong. I wasn't going to get the benefit of any doubts. I had gone fishing with Les Hart, I had played shuffleboard with him, and I had even taken his buck-toothed sister to a dance once. But there in that bleak office, lighted only by a naked bulb in the middle of the ceiling, we didn't have a thing to say to each other.

The chief came back in about ten minutes. He was a heavy, gray-haired round-shouldered man, and his feet came down solidly with each step. He ignored me and went straight to his desk, standing with his back toward me.

"I'm trying to get something straight in my mind," he said abruptly. "Your stories don't seem to gibe. Nothing important, but I just want to get the picture straight in my mind. Now when you came out of the house after the ladder fell, did Sturgis come from the north or south end of the beach?"

I felt myself freeze. For a minute I wondered wildly what Buster had told him and Gilmartin. I knew Buster would do anything to keep himself clear of this mess. But I didn't have anything to panic about; I was in the clear, and all they were trying to do was trip me up.

"I wasn't in the house, Chief. I was down on the dock with Miss Sturgis. We were talking."

"You were?" His tone implied extreme skepticism. "Well, maybe I'm a little mixed up, getting both sides of this. You were down on the dock. That's right. I remember now. Sturgis called to you—"

"He didn't call. I heard Floyd yell when the ladder went over and I ran up to the house."

"Oh, I get it now. The ladder started to go over, and he yelled—"

"All I heard was the yell. I'm just supposing it was when the ladder went over. I don't know."

"Why didn't you say so in the first place?"

"I did. I said I heard the yell and ran up to the house and found Floyd and the broken ladder."

The chief sucked at his teeth, looked vaguely at the far end of the ceiling, then looked at Hart. "I'm a little mixed up. I'll have to talk to Sturgis again. You talk to Tucker here and see if you can get things straightened out. I'll be gone about ten minutes."

"Right, Chief," said Hart and opened the door to the main room and looked out. I could see Sergeant Walt Bivens perched up there in his pulpit just before Hart closed the door. The chief went into the other office, and Hart came toward me, saying, "Now Jeff—"

If it hadn't been for Buster, I wouldn't have been ready for it. But Buster had said, "They'll crucify you," and when Hart came toward me, I knew he was going to swing. I deflected his fist with my left forearm and, stepping in, hit him as hard as I could right on the jaw.

If he had gotten in that first punch, he would have gone to work on me; one right after the other—getting things "straightened out," as the chief had ordered him. He fell into me, and I hit him on the back of the neck and caught him before he fell to the floor. I picked him up and laid him on the desk. He was just beginning to groan and move when the chief walked in ten minutes later.

I didn't say anything and the chief didn't say anything. Hart sat up dizzily, propping himself on one arm. The chief ignored him entirely, ignored the whole episode. It hadn't happened. He hadn't ordered Hart to slug me, and Hart hadn't muffed it. Everything was normal. But tomorrow morning, I imagined Hart would be walking a beat out there among the lumber yards, the concrete works, the gravel pits, and the hibiscus nursery, at the other side of the railroad tracks.

"All right, let's go and take a look at it," said the chief. We went down to the dock in the chief's car. In addition to the chief and Gilmartin, there were two harness cops with us. We took the police boat out to the Key, leaving the *Skidoo* at the dock.

Every light was on in and outside the house when we got there, but Letty was nowhere to be seen. We clustered around Floyd's body, and they looked at the broken ladder and at the scrape mark that curved down the side of the house from my window. Gilmartin wandered off and came back about twenty minutes later. He told the chief he had found Floyd's boat hidden in the mangrove a hundred yards south of my dock and only Floyd's footprints leading away from it in the sand. That was the first time I got really bitter about it.

It was perfectly obvious how Floyd had sneaked into the Key, crept up to the house, and what he had been up to. It was all there, but they didn't want to believe it. They wanted to hang it on me, but they didn't have a leg to stand on.

If you wanted to look at it one way, they didn't fake any evidence and they didn't try to frame me, but they sure hated to come right out and give me a clean bill.

"Well, we better get a statement from Miss Sturgis," said the chief after awhile. "Where the hell—"

I don't know what I did or said, but when he came out with that

"Where the hell," something exploded inside me. The next thing I knew Buster had me gripped in his two great hands and was whispering in my ear, "Dammit, don't blow your stack now!" The mist cleared, and the two harness cops and Gilmartin were looking at me incredulously.

The chief's drawn, lined face was taut. "Let him go!" he said sharply to Buster.

Buster released me, but I heard him swear under his breath. I didn't move. I just took a breath. I knew what the chief wanted. He wanted me to go for him, but I didn't.

"Miss Sturgis is probably up in the house," I said evenly. "She's not accustomed to bastards trying to peep in windows and breaking their necks. Do you want to send Gilmartin up first to get her 'straightened out' before we go up with you?"

"You got quite a temper, Tucker," said the chief. He nodded his head at Gilmartin and the two cops. "Let's wind this up."

We went toward the house. Remembering Daly, my stomach churned. But when we got up there, he was sitting in the big lounge chair in the living room in a white, clean shirt, freshly shaved, and hair combed. He was gray-faced and sunken-cheeked, his hands trembling, and he was breathing shallowly through his mouth, looking every inch an invalid about to meet his Maker. Even his eyes didn't focus.

I knew Daly, and I knew he was just plain scared witless. But to the others he looked seriously ill. Letty stood behind his chair and, for some reason or other, managed to look like a nurse, starched and prim. I breathed a prayer of thanksgiving. She had stage-managed this. She was a girl in a million. She had kept her head.

The chief took one look at Daly, and his voice dropped an octave when he asked the first question. It was obvious to everybody that Daly was a dying man, and in the face of death you must show a certain amount of decent reverence. I looked at Buster, but his face was as bland as an uncut tombstone.

"Who is this man?" the chief asked, looking at Daly.

"He had my room," I said, "the room Floyd leaned the ladder against. He's sick."

The chief looked at Daly. Daly coughed. It was a comedy, but horrible.

"What's the matter with him?"

"TB," said Letty in a brittle voice.

Gilmartin, who apparently knew shorthand, took Letty's statement. She gave it in a hard, antagonistic tone of voice and, fortunately, it substantiated mine. We had been down at the dock when we heard Floyd's yell, we hadn't been near the house, and Floyd had been dead when we got there. They questioned Daly, and though he was almost inarticulate from fear, they got the same answers. It was his room the ladder had been leaned against, and he had been awakened and frightened by the sound of the ladder scraping down the side of the house. He was sick, sick, sick. He coughed and there was no doubt about it that he was sick. I was afraid he was overdoing it, but he, himself, was convinced that he was a sick man, and so, at least, were Gilmartin and the two harness cops.

"Are you sure, Mr. Daly, that you saw and heard all these things," said the chief stiffly, "or did someone suggest them to you?"

"The son of a bitch!" Daly whispered. "He had his ladder against my window. I saw him—"

"Nobody told you about it later?"

"I saw him."

And that was it. There was nothing more to be said. Everybody was convinced. Floyd had tried to play Peeping Tom and had broken his filthy neck. It was all very obvious—the broken ladder, the slyly hidden boat, the footprints up the sand through the mangrove, and the scrape-mark down the side of the house.

"We'll take your statement down at headquarters, Tucker," said the chief woodenly. "The rest of you can stay here."

I wondered vaguely why he wanted my statement when I had seen no more of what happened than Buster, but didn't think any more of it. And I had to pick up the *Skidoo* anyway. I went along with them in the police boat. They took me to headquarters and a male stenographer, a harness cop, took my statement in shorthand in the chief's office.

"Type that up in triplicate and bring in all three copies," said the chief curtly. I waited another ten minutes and then the stenographer brought in the typed copies. I signed all three, and the chief waved his hands. "That's all, Tucker, you can go now."

And me, I thought that was all. I was tremendously relieved and I went out.

I got about thirty yards away from the entrance to headquarters when somebody gripped my arm just above the elbow and said, "I want to talk to you!" He gave me a staggering shove into the shadows of the giant banyan tree that grew in the courthouse square. It was Matt Burkitt. I knew his heavy, toneless voice, and I had just barely realized that this was why they had brought me back to Sanibar when he hit me across the back of the neck. I plunged forward into the aerial roots of the tree and clung to them.

Dizzily, I could still see the lighted doorway of headquarters. Two uniformed policemen were standing there, watching impassively. When they saw that Matt Burkitt wasn't going to need any help, they turned and walked back into the room. I wouldn't have had much of a chance with Burkitt even under ordinary circumstances, but that first savage clout across the back of the neck definitely settled it for me. My legs kept collapsing under me, and there was hardly strength enough in my hands to hold myself upright against the banyan tree.

Burkitt pulled me away as easily as he would pluck an overcoat from a clothes hanger. "Now we're going to find out what really went on between you and Floyd out there!"

He pushed me away and hit me in the stomach. He hit me several times. I didn't really feel him hit me but, oddly, I could hear the thuds as his bony fists struck me on the ribs, belly, and kidneys. Burkitt knew his business and, though I was helpless, I was never entirely unconscious. He propped me against the tree and my head rolled on my limp neck. His face wavered and pulsed before me.

"Now let's have it, Tucker, and let's have it straight this time! Floyd was up on the ladder and you tipped him over. That was the way it went, right?"

"No."

He hit me again. There wasn't a thing I could do to stop him, but he couldn't make me say I had killed Floyd. The truth was the only weapon I had, but it was heavier than his fists and stronger than his muscles. Crazily, I felt that I could beat him with it. But I wasn't really sane. I was in a delirium. His clubbing fists beat me down; and I gibbered and laughed and croaked. When he picked me up, I tried feebly to bite him, but he couldn't make me say that I had killed Floyd.

I remember lying with my face in the harsh St. Augustine grass, vomiting; I remember being dragged to my feet and his fists slamming into my body; I remember the blackness of a chaotic universe thundering around my head, slashed with the lightning of pain. And I remember the white slab of his face hanging over me like a demented moon in a nightmare sky and my mumbling hysterically, "You can't make me, you son of a bitch, you can't make me—" Then his fists slamming into me again and the voices that drifted foggily through the dark.

"Floyd didn't just fall off that ladder, Tucker."

"No ..."

"You tipped the ladder."

"No ..."

"You did it."

"No ..."

"Make it easy for yourself. You tipped him. Ladders don't fall down by themselves. You tipped it."

"Nononono ..."

Burkitt couldn't make me. He thought he was killing me, but really he was killing himself. Because he couldn't make me say it, he was just killing himself. And every time he hit me, it took just a little more out of him because he couldn't make me say it. He knew it, too.

"We're getting out of here," he said breathlessly. "This is going to take time."

Time. To the end of his life. He was killing himself. Matt Burkitt picked me up. I was so limp that I sagged through his arms like wet wash. He carried me to his car and set me up in the front seat, opening the window beside my head so the fresh air would revive me as we rode. I couldn't move, but I could see. I could see pretty plainly, and I almost laughed again when I found that I could identify the spots we were passing—the bank, the chamber of commerce building, the yacht club, the Quonset huts they used for hangars at the air field, the Gulf & Bay Fishhouse. He thought he was killing me, but I knew where we were going. I knew. I could see.

We were going out the old beach road, out among the scrub pine, the palmettos and rattlesnakes where nobody ever went, even the tourists, and we'd be alone with miles of nothing but beach and gulls and ghost crabs all the way down to Boca Grande. There was the sweet-salt taste of blood in my mouth, but I giggled to myself because I had the secret. He was killing himself and I was going to be there, but that wasn't the secret. I knew the answer and he didn't. The secret was that no matter what you do, you do it primarily to yourself. He didn't know that. He didn't know that I was going to kill him.

The car lurched like a boat caught broadside in the trough of a wave. I fell against him. The tires screamed and we bounced heavily in the soft shoulder of the road, and his elbow battered me as he fought the wheel to keep the car from turning over. With a noise like crumpling sheets of thin plastic, we nosed into a palmetto clump and stopped.

Angled across the road ahead of us, cutting us off, was an old '39 Chevvy with a broken muffler that panted gutturally. Burkitt walked ominously toward it. Buster got out of the other car. I knew something was going to happen and, also, that there was a reason why I should be especially interested, but I couldn't think of it. I felt very detached. I wasn't even very curious. I was dreadfully, terribly tired. I wanted to shut my eyes, but not there in Burkitt's car. There was a reason for that, too, but I couldn't figure it out. I began to get a little panicky. Something unpleasant was going to happen out there.

Burkitt held out his hand and demanded something. Buster slapped it aside, and then they were standing in the middle of the road, hitting each other. It was a terrible thing to see. They were both such huge men, and the sound of their fists was terrifying. Now I knew I had to get away from there, because something bad was going to happen to everybody. I managed to get the car door open, but I could hardly move.

The noise of the fight was getting worse. They were like two large, savage animals, and I had to get away. I rolled out of the car and landed on my side in the soft sand of the road shoulder. It took me awhile to get to my hands and knees, and I began slowly to crawl away. In my condition it was very hard to do. First I had to put out one hand, then drag up one leg a few inches, then put out the other and drag up the other leg. Several times I fell over, but I knew I couldn't lie there because they'd come and get me. So I pushed myself up painfully to my hands and knees again.

I crawled for hours and miles, and then somebody touched me on the shoulder and I screamed.

CHAPTER FIFTEEN

Buster told me later that, weak as I was, I fought him like a wildcat before he could get me into his car. He thought I had gone completely out of my head. But I had no recollection of that at all. The first thing I remember was the taste of rum in my throat, and after awhile there was Buster beside me in the front seat of the car.

"Okay now, sport," he was saying anxiously. "You okay now?"

"Burkitt ...?" I whispered.

"Don't worry about that guy, sport. He ain't going to push nobody around no more tonight. But it's lucky for you I come when I did, sport. That guy would of taken you apart in little hunks. I knew they were going to put the boots to you, the way they took you and left the rest of us out there on the island. I could see it in the looks they gave each other. I didn't know what the hell to do, but they were so damn anxious to give you the business, they forgot all about that other clunk's boat—Floyd what's-his-name, the guy that busted his neck.

"So I give them a little head start and follow them. I got there just as Burkitt was loading you in his car, and I know he's going to take you someplace where he can work on you in peace and quiet. So I tail him and when he gets out here, I cut him off the road. It was just dumb luck, that's all. They could of taken you down in the cellar and put it to you there ..."

My body was a furnace pit of smoldering pain, but the rum made it easier to bear. "You took an awful chance," my voice was weak and quavery.

"You got to take a chance sometimes, sport. Have another shot. You'll feel better."

I held the rum bottle in both hands, but it still chattered against my teeth when I drank from it. "I hope you killed him," I said bitterly.

"Well, he ain't far from it, sport. If he wants to eat steak from here on in, he's going to have to buy teeth."

"They planned it. They knew I didn't have anything to do with Floyd getting killed, but they turned Burkitt loose on me. Why?"

"That's the way cops are, sport. Maybe they thought there was an off-chance you knocked the guy off, so they gave you to their muscle man. You can't tell a cop nothin', never. And you're not the first guy that monkey worked on. He was real scientific. There ain't a mark on you, I bet. He didn't touch your face at all. He gave you the whole works in the belly and the kidneys where it really hurts and don't show. But don't be scared if you pass blood for awhile. Most guys do after a workout like you got. It ain't necessarily serious."

"They planned it," I went on almost hysterically. "They knew exactly what Burkitt would do ..."

"Don't let it get you down, sport. This goes on all the time with cops."

I thought of Burkitt's reputation and of the drunks and tramps he'd beaten up; how he prowled the town, even when he was supposed to be off-duty, looking for trouble, looking for somebody to beat up. And he was a good cop. Everybody said he was the best cop on the force. Now I knew what they meant when they said Burkitt was a good cop.

"I'd have killed him!"

"Take it easy, sport. You'll feel different tomorrow. That's the way cops are, and there's nothin' you can do about it. Just don't let it get you down."

"Then why'd you stick your neck out for me?"

"You sound kind of cynical, sport."

"Cynical? Maybe it's because I know you, Buster. You don't give away something for nothing."

"Who does?" He shrugged and gave me that big grin. "Okay, so maybe I had an angle. Maybe I had two, three angles. One is Letty's nuts about you and, believe it or not, I want the kid to be happy. That's a fact, but how happy could she be with a husband with half-a-kidney because some dumb cop kicked out the other one-and-a-half? That's part of it."

"A damn little part of it!"

"Don't be like that, sport, or the next time you shave you'll think maybe, oh what the hell, and let the razor slip and slice yourself from ear to ear. It's happened before. I've known guys. But the whole world ain't against you. The cops around here might be a bunch of foul balls, but they don't own the earth, know what I mean? And me, I ain't against you neither. You've had that idea all along, but I ain't. I seen right in the beginning Letty had a yen for you.

"But you'll never know how close you came to a busted neck that first night, sport, and I'm tellin' you that straight. I knew she'd given herself to you, the way she run in the house, and I was ready to give it to you. If you'd been George Daly, I'd of done it and no questions asked. You beginning to get the idea?" He put a cigarette in his mouth, but before he lit it, he held the match and looked grimly at me over the flame. "I'm not the bastard you think I am."

I couldn't think very clearly. I couldn't separate the different ideas and thoughts that skittered through my mind. I could take only one at a time.

"But you've got a proposition," I said. "You've had a proposition from the beginning, and you've been nursing me along, using Letty and everything else."

"That's right. I had a proposition, only I didn't know what it was myself. But you got one thing wrong. You ain't the guy I was nursin' along; it was Daly. And I got it out of him tonight, and had to scare the livin' life out of him to do it, too. I had an idea, you might come in handy, but I wasn't nursin' you along. It was just a hunch, and it turned out. I need you now. I know it, but if you ain't interested, you can tell me to go to hell and no hard feelings. But let me say this first: it ain't against the law."

"The law! The hell with the law!"

"Don't be like that, crumb!" he said angrily. "You got pushed around tonight, and now you feel sorry for yourself. Well, lots of guys get pushed around, but they don't throw up their hands. The minute you start thinking the hell with the law, you're behind the eight-ball!"

"That's funny, coming from you."

"Yeah? Well, you don't see no cops trying to beat me up, do you? I got more sense. And this proposition I got *ain't* against the law. Are you interested? There's money in it."

"What do you think?"

"I don't think. I always make sure first. For one thing, you're so damn near broke it ain't funny. You got a couple hundred bucks in the bank, you got the boat, and you got that desert island out there that you couldn't give away. Your fishing business is all shot to hell on account of that thing you call the red tide, so you're up the creek without a paddle. And don't tell me I'm wrong because I been nosing around and I know. So I'm offering you a chance to make some real dough and it won't be against the law. If things work out, it'll be as easy as putting salt in your soup. Only we'll have to go out of the country afterwards, if that's okay with you."

"Okay with me?" I laughed harshly. "I'll be *glad* to get out of this damned country, and when I get out, I'll stay out!"

"Listen, sport." He put his hand on my knee and spoke earnestly. "Don't *be* like that. I love my country. We can lick any other son of a bitchin' country in the world, and I never want to be nothin' but a U.S. citizen. I'm proud of my country. There ain't no country like it and anybody tries to tell me different, I'm givin' him such a goddam poke in the snoot he'll be drinking coffee out of his ear for the rest of his life.

"I never said nothin' like this to nobody ever before, but you're practically a member of the family. Even so, if you try to give me this Communist crap I'll break your damn neck for you. And I ain't kiddin'!"

I was sick, exhausted, and confused. Buster wasn't making sense and his flag waving, considering the type of person he was, seemed out of order.

"Oh, go to hell," I told him.

"Shut up and *listen* to me for a minute, sport. I'm talking like a Dutch uncle now. You got the wrong attitude. You're sore. Okay. You got a right to be sore. But just a couple tanktown cops ain't the whole U.S. You got to take this in the right perspective. You got to think the right way, and you ain't. You can't think when you're sore. And damn it!" he said furiously, "if Letty wasn't nuts about you, I'd beat your brains out on the road.

"When a guy as smart and respectable as you starts thinking like a bunch of damn Communists, it makes me see red. If the whole lot of you had one neck, I'd take it in my hands and squeeze it like walnut shells and throw it in the ocean. You hear me, sport?" He shook me roughly. "You listenin' to me, damn you?"

I don't think I was ever closer to death. Buster meant every word he said. He was an actor. He had many parts, and he knew just when to play them, and for whom, but he wasn't playing to me. He was in deadly earnest. His whole, tremendous face blazed with the light. He was a fanatic—and for no reason that I could think of. He was an outcast (actually, he was) who operated outside, or at least on the fringes of the law, and this was his pride. *He was a U.S. citizen.* Now he had shown me himself naked, and that was all he had left, that he was a U.S. citizen.

As for the rest of it, he knew exactly where he stood. He had this great body, and nothing to do with it; he was intelligent, probably more so than I, but he didn't know what to do with his intelligence except make a quick buck. And he was all torn up about that, too. He had the right and loyal instincts, but because they had never been channeled, he was committing a kind of moral suicide.

But that was no reason why I should commit suicide also.

"I'm not a Communist, Buster, and if you don't take your damn' hands off me—"

He laughed, shamefaced, and eased me back gently against the front seat of the car.

"I'm sorry, sport. I kind of got out of control. But how's about it, now? I can't give you the whole proposition yet, because I don't know it myself, but I promise you, it ain't against the law. You need the dough, and so do I. The heat'll be on us for awhile, but all we got to do is stay out of the country. There's nothin' to it.

"The whole operation won't take more'n a couple hours, if it works out—and that part of it's up to me. And if it *does* work out, you and Letty can live the rest of your life on it. I'm telling you, sport, I'd do anything for that kid. I wouldn't hurt you, honest, even if you say the hell with you, but what do you say?"

I smothered the impulse to blurt "I'll do anything if it means money to get out of here."

"Well?" he said eagerly.

"I'll go along with you, Buster. I'm not quite broke, but I'm damn near it. Now what's the proposition?"

He sat back against his side of the car, threw his cigarette out the window, and dug into his shirt pocket. He came up with another of his cigar butts and smoothed it out very carefully in his fingers. Then he bit off a piece of loose leaf and spat it out. Tilting his head so he wouldn't burn his nose, he put a match to it.

"I ain't going to tell you nothing about it, sport," he said finally.

"Because if something goes wrong, I don't want you to know nothing. I got it out of Daly tonight, like I said, but the bastard might have been giving me a bum steer. He's a yellow son of a bitch, and he might have been just trying to get out from under. But that's my worry. I gotta go to Tampa tonight, right now. There're a couple details that got to be straightened out, but I should be back in the morning. Can you take that boat of yours over to the island without any help?"

"I'm all right."

"The hell you are. You've had the guts kicked out of you tonight. That bird, Burkitt, can really hit." He fingered his jaw and grinned. "But, honest, sport, if you can do it by yourself, it'd save me a trip back and forth, maybe an hour, and I'd like to get up to Tampa and get this thing settled. But if you're not okay, just say so and I'll take you back."

"I'm okay."

"Okay, sport." He reached for the ignition key and stepped on the starter; the engine lurched to life with a noise like a sewing machine. "I'll get things set up."

Buster looked back, leaning out of the window. Burkitt's car was still there on the soft shoulder, the twin cones of headlights stabbing the night. Burkitt, himself, was a dark, oblong bundle off the side of the road, unmoving.

Buster nodded. "He'll be okay."

He pushed the old-fashioned gear shift lever into second, saying peevishly that first gear was worn out, and the old car panted down the road back toward Sanibar.

I expected all the way to be stopped by the police. The prowl car passed us as we turned off toward the municipal docks, but it headed east. We knew it would be quite awhile before they found Burkitt. I hoped they'd never find the son of a bitch, but that was silly. It wasn't Burkitt's fault. He was just part of it. He, himself, was just a poor, lonely jerk; the rest of them just used him as their hatchet man, and he didn't know any better.

Buster must have sensed what I was thinking. "Cut it out, sport!" he said as we drove. "You'll just end up behind the eight ball. The law's the law!"

I couldn't help laughing. He gave me a funny look, probably putting it down to the beating I'd gotten from Burkitt. Then he shook his head and muttered something under his breath.

We stopped at the end of the dock and he turned off the ignition. I could see the *Skidoo* rising and falling out there, leaning against her ropes.

"You're sure you can take her out to the island all by yourself, sport?" he asked me again.

"I could take her down to Cuba."

"Good. Now look," he put his hand on my arm and his fingers tightened, "I should be back before nine in the morning. If I'm not, just forget the whole thing. Forget I ever said anything about it. Just take Letty the hell out of here, because—well, because things didn't just work out right. Know what I mean?"

I knew what he meant. If things didn't work out right, he'd be dead. I was in a numb state, and there were implications that I didn't get, but all of a sudden, I didn't want Buster dead. He gave me that great big All-American Boy grin, and I wanted him to come back. He had saved me from that lousy Matt Burkitt, he had figured things out when the Sanibar police department had it stacked against me, and I didn't want him dead. I don't know if you know what I mean. There he was—big, blond, grinning, and, as far as I was concerned at the moment, the only friend I had in the whole, wide world ...

"Take care of yourself, Buster," I said shakily.

He laughed. "Buster is the guy Buster always takes care of, and don't let nobody tell you different. See you in the morning, sport. Next week by this time, we'll all be millionaires!"

I got out of the car and held on to a post on the dock so I wouldn't fall down. He backed the car in a tight U, slammed it into second gear and, with a wave of his hand out the window, rumbled east toward the Tamiami Trail and Tampa.

CHAPTER SIXTEEN

Letty was waiting for me when I docked the *Skidoo* at the Key. Calling my name, she flew aboard, and flung her arms around me. She held me so tightly that I could feel the shudders of her body against mine.

"I was so scared, honey," she whispered. "I thought they were going to do something to you. Buster wouldn't let me go with him, and it was awful just sittin' and waitin' for you to come back. Are you all right, honey? Are you really all right?"

"Just tired." I didn't want to tell her about Burkitt.

"Oh honey, honey. I'm so glad to see you!"

She kissed me wildly, but I was so exhausted that I could barely respond. When we went out to the dock, I saw the spear-gun lying there.

"What was that for?" I asked.

Her chin lifted. "If they'd hurt you—"

I put the gun on the boat. "You've got spirit, Letty, but don't try anything like that," I told her. "Dammit, these cracker cops down here would throw you in jail for the rest of your life."

We walked very slowly up to the house, and I pretended that it was because I was so tired. I knew her temper. If I told her about the beating I'd taken, she'd storm Sanibar with an ax in her hand.

A terrific racket came from Daly's room when we walked into the house, and I looked at Letty in surprise. He was banging on the door and yelling, and then there was a noise as if he'd flung a chair across the room.

"Don't pay any attention to him, honey," said Letty. "He's in an awful mood, stinkin' drunk and everything else. I thought he was going to shoot me once, but I got the gun away from him and locked him in his room. Don't even talk to him, honey."

There was a crash. This time Daly must have knocked over the chest of drawers.

"Let me talk to him!" I said above the noise. I went to the door. "Cut that out," I yelled, "or I'll come in there and beat the living daylights out of you!"

He snarled obscenities, but that was the end of it. Then I heard him stumble across the room, muttering to himself, and the bed creaked. I went back to the living room for a drink.

As I relaxed in a chair with my glass, I noticed a camera with a flashlight attachment standing on the table. In the reflector was a burned-out infra-red bulb for taking pictures in the dark.

"I found it outside in the bushes near where the ladder fell," Letty explained. "It belonged to that fella that killed himself. His name's on it."

It was Floyd's camera, all right. "Too bad we didn't find it when the police were here," I said bitterly. "I'd loved to have shoved it down their throats."

"But why'd he want a camera, honey?"

"To take a picture of you and me in bed together."

She looked disgusted. "You can't even feel sorry for people like that. But talkin' about bed—" She took my hand and led me toward her bedroom, "You look ready to drop."

Letty lay down beside me on the bed. I fell asleep in her arms.

When I awakened, Buster was sitting in the lounge chair by the window. He looked different. His eyes were bloodshot and his mouth was a lipless slash in a harsh face.

"I was just going to wake you up," he said. "It's gettin' late."

I sat up and groaned. I was stiff and I ached all over, but especially around the middle. Buster watched me, and there was a new hard coldness in his face. His eyes were like January ice. He looked as grim and forbidding as a figure out of a dark Norse saga.

"Feel good enough to drive the boat?" he demanded. "We'll have to start soon."

I rubbed my eyes. "Start for where?"

He got up slowly, came over to the bed, and handed me a piece of paper. The first thing I saw was a bloodstain in the upper right hand corner. I looked at Buster, and his face was a rock.

"That's where we're goin'." He jabbed his forefinger at the lines of very shaky handwriting on the paper. "Right there."

It was written in pencil and it was hardly decipherable. The man who had written it had been drunk or sick—or barely conscious. It took me awhile to figure it out. It said:

Long. 83°
Latt. 27°
10:30 P.M.
Blink 1-3-1

"That mean anything to you?" Buster asked harshly. He was as tense as a steel cable that had been tightened with a winch.

"It means longitude eighty-three, latitude twenty-seven."

"But does it *mean* anything, damn it!"

"That's about thirty-five miles off the town of Englewood, out in the Gulf. Now you tell *me* what it means."

A little of the tenseness went out of his face. "So the son of a bitch wasn't lying," he said softly.

"Who wasn't lying?"

Buster sat down on the edge of the bed and took a foil-wrapped cigar from his shirt pocket. He sniffed it and smiled grimly. "He smoked good cigars, too."

He peeled the foil carefully, folded it, and put it back into his pocket. Biting a small piece from the end of the cigar, he spat it on the floor. He lit up, inhaled deeply, and I looked at the paper in my hand. The bloodstain was a smear. Buster saw me, and took the paper from my fingers.

"Don't let it bother you, sport. I just had to get a little rough before this guy saw the light. I'll tell you about it. Daly worked for this outfit up Tampa, and he gave me the name of the guy that wrote this stuff on the paper for me. He was the kingfish, but don't worry about that. I got him alone in his apartment. Nobody knows nothin' about it and they ain't gonna find out till too late. He wasn't as tough as he thought he was when I really put it to him." He laughed shortly, without amusement.

"Now, here's the pitch," Buster went on. "This outfit's been bringing a lot of, uh, diamonds and stuff like that into the country out of Cuba, and they don't pay no duty on it. There's a boat between Cuba and Tampa that passes that longitude and latitude stuff you read there at ten-thirty tonight. We blink a light once, then three times, then once again, and a guy on board the boat drops this package over the side. The package is wrapped in cork and it's got some kind of paint on it that glows in the dark, know what I mean?"

"Phosphorescent," I said automatically.

"Yeah, like that. Well, in this package is the jewelry these other guys brought into Cuba from Europe, and they want to smuggle it into this country. So they drop it off this boat and another boat comes out of Punta Gorda and picks it up, only this time there won't be no boat out of Punta Gorda. It'll just be us. You beginning to get the idea now, sport?"

"So *we* smuggle it in," I said.

"That's where you're wrong," he said with satisfaction. "We ain't gettin' tangled up with no law. We *don't* smuggle it in. We take it back to Cuba and we sell it there. We take a loss. Okay! But there's still plenty in it and we ain't taking nothin' from nobody except a bunch of crooks. And the beauty of it is, we ain't doin' nothing against the good old U.S." He threw back his head and gave a shattering laugh. "How's that for figuring things out, okay? See what I mean now? We ain't doing a thing against the law. All we're doing is hijacking a stake from a bunch of crooks. How's it sound, sport?"

My mind went back to my treatment at the hands of Burkitt and the Sanibar police. "Okay. But if you have this all figured out, why cut me in?"

"I need you, that's why. That longitude-latitude junk don't mean a thing to me. Thirty-five miles out in the ocean there is a long ways; if I tried to do it, I'd probably wind up in Coney Island or somewhere. Now you know how to get there and you got the boat. If we don't make the connection with that Cuba boat, we might just as well row around the lake in Central Park. You can do it, sport. You don't need no signposts. Okay?"

I thought of Burkitt again. "Okay," I said wearily.

He slapped me on the shoulder and gave a loud, blatting laugh. Buster was really under terrific tension. His eyes were staring and his fingers kept kneading his palms, and the right side of his mouth curved up in a twitching, snarl-like grimace. He was as taut and nervous as a cat in a dog pound.

"How much is in this for us?" I asked. Not that I particularly cared. All I wanted to do now was get out of Sanibar and be able to stay out.

"More'n you'll ever spend in your life, sport!" he said, his eyes glittering. "More'n we'll both ever spend in our lives. But let's get out of here. Letty's waitin' down on the boat. Need anything from here?"

I shook my head. My hands were shaking. The excitement was beginning to get to me. Buster helped me out of bed, and I found I was so stiff I could hardly walk. He held my arm and walked me around the room a few times till my muscles loosened up. Then he helped me outside and down the porch steps.

"Oh, hell!" he said. "I gotta get Daly. We can't leave that poor son of a bitch here all by himself. You go down the boat, and I'll be right along."

I envied him as he sprang lithely up the steps to the house. I moved like an invalid. My middle hurt so much that I had to bend over as I shuffled down the path. Then I heard Daly start yelling. I stopped and looked back at the house. Daly was screaming incoherently at Buster. He sounded as if he had gone crazy again. I turned, crabbed awkwardly back to the house, and pulled myself up the porch steps.

Staggering into Daly's bedroom, I saw him sitting up in bed. His eyes had a crazed sheen over the gun he had pointed at Buster. He was screeching and his voice sounded two octaves higher than soprano.

"You're gettin' us all killed, but I ain't gonna let you! I ain't! I ain't! I ain't! I ain't gonna let you, I ain't gonna. I'll kill you, you bastard! I'll kill you first …"

I had nothing to throw at him or shoot him with, and I wondered how to distract him. Slamming the door as hard as I could was all I could think of to do. It worked. Daly's head jerked around, and, in one quick, fluid motion, Buster took a gun from his hip pocket, aimed it, and shot him. Daly's hand's flew to his chest and his eyes spread incredulously. He folded, fell face forward to the edge of the bed and slowly toppled to the floor. I didn't have time to be shocked or startled. Buster grabbed my arm and ran me out of the room.

"The son of a bitch!" His voice had a curious lilt, but, confused and lightheaded as I was, I felt the same way inside; it was the high intoxication of the whole thing. Buster was laughing shrilly and I laughed with him. "He asked for it!" he said. "He asked for it!"

"But where'd he get the gun?" I asked as I stumbled along with Buster.

"I gave it to him. He asked for it, and I gave it to him." Something struck me. "You knew he'd try to shoot you?"

"Sure, sport. I knew he'd try, but I thought I had him under control."

"You're a liar!"

His face congested, but he laughed crazily again. "Maybe I am. I'll never know, and neither will you. Anyways, he's better off dead. He tried to give it to us first, remember? He tried to give it to us first! And if it wasn't for you, he would have, too! You really clobbered him, sport!"

"Yeah, I really clobbered him!" I felt drunk, but not falling-down drunk; just crazy drunk. All I did was slam a door.

And maybe Daly wasn't really dead. He was just lying there on the floor, but he was out of our way. He wasn't going to bother us. It was all very unreal.

Punch-drunk and groggy from the beating I had taken from Burkitt, at the moment it seemed gratifying to me that Daly had been disposed of permanently. I was in a very high state of elation. I was going to make a million dollars. Everything was wonderful.

We cast off from the dock, and Letty worried over me. But Buster took her out to the cockpit, giving her that wonderful grin of his. "Daly didn't want to come, baby," he said, and I almost laughed right out loud. "Daly really didn't want to come."

Buster planted Letty in the cockpit and then later came in to me. "We got to let her off somewhere, sport," he said seriously. "It might get rough out there and I don't want her hurt. Where can we drop her off?"

I tried to think. "Venice. We can drop her off at Venice. There's a dock. And we can pick her up there afterward."

"Venice it is then, sport."

Buster kept Letty out there in the stern cockpit, although I could see she was anxious to come in to me. She kept turning her head, but he kept her out there, and it was just as well that he did the way I felt. But he kept her out there, and I kept the *Skidoo* on course.

Tomorrow would be plenty of time for Letty. Tomorrow I'd have a million dollars and would be able to do things for her—the things that made me feel so foul I couldn't do for her now. I would have given her my guts if it would have made her happy, and I wanted to make Letty happy.

Buster came into the cabin as we approached the twin jetties at Venice inlet and leaned against my chair. "You know, sport," he said in a low voice, "I don't think it's such a good idea to dock at Venice. I beat that Sanibar cop up pretty bad and there might be a call out for us. And if we're held up even a couple hours, we might just as well kiss that package good-bye."

I nodded, as if it were the most natural thing in the world now to have to dodge the police. "Then I guess we'll have to take Letty with us."

"No, that ain't such a good idea neither, but here's what I been thinking. How close can you run to the shore?"

"Go to hell, Buster! You're not dumping Letty over the side."

"Shut up, will you! I already talked to her and she said okay, and anyway, she can swim like a trout."

"I don't care if she can swim like a goldfish! She—"

He put his hand on my shoulder and enveloped me with that warm, spreading grin of his. "Ah, now, Jeff, what's the sense in us gettin' in a free for all? I'm just thinkin' of Letty. Like I told you, this guy in Tampa was supposed to give the word to a boat in Punta Gorda to meet that Cuba-to-Tampa boat and pick up the package. Now I'm pretty damn sure that *he* ain't going to give no word to no boat to meet no other boat—but suppose some other guy gives the word? Suppose this boat from Punta Gorda does show up out there? They might take a few pot shots at us, and how'd you like Letty aboard with a chance of getting a bullet in her maybe? Damn it, she's my kid niece, and I ain't letting her get hurt!"

I had no answer to that. Buster was right. I was the one who wasn't thinking straight. But it was very hard for me to think because I was hurting pretty badly around the middle and in the kidneys. And every once in awhile my eyes would go out of focus and the numbers and letters on the compass would swim like drowning flies in a bowl of water. There was also a painful lump behind my left ear. This and the occasional and passing dizziness that came over me spelled a concussion. Even in the lucid periods I didn't feel that any of this was exactly real.

"You're right," I said. "You're absolutely right, Buster. I'm wrong and if you want to take a poke at me, go right ahead. I was just being a pain in the neck. This neck—" I touched the bump behind my ear and giggled almost hysterically.

His hand tightened on my arm. "You feeling okay, sport? You can run the boat?"

"I can run the boat in my sleep," I said peevishly. "Don't worry about my running the boat. If I had to, I could run this boat right into the lobby of the Paramount Theatre in Times Square and buy you a ticket to the matinee. We can put Letty ashore about a half mile south of the Venice beach. I'll go inside the bar and she can wade ashore."

"Okay. But listen: I didn't tell her what we're going to do because she'd worry. I told her we were *delivering* a package for a guy, so if she asks you, you'll know what to say."

"You don't have to tell me what to say. I can think for myself. Just leave me alone and I'll run the boat."

His voice droned on, but I was getting dizzy again. I thought I was going to be sick, but it passed away. When I felt all right again, we were inside the bar south of Venice and the bow was gently nosing the shelving sand in the shallows. I had to stay at the wheel to keep the stern in the deeper water with the rudder and the props. I didn't exactly know how I'd gotten there, but I was there and I seemed to know what I was doing when Letty came in to say good-bye. She kissed me and held me tightly for a moment.

"Take care of yourself, honey," she whispered. "Please take care."

"Nothing to it, sweetheart," I said airily. "We're just running a special delivery service for the post office." Suddenly I saw she was holding a thick wad of bills. "Where'd you get that?"

"Buster wants me to hold it for him. It's what the man's paying to have his package delivered."

I knew there was something wrong, but I couldn't think what it was. Buster didn't have any money, and nobody was paying us to deliver any packages. But I knew I wasn't able to think straight, so maybe there was something I had missed.

"Sure," I said. "Well, don't buy any Florida oil wells while we're gone. Next year we'll laugh about all this." Letty leaned back and looked anxiously into my face. "You don't sound like yourself, honey."

"I don't? Who do I sound like, Groucho Marx? The trouble with me is—" Things were going all blurry again as I fumbled for words. "The trouble with me is, I'm crazy about you."

That must have been the right line to take because she flung her arms around me and said, "Oh honey!" And then Letty was gone. I watched her climb over the transom and drop down into two feet of water. She waded ashore, holding her skirt up round her hips. Damn, she had beautiful legs! I loved her so much. I waited until Letty was high on the dunes, waving, and then I took the *Skidoo* around the bar and out into the Gulf.

CHAPTER SEVENTEEN

I kept sliding in and out of full consciousness. The motion of the boat in the heavy swells made me dizzy and sick to my stomach, but I didn't throw up. I remember getting out the sextant and taking a shot at the sun, just to make sure that we were on course. And I remember two or three savage mouth-fights with Buster and telling him if he didn't like the way I was running the boat to run it himself.

I remember shoving him away and telling him to stop breathing down my neck. And I remember looking at the spear-gun and swearing to myself that if he bothered me again, I'd sure as hell lock him out of the cabin in the stern cockpit. Half the time I had to grip the wheel to hold myself upright and the yellow light in the compass was of no more use to me than a fried egg. My head hurt, and the motors throbbed inside my skull.

It was quiet now. The motors weren't running, and the *Skidoo* rose and fell on an oily swell. The only light was the weak compass light. The water lapped monotonously against the hull. It was dreary.

"It's twenty after ten," said Buster heavily. "You're sure you know where we are?"

I raised my head from my forearms which were folded across the top of the wheel. "Longitude eighty-three latitude twenty-seven, thirty-five miles due west of Englewood, Gulf of Mexico. Anything else you want to know?" I don't know how I knew it, but I did.

"Go to hell!"

"You, too," I spat at him. "And double!"

I turned and switched on the ship-to-shore radio. In a minute or two we started getting the usual chatter between the fishing boats out in the Gulf.

"... Eight hundred pounds of red snapper this afternoon, running good, got a whole mess of octopus for the Portugees up the coast ..."

"... Kingfish coming in strong ..."

"... Loaded down with black grouper, putting in tomorrow morning, Vance busted his arm ..."

"Shut that damn thing off!" said Buster savagely.

I showed my teeth. "The hell with you!"

He started up from the bunk and seemed to freeze in mid-air. I stared at him. He was standing there, crouched, his right hand extended, his left in a fist at his hip, but it was as if somebody had paralyzed him in that position. His mouth hung open and his eyes were like headlights.

I continued staring at him. I had a monkey wrench in my right hand, but that wasn't what had stopped him. Then the radio came in to my consciousness.

". . *Skidoo*, registration number N103,273, repeat, half-cabin cruiser the *Skidoo*, registration number N103,273, painted white. Sturgis is probably armed and must be considered extremely dangerous. Over."

"Coast Guard cutter Hamilton to Sanibar police, regarding killing of George Daly, will watch for half cabin cruiser *Skidoo*, registration number N103,273. Sturgis armed, considered extremely dangerous, will take due precautions. Any idea where *Skidoo* may be heading?"

"It was last seen off the jetties at Venice, probably heading south, repeat, probably heading south, but witnesses seem confused on this point. Don't take any chances. Sturgis is extremely dangerous."

Buster settled back to the edge of the bunk. He was white. "The Coast Guard, that's part of the U.S. Navy, ain't it?"

"Yes, but they can't touch us out here," I said inanely. I wasn't reassuring him; I was merely giving information. "We're out thirty-five miles."

"But, hell, we didn't do anything against the U.S.! Why do they have to call out the Navy?" Buster looked at me with real hatred. "Why—"

I heard the freighter coming. You could feel the beat of the heavy propellers. I ducked my head, looked through the port to the south, and I could see her lights. She was pounding toward us, and I blinked the running lights according to instructions.

"Here comes your Cuba-to-Tampa boat," I said.

Buster twisted in the bunk and stared through the glass. For the first time I saw that he had a gun in his right hand. Who was he going to fight, the Coast Guard? And with a hand gun? That was a funny one.

"The signal, the signal!" he said hoarsely, as he watched the freighter come up to us. "Give them the signal."

"I did, Buster. One-three-one. I blinked the running lights."

"Give it to them again, sport. Maybe they didn't see it."

I repeated the signal, and we watched the freighter pass, no more than fifty yards astern of us. A luminous circle arced from her stern, and I saw it bob in the sea.

"They dropped it," I said, and revved up the motors that I had kept idling. I made a slow circle, keeping my eyes on the bobbing luminescence, and then switched on the bow floodlight. "Pick it up," I told him, keeping my eyes on the thing and sliding the *Skidoo* toward it. "I'll come up alongside. There's a net in the cockpit ..."

I was vaguely conscious of his going by me. Then there was a hoarse shout of triumph and Buster came back into the cabin with a dripping round shape in his arms. It was a cork ring and, securely lashed to the center of it, was a square package wrapped in oilskin. His hands shaking, Buster set it down on the bunk and slashed at the lashings with a knife. I cut the bow floodlight, and leaned shakily sideways on my chair, watching him. He grumbled and swore, slashing with the knife and ripping at the oilskin with his fingers. Then he pulled the package open and it spilled over the bunk.

I had expected a glitter of diamonds and jewels, but nothing came out of it but a number of small, flat aluminum cans. He snatched one up and twisted the cover from it. A white, powdery dust spilled over the back of his hand, and he gave a harsh, guttural cry. He held up his hand, dabbled the fingers of his other hand in the dust and licked at it.

"It was a fake," I said stupidly. "They—"

"A fake!" Buster laughed wildly and threw out his arm, indicating all the other little round cans on the bunk. "There's a million bucks here, sport!"

"You said diamonds—"

"Diamonds! This is better'n' diamonds!"

"What the hell is it?" It came flooding over me in waves of nausea. Jewels. Diamonds. I had been taken for a sucker. This was dope. Cocaine. The sudden sobering was almost like death itself. When I spoke, my voice was like lead. "You knew it all the time, didn't you?"

"Sure I knew it, sport. So what? There a million bucks here. A million bucks! I couldn't tell you ahead of time because you're such a holy son of a bitch. But here it is, sport!" He lifted two handfuls of those little cans in his hands, showing them to me, his eyes shining. "A million bucks! Would you turn down a million bucks?"

"That kind of million bucks, yes!"

Very slowly, Buster put down the double handful of those little cans. He laid them very carefully on the bunk. He looked up at me, his face grim.

"I knew I was going to have trouble with you, sport. That's the reason I let Letty off at Venice. Now let's get sensible ..."

"Not with that stuff!" I said violently. "What do you think you're going to do with it?"

"Sell it!"

"It's dope, it's walking death, and you're going to sell it?"

"It's a million bucks, and I'm going to sell it," he snapped. "What're you going to do about it?"

"I'm going to throw it overboard!"

He pointed his gun at me. "Over your dead body, sport," he said, grinning. "I mean it, so don't try anything."

I had the monkey wrench in my hand, but his grin just widened a little when my eyes flickered at it. I opened my hand and let the wrench drop. He laughed.

"Now, listen, sport. There's no reason we should have a free for all. There's plenty here for both of us and Letty too. Hell, I'm cutting you in for fifty percent. I could knock you off right now and have the whole thing for myself. Dammit, what more do you want?"

"You killed Daly deliberately," I said unsteadily.

"That's right. I gave him a gun, but it wasn't loaded. I knew he'd make a pass at me. He was scared witless."

"And you killed that guy in Tampa."

"You're damn right I did! Whattaya think, I'd leave him alive to ruin this for us?"

"And—" it came in a burst—"you killed Floyd Hammond, too. He heard you and Daly talking in Daly's bedroom. You had to kill him because he heard Daly tell you about *this!*"

"That's right, sport." He chuckled in reminiscence. "He heard us, and I tipped over his ladder. Then I went down and busted his neck while he was laying there on the ground. And in just about one minute I'm gonna pull this trigger and knock you off unless you come to your senses. Damn it to hell, sport," he pleaded, "don't make me do it. This is my stake. This is the most money I ever had in my hands all my life, and nobody's gonna take it away from me. You can't, anyway, so don't try!

"I'm only giving you this chance because Letty's nuts about you, so use your brains. Look," he said eagerly, "we'll take this stuff down to Cuba and we'll sell it there, and we won't be doing nothing against the U.S. We'll sell it down there, so what're you worrying about?"

"And they'll ship it right back up here!"

"Oh, hell, why be such a pain in the neck? Look, I'm giving you— Keep your hand away from that wrench!"

I dropped the wrench and stood up. Buster was a madman and there was no reasoning with him. Nothing was going to prevent his selling the stuff, and he'd kill me the way he'd squash a fly. But I had to stop him! Somehow I had to ...

Turning away, I walked shakily down the narrow passageway toward the stern as he called after me threateningly. I ducked to go out to the stern cockpit, then snatched up the spear-gun that was leaning there. Crouching, I whirled suddenly and pointed it at Buster. My head was spinning like a top and I could barely see him.

"You're not going to sell that damn devil's dust anyplace!" I shouted hysterically.

His gun bellowed and something slammed against my left shoulder, as my finger tightened against the trigger of the spear gun. I heard the *zing* of the released spear just before I passed out.

Coming to this time was horrible. It wasn't only the pain and the dizziness and the nausea. In front of me, with his head back at a horrible angle, was Buster. The spear had gone through his throat. He was pinned to the partition behind him, and there was a long, jagged beard of blood down the front of him.

I tried to crawl, but my left arm wouldn't move. I looked down and my whole left side was drenched with blood. I held on the door jamb with my right hand and, after an eternity, pulled myself up to my feet. I wavered down the passageway and spilled into the chair beside the ship-to-shore. I reached up and switched over to "Send."

I started talking. I gave them the whole works, everything, and I kept talking. I told it over and over again. I sagged against the radio and kept talking. I wanted to tell them exactly how it was. All I did was talk. I told them and told them and told them. I just wouldn't let Buster get away with that cocaine, I just wouldn't, I just couldn't do that, I didn't want to kill him, but I just couldn't let him spread that infection....

Later, they told me they had to drag me away from the ship-to-shore.

It took three husky gobs from the Coast Guard to do it. I hung on, they told me, with both hands. Even when they did break me loose, I kept yelling to the Coast Guard to grab that Cuba-Tampa freighter, because somebody aboard was part of the dope-smuggling ring, and don't let them get away with it....

I damn near died. I had a fractured skull. That smack Burkitt gave me behind the back of the neck had done it. He had hit me just a little too high. And Burkitt, himself, was damn near dead. Buster had fractured his jaw in three places, broken eight ribs, and crushed something in his throat so that he'd never again speak above a whisper. And, of course, Daly was dead. But he'd been found by the Sanibar police before he died. He'd told them about Buster.

But I was worse off than Burkitt. He came into my hospital room, sat down beside my bed, and looked down at me with those dead-fish eyes of his. I didn't recognize him, he was so bandaged up. He looked down, and his eyes froze me. I couldn't see his mouth because it was covered with bandage, and when he spoke, his voice came through it, muffled.

"You're not getting away with a damn thing, Tucker," he whispered. "You were in it up to your neck, and I know you were. But you've been cleared right down the line from here to the Coast Guard. I'm letting it go at that for the time being, but get this!"

He leaned over the bed. He didn't touch me, but his hand clenched and gathered up a knotted fistful of sheet. "I'll get you some day. You're going to trip again, and this time I'll get you for sure. And when they fry you," his eyes were mad, "I'll put a pan under you and catch the grease. And the next day I'll eat my pancakes in it!"

Burkitt wanted to hit me, but he wouldn't. His face suffused and he hit the side of the bed with his clenched fist. He got up and walked out. I saw the blood trickling down the back of his hand from where he had struck the bed.

Sickeningly, I knew he was right. I *had* been in it up to my neck. I hadn't had any part in any of the killings, but Burkitt was right. I had known right from the beginning that Buster was destructive, and I had gone along with him all the way ... All the way to hell and back.

The nurse came into the room, brightly professional in her, white, starched uniform. She fluffed my pillow and fussed about me until I complained.

"There's a beautiful blonde outside to see you," she whispered, as if it were a state secret. "And I'll lose my reputation if you're not bright and cheerful. Now be a good boy and perk up. Where's that big smile?"

I looked up dully, expecting just another newspaper woman.

It was Letty. She was crying and smiling through her tears.

"Honey," she said, "Oh, honey ..."

THE END

LORENZ HELLER BIBLIOGRAPHY
(1910-1965)

As Frederick Lorenz

Novels:
A Rage at Sea (Lion, 1953)
Night Never Ends (Lion, 1954)
The Savage Chase (Lion, 1954)
A Party Every Night (Lion, 1956)
Ruby (Lion, 1956)
Hot (Lion, 1956)
Dungaree Sin (Chariot, 1960)

Stories:
Backbite (*Justice*, Jan 1956)
Big Catch (*Justice*, July 1955)
Living Bait (*Justice*, May 1955)

As Laura Hale

Novels:
Wild is the Woman (Rainbow, 1951)
Lovers Don't Sleep (Falcon, 1951)
Kiss of Fire (Rainbow, 1952; reprinted in Australia as
  Kiss Of Death, Phantom, 1953)
Woman Hunter (Falcon, 1952; reprinted in Australia,
  Phantom, 1953)
Desperate Blonde (Beacon Australia, 1960)
Lessons in Lust (Beacon, 1961; re-write of *Woman Hunter*)
Sensual Woman (Beacon, 1961; re-write of *Lovers Don't Sleep*)
The Zipper Girls (Beacon, 1962; re-write of *Wild is the Woman*)
The Marriage Bed (Beacon, 1962; re-write of *Desperate Blonde*)

As Larry Heller

Novels:
I Get What I Want (Popular, 1956)
Body of the Crime (Pyramid, 1962)

Story:
Blood Is Thicker (*Guilty Detective Story Magazine*, Mar 1957)

As Larry Holden

Novels:
Hide-Out (Eton, 1953)
Dead Wrong (Pyramid, 1957)
Crime Cop (Pyramid, 1959)

Stories (alphabetical listing):
...And Death Makes Ten (*Detective Tales*, June 1947)
Another Man's Poison (*Shadow Mystery*, Apr/May 1948)
Any Corpse in a Storm (*Dime Mystery Magazine*, Aug 1949)
Anybody Lose a Corpse? (*Mammoth Detective*, Aug 1946)
The Big Haunt (*10-Story Detective Magazine*, Oct 1948)
Blackmail Means Homicide (*15 Story Detective*, Feb 1950)
Bloody Night! (*Dime Mystery Magazine*, Oct 1949)
Bodyguard (*Thrilling Detective*, June 1951)
Bullets for Beethoven [Dinny Keogh] (*Mammoth Mystery*,
  June 1946)
Coffin Key (*Detective Tales*, Oct 1951)
A Corpse at Large (*Ten Detective Aces*, July 1949)
Corpse in Waiting (*New Detective Magazine*, Nov 1950)
A Corpse to His Credit (*Dime Detective Magazine*, May 1947)
Criminal at Large (*Suspense Magazine*, Summer 1951)
The Crimson Path (*Detective Tales*, Sept 1947)
Cry Murder (*New Detective Magazine*, Oct 1952)
The Crying Corpse (*Ten Detective Aces*, Sept 1948)
Death Brings Down the House (*10-Story Detective Magazine*,
  Apr 1948)
Death Carries the Mail (*F.B.I. Detective Stories*, Aug 1950)
Death for Two! (*Detective Tales*, Dec 1952)
Death in Dirty Linen (*Shadow Mystery*, June/July 1947)
Death in Six Reels (*Doc Savage*, July/Aug 1948)

Death in Thin Ice (*Shadow Mystery*, Feb/Mar 1948)
Death Is Where You Find It (*Suspect Detective Stories*, Nov 1955)
Die, Baby, Die! (*Detective Tales*, June 1948)
Don't Crowd My Shroud (*10-Story Detective Magazine*, Dec 1948)
Don't Ever Forget (*Detective Story Magazine*, Mar 1953)
Don't Wait Up for Me (*Triple Detective*, Fall 1955)
The Eighteen Screaming Corpses (*Detective Tales*, Jan 1948)
The Expendable Ex (*Dime Detective Magazine*, June 1952)
Face in the Window (*Detective Tales*, June 1951)
Fall Guy (*Detective Tales*, Aug 1953)
Forger's Fate (*Dime Detective Magazine*, Apr 1951)
The High Cost of Chivalry (*Dime Detective Magazine*, Dec 1951)
Home for Christmas (*Thrilling Detective*, Dec 1947)
House of Hate (*10-Story Detective Magazine*, Apr 1949)
Humpty-Dumpty Homicide (*Detective Tales*, June 1949)
If the Body Fits— (*Dime Mystery Magazine*, Dec 1947)
If the Frame Fits— (*Detective Tales*, Dec 1951)
I'll Be Home for Murder! (*Detective Tales*, Apr 1948)
I'll See You Dead! (*Detective Tales*, May 1947)
In Her Mother's Best Bier! (*Detective Tales*, Dec 1948)
Keeping Honest (*Doc Savage*, Winter 1949)
Kickback for a Corpse (*All-Story Detective*, Apr 1949)
Killer's Kiss (*Detective Tales*, Aug 1949)
Lady in Red (*Detective Tales*, Oct 1948)
Lady-Killer (*Dime Detective Magazine*, Dec 1952)
Lethal Boy Blue (*Detective Tales*, May 1949)
Love Me, Love My Corpse! (*Detective Tales*, Aug 1948)
Make Mine Mayhem (*New Detective Magazine*, Jan 1949)
Man with a Rep (*Detective Tales*, Dec 1949)
Mayhem at Eight (*New Detective Magazine*, May 1950)
Mayhem's Mechanic (*Detective Tales*, Sept 1946)
Morgue Bait (*New Detective Magazine*, Dec 1951)
Murder and the Mermaid (*Dime Detective Magazine*, Oct 1952)
Murder Never Gets Too Old (*Private Detective*, Jan 1950)
Never Dead Enough (*New Detective Magazine*, Sept 1947)
Never Turn Your Back (*Mike Shayne Mystery Magazine*, July 1959)
Nightmare (*Detective Tales*, Oct 1952)
No Dead End (*Triple Detective*, Spring 1955)
On a Dead Man's Chest (*Thrilling Detective*, Apr 1953)
One Dark Night [Dinny Keogh] (*Mammoth Mystery*, Dec 1946)
One for the Hangman (*Suspect Detective Stories*, Feb 1956)

Operation—Murder (*F.B.I. Detective Stories*, Aug 1949)
Orphans Are Made (*Mobsters*, Feb 1953)
Out of the Frying Pan... (*15 Mystery Stories*, Oct 1950)
Port of the Dead (*New Detective Magazine*, July 1947)
Prelude to a Wake (*Dime Detective Magazine*, Feb 1952)
Red Nightmare (*Dime Mystery Magazine*, July 1947)
Sailor, Beware! (*Detective Story Magazine*, May 1953)
Save Me a Kill (*New Detective Magazine*, June 1953)
Self-Made Corpse (*Detective Tales*, Apr 1949)
She Cries Murder! (*New Detective Magazine*, June 1952)
Sing a Song of Murder (*Dime Detective Magazine*, Aug 1952)
Snow in August [Dinny Keogh] (*Mammoth Mystery*, Aug 1946)
The Spice of Death (*Private Detective*, Dec 1950)
Start with a Corpse [Dinny Keogh] (*Mammoth Mystery*, Jan 1946)
There's Death in the Heir [Dinny Keogh] (*Mammoth Mystery*, Aug 1947)
They Played Too Rough [Dinny Keogh] (*Mammoth Mystery*, Mar 1946)
This Shroud Reserved (*New Detective Magazine*, Oct 1951)
Those Slaughter-House Blues (*Mammoth Detective*, Feb 1947)
A Time for Dying (*Dime Detective Magazine*, Aug 1951)
Too Many Crosses [Dinny Keogh] (*Mammoth Mystery*, Feb 1947)
Tragedy in Waiting (*Invincible Detective Magazine*, Mar 1951)
The Trouble with Redheads (*Mike Shayne Mystery Magazine*, Apr 1959)
Two-Headed Killer (*15 Mystery Stories*, Feb 1950)
Undressed to Kill (*New Detective Magazine*, Sept 1949)
Vicious Circle (*Detective Tales*, Nov 1949)
The Voice That Kills (*15 Mystery Stories*, Aug 1950)
Wake of the Ermine Chick (*15 Story Detective*, Dec 1950)
When Cops Fall Out (*Detective Tales*, June 1953)
With Hostile Intent (*Fifteen Detective Stories*, Dec 1954)
With Love and Bullets! (*Detective Tales*, Feb 1953)
Written in Blood (*Ten Detective Aces*, May 1948)
You Can't Live Forever (*New Detective Magazine*, Aug 1952)
You Die Alone (*Fifteen Detective Stories*, Oct 1953)
You'll Die Laughing (*Detective Tales*, Oct 1950)
You're Killing Me (*Detective Story Magazine*, Sept 1953)

Dinny Keogh series:
Start with a Corpse (1946)
They Played Too Rough (1946)
Bullets for Beethoven (1946)
Snow in August (1946)
One Dark Night (1946)
Too Many Crosses (1947)
There's Death in the Heir (1947)

As Lorenz Heller

Novel:
Murder in Make-Up (Messner, 1937)

Stories:
Blood Money (*Suspect Detective Stories*, Nov 1955)
A Tasty Dish (*Suspect Detective Stories*, Feb 1956)
Twilight (*Short Stories*, Nov 1956)
The Hero (*Mystery Tales*, Dec 1958)
The Last Hunt (*Adventure*, June 1959)

As Burt Sims

Television Scripts:
1953: "Death Does a Rumba" (Season 2, Episode 12, *Boston Blakie*)
1953: "Island of Stone" (Season 2, Episode 1, *Chevron Theater*)
1954: "Tailor-Made Trouble" (Season 1, Episode 11, *Waterfront*)
1956 - 1959: Seven episodes of *Sky King*
1958: "Beautiful, Blue and Deadly" (Season 1, Episode 14,
  Mike Hammer)
1958: "Texas Fliers" (Season 1, Episode 18, *Flight*)

A TRIO OF LIONS

From the early 1950s—the golden age of the paperback!
Three noir crime novels in each volume!

Lion Books began in 1949 as Red Circle Books, part of the Martin Goodman publishing empire that also included such magazines as *For Men Only, Stag* and *Movie World*, as well as various pulps and the early version of Marvel Comics. Lion Books only lasted for nine years, but during that time at least a third of their books were noir reprints and originals, and featured authors like Jim Thompson, David Goodis, Robert Bloch, Richard Matheson and Day Keene.

Kermit Jaediker: Hero's Lust
Shel Walker: The Man I Killed
Clayre & Michel Lipman: House of Evil
978-1-944520-02-1 $19.95
"A real ten-knuckle page-turner."—Kristofer Upjohn, *Noir Journal.*
"Reading these books are like watching late night film noir on late night TV with the lights out."—Rick Ollerman.
Introductions by Gary Lovisi and Dan Roberts.

Kermit Jaedeker: Tall, Dark & Dead
Frederick Lorenz: The Savage Chase
D. L. Champion: Run the Wild River
978-1-944520-75-5 $19.95
"As hard-boiled as they come."—Paul Burke, *NB.*
"…really races along."—James Reasoner.
"…unequivocally recommended."—*Paperback Parade.*
Includes an interview with editor Arnold Hano.

"Lots of tough-guy, wisecracking fun… reads like a 65-70 minute RKO private-eye movie."—*GoodReads*

Stark House Press

1315 H Street, Eureka, CA 95501, 707-498-3135, www.StarkHousePress.com